EVERYTHING

NATALIE TRIUMPHS

First edition February 2024

Paperback ISBN: 979-8-9887681-4-2

Ebook ISBN: 979-8-9887681-5-9

CHAPTER 1

As the plane boarded, I was leaving behind everything that mattered. That is everything but Everything, my five-pound Papillion. Unless I could find a way to return, I was leaving behind my friends, my dance team, my home, and possibly missing my high school graduation. There was something ironic about being forced to fly, right after my parents had died in a plane crash. "Died" was a word I still had trouble connecting to thoughts about my mom.

As I sat down, contemplating whether I could sneak out of the plane before takeoff, I realized that mine was not the only dog on the plane. Down the aisle came a dog that reminded me of the ones in the photos of Abu Ghraib. I supposed that was fitting as Cruella de Vil, AKA my Aunt Juliet, my warden so to speak, could teach torture to Blackwater field operatives. No. Cruella had more redeeming qualities than Juliet, more warmth in her little toe than my aunt had in her whole body. And then, there was the Iceman Brian, Cruella's husband.

My life before was far from perfect. In fact, at times it was pretty awful. However, less than a week before, I was at least on the verge of escaping to a top college—even though I was only fifteen. Now that I was being forced to leave my high school two months before graduation to head to Juliet's dungeon, my college acceptances were in jeopardy. My parents had been declared dead. People were insisting I accept that reality. I was being dragged away from all my friends. On the plus side was Juliet's little boy Jonah, a kid to whom they barely let me speak—as if I had the plague and he might catch it. Maybe I did have the plague. Maybe that's why my life had fallen apart.

I thought back to the day everything turned from bad but hopeful to hopeless. My father—I could do without my father—was insisting we go flying with him on a short trip to Maryland. He was an amateur pilot. If he had gone up alone, a plane crash would have been a good thing. No remorse there. If you think I should feel bad about his death, it's because you didn't know him.

But my mother, she always had my back. She was my best friend. She had been forced to go on the plane with that rabid animal. My mom was the only one who loved me, and now she had been taken away from me by my father who only cared about himself.

It was as if some demon had cursed me and my life that day. My mom and I were close to running away. We had discretely started packing. We were just waiting around for my graduation. Instead of going to my graduation party, my mom and I intended to hit the road. I would wind up at the college of my choice and my dad wouldn't know which one. He never even bothered to ask where I applied. I had been offered scholarships at a lot of universities. While my dad didn't even know I had early acceptances, my mom was excited about each acceptance and scholarship.

My mom and I both came up with excuses not to go on the airplane. We both lied.

"Dad, I have dance practice. I can't let the team down."

"I promised to watch Meadow's practice, dear," my mom said.

The truth of the matter was my dance team was on hiatus, studying for AP exams. We weren't the official dance team of the school, but we had performed at some of the assemblies and always received a lot of praise from the other students. We were expected to perform at the graduation. We had already planned out our number and would be rehearsing in May to recover from our break for AP prep.

My dad could always be trusted to dim the mood. "The dance team is a dalliance. It's time you stopped being a failure, Meadow, and started listening to me."

But I could always count on my mom. "Rick, Meadow is a huge success at everything."

My father glared at my mom. "Don't you dare cross me!"

She braced herself. His anger all too frequently had escalated into hitting, choking, grabbing her hair and smashing her head against walls and tables. "Then, don't talk to our daughter that way," she insisted. No matter the consequences, she never backed down where I was concerned.

"Are you telling me how to talk?" He started to come at her.

"Dad, leave Mom alone."

I picked up the landline phone and started to dial 9-1-1. He twisted my arm and got the phone away, putting it against the side of his head. "I'm sorry," he said. "My little girl was just goofing off."

"Not true!" I yelled as he pressed the mute button.

"Thank you," he said, after unmuting it.

"Meadow, if you dare do that again, you'll regret it. And Theresa, we're all going flying—unless—you want to die here."

How ominous those words were. Still, he'd threatened us with death a zillion times and we were still alive. I figured we would survive—again. But nobody wanted his wrath, and so we agreed. By the time we got to the airport and after an hour of my dad telling me I was worthless while my mom defended me, amidst insults and threats to her safety, I knew I had to get away. Going with him was more than I could handle. My dad was first onboard, as he was planning to pilot the private Lear jet. He went straight up to the cockpit. I noticed nobody was boarding but the three of us.

"I can't do this, Mom. Come with me," I whispered to her as my dad was distracted with preparing for the flight behind the cockpit wall.

She looked a little perplexed, but I didn't have the energy to convince her to dump Dad on the spot—especially with him calling, "Theresa, are you and Meadow buckled in?"

I ran down the steps as my mom blurted, "Sweetheart—" I didn't have time to listen to her excuses for staying. The stairs began to retract into the plane, undoubtedly controlled from the cockpit. Unless he did a check, my dad wouldn't know I was gone until he was in the air.

That was the last time I saw my mom. She was looking at me through the closing door as I turned and continued on my way.

As I ran, it occurred to me that he would take it out on my mom when he discovered my absence. She'd have to fight her own battles with him. She should have left long ago as far as I was concerned. Part of me was angry that she hadn't. Moving towards the entrance to the private plane airstrip, I looked back and saw the plane taking off into the air. It wasn't until later that I learned of its fate, that I had no more parents, that my family and my plans had been wiped out.

I didn't have the car keys or a license. So I just ran towards home. I had to walk through the industrial area of Elizabeth City, where most of the homeless hung out. That area of town always made me feel weird with its boarded-up once-thriving businesses that hadn't survived the collapse of the American economy. North Carolina's Elizabeth City had often been classified as one of the ten best cities in America to live in and most of it was beautiful. Because of the economy, the homeless population had been growing and was now overwhelming certain parts of the city. With all the empty buildings, particularly the warehouses I was passing, I didn't understand why we didn't just house the homeless. Then, no more problem.

Men kept trying to talk to me as I walked by, but I wasn't in the mood to talk. Ordinarily, I would speak to the homeless, and treat them like human beings, but I didn't even feel human that day. I hated my life but not as much as the life I was about to enter.

As I rounded a corner, I saw a flash of something that came flying into my arms. Not a thing, a dog. It was a girl dog. She was beautiful, but tiny, with Lassie-style markings on her face and large ears that looked like butterfly wings. The fur on her back was long and mostly white. She looked at me with eyes that almost melted my heart and made my day. She wagged the big fluffy tail she held high above her back as if to say she liked being in my arms.

"Where did you come from?" I asked. She must have fallen from a window, but I couldn't tell which one. I went to the nearest door. It led to an adult massage shop. *Wonderful.* Even in Elizabeth City, there were erotic massage parlors. Well, everyone needed to make a living, and if it pays the bills, who was I to judge? I opened the door and asked, "Is this your dog?"

A woman with tattoos looked at me as if I was a juvenile hall escapee and gruffed out the words, "I'm allergic, honey. Get that thing out of here!" Most of the other doors in the area were locked. I knocked for some time but mostly got no responses. One man invited me in. The dog growled at him. I guessed he wasn't the owner. I declined his invitation. After half an hour of searching, I still couldn't find anyone who seemed to be attached to the dog. So I gave up.

I put her on the ground. "I'm sure someone is looking for you. Run along home," I told her. She just looked at me with her warm dark brown eyes. I figured if I walked off, she'd go her own way. Instead, she followed me home, ignoring my repeated urgings for her to return to her owner. I wasn't about to call animal control. PETIS, a dog slaughter organization, had taken over the town shelter. Nationally, PETIS had a ninety-seven percent kill rate at its shelters. That's three out of every hundred dogs at their shelters who were *not* put to death. I wasn't going to let this little dog fight those odds.

At my home, a large two-story house, I let her in and offered her a bowl of mushroom soup, which she lapped right up.

A knock came at the door. I looked through the edge of the curtain and noticed a police car. The officers at the door weren't looking my way, which gave me some relief. My dad had probably sent them to harass me for getting off the plane. They had never helped my mother when she tried to tell them about the beatings. So I pretended not to be home.

I tried to read and found that I couldn't concentrate. I was weeks away from my final set of AP exams. But I had finished reviewing all the course material and mostly just had to review my subjects and take practice tests. I turned on a rerun of the old *Dinosaurs* series, the only cartoons I liked. My dad had forbidden me to watch it, saying it was propaganda. My parents weren't supposed to be back until early evening. Hours passed and they still weren't home. I made myself dinner. I worried about my mom but figured my dad might have forced her to have dinner out with him. Still, she didn't call, and she usually would have checked up on me. I thought about calling her cell but didn't want to talk to her with my dad listening.

I made myself some vegan lasagna. It was almost done when I heard the doorbell ring. My parents never rang. Maybe it was someone from my dance team.

I opened it to find our next-door neighbors, Susie and Everett Shirelle. Susie came in, followed by Everett. She wrapped her arms around me. "Honey, are you okay?

"Yeah. My parents aren't here."

Susie and Everett looked at each other. "Honey, let's sit down," Susie said. This couldn't be good. She escorted me to the couch and sat beside me. Everett sat on my other side. "Meadow, there's been a terrible accident." She looked at Everett as if waiting for him to speak.

I held my breath. My mom. She had to be okay. My dad could go to Hades. Everett gave me the details. "Your parents' plane had some mechanical problems and went down."

"Where are my parents? My mother? Where is she?" I found I was having trouble breathing.

Kneeling down in front of me to look into my eyes, Everett replied, "They haven't recovered all of the plane. It bounced off some trees as it went down. It came apart and exploded on the way into the ocean. Your parents are—"

"Everett," Susie cautioned. She looked at me. "They don't see any way anyone could have survived the crash."

"No bodies?" I asked, hoping my mom would turn up alive.

"They don't expect to find anything whole, given the way it exploded," Everett went on. "I wish we had better news."

"I'm so sorry," said Susie. It was as if the rest of her words were coming through an auditory cloud. "Everett and I would like you to come stay with us for now. I imagine your relatives will want you to live with them, but you should be able to decide for yourself. You are fifteen. We love you and our children love you. Your mother was my best friend. She asked us to take care of you if something happened to her."

Yeah, I thought, *my mom would have made plans for me, given the way my dad treated her. She probably didn't know from one day to the next whether she would survive. But she had always survived. She did not perish in that plane,* I told myself.

Susie looked at the dog, who had jumped up on my lap and was licking my face, almost as if she were trying to comfort me, too. "Your mom told me she wanted to get you a dog. A Papillion is a great choice. They are such sweet dogs. He's welcome at our home, too." She looked a little more closely. "Oh, it's a girl. She's welcome."

I thought about the offer. I didn't want to be alone. Susie and Everett were like family. But there had to be some mistake. Someone had to find my mom safe and alive and tell me that she was lucky. I planned to keep thinking that. There was no way I was going to allow myself to picture her any other way. I'd stay at the Shirelle's until my mom was found alive. Their daughter Trisha was my best friend and their son Dave was always sweet to me. He was older and had recently joined the military.

The doorbell rang again, and Everett answered it. It was Trisha. As I stood up, she rushed in and hugged me. "My mom called me at the library. If there is anything I can do?"

"There has to be some mistake. My mom can't be gone."

She looked at her mom. "Is it possible?"

"No," Everett said. "The examiners found enough of the remains of the plane to be certain they both perished." He turned to me, "I'm sorry."

CHAPTER 2

Three days later, there was a funeral; no bodies but a funeral. The Coast Guard had pronounced my parents dead.

The funeral had an odd mix of people. Some of my teachers and quite a number of students from my school were there. Though it was a Tuesday, they had been given permission to attend the memorial. Of course, my next-door neighbors were present and so were a number of others from the neighborhood.

My Aunt Juliet arrived. She was even more horrible than I remembered. I never liked her. When I was nine, she threw me out of her Michigan house into a freezing snowstorm because I said something she didn't like about a former President. My comment had been very factual, but she told me I'd know better when I grew up. Later, Juliet had moved to Southern California. There were no snowstorms in Carlsbad, and so she couldn't do that to me, now. Of course, with her and Brian residing there, maybe coastal Southern California would be hit with a first-time blizzard. Or perhaps, she'd drown me in the ocean if I ever came to visit, which I had no intention of doing.

There was a little boy with Juliet and her husband Brian. They stood on each side of the young child and pulled him by the wrists as they started to move past me. Juliet's acknowledgment of me was merely a nod.

"Hi," I said to the little boy. "And who might you be?"

He started to speak but Juliet interrupted him. "He's my little son, Jonah." She looked at my dog. "You brought a dog to your parents' funeral! How uncouth!" My dog growled at her. "He looks rabid."

"She's family. Now, she's everything."

"Everything? What a stupid name."

"I like it." I hadn't found her owners and I hadn't been planning to name the dog "Everything," but somehow, if Juliet hated the name, it seemed like the most perfect name in the world. The dog was all I had, outside of Susie, Everett, Dave and Trisha. I didn't know what I would have done without them.

Jenna from my dance team came up and gave me a hug. "I hope this doesn't mean you will be quitting the dance team."

"Why should I?"

After she went to sit down, Tara, another dance team member, approached me. "Don't let Jenna get to you. She's jealous of your abilities and is talking as if she hopes you'll leave and let her take the lead on the team. Don't you dare!"

"I know. Jenna always wants the spotlight. I'm not about to quit the dance team. Thanks for being my friend."

Tara gave me a hug. Tara had always been nice to me. We hit it off when she arrived from Chicago, the new girl in town. She was really talented and a great addition to the dance team. I was glad she had my back.

An older man with grey hair whom I didn't recognize walked in the door. He glared at Brian, who was standing in front of the side section that was arranged for the family and close friends. Brian glared back at the old man. I got the impression of mental knives being flung by one at the other. Brian started to move towards the man, but Juliet caught Brian's arm and guided him to their seats.

Dave was wearing his Marine uniform. I wasn't into uniforms and I definitely didn't care for crew cuts on guys, but he looked pretty good in the uniform, even with the haircut. *Why hadn't he joined the Seabees so he could wear his hair long? What a stupid thought at a funeral for my parents.*

He came over to me. "Meadow, if you ever need anything, here is my cell number," he said, writing it down for me. "I am supposed to go somewhere to do some special assignment later today. When I'm back, maybe we can go out?"

"I—" I didn't know what to say.

"I know. It must be difficult to make plans now. We used to have a lot of fun together and I have always liked you a lot and not just because you are my sister's friend. That's why I used to butt in on your playdates with her."

"Sure. Maybe we can go out when you come back," I said. I didn't feel any emotion about it. I felt like crying and running away. My mother wasn't dead. This was a stupid funeral.

Trisha came up to me and turned to Dave. "You aren't going to monopolize my best friend today. Meadow, you look really beautiful for this awful occasion."

"I'll second that," Dave said.

I sat between Trisha and Susie with Dave on Trisha's other side. Everett sat between Susie and Juliet. I was glad for the buffer between me and my blood-sucking relatives.

"This section is for family," Juliet whispered to Everett and Susie.

"They're family," I said, firmly, but maybe a little too loudly as I saw a couple of heads turn in our direction.

Looking at the crowd, I saw two men I didn't recognize enter and stand at the back. There was something odd about their suits. There were bulges under their jackets. It occurred to me that they could have papers under their jackets, but I fancied the idea of those being guns and of Juliet and Brian being on the verge of being arrested. I held Everything tightly in my arms.

Though there were no bodies, portraits of my parents had been placed at the front. A Unity minister named Margaret spoke about what a perfect child of God my father was. I had heard that before. I had once tried to tell Margaret he was a monster, to which she had told me to keep such talk to myself and recognize the divinity in him. I recognized the divine purpose of his death. He couldn't hurt anyone, anymore. But my mom's death. That didn't make sense. I needed her.

Brian looked bored as guests started giving testimonials, mostly about my mother and what a kind, helpful person she was. Principal Carmen shared, "Theresa was the most attentive mother at our school. She always showed up to assist whenever we needed a helping hand. I know she loved Meadow and was very proud of her. The teachers have taken up a collection to donate to her favorite charity, Greenpeace." I saw Juliet and Brian smirk. I surmised that, like my dad, Juliet and Brian weren't fans of Greenpeace.

Juliet got up to speak, releasing her grip on Jonah's arm. She looked at Brian who put his arm on Jonah's shoulders in a way that looked as if he were strong-arming Jonah and keeping him in place, rather than nurturing him. Neither seemed to be significantly warm towards the little boy.

"My brother, Rick, was an example of a great man, a loving husband and a dedicated father. I speak for the family in saying that his death was tragic and he will be missed."

Yeah, right. He loved himself and was dedicated to making my and my mother's lives as miserable as possible.

After she finished with some more fantasy fiction comments about my dad, she sat down and took hold of Jonah's arm again. Brian kept looking at the older man in the back. Jonah was restless, trying to wiggle out of Juliet's grasp, like there was somewhere he wanted to go or something he wanted to do. The more he wiggled, the more firmly Juliet held him. Jonah was also looking at the older man. I could almost swear Jonah was trying to pull away to get to the man. Maybe it was my imagination. If I were their kid, I'd have run away before I was old enough to speak.

I got up and went to the podium. I hadn't prepared a speech. I just said what came from my heart. "People tell me my mother is dead. I haven't seen a body. I haven't seen any proof. So, I will talk about her in the present tense." People were looking at me with sadness in their eyes. "My mother is a good person. She deserved better. She certainly deserved much better than the beatings she received at my father's hands." People gasped. "She has always been kind. She never beat anyone or ever hurt anyone in any way. Her only fault was in giving too many chances to a man who didn't know the difference between a wife and a punching bag. *She* didn't belong on that plane." Leaving the implication that my father did belong on the plane, I went back to my seat.

Brian got up, but instead of going to the podium, he walked around the edge of the audience to the back door and out. The older man got up and went out the door after him. I turned to Susie. "My dog needs to pee."

"Get some fresh air, honey. This has to be tough on you."

I got up with Everything and followed Brian and the old man. As I walked, I noticed that the two men in suits with bulges had already left. When I got outside, neither Brian nor the older man was visible. There was no sight of the bulging suits either. I saw a door to a room to the side of the main hall closing. I went over to it and slightly opened the door to listen.

"I could kill you. You are the lowest low of any human being." I gathered this was the older man's voice.

"Go home or you'll meet the same fate as Tammy or Preston," Brian said.

"What have you—you—" Suddenly, the older man was crying out in pain. "Oh, oh."

I heard a crash. I looked in, and the older man was on the floor. I pushed the door back into place and dialed 9-1-1.

As the operator answered, I reported, "A man has collapsed. It might be a heart attack. He could be dead. Please hurry."

"Where are you?"

"Elizabeth City Unity Church. Side room, right of the main hall. Hurry."

I opened the door and saw Brian dragging the man across the floor toward what I thought was a walk-in closet on the other side of the room. "Stop!" I yelled as I stepped inside.

"What are you doing here? I'm trying to help him get somewhere comfortable. Go back to the service!"

"The police and paramedics are on their way. Don't move him."

"You called them?" Brian moved from the man towards me, angrily. I backed up. He continued moving towards me.

Everything started barking angrily at Brian, causing him to pause.

He reached to grab her from my arms. I turned her away from him.

Everything jumped from my arms and ran over to the man on the floor. She sat on his chest and vigorously licked his face. Brian went for the dog as I ran to protect her. He started to reach down but stopped and turned when the sound of sirens suddenly blared out, loud and clear. He turned back towards the man and Everything.

"Don't touch that man or my dog!" I shouted.

Brian turned to me. "Little girl," he icily said, reaching towards me. "Don't touch me either or I'll scream."

I leaned down and took the older man's hand to try to see if there was a pulse. I didn't know much about CPR but had seen shows where people had saved others. *Had I delayed too long?* Before I could get a good feel for a pulse, a couple of paramedics rushed through the door as Brian slipped out.

One of the paramedics kneeled down and checked for a heartbeat.

"Is this his dog?"

"No. It's mine. She is trying to help him."

The lead paramedic handed me Everything. Then, he listened to the man's chest and gave him an injection as another paramedic put an oxygen mask over the man's face and a blood pressure cuff over his arm. As they wheeled him out on a gurney, the man was still unconscious. They didn't do CPR and I saw that as a good sign.

"Will he be alright?" I asked.

"Don't know," the first paramedic replied. "Does he have family?"

"I think he came alone," I said.

The paramedics continued towards their van. As I followed, the one who had spoken said, "See if you can locate some family. He is in serious, possibly critical, condition. We will be taking him to SAMC." I knew that to be the local trauma center.

I went back into the church. Susie, Everett, Dave, Trisha and Juliet were in a receiving line. I checked to see if the suits had returned, but there was no sign of them.

Juliet looked as if she wanted to kill me. "It's such bad character for you to have run out on your parents' memorial and what you said about your father. Disrespectful."

I didn't have time to respond to Juliet's nastiness. I turned to my friends. "A man who was at the memorial had a heart attack or something. The paramedics took him to the hospital."

"Oh, no!" Susie exclaimed. "I heard sirens. I didn't realize it was for anyone here."

I turned to Juliet. "You and Brian knew him. We need to contact his family."

"Never saw him before," Juliet said, coldly.

How did Juliet know who I talking about? "Do you know him?" I asked Susie. "It was the older grey-haired man in the back."

"I'm sorry." She looked at Everett.

Everett shook his head.

Susie continued, "I didn't recognize him. I don't think he's from around here."

"I'll make an announcement," Everett said. "You say, it was the grey-haired man in the back?"

I nodded. Everett went to the microphone and informed the group, "One of the guests has been rushed to the hospital. I don't know his name, but if anyone knows the grey-haired man who was sitting in the back row, they need to go to the hospital or inform his family."

Susie had the reception at her home. She was baking pasta in her oven and cookies in ours as Trisha made a salad. Susie had already prepared finger sandwiches, which Dave and Everett were passing out, along with fruit punch.

"I'll go get the deserts," I said.

"No, you should relax today," Susie responded.

"It will relax me to do something."

"I understand."

I ran to my house to pull the cookies out of the oven. As I got to the house, I noticed the door was slightly open. I slowly entered to see the two bulging suits from the memorial sitting in the living room. I turned to run.

CHAPTER 3

"Please. Don't leave."

Please was a good sign if there was such a thing as a good sign coming from intruders.

The one who had spoken seemed a bit more distinguished and possibly in his late thirties or early forties. I suspected the other was early thirties. From their clothing to the professional way they looked, my guess was they were IRS agents, attorneys, accountants, hitmen or extortionists.

"You just walked in?"

"You left the door unlocked. We rang."

"Everyone is next door. They'll hear if you—"

"We aren't here to harm you," the more distinguished-looking man said. "My name is Stan and this is Justin."

"Well, Stan and Justin, entering without permission is trespassing."

"We need to speak with you."

"About what?"

"Your dad was working on some sensitive stuff."

"My dad? He was an accountant." I wondered if they were mobsters.

"We'd like to see if he left anything in his records that he had been planning to give to us."

"And why would I show you anything he was working on?"

"We worked together."

"I suppose you have ID. Because he didn't mention you."

Stan pulled his photo identification out of his wallet that listed his name under the heading of Central Intelligence Agency and his position as "Special Ops V." Justin pulled out a government ID that categorized him as a field agent.

"My dad was working with the CIA?"

"It's not the kind of agency the movies romanticize."

"I was thinking more of how Edward Snowden pointed out you were spying on Americans."

The men looked at each other. "Snowden was a systems administrator, not an agent. He quit the Company and later was a contractor for the NSA. We're not with the tech section or with the NSA."

"I see. Well, still you must have the wrong Rick Clarkson."

"I'm afraid not."

"It's not that uncommon of a name. Anyone who knew my dad knew that he definitely wasn't the CIA type. His only patriotism was to himself. So, you've got the wrong father."

Stan continued, "The image at the front of the service was the same Rick Clarkson I knew."

That took me aback. "Was my dad helping the Department spy on people? Whatever. You've got the wrong father."

"No. He was just assisting us with some matters."

"That would help you spy on Americans?"

"No. That's the NSA. The CIA is not chartered to spy on Americans." As Stan spoke, Justin looked away, almost uncomfortably. Guess he didn't agree with something about the CIA. "We're about gathering foreign intelligence," Stan continued.

"I see. Well, anything he was working on would be at his office. You'll have to talk to his secretary. I'm sure everything is on his work computer or at his desk there."

"Ms. Talbert gave us his computer and the contents of his desk, but we need to know if there was something more?"

"He didn't like working from home. So anything more is not here."

"There was a little boy at the funeral."

"My cousin, Jonah."

"How old is he?"

"I don't know. He looks about three or four."

Stan shook his head as if something about my response bothered him. "So you were probably in late grammar school or junior high when he was born?"

"I guess. I didn't know Juliet and Brian had a son until the funeral."

"Isn't that a little odd?"

I didn't say anything.

"When was the last time you saw your aunt and uncle before today?"

"They visited briefly about six months ago."

"And he wasn't with them?"

"I guess they left him in California, maybe with Brian's parents."

"Did they mention him?"

"I talk to them as little as possible."

"So, no?"

"I don't remember."

"Do they have any other children?"

"Not that I know of."

"Do you know Brian's parents?"

"No. Is there a problem?"

"No." Stan looked at Justin and the two started to rise.

Did I dare open up a can of cockroaches that would give them more reason to hang out here? Yes. "Did you know the man who was taken to the hospital?"

The men looked at each other. "Someone was taken to the hospital?" Stan asked.

"I guess you had left by then. I saw Brian and a man leave and I followed. The man threatened Brian and then collapsed."

"You think Brian may have done something to him?"

"I don't know. I know they argued." It may have been inappropriate to get Brian into trouble with the Feds, but tough. I didn't like Brian.

"What did the man look like?" Justin asked.

"I think we've asked this young lady enough questions," Stan said, cutting him off.

Everything ran into the living room and jumped into my arms, growling at the men.

"My dog doesn't trust you."

"Cute dog," Justin said. Everything continued to growl.

"Well, if you come across something, here is my card," Stan pulled out a card and wrote on the back. "And here is the best email address for me." He handed me the card.

"I'll contact you if I come across my father's secret identity, but don't count on my finding it."

"It sounded like your mother was a beautiful woman," Stan said. "I'm really sorry for what happened to her and that you had to lose someone you loved."

He must have heard my speech. I nodded, feeling choked up and unable to speak.

"I didn't know your dad that well. My contact with him was limited to a particular project he was handling. I wish you the best and am sorry for any stress this visit has caused you." Stan came across as sincere and part of me was tempted to like him.

"Good day," Justin said as they left. Everything barked as if threatening the men.

"I guess you don't like spooks," I said to her after they left.

Back at the Shirelles, my Aunt Juliet came over to me. Everything growled at her.

"That dog belongs in a shelter."

"This dog belongs with me."

"Well, maybe we can find someone to take Everything," she said with disdain. "When you come to live with us."

"Oh, no. There is no way I'm coming to live with you."

"We are your closest relatives. Of course you will."

"The Shirelles have asked me to live with them, and that is what I plan to do."

"It's not up to you."

"I'm fifteen."

"You are still a minor."

"Well, I'm not leaving Everything, and you don't like dogs."

Juliet looked up. "We'll make room."

"I'm staying here, and nothing could make me go with you." I walked out of the room. Though I had left the room, I could hear the fight that had started between Juliet and Susie.

"She needs to stay here until the end of her school term. She needs her final grades to make sure she gets into the right college. It was her mother's wishes."

"No. We think not. It may have been her mother's wishes but not her father's."

"But she's been advanced two years in school and is less than two months from graduation. She also has her AP exams coming up and activities like dance team."

"Well, my sister-in-law should have let her hang back with kids her own age. Advancing a kid could mess her up for life. That's probably why she is so oppositional. She needs to go back into tenth grade. As for her APs, she'll probably do better on them next year."

I walked back in there. "I will not go with you, Juliet, and I am certain that I could get emancipated if you try to take me."

"Honey, I'm an attorney and there is no judge who will turn you loose."

"Really?"

"Really."

"I have AP exams, next month. I need to stay here to prepare for them and take them."

Susie joined back in. "She's not oppositional. She is a great girl. If you try to put her back, Everett and I will fight you. She's the highest AP achiever in her school. If you stop her from taking those exams, you'll have the whole school lined up against you."

Juliet rolled her eyes. "She can take the exams in California."

"I'm already registered, here."

"I'm sure we can arrange for you to register late in California. And those are standardized tests. You can study for them, anywhere."

I threw up my hands.

Susie looked at Everett, who next spoke. "We could take this to court." Everett was also an attorney but not a family law or probate attorney. He practiced criminal law. He did put together Mom's will as a favor to her, though. I didn't know what kind of law Juliet practiced.

"And you would lose," Juliet said. "I'm family."

Susie looked thoughtful for a while. "Well, perhaps, you could visit with your aunt for a couple of weeks and get to know her. We can have your instructors provide work for you to do while you're gone."

"If you really hate it, we'll go to court," Everett told me and then glared at Juliet.

From out of nowhere, I heard a quiet, almost inaudible voice. "Don't go with her." I turned and looked but couldn't find the source. It had sounded female, almost melodic. The others were looking strangely at me.

"What is it?" Susie asked.

"Did you hear that?"

"What did you hear?"

"Don't go with her." The expression on Susie's face was interesting, and I couldn't make out what it meant.

"When we get to California, we'll have a doctor check you out," Juliet said.

"I'm fine. I don't want to go with you, not for a trial visit, not at all."

Juliet grabbed my arm.

"Let her go," Susie said firmly as Everything growled and jumped at Juliet, catching her off-guard and knocking her back, quite a feat for a dog that was about five pounds.

"I knew that dog was rabid. I'm going to have animal control pick him up."

"It's not a he and she's fine. She was protecting me. You are the real danger," I said, picking Everything up off the floor.

"Listen, little girl," Brian chastised me.

"I'm not a little girl." I heard another growl. Everything seemed to be glaring at Juliet. "You are to stay away from my dog. It's you who should have your rabies shot. She's been vaccinated." I didn't know if she had, but it sounded good.

Juliet looked furious. She settled down in a way that looked phony like she was trying to appear calm while there was a raging storm underneath. "Fine. If you go with me, I won't call animal control."

"That sounds like extortion," Everett said.

"That dog is a danger to the public," Juliet hissed.

I held Everything close as she glared at Juliet.

"It's your word against ours," Everett interjected.

"And mine," Brian told Everett. "This is the third time the dog has become violent."

"She's not violent. She just doesn't like mean people," I said. Susie patted me on the shoulder.

I reflected on all the dogs PETIS with its ninety-seven percent execution rate had killed in Elizabeth City's shelter. I suspected that Everything's survival chances were slim to none if Juliet was successful in having her picked up and sent to that death chamber.

I remembered a kid at school talking about visiting the shelter every day looking for his missing dog. They said they didn't have it. After they executed it, they acknowledged they had had the dog all along, but they countered the owner's claims by saying nobody had called for it. Knowing Juliet, she'd probably insist on being the one to carry out the execution in the case of my newfound friend.

I could pack and run and disappear, but then I couldn't finish school. Would running be worth giving up my exams and graduation? Maybe. Perhaps, I could get a guarantee that Everything would be safe if I agreed to go for just a visit.

"Will you agree that Everything will stay with me and you will not cause her any problems and that I will be in charge of her at all times?"

"And you will come without any more hassles?"

"Only for a visit. You will agree it is for a visit, too, or there is no way in hell you are taking me with you at all."

"Did your mother teach you to talk to your elders that way?"

I glared at Juliet and didn't respond.

Juliet stomped her foot. "Fine."

"She flies with me on the plane, not in cargo and she sleeps in my bedroom, and that will also be on the paper you sign."

"That's going too—"

I gave her a stubborn look.

"Fine."

"And I want that all in writing, notarized."

"You don't trust me."

"No. I don't. And we don't leave until I get my make-up assignments for school and speak with my dance team."

"We leave tomorrow afternoon. That should be enough time to get some schoolwork and make a few calls," she said, turning to Everett.

"No," the voice I heard before said. There was no indication that anyone else had heard it. Maybe it was my inner voice, my conscience, my sense of foreboding telling me to get the heck away from Juliet.

"You don't have to do this," Susie advised.

"As I said, I am her only living relative. We could see what law enforcement has to say," Juliet snapped at Susie. "I could have you two arrested for interfering."

"Not without a court order," Everett corrected her.

"I'll go for a visit. A visit."

I again considered my options. I could run away tonight. But where would I go without my mother? I resigned myself to going to California.

"Just so you understand," Everett told Juliet and Brian. "This is just a visit. If she doesn't like it, she's back here with us. I want that in the paperwork."

"We'll see," Juliet said.

"No. We won't see. I'll have a notary here first thing in the morning," Everett firmly replied.

With that, the debate was over, and I was a prisoner of my Aunt Juliet. I fingered the CIA card in my pocket. For all I knew, Brian and the men I met could all be rogue agents. It was still hard to imagine my dad having been tied to the CIA.

CHAPTER 4

I asked Susie to store some of my mother's mementos. I decided to take a ring my mother had kept from her Alma Matter. Our finger size was close enough. Mine was larger and it was a very snug fit. It was the one thing I could take to remind me of her that would be hard for someone to take away without cutting off my finger. I took it out of her jewelry box and put it on.

After I left the room again, I heard Juliet talking about selling my parents' home. I was sure that she expected to get a profit. She was the executor of my dad's estate, but Susie was the executor of my mom's and Everett was my mother's attorney and had done her will. My dad had yelled extensively at my mom over that, but my mom had held firm. She got a beating over her refusal to obey my dad, but she didn't care. She took lots of beatings to get me what she felt I needed. She had also put money into an account in my name for which she had gotten another beating. Despite the beating, she refused to let him have access to the account.

Susie told me not to worry. My mother and dad had both willed the house to me and Susie would try to block any sale. Everett whispered that he would work with a family law attorney to try to get full custody. If all went well, the visit would be short. He suggested I not make a big deal over the custody dispute so as not to prepare Juliet for the fight.

I called my high school instructors, who were agreeable to giving me advanced assignments in all my subjects. Principal Carmen said she wanted to see me when I came by the next day.

That night, I had trouble sleeping. Susie and Everett had been letting me stay in the spare bedroom at their home since losing my parents. Trisha had said she would like me to stay with her in her room but understood my need to have privacy to get my thoughts together. I missed my mom and kept wishing her back.

"Don't go with Juliet." The voice was clear, distinctively female, much louder than before. I sat up in my bed.

"Who's here?" There was no answer. I got up, being careful not to knock Everything off my bed. I went to the door. Nobody was in the hall. I turned on the light and looked in the closet and under the bed. I looked out the window. It must have been a dream.

I lay back down and turned off the light. I started to close my eyes. Again the voice came, "Please don't go. It isn't safe."

Well, my imagination had no trouble speaking in clear English. "Is someone here or am I going crazy?"

Everything crawled up toward my face and licked my nose.

"You are so cute. You should have picked someone who was a little less crazy."

"You aren't crazy," the voice came again.

Someone must have a transmitter in my room. Maybe it was one of those talking dolls. There were several dolls in the room. Susie seemed to be a collector.

The last several days had been both awful and weird. People collapsing, my dad being tied to the CIA, not to mention losing my very best friend, my mom. I closed my eyes. I needed to sleep. Maybe in the morning things would seem more normal.

Principal Carmen was very disappointed about the news of my leaving. "You are one of our top students. I hope this is temporary."

"It is," I said, thinking positively.

"Good. Because, though you won't be valedictorian, we'd like you to speak at the graduation."

"Me?"

"You are one of the top ten students and the youngest in the graduating class. You are also a National AP Scholar, a giant feat for someone your age. You will be an inspiration to other kids who want to excel." She smiled. "You make our charter program look good. I understand Harvard has sent you an acceptance."

"Yes, but I don't know if I want to go there. I'd rather go to some place that has a dance team."

"Will you and your dance team be dancing at the graduation? It would be a real loss if you aren't available to perform."

"That's my plan. I have been assured the California trip is just a visit."

"I am sure you will do well at whichever university you choose. If you need assistance with anything while you are in California, please feel free to call."

Susie had made an appointment for me to see my doctor to get a PTSD diagnosis and have Everything declared a service dog. "We don't have to be at Doctor Mason's for an hour and a half. Would you like to have some lunch?"

"I'm not really hungry. Can we go by the medical center? I want to see how that man is doing."

The receptionist asked me for the name of the patient. "I don't have it. I didn't have it when he was taken from my parents' memorial. I was the one who called the paramedics. I need to know if he's okay."

The receptionist spoke with a nurse and then came back to me. "I'm really not supposed to do this. What time was he brought in?"

"About eleven-thirty yesterday morning."

She looked at her computer. "That might be Anthony Townscend. He was moved from CICU to a private room this morning in the cardiac wing."

"Then it was a heart attack?"

"I'm not at liberty to say. Room three eleven."

"Thank you."

"No dogs."

"Service dog."

Susie and I got into one of the two elevators. As the door was closing, I thought I recognized the person coming out of the other elevator. The door closed as it dawned on me. "Was that Brian?" Everything started barking.

"I didn't see."

"I didn't get a good look either. It just looked like him."

When the elevator door opened, Everything jumped out of my arms and ran down the hall. The nurses were all preoccupied and didn't appear to notice. According to the signs, Everything was going to the correct wing for Mr. Townscend. I followed the signs to the wing containing room three-eleven and opened the door. The IV pole, along with the bag, and the monitor had been knocked over, and it looked as if there had been some kind of struggle. Mr. Townscend was gasping for air. "Help me."

CHAPTER 5

Everything jumped onto the hospital bed and started licking Townscend's face.

"Nurse," I shouted out the door. "Code blue." I didn't know for sure what that meant, but I had seen it called out in hospital shows. A nurse and an orderly ran into the room. "What happened here?"

"Poison," Townscend gasped and then went unconscious.

"What is that dog doing here?" the nurse demanded to know.

"She's a service dog. She's trying to help," I said, picking up Everything.

"Why weren't you watching him?" Susie demanded of the nurse.

"He was sleeping peacefully," the nurse replied.

As Susie and I cleared out of the room, I told the nurse "He said he was poisoned," in case she hadn't heard him. From the discussion between the nurse and the orderly, I picked up that Townscend had gone into full cardiac arrest.

I waited by the nurses' station, praying Townscend would recover. The head nurse walked up to me with a security guard, who asked me for a statement. It was as if they thought Susie and I had done something to Mr. Townscend.

"I just opened the door and found him that way."

"I hear your dog did a lot of damage," the security guard accused as if he hadn't heard a word I had said.

"It was like that before my dog entered the room. Mr. Townscend said he had been poisoned before he passed out."

"You were there when he collapsed the first time at the church, is that correct?" the security guard continued his questioning.

"I called 9-1-1."

"Did you know him from before?"

"No."

"Brian. You thought you saw Brian here," Susie reminded me.

"Right. I can't be sure, but I thought I saw Brian Pretzel leaving as we got into our elevator. He was the guy who was arguing with Mr. Townscend when he collapsed the first time."

"And how did you know the patient's name?"

"The receptionist downstairs told me." After saying that, I worried that I might have gotten the helpful lady in trouble. "It was because I was the one who called the paramedics, yesterday."

A police officer approached us and spoke with the nurse. Then he turned to Susie and me. "I need your ID cards."

Susie handed him her license and I handed him my school ID. He jotted down the information.

"Your address, Ms. Clarkson?"

I rattled it off.

"Our department received a call that you threatened Mr. Townscend yesterday."

"Did Mr. Townscend say that?"

"I'm asking the questions. Did you blame him for your parents' crash?"

"No. I never saw him before yesterday."

"Why are you here?"

"We came to see how he was doing. He collapsed at my parents' memorial. I was hoping he had recovered. Aren't there security cameras, here? If there are, you can see we just entered the room before we called for help."

"It seems the cameras have been shut off. Are you one of those teen computer hackers?"

"I'm not that good with a computer." Actually, I lied, though I shouldn't have. I was acing my AP computer class, but I didn't consider myself a hacker.

"Officer. You are out of line," Susie defended me. "This girl saved Mr. Townsend's life twice. Yesterday and today. She's a hero. I'm a witness."

"We may have more questions. We will need to take the dog."

"The dog only tried to help after someone else did this to Mr. Townscend."

"Meadow's service dog will be staying with Meadow at our house. When Mr. Townscend wakes up, he will verify that the dog was only helping."

I held my dog closely making sure that the officer didn't touch her. "If you have more questions, I guess I can't go to California," I said optimistically.

"California?"

"My aunt and uncle want to take me to California. But I can't go if I have to stick around for an investigation."

"You will need to supply us with the address and phone number where you will be staying in California. At the current time, you may leave."

"Then, I'm not a suspect."

"I didn't say that."

Susie pointed, and I turned to see Mr. Townscend being wheeled on a gurney towards the elevator, presumably back to the Cardiac Intensive Care Unit. He appeared to be slightly conscious but his eyes were barely open. His hands were trembling.

I rushed over towards him, but the officer pulled me back. "Is he going to be okay?" I asked one of the nurses escorting Mr. Townscend's gurney.

"That's her," Mr. Townscend gasped, looking at me. Then, he appeared to fall unconscious again.

"He's in critical condition," an orderly whispered to me. "We won't know for a few hours."

He has to recover, I told myself. I didn't know Mr. Townscend, but I felt a connection. Once he was awake, we'd know what really happened to him.

In the background, I heard the nurses talking about him. "We need to call his son. The poor boy sat with him all night in CICU and only left to get some rest when Mr. Townscend was well enough to be moved to a regular room."

"He is such a good-looking boy. What about the older son?"

"It seems, nobody knows where he is."

"You will have to leave," the officer stated, handing us back our identifications. The tone of his words sounded like an accusation to me. "Don't leave town without supplying us with that address."

In the car on the way to the doctor, I asked, "Who would have lied to the police? Brian?"

"I am liking this trip of yours less and less."

"I don't want to go at all."

"Everett is going to consult with Mars Brawn about custody when he gets back from vacation the day after tomorrow. It's your mother's wishes against your fathers. Maybe we can get the trip postponed until then."

"Mars does family law?"

"Yes. He's one of the best."

Doctor Mason gave me a diagnosis of Post-Traumatic Stress Disorder, but she pointed out that a service dog was required to perform at least one service task.

"She can call attention to me if I have a panic attack or collapse," I said. I was just making that up, but I had seen the dog go twice to someone who was in distress.

"I would have to see it."

From my Children's Theater Workshop performances, I knew how to fake a faint, and I did just that on the doctor's floor. Everything rushed over to me and barked excitedly at the doctor. I had an eye slightly open and was very impressed at her performance. She next ran to the doctor, grabbed at the doctor's hand, then took her pant leg in her little mouth and started trying to pull the doctor over.

"That works for me," Doctor Mason said. "Her name is Everything?"

"Yes."

She typed a note into the computer and then asked her secretary to print it out. Now, I had a medically approved service dog that was to accompany me at all times. I asked her to make three copies of the letter: one for Susie, one for me, and one to put into a pocket on a vest for the dog.

"I don't have any vests, but you can order one," Dr. Mason said. "No physical identification or vest is necessary. An establishment can only ask if she is a service dog and what service she provides."

I was all smiles, hugging and kissing my dog.

As Susie and I stopped for a late lunch, I professed, "For a while, I thought maybe she was Mr. Townscend's dog, but apparently she is protective of anyone in trauma."

"She is definitely your dog. Your mother did get her for you, didn't she?"

"Of course," I lied. "Papers. I don't know where the papers for the dog are and I'll need a health certificate in case I can't get out of flying. Remember what United did to that little pug?"

"That shouldn't be a problem. There is a vet not far from our houses. We can stop there on the way home."

We called the hospital. They informed us that Mr. Townscend was resting and his son was with him.

"I'm glad he has someone to take care of him," I told Susie.

At the vet's office, Dr. Baucus had no problem giving us a health certificate, saying "This dog is in excellent health. She'll need a rabies certificate to fly, though."

"Don't shots often cause cancer?"

"Yes. Often cancers will form right at the vaccination site. I have some thimerosal-free, aluminum-free vaccines. She's small. The dosage is the same for all dogs of all sizes. I'm supposed to give the full dose, but I've seen little dogs die from the one-size-fits-all dose that is better designed for a hundred-pound dog. I'll provide a limited dose, but if anyone asks—"

"She got the full dose."

"In two years, get her a titer test."

"Could you do a titer for the airlines?'

"I could, but they might not accept it, and you might have to delay your flight." I thought about the possibilities and then realized that Cruella would just use any flight problems to separate me from my dog. As far as I was concerned, Everything was my dog. I never could have survived what was going on but for her. I hugged her, again.

"So you want the shot?" I asked her.

I could almost swear that Everything nodded as she walked across the table to the doctor. "I guess it's okay with her."

But as the needle almost touched my little Papillon, she jumped away and the fluid spilled onto the table. The vet smiled, tossing the hypodermic into the toxic waste can. I wondered if he had pushed the plunger at the wrong moment on purpose. "As far as I'm concerned, she's vaccinated."

"And I've been told there aren't any honorable vets left. I'll recommend you to all my friends."

As he handed me the certificate, he said, "If you ever lose this, I will have a record."

"Thank you."

When we got home, Juliet was furious. "We missed our afternoon flight!"

"You didn't tell me what time it was taking off."

"You said you were going to the school this morning. That was hours ago."

"Where is Brian?"

"He's here. He's been waiting for you all day."

"Really."

"And this morning, I went to court and got an order granting me custody."

CHAPTER 6

"What!"

"They wouldn't issue an order that fast," Susie said.

"It was ex parte."

"Without notice," Susie said. "I know you have to give notice even on ex partes." We looked at the clock. It was after five. "We'll have to take care of it tomorrow," Susie whispered.

As if knowing what Susie had whispered, Juliet said, "If your—" She glared at Susie. "Friends try to interfere, the police said they would issue a warrant for their arrest. We're flying out first thing in the morning at a higher cost after missing today's flight."

Susie went to the phone and called Everett. After speaking with him, she said, "You need to provide us with a copy of the order. Everett confirmed that you also had to give us notice of the hearing, given that you knew I had been given custody by the mother."

"I'll give you a copy, but if you interfere with her leaving, I will have you and Everett both put in jail."

I resolved myself to the inevitable: flying into the dungeon of horrors with Lady Macbeth.

Later that night, I woke up to that voice again. "Run. You can hide out until the Shirelles get things handled."

"But then they'd accuse them of hiding me, and they could wind up in jail," I said. *What am I doing? Talking to a voice that doesn't exist?* If I had told Doctor Mason about the voice, instead of getting a service dog, I'd have been committed. *What is wrong with me? That would be good. It would have helped me avoid going to California with the Borgias.*

I lay there, trying to figure out what to do. If I ran away in California, they couldn't accuse the Shirelles of anything as they would be over two thousand miles away. That was the smart way to save myself. In California, maybe I could become a beach bum for a few days until things worked themselves out.

The next morning, we got to the airport early for a 6 A.M flight. Everett drove Susie and Trisha there to see us off. We would be taking a connecting flight in Atlanta. Brian was fuming over learning of an expected delay in Atlanta. The earlier connecting flight out of Atlanta had been canceled.

"Why don't we take a later flight from Elizabeth City?"

"You'd like that," Juliet growled. I was starting to wonder who was the dog and who was the human.

Before saying "Goodbye" to me, Susie handed me a service vest for Everything that she had sewn the night before. It included a waterproof pocket for the doctor's letter. Sewn onto it were a disabled symbol and the words, "ON DUTY" and "ACCESS REQUIRED."

Trisha hugged me. "I can't stand you going with that awful woman. Call me when you get in."

"I will."

And now I was flying into the abyss. If the plane met the same fate as my parents' plane, at least I'd be joining my mother. That thought was more inviting than the thought of going to live with Juliet and Brian.

The airport in Atlanta was huge. My aunt complained as we walked a distance for our connecting flight. Brian was still upset over the cancellation of the earlier connecting flight and over having to wait an extra hour. "I don't know why we didn't charter a plane to fly straight through," he grumbled.

I was happy we didn't have to go through the check-in procedure again. Though Brian seemed to have some pull and had managed to get the airport to agree to give us a fast check-in without the scanner in Elizabeth City, I still found the security procedures offensive and degrading.

Juliet and Brian seemed to be trying to ignore me while keeping an eye on me at the same time. I hadn't had a moment to say more than a hello to Jonah. My dog was in a soft kennel. As a service dog, she was allowed to accompany me in the passenger section.

Against my better judgment, I asked my aunt to watch Everything while I went to the bathroom while we waited for our connecting flight. She nodded and didn't say anything. I had no doubts she disliked me. So why did she want me to live with her? It didn't make any sense.

When I came back, Everything was gone.

"Where is Everything?" I demanded of Juliet.

Juliet looked at me and shrugged. "You shouldn't have left her. You never know what can happen in an airport."

CHAPTER 7

I started running around, calling, "Everything! Everything!" People looked at me as if I had lost my mind, but nobody came to help. I spoke to someone at the airline counter who called the TSA. A TSA official took a report about my stolen dog. I really didn't have time for paperwork. While they were writing reports the thief could be getting away.

I excused myself and walked up and down the corridor, calling for my dog. Finally, I heard a familiar bark. It wasn't an angry or frightened bark. It was more of a playful bark. It was coming from a Starbucks. I ran over to the small airport coffee shop.

A guy about my age, maybe a little older, was holding Everything and feeding her some potato chips. "That's my dog!" I yelled, running up to her. She jumped into my arms. "You took her!"

"It wasn't like that."

A TSA worker, who had followed me over, addressed the guy. "So, you admit that this is her dog."

"Someone put her into a trash can. I got her out and was feeding her."

"Trash can!" My thoughts went to Juliet. *But why should I trust this guy any more than Juliet? I don't know him.*

"Putting a dog in a trash can is unhealthy," the thief or suspected thief protested. "I was trying to help."

"I assure you, she didn't wind up there with my permission. I asked my aunt to watch her while I went to the bathroom. Can't you see she's a service dog?"

"That's why I felt the rightful owner would come find us. I figured that if I went to security, the owner might get accused of abuse for putting her in the trash can," the guy responded. "I was doing you a favor by watching her."

I glared at him. "Stealing my dog isn't a favor."

"Who is your aunt?" the TSA agent asked.

"Juliet. I'll take you to her." I picked up the open soft crate, which seemed dirtier than normal. In case the guy had told the truth about it being in the trash I pulled out one of the antibacterial wipes I always carried in one of my boots. I noticed the guy watching me as I carefully wiped the crate while holding the dog close to me. I wasn't letting Everything out of my arms, again, before boarding.

As I introduced the TSA agent to my aunt, I noticed that the suspected thief had disappeared. "My dog was found in a trash can!"

"She left the dog and walked off. I guess someone picked it up."

"I told you I was going to the bathroom and asked you to watch her."

"Did you see who took the dog?" the agent asked.

"I didn't realize she was gone until my niece came back. I told her not to leave the dog unattended. I have to watch my son."

What a liar, I thought.

"The TSA requires that all animals be watched at the airport," the agent declared, looking around.

"If I had known that Juliet would throw Everything into the trash can, I would have just peed in my pants," I reproached her, treating the possible thief's accusations as legitimate. "Is that how you treat your son? Should we check him for trash debris?"

Juliet looked furious. But I didn't care. I was being forced to go with her, and she had just lied about me.

"Where did that man go?" the agent inquired of me.

I shrugged. It was his job to keep tabs on suspects.

"Man?" Juliet asked.

"We'll find him. And we'll check out the videos," He looked sternly at Juliet. "If you did throw the dog in the trash can, that would be a serious violation."

"I assure you I did not," Juliet insisted, indignantly.

I hugged Everything and spoke softly to her. "I love you and I will never trust an untrustworthy person with you again."

A little while later, the TSA agent came back and asked Juliet to come with him. Brian stood up and spoke to him out of earshot. The two wandered off together. A little while later, Brian came back and told Juliet it was handled. Maybe the guy who took her had lied and they caught him.

As we were waiting in line at the gate, there was a delay due to an argument between two passengers in front of us and the girl checking the boarding passes.

"But we had our tickets and our passes," the man insisted.

"And what seats were you in?"

"Fifteen B and C."

I was ticketed for fifteen A. These people were supposed to be next to me.

"I don't know what could have happened to our tickets and boarding passes."

"Just go back to the desk and show them your ID. They'll be able to print you up two more tickets and boarding passes. As they walked away, the girl checked our boarding passes and our party proceeded onto the plane.

Brian and Juliet were sitting with Jonah two rows ahead of me. I was surprised they hadn't gotten our tickets in a block of four. Maybe it was because of the last-minute changes. I had hoped to speak more with Jonah, but every time we started to speak, Juliet would interrupt us. So, maybe the separation was intentional. Maybe, it was because they didn't want me to infect Jonah with my rebelliousness. There was something sad about Jonah and I got the impression that he would have liked to have talked to me, too. Perhaps that was just my overactive imagination.

I put Everything's crate, with Everything in it, under my seat, sat down, and buckled in.

"Today is my lucky day," my dog's abductor said, taking the seat next to me.

"A couple is supposed to be in those seats. I wouldn't get comfortable." I pointed to the two seats next to me.

"Maybe they had the wrong number or flight. My name is on the flight manifest for this seat."

"That's interesting—because they said their tickets and boarding passes were stolen, sort of like my dog."

"I really did rescue your dog from the trash can."

"Tell it to the CIA."

"Are they here?"

I looked around in case the two agents had wound up on the plane. "Who knows? The Agency is not what they romanticize it to be," I said, recalling what Stan had told me.

He smiled. "Please, let me introduce myself. I think we got off on the wrong foot. My name is Cal."

"Perfect. I'm sure they will love you in California."

He laughed. "I'm sure my parents didn't have California in mind when they named me."

"Look. I appreciate that you are being talkative. But in four hours, I and my dog will be on our way to our new-um-dungeon. And you will be out of our lives."

"That bad, huh? I think it's fate that we met. Maybe I can rescue the princess."

"No, thank you. You've been reading too many fairy tales. Real life doesn't end like that."

"When I bought my ticket, I told the travel agent I wanted to sit next to the most beautiful girl on the plane."

"Now, I know you're lying."

"Seriously. I didn't think it would happen."

I shook my head and looked out the window. Without facing him, I replied, "Flattery won't get you my dog."

"She belongs with you. Anyone can see that."

"Not quite everyone."

"I don't trust people who don't like dogs."

"Neither do I. Look, it's really great speaking with you, but after this flight, I'm never going to see you again. So maybe I'll read a book."

"Am I that bad of company?"

"No. I just don't like getting to know people and then saying 'goodbye.'"

"I didn't even catch your name."

"Let's keep it that way." I looked out the window.

"You don't like your family or rather you don't like your aunt."

"Not that it's any of your business. But the dungeon comment was a joke."

"That's not why I said that."

"I'll bite. Why? You don't really think I believe your story about the trash can do you?" Actually, I was believing him more and more.

"The way you looked when you were with them."

"You saw me with them? Then you knew she was my dog."

"Clarification. I saw you with them after you rejoined them. You're very spirited. But there is a real sadness about you."

Ouch. He had picked up on the unhappiness that I was supposed to be trying to hide. "What are you? One of those phony new age psychics?"

"I am pretty good at reading people."

"Then you know I like to keep to myself on planes."

"Sitting two rows behind your family. I guess so. I think that woman you are with, your aunt, is the one who put the dog in the trash can. I saw her walking away from it right before I heard the barking."

"If you could identify her, why did you disappear?"

"Confrontations are not my style. I spoke with the TSA later and was cleared. They went and watched the video and said it showed me getting the dog out of the trash can."

"Says you."

"They let me board."

"Did the video show who put my dog in the trash?"

"They didn't say."

Why should I trust him? He might even have stolen someone's seat. On the other hand, I wouldn't put throwing Everything into the trash past the aunt from hell.

After takeoff, Everything whined a little and I pulled her out of her bag and put her on my lap. I figured, if he reached for her, I could scream. While Cal didn't make a play for her, he pulled out a copy of *1984* and seemed to be faking reading it. I wasn't about to tell him it was my favorite book.

"Usually, people read books right side up," I told him.

"Oh, right," he said, flipping the book upright.

Everything pulled free from my arms and jumped into Cal's arms licking him, and then returned to my arms.

"There's no accounting for taste. I guess she liked those potato chips," I remarked.

"I can get her more when we stop."

"Not necessary. I'm sure they have plenty of chips in Carlsbad."

"Is that where you are going?"

"Is it any of your business?"

Everything started behaving very strangely. She kept jumping back and forth between us. With her nose, she tried to nudge my hand towards Cal.

"Your dog is a matchmaker."

"Definitely no accounting for taste."

"Does your dog talk, too?"

"What?"

"I don't want to sound crazy. But amongst the barking, it sounded like I heard the word 'help' coming from the trash can. Probably my imagination or it could have been coming from elsewhere."

"You know what they say about mental illness and criminals," I responded.

I thought back to the voice I kept hearing. There was no way it was anything but my imagination or the PTSD. Maybe my imagination was catching. But I didn't need some crazy guy putting ideas into my mind. I certainly wasn't going to say anything about the voice to anyone. Juliet would have me hauled off to some medical professional and probably have me drugged. That's one obvious difference between me and Cal. I wasn't about to broadcast my insanity in public.

I tried to ignore Cal, which wasn't easy with him sitting next to me. The stewardess came by and asked if I wanted to order something to eat. I had noticed Brian and Juliet ordering food.

"The couple two ahead, Brian and Juliet Pretzel, are covering my expenses with their card," I told her. "I'll order your vegan meal. You do have one?"

"A salad?"

"That's fine. Bring me two. I'm hungry. Also, do you have something my service dog might like?"

"We're not supposed to." The stewardess paused. "I could bring her a sandwich."

"Excellent. Put it on the same tab."

Cal ordered a salad, paying with cash. I wondered if he was doing that just to impress me.

The plane was playing an old video. That was weird. Usually, they played much newer stuff. The selection was *The Adjustment Bureau*. I thought about handing the stewardess my debit card to charge the movie. But I didn't want Juliet and Brian to know I had a debit card with me. So I charged it to them as well. Cal also ordered the movie, paying again with cash.

Cal seemed very interested in the concepts in the movie and started talking about his interpretation. "So the idea is that when two people truly love each other, no force in the universe will keep them apart," he remarked, as Matt Damon grabbed the girl and ran off.

"If that were the case, why are there so many bad marriages?"

"Men are no longer men. Most behave like animals. There was a time when marriages were expected to last until death."

"That was when women were treated like chattels."

"Not by men of quality."

I did a double-take. He didn't strike me as the kind of guy to care about how men treated women.

"And you would treat women differently or would pretend to until you catch some poor naïve girl. And once you trap that unsuspecting girl, suddenly you'd treat her like trash?" My anger about my father was fueling my comments. I needed to get myself under control before I gave away too much information about myself.

"A decent guy doesn't need to trick a girl into liking him. He treats her well and is loyal to her for life."

What rock did he crawl out from under?

"Have you noticed that your aunt and uncle seem more like business partners than like a husband and wife?"

"I try not to think about them at all."

"And that kid with them looks like he has no freedom."

"Maybe they are afraid someone will carry him off and feed him potato chips."

"How much would you like to bet they've never fed him even one potato chip since they've had him?"

"I don't know. But they are his parents. So, they probably feed him what they think is best." After saying that, I turned back to the movie. He was too observant and I didn't feel like going into my life's tragedy with a stranger.

But as I continued watching the show, I found myself observing Cal out of the corner of my eye. For a dog thief, he was really good-looking. He had dark hair, cut Aladdin style, and dark eyes that were full of questioning. He had a suntan on what appeared to be fair skin. His arms looked strong but otherwise, he appeared a little on the thin side. From having seen him standing, my recollection was that he was about 6 feet. There was a real innocence to his look. He turned and caught me looking. I quickly glanced away. I had been told that dogs were good judges of character. Everything seemed to like him. *However*, I told myself, *even dogs can misjudge people.*

"See true love wins out after all," he proclaimed as the movie ended.

"Tell that to the over fifty percent who are divorced."

"But what if that over fifty percent just gave up and chose what was easy and didn't go for true love?"

"I'm not sure I believe in true love."

"Rather cynical for someone your age."

I thought of Susie and Everett. They had a good marriage and seemed to be in love. Maybe, it was just that my parents had short-cutted true love and settled for each other.

"Do you believe in fate?" he queried.

"What?" I asked. *Is he back to that pickup line nonsense about fate putting us together?*

"There is a theory that, if you run into someone once, it's a coincidence. But if you meet them by chance a second time, it's fate. I saw that in a movie."

"You don't seriously believe what you see in the movies, do you?" I responded, flipping my palms up in disbelief. I pulled out a copy of a book I was reading for school: John Locke's *Two Treatises of Government*.

"Great book," Cal said.

"You've read it?"

"Yes. I agree with Locke's philosophy."

"I'm sure he'd appreciate your approval. Or rather, he would if he were still alive."

He held up his copy of *1984*. "I'm sure that Locke and Orwell saw things similarly. Man is a positive force until society messes him up."

"Good analysis."

"Have you read *1984*?"

"Several times."

"This is my first," he admitted.

"Oh. Well if you look at the direction our society is going, *1984*, the government, not the year, is already here."

"I have noticed that. So, you are in high school, right?"

"Not that it's any of your business, but I'm supposed to graduate in a couple of months."

"Me too. You attending a high school in California?" he inquired.

"Not if I can help it," I replied, looking out my window and hoping the conversation was over.

He pretended to go back to his book, but I caught him looking at me.

"So are you going home or visiting?" *Why did I ask that?* The last thing I needed was for him to ask a return question about my reason for traveling.

"I've never been to California before, and I thought I'd finish high school there."

"Shouldn't you have decided that earlier in the year? I mean, it's late in the term for most high schools."

"It's a formality. I've been taking most of my high school courses online and am mostly through the curriculum. I've already been accepted at Georgetown."

"Then, you won't be in California long."

"I've also been accepted by USC and Berkeley, but I haven't decided which to accept."

"Oh. Congratulations." I wasn't going to mention that I had been accepted at Cal and Georgetown as well. I had been accepted at a number of other universities and conservatories, too. "I wouldn't go to Berkeley if I were you. You wouldn't know if someone was addressing you or saying the nickname of the school."

He smiled. "You seem young to be graduating."

"Not that it's any of your business, but I skipped two grades. I don't know if that will hold when I get to California. So, yeah, I'm supposed to graduate this year."

"How about your APs?"

"National AP Scholar."

"And I was impressed with myself for reaching that level. What is your average?"

"Fives on eight APs. And you?"

"Fives on nine APs."

My ego instantly deflated. What were the odds? Most students in my high school weren't even regular AP scholars. *Of course, the possible thief could be lying.*

"Have you been offered scholarships?" he inquired.

"A few. And you?"

"A few. Which colleges are you looking at?"

Why was I doing this with him? What reason did I have to believe anything this guy said? For all I knew his AP history involved looking at the AP promotionals in a bookstore. He did seem really nice for a possible dog thief, though. Besides, I suspected he was telling the truth about Juliet putting the dog in the trash. "I was planning on Columbia. I also got into Cal, interesting your name." Why did I tell him that? Despite my attempt to ignore him, there was something irresistible about him that kept me talking against my better judgment.

"I may have to seriously consider Berkeley. So, if you've skipped two grades, you must be sixteen?"

"Fifteen. And you?"

"Sixteen. With homeschooling and distance learning, students often jump ahead grades."

"Cool. I wonder if I could get my old school to let me finish by distance learning."

"You should ask."

I turned back to the window. Enough conversation.

"I am really glad I've gotten to meet you," he continued, not taking the hint.

"It's been interesting, but like I said, we'll soon say goodbye. I'll go my way. You'll go yours, and maybe you'll meet some nice girl, else-where, who will want to share her dog."

"What if it's not goodbye? We are flying to the same destination." He pulled a notebook out of his pocket, wrote down a phone number and an email address, tore out the page and offered it to me. "Now, we don't have to say goodbye."

"So this is a pickup?"

"In case you ever need a friend to talk with."

I put it in my backpack. "This doesn't mean I will call. I just don't like littering."

He smiled. "When you call, how should I address you?"

"Number one: I won't call, and Number two: 'Hey You' will do."

The stewardess came by to ask if we needed anything further. I asked to use the airplane phone.

"Do you have Gagemvoice?" she asked.

"Yeah, sort of, but I don't use it."

"You can plug in your computer and call home through it. This isn't two-thousand-one or the days when we were limited to Airfones. Would you like to buy one of our headsets with a microphone?"

"Charge it to my aunt and uncle."

"As before?"

"Yes."

I called Susie and tried to whisper so Cal would hear as little as possible. I asked her to check on whether I could finish my high school online so I didn't have to start a new school from scratch. She planned to speak with my principal in the afternoon and have an answer for me. As long as I was calling on Juliet's dollars, I asked to talk to Trisha.

"Hey, I already miss you," Trisha said.

"I wish I were there."

"How is Attila the Hun?"

I laughed. I whispered lower so Cal wouldn't hear. "I call her Cruella."

He smiled. *He must have good ears*, I thought.

As I watched the live show two rows in front of me, Juliet and Brian continued their obsessive attention towards Jonah, but more than overprotective parents, they seemed like his jailers, intercepting any discussion anyone on the plane tried to have with the child. Maybe Jonah had some personality problems, but more than anything else, I got the impression that he didn't like his parents. I didn't like them either, and Cal had picked up on that. Every now and then, I caught Cal looking at Juliet, Brian and Jonah. I figured he must have been thinking the same thing I was about them. I didn't plan to ever contact Cal, but I decided to keep his number. So far, he was the only person I knew in California.

CHAPTER 8

We landed at the San Diego International Airport and Brian drove us up to Carlsbad. I was surprised by the crowds of homeless individuals everywhere. Elderly people, veterans still wearing their military uniforms, children, disabled women in wheelchairs. I had seen homeless populations in North Carolina and other places where I had lived, but those were small compared to what I saw on the drive to Carlsbad.

"Why can't the richest state in the nation afford to house their homeless?" I asked.

"Those people are lazy. And they are dangerous. They should be locked up or forced to leave," Juliet replied, wrinkling her nose in seeming disgust.

"That woman with no legs holding the baby in her lap looks really frightening. I fear for my life," I said, sarcastically.

Carlsbad was an older city. Many neighborhoods didn't even have sidewalks. The homeless population had exploded in the main parts of town. Brian's and Juliet's home was in the Spinnaker section of Carlsbad, which had sidewalks. It was on a hill, away from what Juliet called the "bulk of the riff-raff."

As we approached Spinnaker, I saw two police officers dragging what appeared to be a homeless woman from a dog park on Carlsbad

Village Drive. She appeared to be bleeding from the head. I felt for her, but I was a prisoner too. They roughly shoved her into the back of a police car.

The Pretzels' house was set in what looked like one of those quiet two-million-dollar-plus neighborhoods where everyone minded their own business. I got an eerie feeling walking in the front door as if I had just entered Bluebeard's dungeon.

I was given an upstairs bedroom at the opposite end of the hall from where Jonah's room was. My room was like a little kid's room with cartoon figures on the walls. I looked more closely and it occurred to me that the poses could be mistaken for sexual acts. I wondered if Juliet and Brian had noticed that when they selected the wallpaper. Imagining what might have been depicted gave me a headache and I hoped it was just my imagination. The room had its own bathroom. That was handy.

There was a desk and a Samsung smart TV on the wall. I had read *Vault Seven* and decided it needed to be unplugged when not in use. When Juliet left my room, I followed the electrical cord to a socket above it, near the ceiling where I could plug in my computer. Unplugging the TV was easy. At least, I wouldn't have to pull out the TV to break the connection to a power outlet behind it. I got out my laptop and plugged it in. I had trouble patching into the Wi-Fi network. Trouble was an understatement. I couldn't locate a Wi-Fi network. Even if my relatives' network was down, I'd have expected to find other neighborhood networks. Nothing showed up. I planned to ask Juliet when their network would be up and for the code later. *Maybe they are directly connected.* I looked for a cord from a router and didn't find one.

Something about the door caught my attention. I opened and closed it and noticed there was a lock, but it was on the outside. I went over to the window. It didn't seem to open. I noticed that it had some kind of locking mechanism holding it shut as well. I'd have to get a key. Fortunately, the place was air-conditioned.

Juliet came in. "We have a place for Everything in the garage."

"One of my conditions of coming there was that Everything would stay in my room."

"Well, we've had a change of mind."

"Over my dead body." So what if I was declared to have oppositional disorder. I didn't trust her with my dog. I stood between her and my dog and added. "She is a service dog. The law says she gets to be with me at all times."

"In this house, we are the law."

"I don't want to stay in your home. I'm fifteen and I'm sure at this age, the court will listen to me. Either Everything stays with me or I take the next plane home and report you for abuse."

"You won't be able to take her to school."

"Want to bet? The doctor tested her out and she is an official service dog. She is trained and obeys all commands the doctor gave her. The doctor says there are all kinds of abuse laws that apply if anyone tries to take Everything away from me." I was embellishing, but tough.

"For what condition?"

"PTSD."

"I wouldn't wave around a PTSD classification if I were you. Laws are being passed removing rights from PTSD sufferers. They are a danger to our society."

"Are they going to take away the rights of all the veterans, too? Most of them return with PTSD."

"You are going to need to learn to fit in here."

"I got my right to keep my dog with me in writing. Notarized."

"I'm all too aware of that. Everett had a notary come to the house. You need to be a little less paranoid. We really do need to have you checked out. We have a little boy here."

"If you don't want me, I'm ready to go home any time."

"Don't count on it," Juliet said, leaving in a huff.

I pulled out my cell phone. No signal. That was odd. I needed to call Susie and let her know what was going on. I picked up Everything and wandered down the hall towards Jonah's room. His door was locked from the outside. I unlocked and opened it. "Hi, Jonah."

"You could get in trouble."

I put my fingers to my lips. "Our secret."

His window was different. There was a cross-grid of bars on the window. There was a DVD/TV that was playing cartoons. I hoped nobody was watching from another end.

"Do you like it here?"

"I'm not supposed to talk to anyone. I'll get in trouble."

"I'm family. Besides, I won't tell. Let's be friends. Do you have any friends?"

"My mommy."

"Right, Juliet. She is taking care of me, too."

"No. My mommy and Grandpa T and Grandma and Grandpa R."

"Oh. Brian's parents." My grandparents were gone. But maybe Brian had a father and stepfather.

"I saw Grandpa T sitting by the door." He waved to his door. I looked. Nobody was there. Maybe he was an imaginary grandfather.

"Is he there now?"

"No. You're stupid."

"Sorry."

"Is that a dog?"

"Yes."

"Why is he so small?"

"Some dogs are smaller than she is."

"They have big dogs at school. I don't like them."

"You go to school?"

I heard noises on the stairs. I put my fingers to my lips, backed out, and closed and locked the door.

"What are you doing here?" Brian said as he saw me in the hallway.

"I was looking for you. I need the Wi-Fi Code."

"We don't have Wi-Fi. So, we don't have a code."

"You don't do Internet?"

"It's wired."

"Oh. I need to take Everything out for a bathroom break. I don't want her going potty in my room."

"Down the stairs and through the kitchen, which is towards the back of the house."

He watched me as I climbed down the stairs.

Instead of going to the back, I went to the front. The door wouldn't open. It was dead bolted and even the inside required a key.

I turned and followed the instructions he had given me to get to the backyard. The yard was fenced in. On the drive, it appeared that this house was backed up against the top of a cliff, but I couldn't see over the back fence. I tried to get a cell signal. At first, there was none. Then, I moved towards the fence. There was barbed wire pointed inward below the top of the fence. Because it was below the top of the fence, it wouldn't have been noticeable from the outside. It was even on the gate below the top, which was locked. This really did seem like a prison.

Close to the fence, I got a cell signal that seemed to continue across the back wall and along the back section of the side walls. I made sure my body blocked the view of the cell phone from the house. The closer to the house I got, the weaker it was until it went out. Odd that there was no cell coverage inside. Maybe something was blocking it or perhaps the house was in a dead spot for my particular service. I went back towards the fence and called Susie.

"Good news. Your school will let you finish by distance education so you can graduate with your class. I'll text you the code. But you have to take the AP exams in person. You could take them in California."

"Don't tell Juliet that."

"I don't like her. I know I shouldn't say that about your aunt."

I looked towards the house while keeping the phone on the other side of my body. I didn't see anyone watching. "I don't like her either and I really don't like this place. The windows are locked. There is no Wi-Fi, the bedroom door locks are on the outside of the doors and there is barbed wire on the fence."

"It sounds like a prison."

"Exactly."

"The sooner you get back here, the better. More news. The judge who supposedly signed that document isn't even in the local court-house. The clerk said they wouldn't have issued it without a hearing."

"It's a fake?"

"We think so. Everett called Mars Brawn, but he won't be back from vacation until tomorrow afternoon. He's agreed to help take this to court for an emergency order first thing Monday morning."

"Why not tomorrow?"

"Mars won't be back early enough tomorrow. He has to give Juliet four hours' notice and plans to do so early Monday morning when it will be too late for her to get here. They are hoping to catch her by surprise."

"I'll keep my mouth shut. I don't know how I'll last the weekend. And there is something really weird about Jonah. I am wondering if they kidnapped him."

"They had a passport for him. Juliet showed it to me."

"So much for that theory."

"We can check into it. We got pictures of everyone at the funeral. Brian objected to our taking one of Jonah but Everett got him in a more distant shot when they entered the church. I'll have Everett blow it up."

"Thanks."

"There's more. Your mother gave us documents granting us custody if something happened to her. We looked them over, today, and she specifically said she did not want you to visit or live with Juliet. It didn't say why. With that, we have a good shot at getting custody."

A feeling of relief went through me. "Juliet may have tried to trash my dog at the airport in Atlanta. A guy claims he got Everything out of a trash can when I was in the bathroom."

"That's horrible. It's animal abuse. I'll ask Everett to contact the TSA. If there is video, it will work against her."

"I don't know if I believe the guy who told me, but I don't trust Juliet."

"Be careful."

"Thanks, I'll call you tomorrow. Could I speak with Trisha?"

"Sure, honey."

A second later Trisha was on the phone. "How is Cruella?"

"Worse than ever. I think she accidentally took me to Guantanamo."

"Want me to come to California or rather Cuba and rescue you?"

She spoke away from the phone, probably to Susie. "But she needs me."

"My mother says 'no' but I say 'yes.'" She spoke away from the phone again, "Oh, okay."

"My mom said to wait until Monday as you might be coming back then."

"See you soon, I hope."

"Me too. Bye."

"Bye."

I looked around the yard. I put my phone in my pocket and tossed a branch from a bush up at the barbed wire and I heard a slight crackle. I couldn't be sure, but believed it might be electrified. To get out, I'd have to find a way over the possibly electrified wire onto the top of the fence. "What have I gotten myself into?" I asked Everything.

The kitchen door started to open. I put Everything on the ground. "Good girl, Everything. Do you need to do more?"

It was Juliet. "I am loving the size of your place," I said.

"Did the dog poop in my backyard?"

"She just peed. I could take her out front for a walk if you want her to poop, elsewhere."

"The backyard will do for today."

I figured it was best not to let her know how eager I was to leave. I didn't know if I could wait until Monday. I thought about taking off with Everything late night tonight while everyone was asleep. I had packed a little cash and Susie had made sure I took a bank card with me. I had transferred some of the money from the bigger account my mom had set up for me into a smaller account, and the card only accessed the smaller account. But it was more than enough to survive for a short time on my own and to get back to Susie and Everett.

I went to my room and pulled out my copy of *Voices of a People's History* by Howard Zinn. It was not on my current reading list, but it was one of my favorite books. It had helped net me a five on last year's AP U.S. History exam. *Voices*, the companion book to *A People's History*, contained whole speeches that *A People's History* had referenced. Its contents have been added to since Zinn's death in 2010. Among the included writings were works from Jack Reed, Emma Goldman, Huey

Newton and the original version of "This Land Is Your Land," which was really a song about classism and inequality in America. I wondered if Brian and Juliet would ever let Jonah read this book.

Everything curled up next to me on my bed. I sang some of the familiar songs in the book to her. I could almost swear she was humming along with me. I got up and pulled out some baby food for her to eat. She didn't seem to like dog food, and so I had filled one suitcase with jars of baby food. I had also included some containers of powdered vitamins and minerals that I planned to mix into the food for her to eat. Additionally, I had numerous bottles of alkaline water. Given Everything's size, I had a large enough supply of baby food for several weeks.

I had relaxed long enough. I took out my AP books and took some practice tests to prepare for this year's exams.

Dinner was strange. First, Juliet tried to get me to leave Everything in my room during dinner. Brian interceded and said I could have her with me the first night. I saw this as a postponed fight. Juliet dished up a plate for me and one for Jonah. We didn't have any choices. It contained some kind of stew and some mixed vegetables. She handed us cups of milk.

"I'm a vegan," I said.

"Well, not here."

"Then I won't eat."

She glared at me. Brian relented. "It's fine. I'm sure we can accommodate Meadow." He took my stew and milk back into the kitchen and came back a few minutes later with a plate of vegetables, some soup, and water.

My rebellion sparked a reaction in Jonah. "I want sleepy toes. I want to eat sleepy toes."

"We don't eat sleepy toes, here," Brian told him.

"I want sleepy toes."

"Pretend the carrots are sleepy toes."

"They don't taste like sleepy toes."

The water tasted funny. Maybe, California's water was like FIint, Michigan's. I downed the vegetables, which didn't taste bad. The soup broth tasted off, and I couldn't help but wonder if it had some kind of beef broth mixed in. They kept encouraging me to eat more of the soup and drink the water. I pretended to eat more than I did. At times, when they were focusing on Jonah, I downed some of it into a flowerpot that was next to my side of the table.

Jonah saw my last dump and laughed. They looked closely at him, seemingly trying to figure out why he laughed.

Not wanting him to speak out, I said. "He has such a wonderful laugh. You must be really proud of him."

"We are," Brian replied. "He is a very smart boy."

"I saw," Jonah started to say.

"I bet you see a lot," I said. "Do you know your alphabet?"

He started singing the ABC song.

Juliet looked a little concerned about his outbursts. "Now what have we told you, Jonah? Remember, children should be seen and not heard."

"I'm sorry," he said and looked down as if he had done something really bad.

After dinner, I went up to my room. I hadn't unpacked much and my cases were mostly full. But I knew I wouldn't be able to take all my suitcases in an escape so I packed a combination of baby food, water and clothes into one of my cases. I also packed some of my books, my personal computer, my debit card, and my cash, into my backpack and I waited. My cell phones were tucked under the dresser and I planned to leave them there until time to go. I was still a little hungry so, in addition to feeding more baby food to Everything, I ate a bottle of her organic sweet potatoes. I was going to have to leave a number of jars behind. I knew I could get more after I escaped the Pretzel's Bastille Saint-Antoine.

I started to work on my French literature homework and found I was extremely tired. I started to close my eyes. I had the sensation of hearing something at my door. I opened my eyes and went over to the door. It was locked. I tried to use a nail file to open it but to no avail. I would need to do some planning to get it open. In my tired state, I wasn't up to finding a way to break the lock. I went to the window. It required a key to unlock it as well. What was I to do?

CHAPTER 9

I looked at Everything. If we were going to escape, it would be in the daytime, or else I would have to jam the lock on the door. And what about Jonah? I'd have to send help back for him.

I decided to get a little more rest and then think about it. On instinct, I put my backpack under my bed. Why was I so drowsy? Was it jet lag?

I started to dream. I dreamed about my parents' final argument. In my dream, I heard my mother calling. I dreamt that Everything was speaking. I knew this had to be an illusion, even in my dream. "Wake up," my dream dog kept saying.

In my dream, a light was shone on me and someone started undressing me. *This must be one of those erotic dreams.* It was cold, like I was naked. There were all kinds of clicking sounds, like from a ticket counter or a camera.

Then a man's voice said, "She's too old to be useful. They like them younger."

"She's only fifteen." That was Brian's voice.

This was a weird dream. I couldn't be sure, but I thought I opened my eyes a little? Maybe I was dreaming that I was opening my eyes. The light was almost blinding and I couldn't raise my lids more than a slit. Brian and a man, I could barely make out with my sleepy eyes mostly closed, were standing facing each other and talking. "Fifteen is too old," the other man was saying.

"When they are this beautiful, age doesn't matter." Brian waved at me without looking my way.

"You say both her parents are gone?"

"Both of them."

"No brothers or sisters?"

"No."

"I'll have to talk to my buyer. I don't know if he'll go for someone this old. You are right about one thing. She is lovely, a beauty." They started to turn towards me, and I closed my eyes quickly. I hoped this was a dream. I heard a crash.

"What the—" That was Brian's voice.

"My camera. It's broken."

"You shouldn't have set it on the end of the desk."

"I didn't. It was further on the desk. Where's the flash card?"

"It must have fallen out somewhere."

The words blurred out. I didn't have the kind of energy to stay alert. I felt myself drifting back into sleep. I pictured my parents in some of their earlier fights. I wanted out of this dream. I hated the way my dad treated my mom. When she was alive, she would always protect me every time my dad threatened me. He had a very nasty mouth and he was always saying cruel things. "I'll kill her, chop her up into mincemeat if she doesn't start behaving—if you don't behave." With my mom, he was violent. I hadn't believed in hell, but my mind floated to images of my dad burning as pitchforks stabbed at him. The images brought me peace.

The next morning, I woke up groggy, almost like I had a hangover. "What a weird dream."

"It wasn't a dream," came the voice again. I must be losing it. The only ones in my room were myself and Everything. I got up and checked the closet just to be sure. It occurred to me that Juliet might have put some kind of speaker in my room to make me think I was crazy. I wouldn't put that past her. The voice only started after she showed up in Elizabeth City.

I had to get out of there. I put together some stuff in my backpack, picked up Everything, and pulled my current cell phone out from under my dresser.

"They looked for your phone," the voice said. This was getting weirder. If they had, it was a good thing I had hidden the phone. It was my only device for communicating with the outside world. I hadn't used it in their presence since I had arrived. I figured people who would lock me in without Internet would also likely try to confiscate my cell. If the voice was accurate, it was a good move on my part. I plugged it into my charger long enough to give it enough power for the day. I remembered my dad had deactivated my other phone to punish me for putting down his treatment of my mom one day. That was when Mom got me this one. I had hung onto the old one for the pictures and had stashed it next to my current one under the dresser. I slipped that into the backpack as well.

As I passed the downstairs den with Everything at my side, I heard Juliet talking. "We have a mini-dachshund and an older Afghan."

What? I haven't seen any dogs here besides Everything, I thought. *Weird.*

"The mini is a little over one-half. I have papers. He can be on the next plane to Perth but only if I sell the Afghan." There was a pause. "Two and one-seventh isn't too old when the merchandise is beautiful and very flexible."

Perth is in Australia. Juliet hates dogs. She must have them with a friend. I had never heard of someone trying to sell a dog by referring to it as flexible. Maybe it's because a lot of Afghans and dachshunds have back problems and so people check for flexibility before buying. I moved on, wanting to get out of this madhouse.

The front door was locked. With the talk of dogs, I thought back to the pictures of Abu Ghraib from last year's AP U.S. history class.

I moved towards the kitchen. "You're late for breakfast, but Tulsa can scrounge something up," Juliet said coming up behind me.

"Tulsa?"

"The cook. Yesterday was her day off." Was that why the food was so bad the night before? On the other hand, I hoped to never have another meal in this house.

"No, thank you. I am still full from last night. I should say 'hi' to Tulsa."

"She prefers not to be disturbed. We mind our business and she minds hers."

"I was thinking of checking out the local school today."

"Then, you are thinking of staying?"

"Well, making sure the school is acceptable is part of it."

"It's Friday. We should wait until Monday."

"All the more reason. I'm not going to enroll today, but before I left, Susie called the local high school principal and said I'd drop by this week. If I don't show up, they might send someone here to check on me."

"Really. And what's the local high school?"

"Lancer High." I had done my homework, though the stuff about the call was a lie.

"We can drop by the school later today. Oh, your cell phone won't work here. If you give it to me, I'll get you another one that will."

"I'm glad you said that. I must have left my phone on the plane. I need a new one, anyway." I didn't want anyone messing with my cell phone. I figured it wouldn't do harm to try to play up to Juliet. "Your beautiful house is growing on me."

"Good," Juliet said. For some reason, even when she was speaking in the positive, she always sounded like a wolf waiting to pounce. "So what is the backpack for?"

"I always carry a backpack to school. It has some books I thought I might read so I don't get too far behind. Maybe I can go out in the sun to read while I'm waiting." I didn't mention that I had my debit card, cash, my cell, and some necessities for running away in the backpack.

"Well, there won't be time for that right now. Get dressed and we'll go over to the school and get that out of the way."

"This won't do?" I asked. I pointed to my clothes that would have done on any day at my old high school. I had on jeans, a short-sleeved T-shirt, and an unbuttoned top shirt. "This is how I dressed at my last school."

She rolled her eyes. "I'm surprised they didn't throw you out. "

I didn't respond.

"Okay. We're leaving in five minutes."

"Should I go get Jonah?"

"What? Oh no, he's fine."

"I guess Brian will be here to watch over him."

"He's at work." Odd. She was leaving her little boy in a locked room. Well, Jonah would probably be better off by himself than with either Juliet or Brian. When I got away, I planned to report them. "Your dog will have to stay here."

"Service dog, remember? See. She has on her service vest."

Juliet rolled her eyes again. "Very well," she said, almost under her breath. She was tolerating me. How long would that last? "We will look at Lancer, but I'm sure your father would rather you attended a more appropriate private school."

"I didn't at home. I mean I didn't attend a private high school."

"This is your home now."

———

Purple. Lots of purple lined the halls at Lancer High School. I assumed that purple and grey were the school colors. There was a case of trophies. According to the information sheet in the office, ninety percent of students went on to higher education.

"May I help you?" the receptionist asked.

"Margo, hi," I said, noticing her nameplate that read "Margo Lord." "My guardian called the school and told the principal I would be checking it out. I'm Meadow Clarkson from North Carolina but I'm staying in Carlsbad."

"Who is your guardian?" a nervous looking secretary asked.

"I am her guardian," Juliet said. "And I did not call."

"Susie Shirelle is the guardian my mother appointed. It's something that is being resolved later."

"It is resolved. I have a court order." I held my tongue about knowing her document was forged or faked. "An appointed family member supersedes strangers." Juliet looked furious. She always looked furious.

"That's not what Everett said. Courts are taking kids away from their families all the time."

A student sitting with his back to us in a chair coughed. I realized our conversation had gotten out of hand. Margo didn't seem to notice. She was nervously fumbling through papers.

"Your dog isn't allowed."

"Service dog."

"What is the service?"

"PTSD dog. She is supposed to get help if I collapse or have an anxiety attack."

"You might collapse or have an anxiety attack?"

"I hope not. She also calms me." Margo looked as if she was going through some kind of thought process while taking in my information.

"This is not a good morning. We have something scheduled, and the principal may not have time to see you or the other incoming student."

"I won't take up much time. May I use the bathroom while I'm waiting?" That seemed to relax her a little.

"Go outside. Turn right and it's the third door on the left," Margo advised, almost mechanically.

"I'll go with you," Juliet said.

"Juliet, it is bad enough that I have an adult accompanying me to the principal's office. How would it look to the other students if you escorted me to the restroom?"

"I am sure she will be okay. I have a form for you to fill out," Margo told Juliet, handing her a clipboard as I rushed out of the office. The last words I heard on my way out were from Juliet, who was insulting the school, saying I would probably be going to an academy with stronger academics. I happened to know that this was one of the top schools in the area.

I didn't really have to go to the bathroom—except to make a call out of Juliet's presence. On my way, I saw a couple of police officers in riot gear. One stopped me. "That dog's a little small to be believable."

"Huh?"

"For the drill."

"He's not part of the drill."

"Good. I was going to say this wouldn't work if the dogs were that small."

"I have to take a bathroom break before the drill," I said, playing like I knew what was going on.

He nodded, and I continued on to the girl's room and dialed my neighbor.

"Hello, darling. Are you alright?" Susie sounded concerned.

"Yes. But everything is strange. They locked my bedroom door last night and the food is awful. It's almost as if Jonah and I are prisoners. I pretended I lost my phone, and it doesn't work in the house, anyway."

"I can't wait to get you away from them."

"Please, call the principal at Lancer High and act as if you are reminding them you told them I would be dropping by. It's my excuse to get out of the house. I'm here, right now."

"Sure. Mars Brawn got back from vacation and is preparing the paperwork for an emergency order to get you out of there. He thinks we've got a good shot, especially with the fake order. He confirmed what Everett had learned. There is no Judge Carlton in Pasquotank County and the document is a clear fake."

"Thank goodness." I crossed myself, even though I wasn't Catholic.

"How about Jonah? Any information?"

"Not yet. Everett is checking into the birth certificate. Next week, he's going to have lunch with a friend who has facial recognition software. Hang in there. Sit tight until Monday."

"As long as it doesn't get any weirder."

I left the bathroom. I hadn't gotten more than a few steps when Juliet came up. "You were a long time in the bathroom. The office is this way. Did you forget?"

"Thank you. I did." It was probably just as well that I couldn't flee. Susie had asked me to sit tight until Monday.

"Is the drill about to start?" I heard the secretary asking someone over the phone as we entered the office. "Are you sure the dogs won't get out of control?" She saw me standing in front of the desk. "Okay. Bye," she added, finishing her call.

"Both of you new students came at a bad time," Margo said, turning to me and the boy, sitting with his back to me. He seemed to be reading some literature about the school. "With all the school shootings and other school incidents, we are having a drill today and I don't know if Principal Clippinger will have time to see you. Perhaps, you could both come back on Monday."

Juliet stood and grabbed my arm. She started pulling me towards the door. I pulled back to speak further to the receptionist, and as I stepped back past the front of the boy's chair that was facing away from the exit and towards the principal's office, I gasped, recognizing Cal. He put his fingers to his lips.

Fortunately, Juliet was looking at the door and not me. "We shouldn't interfere with their drill," she chastised me while starting to pull me towards the door, again.

"I'm not an inanimate object. Don't drag me."

Juliet let go and stepped back as if she had been caught taking a cookie out of a cookie jar.

At that moment, I heard shots, lots of them.

CHAPTER 10

Mixed with the shots, were the sounds of dogs barking and howling. I had never heard an assault rifle before, but it sounded like the shots might be from one or even from a machine gun. It seemed as if the discharges were coming from multiple locations and directions and different types of guns. I put my hands to my lips. Margo looked nervous. Cal was sitting very still as if he was trying to be invisible. *Drill.* She had said it was a "drill."

The principal rushed out of his office and told Margo and the rest of us in the room that we had to evacuate. Margo tried to push me and Juliet towards the door, but I could have sworn I heard blasts coming from somewhere on the other side of the outer office door. *Wouldn't it be safer in here, unless it were a shooting drill and we were supposed to join the students evacuating like in a fire drill?* I pulled away as Margo pushed Juliet through the hallway door.

"Hurry!" the principal exclaimed, rushing by us in the direction Margo and Juliet had gone. "You can't," he said to Cal, who had leaped out of his chair, clasped my arm and was pulling me towards the principal's inner office.

"We are," Cal said as the principal continued towards the corridor door.

"Are you injured?" I asked the principal, noticing a big red blotch on his face.

"Shot," he said as he opened the door to follow Margo and Juliet. He didn't look or sound shot.

Before the outer door closed, a very big red dog that looked a lot like a lion rushed through the door, ignoring the principal and coming towards me, Everything and Cal. The big red looked like something out of a Clifford book.

Part of me wanted to hug the dog as if he or she were a big teddy bear, but the protective part of me was worried for Everything's safety. I held Everything tightly in my arms. I felt Cal's arm around my waist as he quickly pulled me into the principal's inner office. I thought about objecting, but I wasn't about to rush away towards an unknown canine that looked like a lion.

The lion-look-alike followed us and managed to wedge itself in the doorway such that the door would not fully close. Cal pulled a table in front of the doorway to make it harder for the large red dog to open it enough to get through. The dog backed away. Cal managed to close and lock the door. We could see the dog through the glass window next to the door. He was trying to climb onto a chair and appeared to be staring at us through the frosted translucent glass.

Our large fluffy pursuer looked strong and heavy as if he weighed more than double and maybe triple my weight.

Cal guided me over to what looked like a closet. The dog was still outside. I could hear more shots being fired. Lots more shots.

"This is a drill. The principal clearly wasn't shot," I said, pulling away from Cal. "Are you part of the drill?"

Through the glass window between the outer and inner office, I could see that the dog was still trying to climb onto a chair. I knew it would not hold his weight.

"No. But haven't you noticed that drills usually precede the real thing? We shouldn't take any chances." He opened the closet door as the dog and chair fell through the glass window, crashing into the inner office.

Cal pushed me into the closet and quickly closed the closet door behind us. "We're safer in here," he said.

We could hear the dog nearby. He pawed the closet door lightly and then I suspected he sat down in front of our location. Everything and I were alone in the dark with a guy I barely knew or trusted.

"The dog looked adorable," I said.

"That's a Tibetan mastiff. It's among the most expensive dogs in the world and also one of the most dangerous. They guarded the temples in Tibet. Your Papillion is very small and fragile. No match for it if it goes out of control, more than it is now."

"Oh."

The shots were continuing. So were the howls and barks. I figured there must be other dogs out there somewhere. I wondered how many dogs were outside. The shots came faster. There was no way they could have been fired by one gun. In less than the last minute, there had already been at least fifty shots, some overlapping each other.

"Margo asked if the dogs were under control. That means they're trained and not dangerous," I pointed out.

"Trained to do what?"

"Good point."

My possible dog thief had shoved me into a closet and we were alone. For all I knew, he was a rapist too.

"What are you doing here? You're not following me, are you?" I quizzed him.

"I just thought I'd check out the high school. I got here first. You're not following me, are you?" I could hear the smile in his voice.

"I thought you were doing distance learning."

"That doesn't mean I can't check out a school. I heard you use GagemVoice to ask someone about finishing by distance education, yourself. How was I to know you would wind up here?"

Plausible, but odd he picked the same high school on the same day. What was more disconcerting was his eavesdropping on my conversation. "What gave you the right to listen to my private conversation?"

"You were right next to me. So, how is your aunt treating you, your dog and Jonah?"

"How did you know Jonah's name? I didn't mention it in the call."

"Your aunt and uncle spoke to him on the plane. He didn't seem happy."

"I don't think he is." *Why am I talking to this guy about my cousin?*

"Well, at least he has you to keep him company. You will look after him, won't you?"

"Why should you care?"

"He seemed like a nice little boy."

"Did you try to run off with him, too?"

"I didn't even get close to him. Your aunt and uncle are kind of like jailers."

Weird. Those were my thoughts about them too. Was it that obvious or was he just observant?

"Look, if there are any problems, call me. I really do want to help."

"Why?"

"You're the only girl I know in California and well, aside from the fact that you don't trust me, you seem really nice. And also your dog is friendly."

"My dog is mine."

"No dispute."

I relaxed a little. "Besides, I can't call out. For some reason, my cell signal doesn't work in the house."

"Well, there is always Skype and GagemVoice."

"There's no Wi-Fi either."

"Next, you'll tell me you're under maximum security."

I didn't say anything in response and he picked up on my reaction. "Doesn't the isolation seem odd to you? Jonah not liking his parents, no phone service, no Internet and them treating you like prisoners?"

"You wouldn't, by any chance, know how to pick a lock, would you?"

"What kind of lock?"

"Little window locks. Door locks. I'm planning to become a cat burglar and want to up my skills."

He took a breath. "Do you think you and Jonah are in any danger?"

"Ah, no. No. I just wanted to know for my enrichment."

"Meadow, do think there is somewhere we could meet? I might be able to help."

I was taken aback by his use of my name until I remembered

announcing myself to Margo. "Not if my aunt Juliet has a say. She watches me like a hawk."

"You are fifteen, right?"

"Yes."

"Would she let you go out for snack food?"

"I wish. Her food tastes weird."

"What would she do if you took your dog for a walk? She would let you take your dog out for a walk, wouldn't she?"

"Unless she wants dog poop all over her house and yard."

"I'll meet you at Hidden Canyon Community Park at 5 P.M."

Why did he pick that park? I had seen a sign for it on the way to my aunt's house. Maybe he had been following me, after all. Was he living near my relatives or had he followed me to their home?

Before I could answer his question, and my answer would have been to turn him down, I heard footsteps and the door to the inner office opening, followed by shots inside the room, a horrifying howl and finally silence.

"If anyone is in here, come out. We will not hurt you."

Was this the acting shooter or the acting law enforcement? *Law enforcement is supposed to announce itself,* I thought but then the answer came. "This is the police."

Cal got out of the closet followed by me. The big red dog was on the floor, bleeding, dead, not drill dead, but real dead. I leaned down to feel his chest as an officer in riot gear asked, "Are you students?"

"Future students. We were here to tour the school," Cal said, kneeling next to me.

"Did you have to shoot him? He didn't try to harm us," I reacted.

"He was dangerous. He mauled two students just a few minutes ago. You need to go outside."

"He couldn't have mauled two students. He was in here the entire time with us," Cal said.

"No. He mauled two students," the officer replied as if reciting a line.

"Is the drill over?" I asked.

"Drill?"

"The shooting drill the secretary mentioned."

"This wasn't a drill. I don't know why someone would say that."

"Oh," I said. Not wanting any hassles with law enforcement, I decided to shut down all my further comments. Cal apparently decided to do likewise.

Cal and I walked outside the outer office door into the hallway. A woman, pushing a make-up tray down the hall, clasped onto me. "Where did it bite you? I need to put the blood in the right spot."

"Blood?"

"How about this?"

She tore the sleeve on my blouse as Cal yelled, "Hey!" Next, she threw some red goop on my arm and then put some on Cal's head.

The officer came out the office door and started to usher us out of the building. "I thought you were part of this. But you almost had me fooled with your comments about a drill."

Cal was looking back and forth between the officer and the woman who had just decorated us.

"That was the wrong girl and boy. Here are the right ones," a man said, as he approached the make-up artist with a couple of teens about our age. He looked at me. "I guess more can't hurt. Are you also with Crowds Unlimited?"

Cal nodded and I did likewise. Something told me we could get in trouble, though we had done nothing wrong, if we didn't play along at this moment.

As we exited the school, we could see news crews while the bulk of the paramedic teams waited beyond the press area as if the emergency crews felt the reporters needed the best view of whatever was happening. Cal appeared to be turning away from the cameras, seemingly not wanting to be photographed. I didn't want to be photographed either.

EMTs were putting empty stretchers in ambulances. Not very convincing.

One girl was sitting up talking on her cell phone as she was being carried onto an ambulance. "What's wrong with her?" I inquired of an EMT who walked by me.

"Shot in the head."

"And that boy on the stretcher over there?" I asked, pointing to a boy taking pictures of the crowd with his cell phone as he was being moved towards another ambulance.

"His neck was half eaten by a Mastiff."

"Where is the blood?"

The EMT didn't say anything. He walked off to help lift the boy's stretcher into an ambulance. I figured a lot of people were supposed to be pretending to be shot in the head or partially eaten: the principal, me, Cal, the girl and the boy on their cell phones and who knows who else.

"I guess they forgot their red goop," I whispered to Cal.

As we got to the street, Cal pulled away from me and seemed to disappear into the crowd of officers and EMTs milling around.

Juliet came running up to me. "Darling, I was so worried." I noticed we were being filmed and figured she was playing to the camera.

"Did you see the shooter," a channel eleven newswoman asked me. "Did one of the dogs attack you?"

"No," I said.

"You're covered in blood. You must be in shock," the reporter remarked.

"No," I said. "The officer shot a dog. It didn't do anything."

The reporter turned towards her cameraman. "A brave girl, caring more about the dog who attacked her than about her injuries."

Another reporter came up. "You were in the school when the shooting and dog attacks happened, weren't you?"

"I heard what sounded like shots and hid in a closet."

"You didn't see anything?"

"A friendly red dog. He's dead."

"How do you feel about gun control and banning dogs?"

I looked at Everything, who licked my face. "I like dogs. Where are the other students? There should be more students out here if they evacuated the school."

Juliet pulled me away.

"You aren't supposed to cause any problems," she reprimanded me.

"I wasn't," I told her.

A paramedic came up. "We need to take you to the hospital."

"I'll drive her," Juliet replied.

I saw officers leading away two other Tibetan mastiffs, a pit bull and two greyhounds in chain link collars attached to leashes as other officers pointed guns at the dogs. The bodies of three German shepherds and four Dobermans were being carried away, followed by the body of the big red Tibetan mastiff that had been shot in the principal's office.

The crowd, that had formed, cheered as the dead dogs went by. Next came a boy about my age in handcuffs.

"That's the shooter," I heard a reporter say.

"Where are they taking the live dogs?" I asked an EMT who walked by.

"To the pound, where they'll be executed. You are lucky to be alive. Nineteen students didn't make it."

CHAPTER 11

As Juliet started up her car, I asked, "May I stop at Target to buy some more underwear?"

"You peed in your pants?"

"I'm fine. But I forgot to bring enough underwear for the visit and I don't want to do laundry every day."

"You should have brought it with you instead of that stupid dog. I have to work this afternoon. And I don't have time to go to the store."

"How about if I go to the store while you go to work?"

"I'll see if I can pick some up for you."

"Am I a prisoner? Because guardians generally allow kids to have freedom and to go shopping."

"Most kids don't go to school and wind up covered in blood."

"This isn't real blood."

"What, you faked being hurt?"

"I didn't fake anything. This girl—never mind." Juliet was just turning whatever I said against me. I might as well stop before it got worse.

At that moment, Juliet's phone rang. She put it on speaker as she was driving.

"Courtney Cohen is at the office right now. You have to come in."

"I'm busy."

"She is about to sue the firm. You need to get here."

A while later, we pulled into an office building. Juliet handed me one of her jackets to put over my blouse. "I can wait here in the car," I said.

"It will be much better for you up in my office."

As we entered the office, a woman about twenty-five or so glared at Juliet. "I want my mother back."

"Excuse me," Juliet said to her. She turned to me. "You can wait in the library." I looked back at the woman, clearly in distress, as Juliet led me to a room with a table, some bookshelves and a bar. "Wait here."

After Juliet left and closed the door, I went to the door and slid it ajar enough that I could hear and see a little. "You've imprisoned my mother and stolen her money. What you have done is immoral. She trusted you."

"Calm down. Your mother is incompetent. I was appointed her conservator by the county and I'm taking care of her."

"She almost died last night. If I hadn't gotten her to the hospital, she would have. She has a heart condition and you withheld, you confiscated, her medication. If I hadn't shown up, she would have died."

A man, who was presumably Juliet's partner, handed Juliet some papers. Juliet quickly looked at them and then addressed the woman again. "This morning the court granted your mother a restraining order against you."

"My mother is in the hospital."

"Jed went there on her behalf."

"That's not what she wants. She wants a new administrator and you out of her life."

"She isn't competent to make such decisions, and she will be returned to the nursing home."

"So you are requiring her to stay in that place without medications and with nobody to help if she has a problem."

"I was doing what was best for her health. Carlsbad Happy House comes with excellent references."

"From funeral homes, I bet. I've checked. Families have been complaining about the lack of care and about the deaths."

"Jed and I have been assigned to act on her behalf. If you go near her again, you will be arrested."

"She's not incompetent. She's just a little scattered. You are a thief. You are only doing this to steal her money. This is an outrage."

"It's the law. She will be leaving the hospital this afternoon and you will stay away from her."

"Her doctor said she needs to stay in the hospital and I am her next of kin."

"Under the conservatorship order, I have the authority to place her where I want. Carlsbad Happy House is where I've placed her, and I will make sure she gets back there later today."

"At your Happy House, she is forced to sleep in her own feces. Nobody changes the sheets and the one person I could find who spoke English said you are in charge of her medication and you have instructed them not to give it to her. You almost killed her. You should be prosecuted for attempted murder."

"You are not a doctor, and I am acting in her best interests."

"You are not a doctor. You have a reputation for being the 'conservator of death' because so many of your wards die!"

"You need to leave now or I will have to have you arrested. Goodbye."

"And what about her house? There's a 'For Sale' sign on it."

"It takes money to administer the estate."

"It takes money to kill my mother!"

"Jed, get her out of here," Juliet said to her partner.

Courtney looked in shock as Jed tried to take her arm. She shook him off.

I had heard that the public guardian system was corrupt. Somehow my aunt had been appointed this woman's mother's conservator. How did that happen? There had been stories in the news and a book done by Janet Phalen about elderly people dying under conservators who got rich off the estates of those who had died. Phalen was a courageous writer and reporter who had dared to expose a corrupt system. But I had assumed that that was just an exaggerated rumor.

Courtney left crying. She made one parting shot. "I won't let you kill my mother. I will find a way to save her." I wished I could reach out to her. I closed the door fully before Juliet turned around. Then I went to the table, pulled Zinn's book out of my backpack and pretended to be reading as she opened the door.

"Are you ready to go?"

"May we please stop by Target?"

"Not now."

There was a phone in the room. I picked it up and dialed Susie's number. There was no answer, but Juliet didn't know that. "Susie, I want to come home today," I said. "I'm not even being allowed to pick up clean underpants. I am a prisoner with no rights."

In the background, Juliet said, "I know it's an adjustment. I'll take you to Target." I knew her concession was because of the phone call and for Susie's benefit, but the reason didn't matter. I was in survival mode and needed to do what it took to be alive on Monday.

"Certainly. I'll call you back later to make arrangements if things don't improve. If you don't hear from me tomorrow, send someone to pick me up." I hung up.

Juliet stood there open-mouthed before regaining her composure.

After a minute, she said. "I guess I'm not used to a teenage girl. What is it you want?"

"More freedom for starters. Like every other teenage girl has."

"It's a dangerous world and a lot of girls have been abducted lately." She paused. "Perhaps, we are being over-protective."

"Your house is like a prison. Are Jonah and I prisoners?"

"No! We're just really protective. It's a new city for you, and unfortunately, Carlsbad is very high in crime."

"I know how to avoid trouble. Tomorrow, I want to be able to tell Susie that all is well."

Susie had actually checked out the crime rate in Carlsbad before I left Elizabeth City. It wasn't a war zone, though Juliet seemed to talk about it as if we were in some Middle Eastern country under attack. In fact, Carlsbad didn't have any real crime problem, at least not more than most other towns. But I was picking my battles and it looked like I might have just won a minimal amount of freedom.

We stopped at Target. I hoped to buy lock-picking tools, but Juliet was clinging to me. I knew that I couldn't openly buy anything questionable in front of her and so, for the first time in my life, I decided to take to shoplifting when Juliet wasn't looking. I held my backpack low like a purse so as to make it easier to slip things into it. I felt something tugging at my backpack a couple of times. I looked. Everything was playing with the zipper. I worried that I would get caught. "Don't," I said to her.

"What are we doing in the tool section?" Juliet asked.

"I was thinking of constructing something to put in my room for Everything."

"Brian can put something together for you if you need it."

She was getting suspicious. So, I brushed through the tool section, quickly putting a small screwdriver into my pocket. With Everything playing with my backpack, I didn't want my pal exposing anything I might be taking. I also lifted some candy bars to stuff into my pockets. I knew there might be GMOs in them, but they would be better than the food at the house. I could see there were cameras in the store, but, if I could take things without prison guard Juliet noticing, the store personnel probably wouldn't notice either. Besides, if the store caught me, jail or juvenile hall couldn't be worse than Juliet's house.

"I also need to look for some dog food for Everything," I said. "I have money."

"This is the people food section."

"She eats human food, mostly baby food, but I'm sure she will like these cans of yams, peaches and pears." Fortunately, the yams were pre-cooked.

"What dog eats peaches and pears?"

"Most do." I had enough baby food to last for a while, but I craved something a little more. Of more concern was how I would escape eating my aunt's food. Maybe the regular cook would provide something a little less suspicious. That weird dream last night left me feeling I might have been drugged.

"How long will that last?"

"These six cans will last quite a while." *At least, until Monday.*

I found a box of organic strawberries, a dream come true. "There is no way your dog eats strawberries."

"They are her favorite food." I didn't know if she liked them, but I did. I showed one of the strawberries to Everything. She started to nibble on it. *Thank goodness,* I told myself. This dog was more than cooperative.

"I'm sure Tulsa could whip up something for your dog. We have fruits and vegetables at home."

"I'd rather pull my own weight where my dog is concerned. My mother always taught me not to shuffle my responsibilities for my pets off on others." I hadn't had any pets when my mother was alive, but Juliet didn't seem to know that.

She rolled her eyes.

After that, she took me home. I went up to my room and opened my backpack to pull out my books. *What!* I was stunned. There were wrenches and other tools inside it, along with an Ethernet cable. Now, all I needed was to find a place to plug in the cable. *But how did it get in there?*

After debating with myself whether I was an unconscious kleptomaniac, I decided to let it go for now and took some practice AP exams that I'd have to send in later. Then, both Everything and I feasted on strawberries, peaches and pears.

Tulsa might make better food than the Pretzels, but she worked for them. I kept thinking about how tired I had been the night before. I knew I was paranoid about my aunt at this point, but it wouldn't surprise me if the food Juliet and Brian were giving me contained either tranquilizers or hallucinogens.

"I wish I knew who to trust," I told Everything. "Right now, there's you and me. There's no guarantee Susie will get custody of me and get me home."

"Cal."

I looked around. "I'm hearing things."

"You can trust Cal."

Why was it that, when I was alone and only Everything was with me, I kept hearing a voice? It was a soft sweet female voice, but there was no female in the room other than myself and, of course, my female dog.

"I am going crazy. It's me and you, and I keep hearing voices."

"I'm talking to you." There was that vocalization again.

"Okay. Who is speaking to me?"

"Me."

"Do you have a name?"

"Rebekka, but you call me Everything."

CHAPTER 12

I looked at my dog and then around the room. "You're kidding. This is a joke. A twenty-first century version of *Candid Camera.*"

"Sorry. No camera. Just me." Now that I was watching, I noticed her mouth move a little. But she wasn't using her lips in the way a human would to form the kinds of sounds that were coming from her.

"How do you do that? I mean your lips aren't moving in the right shapes to form the letters."

"I am projecting from inside."

"And you're a dog."

"Call me a spirit guide."

"Mine?"

"No. But you seem to need me more than the person I assume I was assigned to."

"What?"

"Why else would I be here?"

"Okay. Suppose you are a spirit guide. Won't you get in trouble for being with the wrong person?"

"Maybe. But you seem needy. So I might get a pass."

"I see." I put my hands to the sides of my head and lay down on my bed. "I really am going crazy. I can just imagine the girl with the talking dog trying to tell the court that she is competent enough to pick her own guardian. How do I know my aunt and uncle didn't plant a tiny speaker somewhere around you so that they could have me declared insane?"

"I'm sure they would have if they had thought about it. Give me a bath. If there's an external speaker attached to me, it will likely get wrecked in the water."

"Okay."

I went into my bathroom and filled the tub. Then I put Everything in it. "I wouldn't dare dunk you. You could drown."

"I'm a talking dog. Don't you think I know how to hold my breath?" With that, she dived under the water and came back up.

"Still speaking?"

"Still speaking."

"Maybe it's a waterproof microphone or maybe they had you swallow it."

The Papillion rolled her eyes, something I didn't know a dog could do. I pulled her out of the tub and dried her off.

"Give me a series of commands. Your creepy aunt hates me and you know she hasn't had time to train me."

"Okay. Walk on your hind legs."

The Papillion lifted her front legs in the air and walked on her back legs until her front paws were on my legs.

"Here's a tough one." I pulled out my Howard Zinn book and put it on the floor. "Open this to page three hundred."

That was a mean suggestion. Even if Everything could talk, she'd have a heck of a time turning the pages. But I was wrong. She used her front left paw to hold the book open and her right paw to turn the pages.

"Impressive," I said. That was pretty convincing—no matter what page she turned to. I looked at the number at the bottom of the page. It was three hundred.

"Oh my God. Shut up." I let myself collapse back on the floor. "I don't believe this. It's conclusive. I'm insane." Everything came over to me and curled up in my lap.

"So, your name is Rebekka."

"They used to call me Becky, but I like Everything. It makes me feel like—like Everything."

I sat up. "So, did you used to be human?"

"A very long time ago."

During the rest of the afternoon, I wasn't able to get much more out of Everything about herself. But she did know French and seemed to know a great deal about Thomas Jefferson. She recited the *Constitution* for me—the entire thing.

At four-thirty in the afternoon, I went downstairs. "I need to take Everything for a walk."

"Use the backyard."

"She needs a longer walk. Just around the neighborhood area. Dogs don't just go outside and drop their poop. I won't walk that far. That way, she'll get everything out of her system and you won't have to deal with the smell."

"Dinner is in an hour."

"I'll be back."

"Very well. I'll go with you."

"This is what I meant about feeling like a prisoner. I can't even walk my dog without being watched."

Finally, she opened the door and let me walk outside with my dog, or maybe my hallucination.

I had mixed feelings about going to Hidden Canyon Community Park. What did I really know about Cal? His interest in my dog and Jonah was sending up red flags. But Juliet was some kind of monster, and I needed all the help I could get. The park was close, and I was glad Cal hadn't picked a location across town. I just hoped it was only a coincidence that it was so proximate to the Pretzels' home.

On the way, I called Susie and told her about Courtney Cohen and her mother. "We might have an ally in fighting Juliet. Maybe you could look her up."

"Will do. I am so sorry that you are in this terrible situation. We should have found a way to establish that the order was a fraud before you left.

"You did your best. And thank you for the vest for Everything. It's really helped."

"Were you at Lancer High today?"

"Yes. Did that make the news in Elizabeth City?"

"A little. They said there was an attack from some mentally ill former student who brought attack dogs and guns to the school."

"It was a fake. And they killed a number of the dogs."

"A fake?"

"Right. They told us they were having a drill. They had make-up artists. They even slapped some fake blood on me and Cal."

"Cal?"

"This boy I met."

"Do you like him?"

"He's nice, but I don't know him well enough to know if I trust him."

"Be careful."

"I will."

We said goodbye, and I hung up.

I walked to Carlsbad Village Drive, took that down to Concord, followed that down through a housing tract to Vancouver Street and proceeded to Hidden Canyon Community Park. I had looked up the area surrounding Juliet's address before I left North Carolina and had a rough idea of where I was going.

I didn't see Cal. I sat on the ground by a tree. I heard a voice say my name. "Don't look." This thing with hearing voices was getting crazy. It sounded like it was coming from the trees behind me. But I didn't need to turn. I recognized Cal's voice. "You were followed." He paused. "By the entrance."

I could see a man standing by the sign that listed the park rules. I didn't recognize him. He appeared average height and build, but looked solid as if he had worked out. I didn't think the man could see Cal from where he was.

"There is a dog park up the hill. Meet me there."

"What?" I turned, realizing I shouldn't, but Cal was gone. The man seemed to be watching me.

I saw a man and woman pushing a little boy on a swing. I went over to them. "Look, I think that guy over there by the entrance is stalking kids." I pointed to the man watching me. "I've seen him checking out the kids in the park before. And the other day, a woman said that a man, who looked like that guy, tried to get her child to run off with him."

The woman stiffened up. "Watch Nathan," her companion said to her. Then he walked over to the man in question. I couldn't hear their words, but the watcher threw up his hands, turned and walked off.

I picked up Everything and proceeded up the trail that led to the dog park. Cal was sitting on a bench inside the fenced area. I put Everything down to run around while I sat next to Cal. He may have flirted with me, but he was keeping his hands to himself and hadn't made any inappropriate moves.

"I think you got rid of him or at least he'll be hanging back."

"You don't want him to see you. Why?"

"I have my reasons."

"You disappeared when I took the TSA agent over to Juliet and Brian at the airport. And later at the school, you were there and then you weren't."

I waited for a reaction, but he didn't respond. He was definitely a mystery. My dog trusted him, and now that I knew a little more about her, I was pretty sure she wouldn't have if he had just stolen her. He had heard her call for help. Interesting.

"I have something for you." He held out two key-like objects. One smaller and one larger. "See if these will work on those locks you mentioned."

"What makes you think they will?"

"They are bumper keys."

"So, you *are* a thief. I mean, if you have lock-picking tools."

"No. I'm not a thief," he said, sounding offended. He softened his tone. "You never know when you are going to have to rescue a damsel in distress."

"Damsel." *Oh, the chauvinistic type*, I told myself. *Not for me.*

"I mean Rapunzel would be locked in the castle forever with the current kinds of security it sounds like your aunt and uncle have." He smiled.

"I'm not Rapunzel."

"But you are beautiful."

"I guess you're the shallow type, judging women by looks."

"Shallow," he chuckled. "You are also very smart. You read the same books I do."

"Okay."

"I have something else for you."

"Today's my lucky day."

"It's not much. It's an avocado sandwich. You mentioned the food tasting weird."

"Can I trust this?" I asked, taking the sandwich and shoving it under my blouse.

"I want you alive for the next time we meet."

"What makes you think there will be a next time?"

"Fate. We met up at the airport, on the airplane, at school and now here."

"This was planned."

"True, but what were the odds we'd show up at the school at the same time?"

"I'm reserving judgment on our meetings."

"Fair enough. Do me a favor."

"What?"

"Keep an eye on Jonah. If there is any indication he is in danger, get him out of there."

"Why do you care? What is he to you?"

"I could be wrong but from the way they were pushing him around on the plane, I think they might be abusing him and I'd hate for that to happen to any little kid who can't defend himself."

"Who are you to accuse my—" I stopped myself. I felt the same way.

Everything went over to Cal, jumped onto his lap and started licking him.

"Well, at the least, you certainly have a way with dogs."

"She is really sweet. I guess she takes after her owner."

"I'm not sweet. And don't expect me to lick you. Never happen."

"Well, you are good company, even though you seem to hate me."

"I don't hate you. I'm just not into boys."

"Oh. Well, that's fine."

"I didn't mean it that way. I just have been too busy. Activities, school."

"Ah. I get it."

"I have to get back. Juliet will call out the National Guard if I'm not back for dinner."

"Keep safe."

"That's my plan." A thought came to mind. "The dogs. They were going to execute them tonight."

"If you can get out, meet me at nine tonight at Pontiac and Carlsbad." It was a residential intersection near Juliet's home. That did seem odd. *Maybe Juliet has put him up to stalking me. Can I trust the sandwich?*

"No guarantees. Are you a burglar? Because they're bound to be inside the shelter."

"I'll be a rescuer if I am successful. There is a difference."

I walked around the Ann O. L'Hureaux Memorial Dog Park, as the sign called the place, looking for my watcher. I went over to the path to Hidden Canyon and looked down the hill. There was no sign of him down there, either.

The dog park was on Carlsbad Village Road and so I took that back to my neighborhood. As I turned a corner into the housing tract, Everything perked up and gave out a bark. It wasn't a happy bark. It was more of a concerned bark. I continued on but I could swear I heard footsteps behind me. I wondered if the watcher had seen me use my phone when I called Susie. I'd have to hide it really well in case Juliet was onto me.

As I walked in, Juliet eyed me suspiciously. I went to the dining room table and sat down. "Can't you leave that dog of yours in your room?"

"How about she and I both eat in my room?" I aked and left the table. I actually wasn't too hungry after the afternoon feast. Juliet brought up a plate of food. It looked okay and smelled okay. I shoved it at Everything.

"The smell is off," she said.

"That's good enough for me." I took it to my bathroom and flushed it down the toilet. I opened a can of yams, pulled out the avocado sandwich and chowed away.

While everyone was downstairs, I checked out the bumper keys. The larger one worked in the door and the smaller one worked in the window lock. I just had to wait until the right time. Then, I would be out of there—or so I hoped.

As the evening wore on, I started thinking about the dogs and about Jonah. Jonah was their kid. He wasn't my responsibility. My staying wouldn't help him. The dogs were another matter. If Cal and I could rescue the dogs before they were killed, that would be a worthwhile contribution.

I plugged back in the TV. I might as well see if the school had made the local news. Susie had seen something about it in the national news. The incident was on all the channels. I caught a glimpse of myself as Juliet was pulling me away. A DNN newsman said, *"That girl is lucky to be alive."*

His co-anchor added, *"If law enforcement hadn't shown up and shot several of the dogs, they'd be carrying her to the morgue."*

Everything growled at the TV set.

"I feel like growing at it, too. They are lying."

"The news media in your time is full of lies. Back in my day, some of the press slanted the news, but there were always voices who told the truth and got people to listen."

"They are censoring the honest voices these days," I said.

I turned to Channel Seven. A group of teens that I didn't see at the school were talking about the need to execute dangerous dogs before they kill again. One pointed out that most of the guns had been confiscated after the last school attack. *"But notice, we need ever stricter laws.*

Somehow this student got his hands on guns." I looked more closely at the teens. They looked too old to be in high school.

A Channel Seven newswoman commented, *"Those kids are brave for speaking out. I'm certain something will be done about guns, dogs and mentally ill kids. We have learned that all the college expenses of those brave youth will be covered through graduation for their courage in doing the right thing."*

"Bribes to lie," I said.

"Those should be illegal," Everything replied. "Dogs may die because of their lies."

Everything was more than a dog, obviously, but clearly, she felt a kinship to other dogs. I thought about talking to her about the plans for later that night, but I couldn't be sure that this wasn't a two-way TV. I looked down at Everything. She was out of view of the TV. If they were watching, they'd never think it was my dog who was speaking. They might think I was schizophrenic.

A psychologist came on TV. *"The boy should have been treated for a mental condition. Kids or adults who are depressed or who have PTSD or other conditions should never be allowed around dogs. Or guns. In this case, nineteen dead students would be alive if that disturbed kid had not had access to those dogs and guns."*

I found it interesting that the boy's specific mental illness was not mentioned. For all I knew, his "mental condition" was playing video games, something the World Health Organization had declared to be a mental health problem.

As I switched channels, Raquel Madcow commented, *"We've already put together legislation to remove guns from the mentally ill. The next step should be to remove dogs from anyone with any psychological issues. This kid should not have been allowed anywhere near a gun or a dog and yet he got his hands on guns and dogs. We must start locking up anyone with any psychological conditions."*

"Any psychological conditions?" I reacted, almost under my breath, but loud enough for Everything to hear. "Everyone has psychological conditions of some kind. You learn that in AP Psychology. And guns? How many guns could he shoot at once? It sounded like several shooters."

Everything growled at the TV again. I turned it off and pulled the plug. I had PTSD and a service dog. Would they try to take away my service dog? Would they drag me off to indefinite detention? This was not good. I needed to get out of California as soon as possible.

A while later, as I was reading my Zinn book, Everything started barking. I went to her and calmed her. "Everything, we don't want to call attention to you. They are after dogs," I whispered.

Next, I heard Jonah screaming. "I don't want to go back to the school."

It's Friday night. They are taking him to a school? Why?

CHAPTER 13

"It's not so bad. You need to act like a grown-up," It was Juliet's voice. Even through the closed door, the conversation was loud enough for me to hear.

"It hurts."

"Man up," Brian told him.

"No. Please don't make me go back."

I tried to open my door. It was already locked. I hadn't noticed them locking it. That might have been what set Everything off.

"Please, please," the boy wailed.

I so wished I could rush to Jonah to help him somehow.

I heard Brian's voice, again, seemingly speaking to Juliet. "We'll be back pretty late. There are more than a dozen kids being prepared for initiation."

"Don't wake me up when you come in," Juliet said. It occurred to me that, if the food was drugged, they probably thought I was sleeping during the whole incident and didn't feel the need to lower their voices.

I heard someone walking up and down the hall and someone else, with heavier steps, going down the stairs.

There was a knock at my door. "Meadow, you up?" Juliet called.

"I'm about to take a shower and go to sleep," I said. "See you in the morning." *Oops. I'm probably supposed to sound drugged.* I decided not to worry about it.

I heard the outer garage door opening and the sound of a car driving off. I heard footsteps moving away from my room. It was about eight-thirty. I changed and put on a jacket. I turned on my shower so Juliet didn't think I was lying. It might make her relax and assume I was going to sleep.

I pulled out the smaller bumper key, unlocked the window and opened it. With the shower going, the sound was hidden. Was there some kind of silent alarm? I hoped not. Brian probably wouldn't have wanted a security service tromping in to check out alarms, given what seemed to be going on in this house. The fresh air was invigorating. There was no screen. There was no need for one on a window that didn't open. I took some extra blankets from my closet and stuffed them under the covers, along with some clothes to look like there was someone sleeping. If they pulled the covers to check, they'd know I was gone. I was counting on Brian being out as late as he had said.

I included my cell phones, my wallet, money, ID, debit card and a change of clothes in my backpack. There was still room for Everything. I made sure to poke some air holes in it with one of the sharp tools that had magically appeared in my backpack after the store. I looked at her. *Did she?* I next cut a hole in the box springs and stuffed the remaining tools inside.

I didn't know if I was coming back. Having heard Jonah scream, I wanted so much to help him. Maybe Cal could do something. I turned off the shower and my room light, put Everything in my backpack, scurried through the window, pulled the curtain fully across the area and then pulled the window so it would look closed at a glance from the outside—even though it was slightly open.

My room was on the side of the house above part of the garage, which jutted out a ways to the side. I lowered myself onto the garage roof and walked over to the gate. I held onto the roof and lowered myself onto the top of the gate, above the electrical barbed wire, which was slanted towards the backyard. From the gate, I lowered myself to the ground. A small part of me feared getting caught but most of me felt the exhilaration of being free.

As I got to the suggested intersection, I saw the passenger door open on a blue Mustang. Cal got out. "I wasn't sure you'd come," he said.

"I wasn't sure I would either."

"How's Jonah?"

"Brian took him to some school. He didn't want to go. Brian said they'd be back late."

"See what you can find out tomorrow."

"I was kind of hoping not to go back."

"I don't have the right to ask you to put yourself in danger, but you might be Jonah's only hope."

"You really care about him for a boy you just saw at the airport and on the flight."

"I'm a sucker for little kids." There was something very endearing about his concern for Jonah.

He held the door until I was in, then he closed it, went around to the driver's side, got in and drove. I let Everything out of the backpack and she put her front feet on the dashboard and looked at the steering wheel as if she wanted to be the driver.

"When we get back to North Carolina, maybe I'll get you your own miniature vehicle," I told her.

"I wouldn't be surprised if she could drive better than most human drivers," Cal mused. "But I really think she needs to get down."

"Good idea," I said.

Everything dropped her tail, looking depressed and laid down on my lap.

"I heard someone tell the press the dogs would be taken to the Bayside shelter," Cal informed me.

"I still have my bumper keys."

"I don't think those will help," Cal said as he slowed the car when we saw a crowd of teens, a ways ahead, marching up and down the center of the street with signs calling for the elimination of dangerous dogs.

"After nine at night?"

"It's a Friday."

I nodded.

Cal pulled onto a side street. "Let's try to get lost in the crowd."

I had a scarf in my bag and I put it over my head. I pulled a little cash out of my backpack, though I didn't have any use for it in mind, and put it in my pocket. I put the backpack on the floor in front of the passenger seat. It was unzipped in case Everything needed to hide in it. I was wearing a black jacket over my black outfit. Before leaving the car, I addressed Everything. "Please stay out of sight in the car. These people are out for blood."

"You talk as if you expect her to understand."

I smiled. "That's how I talk to dogs."

As we approached the crowd, I saw a woman who was trying to sleep on the sidewalk with her little kids. "Wait," I said, going over to the family. I leaned down and pulled a little money out of my pocket. It wasn't much, but I had to do something. Cal pulled back my hand and reached into his pocket and handed her more money than I could have given her.

"Thank you." She had a kind voice.

I almost felt like crying as I observed the way she held her kids close. They had nothing and yet the love was so visible.

"I wish we could do more," Cal said, as we continued on.

An elderly homeless woman sitting on the sidewalk near a building was holding a little puppy. It looked like a sable and white Sheltie. A couple of teen boys, maybe a little older than me and Cal, looked at her and pointed. One of them pushed the woman's upper body flat on the ground as another ripped the puppy from her arms. Cal and I ran over to the boys. "Give her back the dog," Cal demanded.

'You mean this killer," one of the teens, responded, gesturing to the Sheltie in his hands.

"It's a puppy!" I exclaimed.

The other boy tried to punch Cal. Cal moved to the side and delivered a kick to the teen's groin and then delivered a high kick to his chin with his other foot.

Nice action, I thought.

The first teen put the dog down and went for Cal. I already had my jacket off and flung it over the boy's head before he got to Cal. I swooped up the puppy and gave it to the woman. Cal kicked the guy in the chest and, as my jacket fell off, gave a kick to his head that knocked the boy to the ground. The teen got up and he and his friend ran off.

"Are you hurt?" I asked the woman.

"I just need my little Charm." She kissed the little pup.

Cal picked up my jacket from where it had fallen and handed it to me and then pulled off his own jacket and handed it to the woman. "Keep the puppy covered and try to get away from this area until the march is over."

"This puppy is all I have left," she replied. Cal reached into his pocket and pulled out some more cash. "Take this. Maybe you can get yourself a hotel room for the night."

The woman got up shakily and gave him a hug.

"Let's get lost in the crowd fast and make sure those two guys don't spot us," Cal recommended.

We walked up to the group. Someone handed me a pre-made sign calling for euthanizing pit bulls and shepherds. Cal picked up a sign calling for beheading chow chows. We used the posters to hide our faces and upper bodies. "Did you know there is a law banning unfixed pit bulls and Chihuahuas in Hollister, California?" he asked me.

"Chihuahuas?"

"It seems, the people in Hollister consider them dangerous dogs."

"Yeah. My biggest fear is being mauled by a Chihuahua."

He laughed. We continued hiding our faces behind the signs as we approached the shelter.

The written slogans and the vitriol were like a psychotic novelty. At the shelter, the crowd was prompting some boy to go speak. "Tell them, Doug!" someone yelled.

I heard a person in the crowd near me tell a boy who was heading towards the front of the crowd, "Don't tell them you weren't at the school." I presumed the boy spoken to was Doug.

"Of course not."

The presumably Doug guy in that conversation was propelled forward by the crowd to a make-shift stage.

"Dogs are being used to hunt, attack and kill students. Pitt bulls, shepherds, huskies, mastiffs, chow chows. We are the future. It's time we controlled dog ownership. Unless a dog can be certified as non-violent, it should be dispatched."

"'Dispatched,' what an interesting name for 'murdered,'" I quietly said to Cal. Someone looked at me but most couldn't hear me as the crowd of students was shouting support for Doug, thrusting their right arms up straight while making fists.

"Doesn't this remind you of the Nazi movies Leni Riefenstahl made?" I asked Cal.

"This is a mob with a mob consciousness," Cal responded. "What has happened to these students to cause such a mass psychosis?"

"I don't know. I mean we had unity at my old school. I guess unity can turn into violence."

"Reminds me a little of Two Minutes Hate?"

"*1984.*"

Doug proclaimed, "There are dangerous dogs in this shelter. Why haven't they been dealt with? Are we waiting for another attack?"

The crowd responded "No! Kill them. Kill them all!"

"Imagine he was saying this about any minority group," I muttered.

"This is how the KKK got started," Cal noted.

I thought back to my history books. "Yeah."

The crowd was terrifying. I was very glad I had left Everything in the car. *She'd probably be mincemeat by now—either that or nailed to a cross —if she had come.*

A chant started in the crowd. "One, two, three, four, throw their guts upon their floor. Five, six, seven, eight. Kill them while it's not too late."

After several rounds of chants and loud applause, Doug continued. "Those students who died were friends of mine. I hid in a closet as my fellow students were slaughtered by the guns and dogs. After prior attacks, they pushed through gun legislation. But where are the laws against dogs? Why are killer dogs allowed in this state? I call on this shelter to send out the dangerous dogs for judgment before more students are killed."

After Doug finished, a woman got up and introduced herself as Griddy Newcastle, the Director of PETIS. "PETIS stands for People for the Ethical Treatment of Inferior Species. We have a ninety-seven percent kill rate at our shelters."

The crowd cheered. One of the teens yelled, "Why not one hundred percent?" He led the crowd in a chant of "Kill them all."

CHAPTER 14

Newcastle continued. "We're getting there. Dogs who are alive, particularly purebreds, have a terrible life, controlled by monsters who breed them and force them to bear more little killers. To this heroic crowd, we will allow you to participate in what we do every day. We will open our doors and allow you to act responsibly with these dogs, preventing those who haven't yet killed from turning into killers and rescuing those who are killers by terminating their killer nature. When you finish, you will find we have a giant walk-in freezer for the carcasses —something we have at all our facilities. Put them in there neatly."

"Shit," I said. I didn't normally use that language, but my classmates did, and it was certainly called for here.

"She's an F-ing lunatic," Cal snapped.

The cheering crowd seemed to disagree with Cal. I didn't want to get to know anyone in this group.

The doors to the shelter opened and the crowd rushed in. Cal and I went through the doors as well. The cage doors in the first several rooms were open and filled with protestors as we passed. I was pushed and shoved by the hate mob as would-be executioners forced their way in to join the butchery. There was nothing we could do about those dogs without getting killed ourselves.

As the crowd slaughtered dog after dog, people in the group held the remains up proudly and then tossed them into the cheering cabal, with some of the remains landing on the floor. We saw dogs, with crushed heads and stab wounds, held up by enthusiastic teens while others were lying on the floor bleeding.

"Oh my God," I whispered. The group had pulled a German shepherd out of a cage and put him on a table. Multiple individuals were stabbing him at once as blood spurted out from various areas of his body. I thought I was going to faint, but I pushed myself onward, past the room.

We made it past the swarm to the chamber with the dogs awaiting official executions. The Tibetan mastiffs weren't there. In fact, none of the dogs that had been led away were there. Had they already been executed? Or were they trained dogs that were returned to their respective homes?

Cal locked the door after us. Among the dogs was a beautiful black shepherd huddled in the corner of his cage. He looked at me with sad dark eyes. Cal opened the cage. "Come on boy," he said. Slowly. the dog moved forward. Cal reached out and hugged him. There were some collars and leashes on a wall. Cal attached one to him. I saw a key turn in the lock. The door opened.

"What are you doing?" It was Griddy Newcastle.

"We are taking these dogs out front for a public execution. Those who couldn't fit inside wanted to see some of the action. Is there a back door? We will never make it around to the front if we have to go through the crowd." As he spoke, I attached collars and leashes to the others in the room. I desperately wanted to save more dogs, but I knew that Newcastle would call in the other human killers if she got suspicious and figured out what we were doing.

She guided us to a back door and opened it. Then, she opened the back gate.

"Meet you out front," Cal said to her.

As she closed the gate to go back inside the shelter, we saw the student who had yelled, "Why not one hundred percent?" He had come around the outside to the back. "Where are you going with those dogs?" he shouted as he came at the dogs with a knife.

Cal kicked the knife out of the guy's hand and then grabbed him, twisted his arm and threw him against the shelter fence. As Cal did so, I undid the leashes. All but the black shepherd ran off. He stayed by my side as if he felt safer with our company.

"You don't want to come after us," Cal said, picking up the knife and pointing it at the kid.

I re-leashed the shepherd, and we bolted off with the dog towards the beach. We ran along the beach, aiming for a back way to our car. Suddenly, we heard shouts. A mob was rushing after us. The kid with the knife must have told the others we were rescuing dogs.

We ran as fast as we could, but they were gaining on us. I knew that it would be bad news for us and our new friend if they caught us.

We headed into a parking lot. There were more people in the parking lot. Beachgoers were coming at us from all directions. Several had rocks.

A rock was hurled in my direction or maybe it was aimed at the shepherd. Cal pulled me behind him as he blocked another one with his arm. I pulled the shepherd in front of me behind Cal.

We were surrounded by a crowd that was closing in and chanting, "Death, death." I feared we and our companion were about to meet our end.

As I prepared for the fight of my life, a car blasted its horn and forced its way through one side of the crowd.

"Run them over!" a voice in the mob yelled.

The white Dodge Charger pulled alongside of us, and the front passenger door was pushed open. "Get in!" the driver called to us.

CHAPTER 15

There was the mob and the open door. We chose the open door. The engine revved up to a roar and the horn blared out as the Charger jolted backwards. People and teens started banging on the windows as the car quickened its pace and people behind it jumped out of the way, rather than getting plowed under. The driver spun the car around, knocking the attackers away from the car and then sped off with us and the dog inside.

The driver looked close to our age. "Hi. I'm Derek. Nice dog you have."

"He's a rescue," Cal said.

"That's the best kind."

"Thank you for helping us," I lauded him.

"No problem. People are going crazy after that attack at Lancer High."

"No kidding," Cal said. "I'm Cal."

"And I'm Meadow."

"Nice meeting you. So where are you going?"

"Back to my car," Cal said.

"Care to drop by my pad for some conversation?"

"I don't know. It's kind of late." I sensed Cal felt as funny as I did about trusting anyone.

"True, but those of us who are sane should stick together, figure things out. Besides, there are two of you and a dog. I'm the one who should worry."

"True," Cal said. He looked at me.

"Either they'll check my bed and find I'm gone or they won't. So sure. But I need to make certain Everything is okay."

"Drop us off at my car and I'll follow you to your place," Cal said. He gave Derek directions to the car. "And if there is damage to your car, I'll cover it."

"Consider it my contribution to the cause."

Derek had to backtrack a couple of times to avoid the crowd but still managed to get us back to Cal's Mustang. He gave us his address in case we got separated. Derek was a student at UCSD and was staying in a university dorm. He mentioned he had been visiting his parents in Carlsbad when the mob scene broke out.

As we got into Cal's car, Everything looked questioningly at the shepherd. The shepherd got into the back and laid down peacefully as my dog watched and bounced forward into my lap.

"Don't worry little one. He'll be staying with me," Cal said to Everything. "Now I'm talking as if she can understand."

Everything settled down in my lap, seemingly okay with the situation.

At UCSD, Derek gave us a temporary parking pass. We left the shepherd in the car. Cal put a blanket running from the back window, over the seats to the dashboard. The shepherd seemed content to lie down and get some rest. I put Everything into my backpack.

Derek signed us in, saying we were his brother and sister. Security bought it. When we got to his room, Derek introduced us to his room-mate Crete.

"Would you like some beer?" Derek asked, going to his mini-fridge.

"No thanks," Cal said. I shook my head. I would already be in enough trouble if Cruella had noticed my absence.

"How about some hot chocolate?"

"Sure," I said.

Derek pulled some instant hot chocolate packets out of a cabinet and put some water in a glass kettle sitting on a portable burner that he turned on.

"I heard that they shot a Tibetan mastiff."

"We were there," I said. "He just hung out near where we were hiding. He didn't hurt us at all."

Derek and Crete looked at each other.

"You were there?" Derek asked.

"Yes. We were in the principal's office. There was a drill going on. The mastiff came in and we hid in a closet. Later they slapped some fake blood on us."

"Drill? Fake blood?" Derek inquired further.

"It wasn't real?" Crete asked.

"Not as far as we could tell," I said.

"And that Doug guy wasn't there. We heard him talking to a friend at the rally tonight," Cal added.

"The mother—" Derek said. He started pacing. "He pretended to be hiding in a closet when the mastiff attacked."

"Parkland had a scheduled drill, too," I recalled. "I wonder if that was fake."

"I've always questioned it," Derek noted.

"Wouldn't surprise me," Cal said. "Most of the attacks lately have been on the same days as scheduled drills in the same location."

"But he hung himself in his cell," Crete responded.

"What?" Cal asked.

Crete went to his computer, and showed a mainstream news story, stating that the shooter, a boy named Mickey Truse had hung himself in the cell. He was found earlier in the evening at dinnertime.

"The article doesn't say whether he had a cellmate, what the guards were doing at the time he hung himself or how he managed to hang himself," Cal pointed out.

"Convenient," Derek said.

"But it's Bull! He hadn't even been arraigned, yet," I blurted.

"Police State. This is all about setting that up," Derek remarked. "They picked up my brother in Washington State a couple of weeks ago. He's a veteran with PTSD. He got a call to me when he saw them coming. He said he figured they were planning to insist on confiscating his gun because of the new gun laws, but next I knew, they grabbed him, instead. He managed to send me a message as they were taking him away. Haven't been able to get in touch with him since. I called both the police and the Feds and they all claim that they didn't pick him up. The police commander said that they went to my brother's condo and he had left."

"You think it was someone else masquerading as law enforcement?"

"I don't know. Right after it happened, I contacted a professor he knew at the U of W, and he was going to check into it and call me back. But he never did."

"I'm sorry man," Cal said. "That's terrible."

"They are going after people with any mental health diagnoses," I said. "I saw it on TV."

"Any excuse to create a police state," Derek reacted.

I pulled Everything out of my backpack.

"She's beautiful," Crete acknowledged.

"What's her name?" Derek asked.

"Everything," I responded.

"People with PTSD and depression are more dangerous to themselves than others," Derek said.

"I'm worried about my dog."

"Is she a Chihuahua?" Derek asked.

"Papillion," I responded. "I was diagnosed with PTSD. She's my service dog."

"You better watch out," Derek warned. "They might confiscate you and kill your dog." He put the contents of the chocolate packets into two paper cups and poured in the hot water. He mixed them with a couple of stirring sticks he had in a jar.

As Derek handed them to me and Cal, I related. "I've been more than a little worried about that since I saw the news earlier today. I'm living with people who hate my dog."

"Can't you get away?"

"Family."

Cal looked down, maybe upset, as if by telling a stranger more than I had told him, I had betrayed him somehow. Then seemingly moving on, he shook his head. "The teens were going crazy. They were running through the shelter, slaughtering dogs, helpless dogs that were in cages."

"Sick," Crete said. "I grew up with Tibetan mastiffs. They are really great dogs if they are trained. Do you know what happened to the ones they captured?"

"We didn't see them in the shelter," Cal said. "Since it was a drill, they were probably nothing more than well-trained actors."

"And still they killed one of them," Crete lamented.

"I want to get out of California," I said.

"It's happening all over. Staged events. Frenzies. Loss of rights," Derek noted.

"Where do you think they took your brother?"

"I don't know. My parents have been trying to find out, but they've been getting stonewalled. The professor I told you about, his phone is now out of service."

"North Carolina isn't quite so reactionary."

"It is, but in more of a right-wing way," Cal commented.

"I'll take that over what I saw tonight," I said.

"You don't have an accent," Derek pointed out. "Cal has more of a southern twang than you do."

"My family traveled quite a bit. We settled in North Carolina about five years ago. It's really pretty."

"Pretty humid," Derek commented.

"There is that," I said.

I had thought I had detected a mild accent in Cal's voice. As if hearing my thoughts, he said, "I spent a lot of my first ten years in Virginia and Pennsylvania. After that, I wound up in Connecticut for most of my next six years."

Derek petted Everything. "You can hide your little one, but your big black one is going to be harder to hide from the crazies."

"My dad leased a townhouse with a private garage," Cal said.

"How does your father feel about this?" Derek asked.

"He couldn't come out here, so I'm staying in the townhouse by myself."

"You don't look old enough to be on your own," Crete said.

"I'm almost out of high school," Cal replied.

"I'm living with a lunatic aunt and uncle," I interjected. "I wish I were on my own."

A thought struck me. "Wait. I spoke to some CIA agents after my parents' memorial. Maybe they can locate your brother."

"CIA?" Derek asked, taking a step back, almost like I had the plague.

"They said, my dad worked with them. I thought he was just an accountant."

I unzipped the front pocket of my backpack and handed Derek the card. He wrote down the information before I took it back.

"My brother's name is Daniel MountClaire. You'll call this Stan guy tomorrow?"

"Sure," I said. "But he might not be at work until Monday."

"Maybe you could leave a message or email him to call you. If you already have an in with him, he might be more ready to answer your messages."

"I will," I assured him.

CHAPTER 16

A couple of hours later, Cal drove a few doors down from my aunt's house. The lights were off. He walked me to the gate. "Stay safe," he said. I had decided to go back because of Jonah. If a stranger could be worried about my cousin, I needed to be worried about him, too. Cal helped me up onto the fence and stood prepared to catch me if I had a mishap as I pulled myself onto the roof. I thought about how my impression of him had changed since the airport in Atlanta. He was really sweet and very aware.

My room was as it was when I left. After letting Everything out of my backpack, I crawled under the covers and tried to get some sleep. I kept worrying about the dogs, Courtney's mother, Derek's brother and Jonah. When I wasn't thinking of them, my mind wandered to Cal. There was something really charming about him. Finally, I dozed off, and it seemed like only minutes before Juliet opened my door. The sun was out.

"Breakfast is ready."

"Fine. Please leave it here. I'm not feeling well." I didn't want to say I was tired. That might send up red flags.

She felt my head. "You feel alright. I can take your dog out for a walk."

Everything growled. "Not a good idea. She's my service dog. She'll alert me when she wants to go."

"She's been cooped up all night."

"She's a Papillion. They don't go much during the night. Please let me sleep and get better."

"You better teach her to stop growling or she will have to go."

"Service dogs are supposed to growl when someone besides their handler goes near them. Most have patches saying not to touch. I'll have to get one of those so you'll understand."

About an hour later, I got up, picked up what Juliet had brought to my room, and flushed it. For breakfast, I had peaches and yams. Everything had some of her baby food. I dressed for the day with my usual layered clothes. I had on a blue short-sleeved blouse and a long-sleeved unbuttoned shirt covering it. California was warmer than North Carolina but less humid and the difference made it feel cooler. So long slacks worked.

Nobody was in the hall so I went to Jonah's room. He was lying in bed with his face down. "Jonah, are you alright?" He shook his head. I went over to him. I tried to turn him over, but he wouldn't move. I felt tears on his face.

"What did they do to you?"

Everything, moved from my arm onto Jonah's bed. She licked the side of the boy's face.

"Dog," he murmured. "No!" he quietly wailed.

"She's friendly. She won't hurt you."

"They had dogs."

"Who?"

"The men in robes." He turned over and the tears were clearly visible.

"Robes? Did they hurt you?"

He nodded. "You have to go. I'm not allowed to talk."

"If you need me, I'll help," I said. Who was I kidding? I could barely help myself. But I wanted to help him. *He was the reason I came back last night or rather very early this morning.*

Juliet and Brian were sitting on the couch. "Meadow, things are not going to work well if you lie to us," Juliet said. She was more controlled than usual. She and Brian had undoubtedly discussed whatever this was. I had thought I got away with getting out and coming back in last night. *Maybe not.*

"What is this about?"

"You know what it's about. What lies have you told lately?"

Was I photographed at the rally last night? Had I been caught? I was trying to think back to whether any news cameras were aimed at me. "No. I don't," I said.

"The phone. You said you left your phone at the airport."

"Oh, that. I did."

"But you had it yesterday."

How would she have known that unless the person who followed me told her? "Oh, you mean the dummy phone," I covered for myself.

"Dummy phone?"

"My old cell phone. It's got pictures and videos, but it doesn't make calls as it was replaced by my new phone. I was listening to some of the music files yesterday. But it's not a working phone."

"May I see it?" Juliet asked with a demanding tone.

"Sure. But it's out of power. I forgot to bring the cord. What I really need is a current one that makes phone calls."

I was now glad I had brought the old phone with me. It had a lot of pictures of my mother. Upstairs, I switched cases with my current phone so it would look like the one I used yesterday. Then I ran downstairs.

Brian looked it over. It wouldn't turn on. He opened it up to check the battery, which was in place. Then he plugged it in.

"Hey, some of those pictures are personal. It's not just my family. It's my friends."

He turned it on and looked at the call and message history, the latter of which showed the phone was deactivated. Then he held it to his ear. "She's right. It's no longer in service."

"Thank you for telling us," Juliet said. Not an apology, but one of her more polite moments.

"I'd like it back."

Brian unplugged it and handed it to me. I went upstairs and switched cases, again, and then returned downstairs.

"I'd like to take Everything for a walk," I said. "As you pointed out, she's been locked up all night."

"I don't think it's safe. It's not just you. Everything isn't safe going outside."

"I'll keep her safe."

As I went out the front door, I wasn't so sure about our safety. A woman walking down the sidewalk glared at my dog as she passed. It wasn't as if Everything could hurt anyone. She was five pounds and looked like a miniature version of Lassie but with big ears. Actually, she resembled a rabbit more than a dog.

On the sidewalk, a little kid walking with his mother started screaming. "A dog. A killer dog."

"It's okay honey. He doesn't look dangerous."

The kid didn't listen. He kept screaming and crying. The mother looked as if she didn't know what to do. She mouthed, "Sorry."

I continued walking. "Hey," someone yelled at me. I saw something fly by Everything's head. It was a rock. *What if it had hit her?* I worried about what would happen to Everything if something else was thrown. I picked her up in my arms and looked for the thrower. It was a girl about my age. "Don't you have any sense of morality? This town has seen enough of dogs."

I decided to ignore her and walk on. *There will always be crazies.*

Water from a hose hit me. Some guy was holding it. As I looked, he ignored me. I started to move forward and he sprayed me again, looking almost as if he had just sprayed an ant.

I quickly moved on. A group of teens blocked my path. A stocky boy tried to grab my dog and I ran across the street. The teens ran after me. I pulled Everything tight against my body. They'd have to kill me to get her.

CHAPTER 17

A man who was gardening across the street picked up his rake and yelled, "Leave her alone or I'll call the police." With the rake he looked threatening. The teens backed off.

"Thank you," I said as I walked over to him.

"You shouldn't take chances like that," the man lectured me. "This is just like what my grandfather told me happened in Germany."

"You mean with the Nazis?"

"First, they went after the communists and then they went after anyone who got a mentally ill label. They believed that anyone who had anything mentally wrong should be euthanized. You've heard the news people going on and on about locking up anyone who might become dangerous. That's exactly what Hitler and the Nazis did before they exterminated them. They had total gun control so the people couldn't defend themselves. Here, they've been passing gun laws. Dogs are our last defense."

It was odd that he had made a big deal about the mistreatment of the mentally ill. Maybe after noticing the service vest he looked for a physical disability and couldn't find one.

"Do you think my Papillion is in danger?"

"You saw those kids. If they had gotten their hands on your dog, they'd have killed her for certain."

I was shaking.

"What do I do?"

"Keep her out of sight. I see she has a service dog vest."

"Yes. "

"They could use whatever you have as an excuse to grab you and her."

"Grab?"

"Make you disappear like they did in Germany."

"What is happening to people? The teens I grew up with seemed normal and these did until they went after my dog."

"The schools have been programming children to conform, separating them from their families and morals. Unless they have a stake in standing up, they won't. They've been trained to go with the agenda, not stand out. My late wife, bless her heart, homeschooled our kids. They got into Harvard and are doctors now."

"You must be proud."

"If they hadn't been homeschooled, they never would have gotten that opportunity."

I took off my outer shirt and put it over my dog. I looked around for someone following me. I didn't see anyone. I discretely pulled my working phone out of my boot. There were a few drops of fluid on the outside of the case. I checked my pocket and it was soaked. I slid the phone back into my boot and continued walking. There were some trees at the end of the block. I moved in between them and pulled out my phone again. Looking more closely, I could see that the water hadn't made it past the case. I called Susie.

"I need to get out of here fast," I said. "People are going crazy and Everything is in danger."

"I've seen the news. Are you alright?"

"Frightened. With the PTSD designation, they might lock me up."

She laughed.

"Seriously. I met someone whose brother with the same diagnosis was taken away. He was former military."

"Just wait there until Monday. We don't want them to think we've grabbed you before the hearing."

"That's two more days. That little boy Jonah. They took him somewhere last night and I think they did something really bad to him. This morning, he was sobbing. He could barely speak. He was stuttering."

"Everett got in to see Mr. Townscend. You might be right about Jonah not belonging with Juliet and Brian."

"Is Mr. Townscend connected?"

"He has been calling for Jonah in his sleep."

"He knows Jonah? Could he be Brian's father or uncle? Was this some kind of family feud?"

"Everett learned that Anthony Townscend has a couple of sons. I don't think Brian's one. He's been in and out of consciousness. So, we haven't been able to ask him if it's even the same Jonah. Everett hired someone to guard Mr. Townscend's room so nobody will sabotage him again."

"That's smart."

"When you or Everett speak to him again, tell him I hope he gets well soon."

"He told the police that you saved him."

"Good. I think Juliet is having me watched. She knew I used the cell yesterday on my walk. I showed them my old phone today and pretended I didn't have this one."

"That's probably best."

"Please, get me out on Monday."

"Mr. Brawn is certain we'll win. Don't give us away, though."

"I won't. Expect a call from me from Juliet's phone later, and I'll act like we haven't talked since yesterday when I pretended to call you from Juliet's office."

"We should set up regular calls until you are out of there to put them on better behavior."

"My thoughts, too."

Next, I left a message for Stan but asked him not to tell anyone I called. I told him I wasn't allowed to speak, but I needed to get in touch with him.

My third call was to Cal. We arranged to meet that night after everyone went to bed. Juliet seemed to go to bed early. So we decided on approximately nine or ten P.M.

I whispered to Everything, "I'm so sorry. I think I need to keep you out of sight for your own safety. People are going crazy."

"I understand," she whispered back. I felt her lick my arm. "I believe in you, Meadow." Those words meant so much to me, especially now when I felt so lost. I hugged her through my shirt to let her know I believed in her too.

As I turned back towards the house, I saw a man just past Juliet's house looking at me. He gave me the creeps. I didn't know if he was anti-dog or if he was the one who had watched me the day before. He looked like the guy from the park, but I couldn't be sure. I chose to ignore him.

"It's time for lunch," Juliet said as I entered the house.

"But breakfast was so filling. I don't know how much more I can eat between now and dinner. I need to keep up with my assignments. May I go up to my room?"

Juliet waved me on. I figured she didn't really want to deal with me, anyway. I kept wondering why she even wanted me.

I needed Internet. My phone wouldn't work there. Maybe the cable outlet for the TV would. The TV was always unplugged except when I was using it. I pulled the TV forward and followed the cable cord. There was another outlet for an Ethernet cable next to the TV cable outlet behind the TV set. I had the Ethernet cable Everything had stolen, yesterday. It was long enough that I could put my computer on my desk and extend the cable to the outlet.

I first went to my email. My friends from school were messaging about the "horrible" incident at Lancer. Most of those emailing me had bought into the official story.

Tara simply asked how I was doing and didn't mention the dogs or the shooting. I sent her back an email that said I considered myself a prisoner of psychos, had to steal Internet and had no phone signal at the house. She sent me back an unhappy face and asked if there was anything she could do. I told her that, if I got free, I'd be in touch. She really had been a good friend. I had kind of taken her for granted. In the dance team, she was generally enthusiastic about my suggestions and very encouraging. I wish I had gotten to know her better on a personal level.

Next, I emailed Stan and asked him to contact me about an urgent matter. I told him I had borrowed Internet and didn't know when I'd have a chance to use it again.

Then, I started looking up Anthony Townscend. There were so many of them. I added in the name Jonah. On the third page of links was a story about a little boy named Jonah who had been taken by his mother. It said she had fled with the boy. There was another story saying the boy had been taken from the mother and she had disappeared. It mentioned that she had identified the father as a Preston Townscend, but he had also disappeared and they couldn't verify her story. One article went on to say the mom Tammy had run away from a divorce to a Brian O'Connor. Interesting, but my Aunt Juliet had been married to her Brian for quite some time. Their last name was Pretzel, not O'Connor. Another article said that Tammy and Brian had never been married and Brian had gotten custody of the child without even a paternity test. That last article said he wasn't related to the child in any way and that Preston was the real father. It hinted that Brian might be a trafficker. It also mentioned Brian's new wife Juliet. Maybe the first names were coincidences. There was no mention of Anthony Townscend in the articles. So the links probably just showed up because of the names Townscend and Jonah. There might be no relationship between Anthony and Preston.

I saw a message from Stan. "What's happening?"

"What kind of stuff was my father into?" I responded.

"I can't tell you that," was the response.

"A guy from Washington State named Daniel MountClaire disappeared a couple of weeks ago. Could you check into it?"

"Isn't that for missing persons?"

"Reportedly, the government picked him up for PTSD. He's a vet."

"I doubt the Company would have any reason to pick up a vet for PTSD. But I'll keep my eyes open and get back to you."

"I have limited Internet and almost no phone. Leave me a message and I'll call when I can. Do you have a cell?" He probably wasn't at his office over the weekend, which is why he didn't answer when I called earlier.

He responded with a number that I assumed was his cell.

Next, I went to *Fakebook*. I knew it had been outed for censorship, data-mining and spying on the users, but I had close to 5000 *Fakebook* friends and there were a lot of honest and fearless posters that I admired, there. I never used *Snaptalk*. My parents had told me that *Snaptalk* was monitored and the videos don't really go down for all purposes when you wanted them deleted. Also, the same people who owned *Fakebook* owned *Snaptalk*. *Screwtube* had more videos than alternate platforms but regularly censored anything telling a truth that wasn't to be told. On *Fakebook*, there were a lot of postings regarding the school event. Interesting. From reading the accounts, the teen speeches from last night made the news but not the slaughter of the dogs. I didn't use my actual name on *Fakebook*. So I hoped my aunt and uncle wouldn't be tracking me. I realized that it listed Elizabeth City as my hometown, but there were a lot of teens living there. If I posted that I was in Carlsbad, they might figure out my fake name.

I private messaged a guy who called himself Rant Edwards. He had claimed that there were oddities in the Lancer videos. People were attacking him and calling him a conspiracy theorist. My message read:

"I'm not in a position to use the Net much or talk and I must remain anonymous. I was there. It was a drill. They said so. They slapped fake blood on me and shot one of the dogs who didn't harm anyone, as far as I could tell. A mob of teens killed a bunch of dogs in Carlsbad last night. All dogs, here, are in danger. And I overheard a conversation with that Doug guy. He wasn't at the school when the drill occurred."

I also sent Rant a friend request and looked through his list of friends and some of his public postings. He had at one time been a Bernie supporter. Weren't most of us?

I remember years ago, my mother had been really excited about Bernie Sanders. I was too young to vote and still am too young to vote, but I went door to door for him with my mom. That was before the 2016 election was rigged and the guy who was supposed to be a fall guy for Hillary was elected in the general election, overcoming the margin of Hillary's cheat. My dad had supported Hillary.

I remember how betrayed my mother felt when Bernie accused his supporters of being Russian stooges. I had decided that politics was a game played by the rich and those who believed in politics. Both major parties were corrupt.

Watching my mom's trust in Bernie get deflated, I found it hard to believe that there was any political solution to anything. There were the Dennis Kuciniches and Cynthia McKinneys of the world, but though they had remained faithful to the people and their principles, they were no longer in Congress. *Maybe I can send them a message about what is going on,* I thought. I debated with myself and then sent them both the same message I had sent to Rant with a note that I was fifteen.

I heard footsteps in the hall. I shut down my computer and pulled out the cord. I quickly reattached the one to the TV, plugged it in and started watching. Juliet opened the door without knocking.

"I'm doing the laundry. Do you have any bath towels you'd like me to wash?" *Juliet helping by washing my bath towels?* She didn't seem the domestic type. I went into the bathroom and got two out. I didn't trust her not to put a topical poison on them, but she had had lots of opportunities to do that already if her plan was to kill me. Her intrusion seemed like more of an excuse to spy on me.

"I was just taking a break from my studying while watching TV. I need Internet to study for my AP exams."

"APs are so meaningless. They didn't help me."

I bet. "They are important to me. I start college next year."

"I told you that was a bad idea."

"This argument is not happening. I need some space."

"You need to change your attitude." She closed the door.

I saw a picture of Lancer High on the news. Raquel Madcow was speaking. *"We have reason to believe the Russians supplied the mentally disturbed student with the dangerous dogs. This is an attack on America."*

Oh really! I thought. *Will she ever get off that Russia kick?*

She continued, *"Anyone with PTSD should be picked up so they cannot be used by the Russians to harm Americans. We can all be proud of those courageous teens like Doug Carson for standing up against the use of dangerous dogs as weapons."* I turned it off, unplugged it and placed a jacket over the top of the screen.

I looked at Everything. "Come here, little weapon."

"People in your time are insane."

"That's for sure. You said you were named Rebekka, long ago. When was that?"

"Back in the Eighteenth Century."

"Were you there when the country was founded?"

"My dad took my brother to meetings with Jefferson at the time of the *Declaration*. I was a couple of years younger than you at the time of the *Constitutional* Convention."

"Your brother?"

"Well, he was less than a third your age back then, but he accompanied my dad to discussions with Benjamin Franklin and Thomas Jefferson."

"Wow. That's really amazing. Were you in Pennsylvania or Virginia?"

"Both. We also knew Patrick Henry, Alexander Hamilton, John Adams, Thomas Paine and a lot of other people in your history books."

"Back when people believed in freedom and human rights." I looked at Everything. "And animal rights."

"This is a different world."

"I saw that last night." I looked at my books. "I really need to keep studying for my AP exams."

"Where will you take them?"

"I'm scheduled to take them in Elizabeth City. I hope I can."

"Do you really think they will try to harm me?"

"That rock today could have done serious damage. You'd best stay out of sight until this is over."

"What if it's not over?"

"Things do seem to be getting worse. One of my subjects of this year's APs is European History. The teens last night and today reminded me a lot of the HJs. Those were the Hitler Youth."

"If you said that publicly, you'd be in trouble, wouldn't you?"

"Of course. People don't like to hear the truth when they are on some bandwagon. If they do try to come for us, I want you to hide. You're small. You could crawl under couches or behind furniture, hide in a towel and sneak away when it's safe."

"Where would I go?"

"Can you talk to anyone else?"

"I don't like to."

I lowered my voice to whisper to her as if the walls had ears. "Well, my phone can be opened on voice command with the password Montesquieu."

"Montesquieu," she repeated.

"You can tell it to call Cal. He'll help, I think."

"Oh, he'll help. He's a nerd and not as nice as you, but he's okay."

"You like him, don't you?"

"He'll do."

"Actually—" I took my phone out of its hiding place and placed it in the zippered pocket on the side of Everything's vest. It barely fit and only did so because the pocket took up half the vest. "You'll have to talk loud, but use it if you are ever in danger."

"Will do."

I turned my computer back on and took some practice AP Physics and European History exams that my school had given me on a flash drive. The physics exam was mostly problem-solving, multiple choice and short answer. The European History exam was a combination of objective questions and essays. I still had to send in the U.S. Government and Politics and English Literature and Composition practice exams I had taken since arriving. The files immediately gave me back the feedback of one hundred percent on everything but my essays, which I was to email in with the exam results. It would give me an excuse to force Juliet and Brian to let me use the Net. I needed to get the practice tests in by the end of school on Monday at the latest. Even though I was already a National AP Scholar, the more credits I had, the more freedom I would have in college. And I didn't want any of my universities to renege on my acceptance. The official acceptances were supposed to be going out later this month, but I had already heard from five of the colleges to which I had applied that they would be sending me acceptances and scholarships. Apparently, Cal had also gotten early acceptance letters. But they were always conditional on completion of expected work.

Dinner time came and Juliet again barged into my room. Fortunately, I was still just using the computer offline. "I need Internet to turn in my practice AP exams. The school is expecting them."

"It's Saturday. The school won't be open until Monday. You need to be part of the family. Now come downstairs for dinner."

"After I finish my next two exams."

"Should I confiscate your computer?"

"I'm supposed to call Susie later tonight. If I don't or if I tell her you took my computer, I'm sure she'll call 9-1-1."

Juliet rolled her eyes. "You better stop threatening me or there will be serious consequences. You can skip dinner tonight."

"Fine." Actually, that was more than fine. I wouldn't have to pretend to eat whatever they were dishing out.

As long as I was on a no dinner punishment, I might have a chance to sneak use of the Internet again. I went online and uploaded my exams. I sent the principal a message asking her to please assist Susie and Everett in gaining full custody of me. My message told her I had to sneak my AP assignments onto the Net as I had been denied official access and my aunt was threatening to stop me from graduating. I sent a similar message to my favorite teacher, Ms. Brown. Ms. Brown was my AP English Lit instructor. She had always been warm towards me and had once told me I was her favorite student. I advised both not to let Juliet know I had managed to get on the Net. I was a little worried that they were monitoring the router, but it was dinner time and I was safer now than before.

I looked through my email. There was a long list of unread emails, mostly from my dance team and other students at the school. There was a very snippy one from Jenna. "Heard you won't be back. We'll miss you." There were a lot of condolences but no new emails from Stan.

I went on to *FakeBook* and noticed I had a private message from Rant. It read.

"Are you the girl with long blonde hair and a torn sleeve? Nothing about

the attack adds up. They are proposing laws across the country to eliminate all dogs. Your voice is needed."

He was too close to identifying me. I responded. *"Give me until Monday night if you want my voice to join in. Otherwise, I might not be able to speak at all."*

Laws. I wondered, *would they really pass laws to kill dogs? Would they pass laws to take dogs away from people like me?*

I saw online that there was a march on the downtown shelter in San Diego scheduled for tonight. How early could I get out? They knew they hadn't drugged me tonight if that was what happened two nights back. So they might expect me to catch them if they checked on me in the middle of the night. On the other hand, Juliet had no qualms about coming into my room unannounced.

I looked at the paper Cal had given me with his email address. I was glad I hadn't thrown it away. I had always been shy about contacting boys and I didn't want Cal to think I was interested in him. I hadn't even asked his last name so as not to sound too interested. I put my qualms aside and emailed him, *"We have more dogs to save. I don't know what time I will be available. I can't let them catch me on the Net, and I don't have phone access here."*

A minute later a response came. *"I'll be waiting around the same corner, starting in an hour. I am borrowing a white van for the rescue."*

"Thank you. I'll come when I think it's safe." I disconnected the computer but did not wire back in the TV. They wouldn't know unless they were watching me and if they were, they'd fix it when I wasn't home.

It was still light outside. I went downstairs to the dining room, where Brian and Juliet were having dinner. "I need to call Susie. The depression is really getting to me, and I want to sleep and be alone for the rest of the night. Tomorrow morning, I'd like to go to a church. It might help me with recovery."

Juliet asked, "Would you like to talk to me and Brian about the depression?"

"No. I just need to be by myself. Please, at least, give me that space."

"Space isn't always good."

"Can I call Susie so she doesn't panic?"

They pointed me toward a phone in the dining room. They were going to listen.

"Hi. It's me," I said, as Everett answered.

"How is it going?"

"Susie, it's so good to speak with you."

"Someone is watching you."

"Right."

"Are you safe?"

"I don't know. But it always feels good to speak with you."

"We'll get you out of there as soon as we can."

"That is so sweet of you. Of course, I'll call back, tomorrow, to let you know how I'm doing."

"There's more I need to tell you when you aren't monitored."

"Yes. I know that rest will help. Juliet has promised to give me some privacy tonight so I can rest and restore my health."

"Call by five tomorrow or we'll do a welfare check."

"That is a wonderful idea. It will help me sleep tight tonight and yes, I will call by five tomorrow."

"If you can get to a phone unnoticed, call back tonight."

"Love you, too. Bye."

Juliet and Brian had been pretending to eat. Jonah looked like he wanted to speak with me. I wished I could figure out a way to get him away from Brian and Juliet long enough to find out what was going on with him.

I said goodnight and went up to my room.

I thought about the fact that they had wired telephones. Cell phones could be tracked and monitored by the government. *How much did they have to hide?*

I covered the TV, though even a smart TV shouldn't be able to pick up anything unplugged—I didn't think. Then I turned on the shower and prepared to leave, opening the window a little. Through the water, I could hear more screams. "I don't want to go. I don't want to go." Brian was taking Jonah wherever, again, but at an earlier time, tonight. An hour hadn't passed, and so Cal wasn't nearby, yet.

I heard the garage door open and the car drive out. I turned off the shower water and waited. My curtain was closed over the slightly open window. My door started to open. I jumped into bed. It was Juliet.

"Would you like to talk?"

"Please go."

"You would do better if you were less resistant to me."

"I told Susie you promised to let me rest, alone. Please. I lost my mother only a week ago."

"And your father."

"Right. And I need to deal with it. It's more than depressing. Please, at least, give me tonight."

"I expect you to be more cooperative, tomorrow." She closed the door. I stuffed my bed and climbed out the window with Everything in my backpack. My window, being at the end of the upstairs hall over the garage and nearest to the gate, made it harder for her to spot me. Unless she walked outside, she wouldn't see me. I didn't think she had that much energy.

On the roof, something crackled beneath my step. I halted. It was some leafy debris that must have blown onto the roof. If I stayed in place too long, Juliet might go outside to look. I slowly and carefully, proceeded, being as quiet as possible.

Once down, I walked the opposite way from where I was meeting Cal. I decided to go around an extra block to avoid any chance of being seen from the front of the house.

When I got to the meeting spot, the van was already there. It was a white van with no windows on its rear sides or tail. But it wasn't Cal who was driving. It was Crete. Cal came around from the passenger side. "I thought we might need some help."

Derek got out of the back.

"I asked Stan to look into your Daniel's disappearance and he said he would. I hope he finds your brother," I told him.

"Thank you."

"Ready to go?" Crete asked. Cal and I got into the front with me in the middle while Derek rode in the back. I pulled Everything out of my backpack and held her in my lap.

"So is this your van?" I asked Crete.

"I borrowed it from one of my neighbors," Cal said. "Crete knows his way around San Diego better than I do. So it makes more sense for him to drive."

"Also, I drive very fast," Crete said.

"The animal shelters in San Diego County already have a very high euthanasia rate." Derek pointed out from behind.

"Such a lovely term for murder," Cal responded. I liked him, more and more.

"How is your shepherd doing?" I inquired.

"I left him at home, inside, with a lot of food. He actually seems happy for the attention, glad to be out of that shelter."

"Can you believe he was in the kill section?" I asked.

"The kill shelters are unconscionable," Crete remarked.

"The shelter we are going to is in Mission Valley," Derek said. "There is a major law school above it. I wonder if any attorneys there will defend the dogs."

"Maybe," I responded. "If we rescue any, where will we put them? I'm certain Cal's place isn't large enough for all the strays in San Diego."

"My parents will help," Crete said.

"You asked them?" I responded.

"No. But they love dogs. They have enough rooms to take in perhaps six or eight."

"That's cool."

"If Crete's parents are helping, I'll pressure my parents into putting a couple in my room, a couple in Daniel's room and a couple in the garage," Derek joined in.

"Any idea how we'll get in?" I asked.

"We'll figure something out," Cal said. "Do you have the bumper keys?"

"Yes, but the place is probably alarmed."

"My uncle's an electrician and I'm studying electro-physics. I know how to cut the power," Crete said.

"Wow." I thought back to the other night. "I hope they don't open this shelter to the mob like last night. So many dogs were slaughtered."

"In a sane society, that would never happen," Crete responded.

"This is definitely not the society our Founders envisioned," Cal remarked.

"After nine-eleven, the government kind of threw out the *Constitution* and *Bill of Rights*," I noted.

"How can they do that? They were to be living documents. What they have done since nine-eleven is treason," Cal responded.

"You go lock up our leaders," Derek suggested. "The military should be doing just that. It isn't."

"What about the Oathkeepers?" I asked.

"Oathkeepers?" Cal inquired.

"It was a group that called upon all public servants who had taken an oath to the *Constitution* to defend it and the public. They had members who were in the military and some of the police forces. I haven't heard much about them in a while."

"The government went after the leadership. They can't have people standing up for the *Constitution,* here." Derek replied. After a pause, he continued. "But you have given me an idea. I'm going to try to contact my brother's unit. Maybe they can use their connections to help find him."

"If he was in the military, he's probably pretty sturdy," I said, trying to reassure Derek.

"You didn't see him after his last tour of duty. I think they made him do some pretty bad stuff over there."

"War is organized murder," I stated.

"I don't think the colonists saw it that way," Cal said.

"The ones at the top who stood to profit from it probably saw it a lot differently than the idealists," Derek threw in.

"Isn't that a little cynical?" Cal asked.

"Read Howard Zinn's *People's History of the United States,*" I said, supporting Derek.

"Great book," Derek agreed.

"I'll have to read it," Cal said.

"You didn't read it for AP U.S. History?"

"No. But I remember hearing that it was a good source."

"It's the number one reference for taking the exam," Derek noted. "What score did you get on your exam?"

"Five."

"Can't argue with that," Crete said.

As we pulled into Mission Valley, the streets were full of marchers. "I didn't realize there were this many students in San Diego," I said.

"There are a lot of colleges in addition to the high schools. There's USD up the hill, San Diego State up another hill, USIU, Point Loma University, and of course UCSD, which contains five colleges," Crete responded.

"You think these are college students?"

"It's a mix. Probably a lot of the protesters are getting paid and the rest are go-alongs," Derek reasoned.

"Paid?" I asked.

"Mobs on Demand and other organizations supply crowds for events, even for staged events," Derek said.

"Like what happened at Lancer?"

"I didn't see many students outside when we got out there. Did you?" Cal asked.

"Actually, no. And they supposedly evacuated the school."

"Some of the organizations even advertise that they will rent out cadavers for the events," Derek continued.

"Wonderful. How do you tell the difference between a staged event and a real one?" I asked.

"In a real one, they don't need actors, the injuries look like real injuries and real paramedics cart off injured people in ambulances. No wheelbarrow rescues or rescues in stolen trucks, and those who are shot are in such bad shape they can't do interviews or walk down the hall with Minnie and Mickey Mouse the next day."

I remembered the event to which Derek was referring. "Well, the fake blood they slapped on me looked pretty real," I said. "I guess, when there is real blood, they don't need make-up artists."

"There are also hybrid events," Derek noted. "Those are events where there is a combination of crisis actors and real injuries. And then there are false flags, which are real events created by someone the victims trust."

"Nine-eleven?"

"Right."

"What has our country come to?" Cal asked.

"Were you born yesterday or did you step out of a different dimension or time?" Derek asked him. "This stuff has been going on a long time. The Maine was a false flag. That was at the turn of the twentieth century."

"And I got a five on my AP without any reference to false flags or staged events," Cal noted.

"You probably wouldn't have gotten a five if you had referenced them as such," I said. "The truth is a forbidden topic. Everyone knows it but, people are afraid of saying what they know for fear of being called a 'conspiracy theorist' or a 'Russian.'"

Crete parked at the Fashion Valley Mall, and we walked towards the shelter. We left Everything in the van for safety reasons. "Be very quiet and stay out of sight," I told her.

"You act like she understands you," Derek remarked. Cal had said something similar the night before.

"I think she does," I responded.

As we approached the shelter, we saw the marchers coming down Linda Vista Road, which led up to the University of San Diego.

"Oh my God," I said as I saw a cathead propped up on a stick. "Whatever happened to animal abuse laws?"

"PETIS and HSUS claim leaving animals alive is abuse," Derek pointed out.

"Right. PETIS has never met a dog they didn't want to kill," I managed to get out, just before I started throwing up.

"If you want, you can wait back at the van," Cal suggested. "This mob is enough to turn anyone's stomach."

"No. This mob is why I need to be here." I pulled myself together, but I was shaking. Cal put his arm around me. I looked at him. Most guys wouldn't put their arm around a girl who had just thrown up. I felt awkward but his arm felt comforting.

Noticing my uneasiness, Cal remarked, "Take a little of my help. The four of us are a team. And, well honestly, you look a little unsteady."

"Thanks," I said. "I'll be fine." A man walked by us with a cooked dog. I worked hard to keep from vomiting again. Cal was right. I might not make it without support.

"Don't look," Cal said, pushing my head against his side.

"What was it?" I asked.

"You don't want to know."

I heard someone else vomiting. It was Crete. When I looked, he straightened up and he turned to me. "I don't think I can stay in this city. The people are completely barbaric."

"It's mob mentality," Cal said. "People will do things, sick things in a mob that go against their principles."

"The media has been programming people the last two days. They've convinced the masses attacking helpless animals is an act of heroism," Derek remarked.

As we got to the shelter, Doug was in front of the crowd. "I had to stand and watch as my classmates were mauled."

"He wasn't even there," I told Crete. "Like I said, I overheard a conversation with him at the last rally."

"He's a publicity seeker. His dad is FBI. Did you know that?" Crete informed me.

"You're kidding," I said.

"And his mom works for the news on DNN," Derek added. "I understand he practiced his speech from last night at her studio before he got to the rally."

"Is anything here real?" Cal asked.

Doug continued speaking to the crowd. "Kids deserve the right to learn without being terrorized by guns and dogs. We are the future and the adults need to listen to us." The audience gave Doug an uproarious applause.

A girl got up before the crowd. "I was there and it was brutal. If the adults won't listen to us and rid our state of these killer dogs, we must take matters into our own hands."

"Hey," Derek said. "She's not a high school student. She goes to Earl Warren College at UCSD."

"Wonder how much she's making," I remarked.

"I heard some of the airlines are offering air free travel for the next year to the students who are faking this nonsense," Derek added.

"Would you lie for a chance to visit Paris for lunch?" I asked, sarcastically.

"Lie, yes, but not if it hurt dogs," Crete answered.

"I've had enough of twenty-first century America. I want out of here," Cal said.

"I just want out of California," I told him.

"California hasn't always been this bad," Derek responded.

Griddy Newcastle took to the spotlight.

"Is she going to open up the doors for another slaughter?" I asked.

"Sick," Derek grunted.

"The City won't let us enter this shelter to protect the students," she started.

"Protect the students by murdering innocent dogs and cats," Cal remarked.

"So we can either break down the doors or march on the Mayor's house and demand that he open the doors for us," she continued.

The crowd echoed, "Make the Mayor open them."

A woman with a German Shepard ran to the front. "Dogs are our friends. Here, I'll prove it." The crowd started to close in on her.

"Hold it." It was an officer from the police station just down the road. At last, the voice of sanity to save the dogs.

The officer pulled out his gun and, with one shot killed the woman's dog, as I and the woman screamed.

CHAPTER 18

Crete rushed towards the officer, but Derek pulled his roommate back and stopped him.

The crowd started moving away, apparently to go to the Mayor's house. Some got into vehicles. Others continued walking, presumably to where their cars were parked.

"Do you really think the Mayor will refuse this crowd?" I asked.

"Not a chance," Derek responded.

"If he were a man of integrity, he would," Cal said.

"You don't know much about modern politics," Derek told him.

"If the Mayor were Dennis Kucinich, Cal would be right. He'd tell them where to go and set up special protection for the animals," I said, coming to Cal's defense.

"If the voters believed in electing idealists, Dennis Kucinich would have been elected President in 2004 or 2008," Crete pointed out. "I'll go get the van and park closer."

"Cal, they'll look up the license plate, and then your neighbor will turn you in," Derek warned.

"I switched the license plates," Cal replied. "I thought of that."

"Smart guy," Derek said. "But I'll get the van. Crete, we need you to cut the power." Crete tossed him the keys.

"Let's go around to the back," Cal suggested to me. "You should stay outside and be a lookout."

"You may need help with the dogs. And I don't want you to cut me any favors."

"What we are doing could get you a record, keep you out of college."

"And you?" I responded.

As Crete went to the power substation on one side of the Inhumane Society facility, we scouted out the other side and the back. Cal put on a cap and handed me one. "Put your hair up under here," Cal instructed. It won't help against facial recognition but might possibly help with a general description."

Most of the doors we could see through the fence had scanner locks. We found a gate that we knew we could open with a bumper key or the bolt cutter my handy accomplice just happened to be carrying under his coat. But the main obstacle I could see through the fence was a card reader next to the nearest shelter door. There was also a regular key lock and cameras at that entrance.

Through the stucco walls, I could hear the dogs barking and howling. It was as if they sensed the danger. Suddenly, the lights went out. Cal handed me some gloves and put on a pair himself. He quickly got us through the gate. With the electricity out, we figured the cameras and readers were out too.

I looked around for any witnesses as we moved inside the fence but didn't see any. I figured everyone was preparing for an assault on the front. As Cal opened the closest rear door, I heard some workers inside talking about going to the backup generator. I hoped Crete was planning to fix that too. The workers took off away from the section we were entering.

Inside the door was some kind of lab, probably where they performed the actual euthanization or execution of dogs. There weren't any dogs there. Maybe the day's executions had already taken place. As I walked, I almost slipped on something wet on the floor.

Cal steadied me. He aimed a little flashlight at it. "Blood," he said.

I did my best to suppress the images that came to mind.

We entered a corridor leading from the lab towards the front. It contained doors and entrances to other corridors. We moved forward along the corridor, following the sounds of barking dogs. With Cal's flashlight, I could see a sign on the first door saying "Quarantine Area." Those dogs seemed best to rescue, first.

The dogs calmed down their barking as we entered the room. I used the bumper key for some of the cage locks while Cal used his bolt cutters on others, doubling our speed. The dogs in this section included Rottweilers, Dobermans, pit bulls, huskies and shepherds.

They actually seemed quite happy. I don't know if they saw us as their rescuers or just the bearers of freedom, but they followed us as we moved towards the next section.

The lights went back on and then off. The next section had large breed dogs, like Pyrenees and Saint Bernards. We opened all the locks in that room as well.

"If we can't get all the dogs in the van, would they really be safer free?" I asked.

"At least, freedom will give them a running chance. We're close to Presidio Park. If any get away from us, they could go there." It was Crete's voice. He had snuck in behind us. He grabbed some leashes off the wall and we attached them to many of the dogs. I would have expected the dogs to be barking or fighting with each other, but instead, they seemed super friendly and cooperative.

Set after set of dogs was okay with the being leashed together with other dogs or with just accompanying their prison mates. They all followed us quietly as if they could sense we were on their side or that their lives depended on it. In the next section, were some Chihuahuas, Pomeranians, poodles, American Eskimos and a variety of other dogs. Crete threw us some collars and leashes and we attached them to our new rescues as we proceeded into the next section.

"Hey, what's going on here?" The voice was coming from the first area where we had rescued dogs. Apparently, the workers had returned and discovered open cages. We quickly attached more collars and leashes to the collies, Labradors, Aussies, golden retrievers and Irish setters in that section. We could hear footsteps approaching the room.

There was a side door from where we presently were that we

suspected led out. We made for that door. Crete picked up a book off a counter and stuck it in the doorway to prop the door open, as we guided the dogs out towards the back side gate where we had entered.

Derek was by the gate with the van running. As Derek, Cal and I assisted the dogs into the van, Crete started back towards the shelter.

"Don't. You'll get caught," Derek whispered. Crete ignored him. Derek helped me and Cal continue putting the dogs into the back of the van and then rushed back after Crete. Everything was in the front passenger section and I was kind of glad, given that I didn't fully know the disposition of the new dogs. Surprisingly, they did not fight in the crowded area. Cal and I started back to try to hurry the other two so that we could rush away without getting caught and losing the dogs we had.

As we approached, the darkness was suddenly filled with brightness from the other side of the shelter and we could hear yells from the front. "Burn it down! Cook them all!" The facility had seemed fireproof, but we could hear explosions and see bursts of light and fire leaping into the sky from the front and filling the air with an odor of gasoline and other noxious chemicals burning.

"No! Stop!" It was the worker's voice we had heard before. It wasn't near the back. At least, the workers were distracted by the crowd at the front. Cal and I went back inside. Derek and Crete each had close to a dozen more dogs.

Cal picked up some badges. "They might come in handy at one of the other shelters." We split up the dogs between the four of us and ran to the van. Somehow, they all managed to fit, inside. Flames were soaring high into the sky and visibility was low.

"We can't let the rest cook," I said.

"Don't worry," Derek reassured me. I heard some rustling nearby and saw hordes of dogs and cats fleeing past us. "We opened all the remaining cages and all the nearby doors. I just hope they are far away when the mob realizes the dogs have escaped.

"If the whole place goes up in flames, they may think they've killed them all and leave," Crete noted. "At least, we can hope."

"Hopefully, the dogs don't circle toward the front or around to the police station," I said.

"Would you?" Derek asked.

"The police are supposed to be peace officers, but notice they didn't stop the mob, just used a dog for target practice," Cal remarked.

I heard sirens and saw flashing lights.

"Fire," Derek said. "At least the fire department hasn't yet turned evil—yet."

The dogs we had escorted out were packed into the van, pressed against each other with no room for movement. Surprisingly, they didn't seem to incur the crowded rat syndrome.

Outside, it was hard to breathe through the fumes filling the air, and I hoped the escaping dogs and cats or innocent observers didn't wind up with any lung damage.

We closed the windows and Crete turned on the air conditioning. Despite almost zero visibility, the van sped away towards Crete's parents' home.

"Wow!" I said. "I don't know how you navigated that. I couldn't see anything."

"I learned to drive in this area."

Everything started lightly barking out something and the other dogs barked back at her, not angry barks but almost like a form of communication. I wondered if she was explaining the situation to them and asking them to make the best of it.

Crete's parents had a large house in Point Loma with a security fence all the way around. Good place for some of the dogs.

It turned out that Crete's sister Jemma was a dog lover. She convinced her parents to take in a couple dozen and to agree to adopt some out to non-killers later. Dogs filled several guest rooms, a recreation room, a garage and a basement. The furry guests were separated by type and personality.

Crete's dad was a doctor and started examining the dogs for any medical problems or injuries.

Derek's parents also took in a dozen when we got up to Carlsbad. Derek told them about my contacting Stan to try to find his brother and that more than won them over. It turned out that Derek's mother had a real soft spot for dogs. The remainder of the dogs went to Cal's for the night.

"You realize we're going to have to find them homes don't you?" I told Cal. "And you're going to have to name them."

"I was counting on you to help me with the naming," he said.

I suddenly remembered I had wanted to call back Everett. But it was too late, Eastern time, now. I decided to call him the next day.

When we got back to Juliet's house, it was quiet. I took my usual rooftop entrance to my room with Everything in my backpack.

———

About sunrise, I was awakened as I heard Brian come back with Jonah. Jonah was sobbing, "I don't want to be a man."

My heart ached as I heard his sobs. I tried to distract myself. There was nothing I could do as I was a prisoner, too.

I had lost my best friend, my mom. I could only hope that I would be able to graduate with my class and go to college.

I hated living with Juliet. But somehow, I had found purpose, here, in California. I couldn't save all dogs, but I had helped save a lot. Maybe, through some miracle, I could help save Jonah as well as Courtney's mother. And I had made friends, really nice friends. So maybe there was a purpose to my being here for this brief time. But new friends couldn't make up for the loss of my mom. What I wouldn't do just to have her back.

Everything curled up on my bed next to me. Juliet opened my door before I was through sleeping. "Haven't you been hibernating long enough? It's Sunday."

"Church. I want to go to church."

"Which one?"

"I don't care. I just want to feel spiritual."

"I think you've missed most services."

"Do you have a Bible in the house?"

"No. Brian and I aren't into that kind of stuff."

"Oh."

"Brian and I need to meet with some people this morning. Could you hang tight with Tulsa?"

"Sure. When will you be back?"

"In a few hours. And given your mental condition and your dog, I wouldn't set foot outside the property."

"I'm sure you're right." Freedom during the day. I was ready to officially agree to anything. I used to be extremely honest. Now? Staying alive meant taking extra measures.

When I went downstairs after my jail-keepers departed, Tulsa was busy cooking. I went to Jonah's room. Jonah was looking as if he was in shock. "What happened last night?"

"I'm not supposed to tell."

"Sometimes it's good to talk."

"They'll hurt me if I talk."

"It will be our secret."

"You won't like it."

"I'm not going to judge you. You're my cousin, and I want to be your friend."

"They made me do it. I didn't want to."

"What did they make you do?"

"Will I go to hell if I hurt someone?"

"You're, what—three years old?"

"Four."

"Sorry. I think at your age, it's not your fault if you do something wrong. It's the fault of the person who makes you do it."

"Brian made me."

"Made you do what?"

Jonah didn't say. He started crying.

I put my arms around him. "Whatever you did, it wasn't your fault. The fact that you are crying means you are a good kid."

"If I tell, they'll hurt me really bad."

"It's okay. You don't have to tell me. I'm on your side."

"May I pet your dog?"

"Sure." I put Everything on Jonah's bed. She went over to Jonah and licked him. "You are a good kid. Don't let them ever convince you otherwise."

"I want to be good."

"If we could get out of here, leave, would you want to?"

"They'll catch me and punish me."

I held him as he cried. He looked up at me as if he almost trusted me. But then he pulled away and went back to lying face down on his bed.

I went downstairs. Tulsa was watching Raquel Madcow on a TV in the kitchen.

"Witnesses said the perpetrators drove off in a white van. The video cameras were turned off. A manhunt is underway for the kids who blew up the animal shelter killing three people."

"What?" I asked.

"Hoodlums. They got into the animal shelter in San Diego and blew it up," Tulsa said.

Raquel continued. *"The police say they have leads and are close to making an arrest."* A minute later, she interrupted her own mouthings. *"Update. They just made an arrest. A young man from the Carlsbad area."*

CHAPTER 19

I sat down. Did they have Cal? Were they about to get Cal? If he hadn't been picked up, I had to warn him. I went to the front door. The deadbolt, the one that required the key from the inside, was locked.

I went to my room, put Everything in my backpack and picked up my bumper keys to unlock the dead bolt. Tulsa was still distracted, watching TV. I looked out through the eyehole in the front door. There was a car in front of the house and I could see the man from the park.

Tulsa had switched to a movie channel that was showing the final *Avengers* movie. I couldn't go out, and Tulsa was in the dining room and would see if I used the dining room phone. What other rooms might have a phone? I looked around the downstairs. On the other side of the stairs, there was a hallway and a locked door. It was the den where I had overheard Juliet speaking about the two dogs the other day. I opened it with the bumper key.

I went over to the desk to use the phone. There was a stack of papers and files on the desk. The first file was marked "bloodline—high-value asset." I opened it. On top were what looked like food orders. Underneath were photos: nudes of Jonah.

That poor kid. His dad must be some kind of pedophile, I thought. I snapped pictures of the file contents with my phone. If I couldn't call out on it there, I could at least take pictures. Under the pictures was an envelope, clasped shut. I opened it. It had passports. A number were for Jonah but they had different last names. They included O'Connor, Sulvan and Riefenstahl—as in Leni Riefenstahl. I thought about all the Nazi-like stuff that was going on. *What are Brian and Juliet up to? O'Connor is a common name. But normal parents don't take nudes of their kids and get passports under multiple names.*

The ringing phone in the study broke my concentration. The answering machine picked up. "Jules, we have a buyer for the Afghan. The day after tomorrow." This was Juliet's home office. I looked back at the envelope with the passports. I had to get Jonah out of there. But I didn't have anywhere I could take him right now.

I opened a drawer. There was a receipt from "Arrowcorp" for two microchipped dogs. *Where are the dogs?*

The receipt also had a note that read: "Trigger: Salmonella." Weird. Arrowcorp sounded familiar. I had seen or heard that name before, but I couldn't recall where.

What was it Cal had said? Juliet and Brian were more like business part-ners than husband and wife? I certainly hadn't seen any intimacy. I didn't even know if they slept together. My room was always locked at night. Under the envelope with passports were nude photos of other little boys. I took more pictures.

I started to lift the phone receiver and then wondered if it would show a record of prior calls. I had to get outside.

I left the office, relocked it and checked on Tulsa. She had fallen asleep on the sofa. *Good.* I went to the front door and looked through the peephole. The car was gone. I opened the door and carefully looked up and down the street. I didn't see the man or his car. I went outside.

As I walked down the street, I saw the older man gardening. I crossed the street to speak with him.

"You protecting that dog of yours?" he asked.

"Yes."

"They are killing dogs all over town."

"I know. What has gotten into people?"

"It's like with the Nazis, the KKK and other extremists. They look for scapegoats. You've read history books in school, haven't you?"

"Yes."

"The Blacks didn't do anything to deserve getting lynched. My grandfather moved from Nazi Germany to the South. My father grew up in the South and said that he often saw bodies hanging from trees. Some were kids. The killers had no remorse. They behaved as if they were stomping out cockroaches."

"Like those wars in the Middle East where nobody cares about the kids being drone bombed."

"That's what I'm talking about. Our society has already degenerated, just like in Nazi Germany and now the North is even more racist than the South. When the government came for the guns, I said it was just a matter of time before it got worse. Most of the legislation was about rounding up the mentally ill, not guns. My son's girlfriend was snatched for being depressed. Never saw her again. That all came out of Parkland. Do you remember that?"

"Yeah. There were oddities there too."

The look in his eyes changed. *Had I said the wrong thing?*

"That word: 'Oddities.' It's a trigger. I said that word to a friend, a normal guy, and he came at me with a knife. Tried to kill me. The media is programming people to react to certain words. The schools are programming kids from preschool on. Does it make sense that teens are running around slaughtering dogs?" He sounded a lot like Derek but crustier.

"No. It doesn't."

"Someone wants them running around in the streets, acting like vigilantes. Otherwise, the media wouldn't cover it."

"But who is behind this and why?"

The man shook his head.

"Do you know Brian and Juliet?"

"Strange family. They keep to themselves. I asked Brian what happened to the other Jonah and he told me I was crazy."

"What do you mean the other Jonah?"

"Jonah isn't Jonah, not the original one, anyway."

I had no reason to believe him but something about his story seemed to fit. "What do you mean Jonah isn't the original Jonah?"

"He's changed. He looks different. He's not the same boy."

"I'm Juliet's niece. I didn't know she had a son until last week."

"This Jonah just showed up about six months ago. But the first time, he looked completely different."

"I see." Someone who hadn't seen the weird stuff I had witnessed might consider the man crazy. But I took his words under consideration. I was keeping an open mind and was ready to accept the unbelievable. "I noticed a man in a car outside the house earlier today."

"He's been hanging around the neighborhood the last few weeks. He showed up after I asked Brian about Jonah. I think he's watching me. This morning he was taking pictures of me."

"You?"

"I see things. They don't like that."

"They? Who are they?"

"I don't know. The people who are doing this odd stuff. Do you really believe dogs attacked that school?"

He sounded like a real conspiracy theorist. Yet, he was right about the dogs and I was suspicious of the man in the car as well.

"The other day I thought he was following you, too," he continued.

"Friday?"

"Friday."

"Do you think he's dangerous?"

"What do you think?" he asked.

"I guess."

"Is he just watching us or is he casing us?"

I had to track down Cal. So, I wished the man well with his gardening. I was only taking what the old man was saying with half an air of seriousness. I knew some of it was true. But part of it might just be delusional. Most people would dismiss the whole thing as paranoia.

I walked down Carlsbad Village Drive to the dog park. I almost collapsed when I got there. The park was full of fluffy, bloody carcasses. A little girl was standing by the park sobbing. "They killed my dog. She was my best friend."

I gave her a hug. "I'm so sorry. I know how you feel. Dogs are like family."

"Next, they'll start killing us kids."

I could see why she was scared. Dogs were helpless in today's society. They looked to people for their protection, just as people looked to dogs for their protection. Kids were also helpless. Where would they run or what would they do if someone came for them?

I wished I could reassure her but I couldn't and so I just gave her another hug.

I moved behind some brush, to be less visible and tried to call Cal. His phone went straight to voicemail. Had they picked him up? If they had him and his phone, would they be monitoring his messages? I sent him a message, saying something innocuous. *"Studying my French literature. Any chance you could help me study?"*

Next, I called Susie. Everett answered.

"What's up?" I asked.

"Townscend. Someone tried to kill him again. Fortunately, the nurse was alert after the last attempt. His son is here. He hired more private security and a private nurse to protect his dad."

"Do you trust the son?"

"Yes. He was really concerned about the attack on his dad. We didn't talk to him much. His dad has him taking care of other things."

"I see."

"There's more. Jonah may not be your cousin. Townscend claims Jonah is his grandson."

"So his son is the father, not Brian?"

Jonah's comment to me that first day in his room: "I saw Grandpa T. Sitting by the door."

"Not the son I met," Everett continued. "He has another older son who has disappeared."

"Disappeared?" There seemed to be an epidemic of that going around. "I keep hearing about people disappearing. There is a guy in Washington, a vet, who disappeared. A neighbor here said the girlfriend of his son disappeared."

"And we're hearing there's a dog-killing frenzy in California."

"That's for sure. How is it there?"

"People, here, are more rational. Some of the high school students tried to create some unrest but the dog owners managed to put it down."

"Put it down? How?"

"They came out with pitchforks and rakes and told the teens that if they wanted to kill the dogs, they'd have to kill the owners first."

"Wow!"

"Society is becoming more polarized though. There are those who feel the kindest thing to do to a dog is to kill it."

"Like PETIS."

"Yes. And of course, there are those who would put their own lives between their dogs and those going after them."

"I found nude photos of Jonah and other boys today and passports for Jonah with multiple last names and passports with other last names for Brian and Juliet. Also, the file said, 'Bloodline-high profile.' One of the last names for Jonah was 'Riefenstahl.'"

"Leni Riefenstahl was—"

"I know. She photographed Hitler."

"It's getting dangerous. No matter what happens in court, I want you home. Call me tomorrow. Susie and Trisha want to fly there to pick you up. It would probably be safer and more effective if I went there."

"I agree. Today, I've got to get back before they discover I'm gone."

As I started towards the house, sirens swept past me. I saw paramedics and a firetruck. I tried to stay out of sight as I continued on. They went to the old man's house. Somebody was wheeled out on a gurney and taken to the back of the ambulance. From my position, I couldn't see much. EMTs appeared to shake their heads and cover the top of the person with a sheet. Across the street, I saw my stalker watching the events at the old man's house.

CHAPTER 20

I turned back and took the long way home, hoping the stalker didn't catch sight of me as I returned from the other direction.

When I got into the house and relocked the door, Tulsa was still sleeping on the sofa. I freed Everything from my backpack, and she followed me upstairs. I put my backpack into my room and then went downstairs, with Everything still following me, to speak with Tulsa. "Do you know when Juliet and Brian will be back?"

She looked at her watch. "I've slept too long. I need to finish dinner. Would you like to help me?"

"Sure."

As we made vegetable lasagna, Tulsa snacked on some of the food in the refrigerator. I made myself a salad to eat while we cooked. She broke the lasagna into three settings.

Then she pulled two containers of some type of powdery substances out of one of the cabinets. "I'm supposed to use this in Jonah's food," she said pointing to one of the containers. "And this in, I think, yours." She pointed to the other container. "I guess it's what your doctors prescribed."

I didn't say anything. I didn't want to set up any red flags that would result in Juliet and Brian finding out that I knew about the drugging. I would be sure not to eat my section of the lasagna. Tulsa seemed to have some afterthoughts. "I'm not sure I was supposed to say that."

"Just in case, I won't say anything."

"You're a sweet girl."

"Thank you."

Everything and I returned to my room. While Tulsa had been distracted with the other parts of dinner, I had snuck some of the powder from each of the containers into a couple of paper towels. I put them into two empty jars of baby food and stored them in my backpack. Maybe someone could get them analyzed for me.

I plugged in my computer, connected it to the Internet, inserted the micro SD card from my phone and emailed my photos to Everett. I also sent them to Cal. If anything happened to my phone, it would be good if more people had copies. There was still nothing from Stan about Derek's brother.

I reattached the TV and turned to news of the shelter explosions and fire. They were expressing anger over the killing of employees at the shelter during the fire. It was all being blamed on unidentified kids in a white van. There was no indication as to the names of the teens, but it was said that the authorities had attempted to arrest an unnamed suspect and that he had killed himself. Fear went through me. I flipped through the news reports. One had the police taking the suspect into custody. Which was it? There were no photographs of either the teen, alive or dead, or of the supposedly killed employees.

Dead perpetrators eliminate trials and unwanted questions. I couldn't imagine Cal killing himself. However, the police were good at killing people and making the deaths look like suicides. I thought about the kid who had supposedly hung himself after the Lancer incident. Then I recalled reading that the Philadelphia police had been caught planting toy guns on people they had shot in cold blood. I hadn't said prayers since my parents perished. I mostly yelled at God in my thoughts. But now I was praying that Cal was okay.

I went back into Jonah's room and looked in on him. He was watching cartoons on his TV. He seemed kind of mesmerized by what he was watching and so I just closed the door. I had wanted space after

I lost my parents, and I figured he probably wanted some space to deal with whatever happened the night before. I determined to find a way to follow him and Brian later that night.

Just before dinnertime, Brian and Juliet returned.

I had filled myself up pretty well with the salad. I wanted an excuse not to eat the food. They brought some dog food for my Papillion and tried to insist I feed her regular dog food. I didn't trust that not to be drugged or poisoned. I wanted to get up to my room for dinner, so I made a nuisance of myself, asking questions about where they went. Their answers were vague, "We were visiting our attorney about your adoption."

Not good. Were they expecting tomorrow's ex parte?

"Are you a family law or an elder law attorney?"

"I do both but I want someone else to handle the case."

She mentioned an attorney named Tsoh and that she was working with a judge named Paddock in matters of this nature. I guessed those were last names. According to Juliet, Tsoh was on the verge of being put onto the bench. It figured that someone helping Juliet steal kids would be made a judge so he could help others like her steal other kids. What were they up to?

"You can't adopt me. I'm fifteen and the judge would ask if I want to be adopted."

"That will be up to the judge."

Do they have access to judges who break the law?

I continued asking questions, trying to learn the first names of the people they met with and what their plans were. Finally, Brian said, "That's enough. We aren't discussing this, anymore."

"We *are* discussing it if it's my future," I insisted.

Everything started barking.

"You're going to have to control that dog."

"She's trained to bark when there is tension. I'll take her up to my room so I can finish my dinner."

"Just keep her quiet," Juliet said.

"So, Jonah." I turned to my cousin. "How do you like Southern California?"

"I-I—"

"He doesn't speak much. Developmental problems."

She said that right in front of him? "Maybe, I can work with him. I used to tutor younger kids when I was in Elizabeth City."

Everything gave a single bark.

"I know you don't like having Everything at the table. I can finish upstairs unless you would like me to help with tutoring Jonah."

Juliet glared at me. Maybe I was too obvious. "Maybe you could get Everything to cut out the barking," Brian said, diminishing the tension.

"I'll work on it," I replied, as I stood up and took my plate to my room.

After putting a sample of the lasagna in another empty baby food jar, I put the rest in the toilet.

"Thank you, Everything. That was right on cue."

"You have to get out of here," she advised. "Did you see what they did to Juliet's neighbor?"

"Actually, no, but I suspect the man in the car may have been involved."

"They are poisoning you and Jonah, and they want to give me special food, too."

"After tomorrow, I may get to go home."

"Don't count on it."

"I know. There is something really scary about them. Why did they want me here when I'm nothing but trouble to them?"

Juliet opened the door. "Were you talking to someone?"

"Just myself." I didn't think we were talking loud enough for her to make out the words. At least, I hoped she couldn't. "I need to take my practice exams for school, and then I'm going to bed. Tomorrow will you give me the Internet access to upload them?"

"We'll talk tomorrow."

I wasn't just saying that. I had been way ahead in my studies, and I didn't want to fall behind. After she left, I heard my door lock. I plugged in the Ethernet cable on the off chance that I wouldn't have access later. I took my AP Computer Science practice exam and my AP French Literature practice exam. I wondered if I would get the state award if I aced all my official AP exams.

"Vous avez bien réussi votre examen de littérature française" (You did well on your French Literature exam), Everything remarked with a perfect accent.

"You speak and read French?"

"C'est ma deuxième langue."

"You just said it's your second language."

"Oui."

"That's great. It's my worst subject."

"I think you just got an A on your exam."

"Maybe, you can coach me some on the subject."

"Ce serait amusant." (That would be fun.)

After sending the exams off to my school, I tried to get a message to Cal. There were still no names regarding the white van on the news. I knew that it was risky to use the Net. They likely had a router with lights to give me away, but as the access was hidden, maybe they weren't checking it. I hadn't seen a router box in the private office. So maybe it was in the garage or somewhere less visible.

I disconnected my computer and slipped into another dark outfit my aunt and uncle hopefully hadn't seen. I needed to try to stay invisible tonight if I was able to follow through with my plans.

There was some commotion down the hall. Jonah was ranting about how he would not go. I heard breakage coming from the direction of his room. I planned to find out where they were taking him. I used the bumper key to open my door enough to peek. Nobody was in the hall. It sounded like Brian and Juliet were both in Jonah's room. I went to my window and freed the lock on that as well, covered the window with the curtain and quickly stuffed my bed. Everything climbed into my backpack. I snuck out my door and quietly closed and locked it. I moved cautiously toward the stairs and then continued on toward the inner garage door. The minivan was open and I got in, hiding behind the back seat. There were some boxes behind me. I hoped those wouldn't be pulled out before I exited the van.

A little while later, Brian carried Jonah down to the vehicle. "I hate you!" Jonah yelled. I heard what sounded like someone being slugged. Jonah wailed. Then I heard the sound again. Jonah was sobbing, hysterically.

I could hear the garage door opening. The minivan pulled out. It made several turns and seemed to be driving down some city highways. It went a ways down a hill. The vehicle made some more turns, went on a flat road and then was moving uphill. Finally, it stopped and Brian carried Jonah out.

I peeked, noticed the coast was clear, and carefully got out of the car. We were in a parking lot by a two-story building. There was a sign that read "Day Country School." I looked around. There was a secured trailer parking area just above the back side. I wandered around the perimeter. There were some exclusive homes up the hill. Cal still wasn't answering his cell. I called Crete. "Do you and Derek think you could help me with another kind of rescue?"

As I waited for them out of sight, I saw more kids being taken into the school, all young, like Jonah. Some were crying. Some were protesting. Others seemed excited as if they thought something fun was going to happen there. Brian went to the car and got some of the boxes out. Men were going in and out of one of the doors to the building. I noticed a number of the individuals were carrying some dark clothing. I didn't dare go too close out of concern I might get caught.

I continued trying to call Cal. No answer. I noticed there were numerous missed calls from a number I didn't recognize. It wasn't Cal's. But whose? No messages were left. Was the caller afraid of letting me know who he or she was or afraid that the wrong person would listen to the message? If my stalker had come across my phone number, he might have been trying to call in case I was dumb enough to answer.

It wasn't long before Derek and Crete arrived. They had been visiting Derek's family in Carlsbad. "My family loves the dogs," Derek said. "The new houseguests are taking their minds off Daniel."

"The police supposedly picked up someone in connection with the white van and he, supposedly, is dead. I haven't been able to get in touch with Cal," I told them.

"There are lots of white vans," Derek tried to assure me. "Remember when they created a frenzy about Chis Dorner, the cop who supposedly wrote the manifestos, and the Torrance police shot up the truck with two women who didn't look anything like Dorner?"

"They referred to the suspect from the shelter they shot as a 'he' in the reports where they claimed they killed him."

"How many white vans were at the shelter last night?" Derek inquired.

"Didn't Cal say he switched the license plates?" Crete asked.

"Then, they might have picked up some innocent dude that wasn't even there. Or gotten a facial ID on Cal from a camera we didn't notice watching us. This is a mess," I said.

"I think Cal is too smart to get caught," Derek reassured me.

"That's what a lot of people in prison think," I replied.

"I suspect the fire-bombing was a false flag, staged by someone the authorities probably knew. Have you noticed that most of the alleged perpetrators in these events wind up dead?" Derek asked rhetorically. "Like the one from two days ago."

"You may have hit the target, Derek. Has anyone seen any funerals for the dead students or the guy who supposedly shot up the school?" Crete queried.

"I've noticed that there haven't been any," Derek said.

"I looked up the students they claimed were injured, killed or witnesses," Crete informed us. "Most had Fakebook pages showing they were in college or attending school elsewhere. Some of those who went public had IMDB profiles."

"And they supposedly incinerated Dorner but not his miracle incineration-proof driver's license in Big Bear and it happened while his mother was drinking margaritas in Irvine as if her son was fine. No body," Derek recalled. "Most of what we see on TV is probably fake news."

"I hope so." Still, fear, no some form of terror, was rushing through me.

"I'm starting to believe your false flag theory," Crete told his roommate.

I needed to focus on the task at hand and tried to put the news reports out of my mind. My new friends seemed to be doing the same.

"I think I can just cut the power to this school. I bet it doesn't have a backup," Crete stated.

I handed Crete my backpack. "Stay outside. If something happens to me, save Everything."

"I'll keep you safe," Derek assured me. He handed me a ski mask. "You don't want your uncle to recognize you."

"I certainly don't."

Derek and I moved towards the door I had seen people entering through. When the lights went out, I tried to open it. I didn't even have to use my bumper key. It was unlocked.

Nobody was in the front room. I heard a scream of horror in one of the back rooms and then sobbing. I wanted to rush in but knew that would be counter-productive. I opened another door a crack. Derek and I looked in. I pulled out my cell phone and started filming. If we were to save Jonah, we'd need evidence.

There were candles and torches blazing all around the room, including one set of torches close to the doorway. Men were wearing dark robes. The boys were stripped naked. Some were hanging in V formats from ropes hanging from the ceiling attached to their feet and hands. I was filled with rage and I wanted to scream.

A cup was being passed around by the men attending to the boys. As it was passed from man to man, each boy was given the choice of continuing to hang or drink the liquid.

There was something on the floor with a tarp underneath. It took me a minute to make it out in the flickering torchlight. Long black hair flowed from it and blood. It was clearly a girl. There was nothing I could do for her. I was too late.

There was another young girl standing naked, sobbing, looking helpless, with a man and boy approaching her.

"Do it," the man instructed the boy. The man put a knife in the boy's hand and held it there as he guided the boy towards the girl. That was when the battery in my cell phone died and my recording stopped.

CHAPTER 21

"Please, please," the girl wailed. The boy paused but the man holding the knife in the boy's hand pushed him forward. The boy wasn't Jonah, but the man was Brian. Derek moved in front of me, blocking my view. The next thing I knew, Derek removed a torch from the wall near the door and threw it into the room, catching a couple of the robes on fire. Flames were everywhere.

I ran to Jonah, who was still hanging from the ceiling. Everyone, especially the men whose robes were on fire, was trying to put out the flames. One man grabbed at me and I kicked him in his privates, and then kicked again, knocking him down. I picked up a knife from the table and cut Jonah down and cradled him in my arms.

Two other men came at me and Jonah, and I pointed the knife at them as I continued holding Jonah. As one reached for another knife, I somehow managed to lift my leg and kick the knives nearest him across the table. My dancing skills were coming in handy. The man who had reached for the knife moved towards me as if daring me to take action. I shook my head, firmly and slowly, to promote the idea that that would be a very dangerous move. He backed off.

Derek had taken another torch and was brandishing it to force the robed men away as he picked up the girl who had, a minute earlier, been close to her own death. Derek carefully carried the girl towards the door while still brandishing the torch.

I moved to join Derek while continuing to face into the room and threaten my would-be assailants with my knife. I hadn't realized someone was behind me until he yelled as Derek's torch lit up his robe.

As we approached the doorway with Derek continuing to threaten those following us with his torch, someone closer to the door managed to arm-wrestle my knife away from me. It was Brian, standing between us and the exit. "Put the kid down."

I nodded as if cooperating while I moved towards the wall and pretended to prepare to put down Jonah. But instead, I clasped a torch from the wall and shoved it into Brian's midsection. My uncle yelled as his robe caught fire, and he dropped the knife. Derek shoved him out of the way, and we ran out the door and raced through the building's entrance with the sound of rushing footsteps behind us.

We were being chased, but our pursuers weren't as young or as athletic as we were. We ran through the parking lot and down the hill as fast as we could. I could hear our pursuers making cell calls, requesting backup. I kept expecting to hear fire alarms, but there were none. Maybe they were turned off for the ceremony.

I started to trip, but Derek reached out and clasped onto me while still continuing to carry the girl. That slowed us down as our pursuers started to close the distance.

Seconds later, Crete pulled up alongside us in Derek's car. Derek and I jumped in with the kids, and then Crete sped off.

"They'll get our plates," I warned.

"I pulled Cal's trick. I stole a couple of plates off one of the cars in the parking lot. It was the wrong kind of car, but the number will trace them back to one of those guys."

"Cool," Derek said.

I was in the back seat between Jonah and the girl. There were some towels in the back seat and I wrapped one around each of the kids. "I need to get back home for an alibi, and these kids need to go somewhere safe for the night."

"Meadow?" Jonah asked, apparently recognizing my voice. I still had my ski mask on.

"I told you I'd help you," I said, pulling off my face-covering. I leaned forward toward Crete and Derek. "Do you think it's safe to go to Cal's?"

"Unless the police are monitoring his place for accomplices," Derek said.

"You think he was caught?"

"Just being cautious. I have a friend Charlie, who is a hacker. Let's see if he can find out," Derek said.

"Is he going to UCSD?"

"Yeah, but I knew him before. We went to high school together. He's from this area. He and another hacker have a place in Oceanside."

A few minutes later, Crete pulled off the road and put on his correct license plates. Derek threw the stolen ones in a little inlet coming from the ocean. Crete went into the trunk and got out some T-shirts. The girl's fit her like a dress and Jonah's went down almost to his ankles. "This is temporary—until we can get you some proper clothes," I said.

Shortly after that, we pulled up to a house. Derek got out and knocked on the door. Someone opened it. Derek and a guy about his age walked to the car, and we all got out.

"This is Charlie."

"I hear that you guys are in a bit of a predicament."

"And she needs to get back before her absence is detected," Derek noted.

"I can't just leave Jonah, though."

"We'll make sure nothing happens to him," Derek said. These guys were near strangers to me and Jonah. Did I trust them? It was a lesser danger than my other options. I trusted them more than I did Juliet and Brian.

"What about your housemate?" I asked Charlie.

"He had to go to Madison on an emergency. He'll be back next week if all goes well with his family. Come on in for a minute," Charlie said. Inside, I noticed he had an Australian shepherd with a tail.

"She's beautiful," I said.

The dog came over to us and sniffed my backpack. Charlie kissed the dog and she turned around and lay down. I pulled Everything out of the backpack.

Charlie smiled at my companion. "I like your dog."

"Thank you. Look, tomorrow evening, I can figure out where to take Jonah. I just need time. I'm trying to arrange to go home. Can you promise to keep him safe until then?"

"To North Carolina?" Derek asked.

"Yes."

"You're doing great work here. We could form a team of super-heroes fighting injustices in California."

"Maybe we could make the team national. You can come and visit me."

"You won't leave me?" Jonah whimpered, grabbing for me.

"Of course not. We'll figure things out. You'll be safer with these guys until tomorrow."

"You and the pretty girl can stay here. I can teach you about computers," Charlie said.

Seeing me cringe a little at the word "pretty" applied to a young girl by an older guy, Derek assured me, "Charlie's okay. He and I worked on some civil rights stuff in high school. He's cool. And both the kids will be safe here. He really likes kids in the proper way."

"I better. I have a little brother and sister who would beat me up if I ever hurt a kid," Charlie said. "And I've got ice cream."

"Ice cream?" Jonah asked.

"And you can eat as much as you like."

Jonah still seemed hesitant, but it looked like Charlie was trying to accommodate him.

"I promise you, the kids will be safe with Charlie," Derek told me, again.

The girl had been quiet so far. "You won't hurt me?"

"No. I'll tell anyone who asks that you're my little cousin come to visit," Charlie said.

I kneeled down to her, hoping I could get her to say more. "Do you have a name? Mine is Meadow."

"Eleanor." Her voice was weak as if she was uncertain about us.

"Eleanor, you are so brave. I will do everything I can to make sure you stay safe."

She nodded as if she almost believed me, but wasn't ready to trust anyone. I could understand, given what she had been through.

I looked at Charlie. "Promise me you won't turn Jonah over to anyone, the authorities or anyone else. Otherwise, they'll probably just hand him back to Brian and Juliet." I pulled the card from my phone that contained video of what we had just seen and also some of the insanity from the dog clinics as well as the still photos from Juliet's home office. "Here is some evidence." Charlie copied it onto his computer and gave it back to me.

"Charlie, can I borrow your car to drive Meadow home?" Derek asked. "They might recognize my car."

Charlie threw him the keys. Then, he went into the kitchen and brought out a half gallon of organic almond chocolate ice cream. Jonah's eyes widened. I felt a little relieved but hoped I wasn't making a mistake.

Before we left, I told Derek, "I can't just go back to my room without finding out about Cal. Can we drop by his place?"

"Sure."

I gave Jonah a hug. Though the girl seemed to be keeping to herself and not saying much, I gave her a quick hug as well. She looked very nervous, and I figured she probably needed space.

We went by Cal's. Dead silence. Nobody answered the ringing. I used his bumper key to get in. No Cal. No dogs. The place looked like a bit of a mess as if it had been ransacked. Maybe the police had searched it.

"Let's go," I said, not wanting to give up for the time being but not knowing what else to do.

"I'm sure he's alive. We'll find him," Derek assured me.

I made it up to my room through the window before Brian got home. I let Everything out of my backpack, quickly stripped, got into my pajamas, threw my outdoor clothes into the bathtub and quietly shut the bathroom door. I closed my window, used the bumper key to relock it and climbed into bed. I heard them speaking in the hall and went to listen at the door.

"Jonah's gone. Some hoodlums broke into the school and got him. This could cost us millions."

"We have judges and CPS on our side. They'll find him."

"One of the hoodlums burned me."

"Did you get it treated?"

"I had Doc Rosen take care of it. A hospital would have asked too many questions."

"Good thinking."

"Is Meadow in her room? The one that torched me was about her size." I slipped back into bed and pretended to be asleep. Brian came and touched my head and I jumped.

"What are you doing in my room?"

"Just making sure you are alright."

"I'm fine. Except I was really sleepy last evening. I've been sleeping more than usual, lately. Maybe I'm coming down with something."

"It's just the adjustment to the West Coast."

After they left my room, I got up and took a shower. I wondered what time Brian and Juliet would get the call about the ex parte hearing. And would the answering machine take it or would my relatives jump into action and send an attorney to court in North Carolina? I laid back down and got more sleep. I really was tired after the night before.

I was surprised by how late I slept. Brian came into my room. "We're going for a family outing," he declared.

"Outing?"

"To our place in Silverado Canyon."

"Can't we stay here?"

"We're leaving in an hour. Pack your things."

What is up? I have to get in touch with Susie, but I can't with Him monitoring me.

"I need internet access to upload my homework."

"You'll get it when we arrive there."

I packed up all my suitcases. It wasn't hard. I had never fully unpacked. I pulled the battery from my phone and put the pieces into a hidden pocket in my backpack, along with the non-working phone, my laptop, the bumper keys, my money, ID and bank cards and then filled it with other important items. "Where's Jonah?" I asked, innocently.

"He and Juliet will be joining us later."

So I was Brian's prisoner.

"I promised Susie I'd call her back today."

"You can talk to her later."

"Is there a phone at the new place?"

He didn't answer me.

He took Interstate 5, northbound, got off at Alicia and then took a circular route down into a canyon. The house was a large one-story house, positioned high on a hill above the road and very isolated. Unless I could get a cell signal, my friends wouldn't know where to reach me.

We were about to enter the house when a car pulled up next to us in the driveway. A man who looked really familiar, though I couldn't place him, pulled out some dogs, big dogs. I didn't recognize the breed. But they didn't look like they wanted to play.

Brian signed for them. He whispered something to the dogs and they looked at me. *What is that about?* I had thought Juliet didn't like dogs—except, maybe, for Chihuahuas and Afghans and these weren't those.

Brian went into what he called his "office." As I walked through the house, trying to familiarize myself with where things were, the dogs followed me. An unconscious chill went through me. I approached Brian's office and his dogs growled at me. I was less concerned for myself than for Everything.

"Brian!" I called. A minute later, he came out. "I'd like to go to my room. Where is it?"

He walked me past the entry area where my bags were. I picked them up and carried them to my new holding cell. Brian returned to his office.

I had to get out of there. As I had feared, my phone signal did not reach here. I started moving around the house, again, and the dogs growled when I turned in apparently unauthorized directions. I kept Everything close in my arms. I didn't trust these dogs with her. It was as if they had been assigned to watch me. The dogs at the pound had all been sweet. I had come to think I had a way with dogs. But not these. There was something odd about them. The way they moved their eyes and heads looked more mechanical than natural. Their teeth were very large and they frequently showed them off.

I thought about Jonah. If I never returned, he'd be alone with strangers.

I wondered what had happened in court. *Had Susie gotten custody? Was this the response?*

About an hour later, Brian took off in his car. This was my chance to go out. I put Everything in my backpack, put it on my back and went toward the front door. I started to grab for the doorknob and one of the dogs lunged at me, knocking me back, away from the door. It growled as if it were about to attack me. This dog was somehow in charge.

I looked around. There were other doors, but by the time I would get them open, either that dog or the other one who was also closely following me would be on top of me.

I went back to my room. That seemed to settle my jailers down. I closed the door. There were no locks on this window. It was a picture window that did not open. *I'm out of here.* I picked up a chair and threw it. Then I used a comforter from the bed to brush away the sharp glass from the bottom.

With my backpack, which currently contained Everything along with other essentials, I hopped through and ran. I hoped the dogs were trapped inside the house.

As I got close to the bottom of the hill, I relaxed a little, feeling slightly out of danger. I just had fifty feet to go to get out of the yard when I heard the snarling. The dogs were almost upon me.

I kept running. I could sense that the dogs were right behind me and that I was about to be their lunch. A car pulled up to the gate. My stalker stopped the car, got out, opened the gate, and drove in. If the dogs didn't get me, the stalker would. The dogs growled a warning at me, as I froze, and then focused on the intruder.

My stalker got out to close the gate. As he did so, the dogs leaped into action, attacking the man. He said something that I could only partially hear. What I heard was "Sam." Perhaps that was the name of one of the dogs. The dogs cut their attack. The man looked injured, weakened and bleeding.

I needed to get out of there while the dogs were focused on him. I ran for the fence, a low wooden fence, like in some of those old western movies. Being a tumbler, I did a handspring over it and quickly landed on the other side.

"Stop her," my stalker yelled.

The dogs bounded over the fence with ease and were closing in on me.

CHAPTER 22

Just as it looked like this might be my last moment alive, a car pulled from the curb a short way up the road along the route we had taken coming there and hurled towards me. It was a blue Mustang and the passenger door was swinging open as it braked to a stop. I jumped in and closed it.

The dogs leaped onto the hood and started working to smash the window as if their front paws were sledgehammers. Cal made a quick U-turn and one of the dogs flew off but the other stayed stuck to the hood as the car raced away.

The one that had flown off, got up and ran after the car at a speed I didn't know a dog could travel. Cal pulled to the left to pass a slower car that had entered our side of the road. As Cal swerved back to the right side of the road, a truck whizzed past us from the other direction, hitting the running dog. The truck didn't stop and I heard loud laughter from its occupants. It struck me that the truck had intentionally taken out the dog. It looked like what remained of it was still animated as it lay in the street.

The other dog was still on the hood, holding on, as Cal kept driving erratically, trying to shake it off. He stomped on the brakes and it rolled off. It turned to rush back to the car. I rolled down the window a crack and yelled, "Sam," hoping the dog would stop its pursuit. It crawled back up to the windshield again and I was expecting a splattering of safety glass.

A memory came back. "Salmonella," I yelled. It stopped. Cal drove up out of the canyon with the dog lying down on the hood.

He pulled off the road up in Rancho Santa Margarita and stopped. As he did so, I looked back down into the canyon road at the remains of the other dog, still squirming in the street with pieces moving in our direction. Even in that state, I believed it would harm us if it could get to us.

"Salmonella?"

"It was on a receipt in Brian's office." The dog lay on the hood as if he were waiting to hear more. "Salmonella. Off the car." It moved off the car. "Stand still."

It seemed frozen, stiff. Cal felt its body. "This thing is cold. It's not alive."

"What? Is this a remake of *Dead Heat* or *Re-Animator?*"

"It's got metal under its fur. It's either had amazing prosthetics or it's a robot."

He opened the trunk. "Salmonella, get into the trunk and go to sleep," Cal said. The dog obeyed.

Cal closed the trunk and off we went. "Darn. I left my clothes and the baby food," I sort of joked, knowing I could get more.

"Baby food?"

"Everything likes baby food."

"Oh."

Luckily, I had kept the powder and lasagna jars in my pack.

"I tried to call you yesterday."

"The Belgian shepherd chewed up my cell phone."

"Ouch."

"Fortunately, the SD card was safe. But as I was pulling it out, along with the sim card, he swallowed the sim card."

I laughed.

"I tried to call you on a new burner phone."

"I thought those calls were a trap. You didn't leave a message."

"I didn't want your family to know you had been in contact with me."

"Your house was deserted and torn apart, and the dogs were missing."

"I had to go see a relative. I didn't have time to clean up from the doggie playtime. A group I found online is standing up against the violence and they adopted most of my dogs and are taking care of Monarch."

"Monarch?"

"My shepherd. It's a joke. You have a Papillion, which means butterfly, and so I named my dog after a type of butterfly."

"Cool."

"I just got back a couple of hours ago and I wanted to make sure you were okay. Brian was totally oblivious to being followed."

"So was I apparently. A friend of Derek's has Jonah."

"Derek told me. I called him on the way from the airport."

"So, where are we headed?"

"How about some lunch and then, we pick up Monarch and off to Charlie's."

"Thank you. I could use a real meal after days of mostly baby food."

"But keep Everything out of sight. There was a dog attack at another high school, today."

"What?"

"Chicago."

"That's crazy."

"A group of supposedly high school kids is flying around the country asking why people don't care enough about children to rid the country of dogs."

"Isn't it odd that all of a sudden there are all these dog attacks at high schools when there were none before?"

"Very odd."

We went to the Veggie Grill in Oceanside. It was a nice, friendly restaurant. Everything stayed close to me in my backpack and I kept sneaking her food from my plate. I tried calling Susie, but there was no answer on her home phone or on either her or Everett's cells.

As we were leaving the restaurant, I spotted someone familiar. It wasn't until we got outside that I realized it was Courtney. "I need to talk to that woman," I said.

I went back in to her table. "How is your mother?"

"I have no idea. You were with that crooked attorney."

"She's my aunt. I heard you speaking. What she did to your mother was terrible."

"Why are you telling me this?"

"I guess, I care."

"My mother is probably going to die and it's your family's fault."

"I don't like my aunt."

She seemed to relax a little. "If you find out anything about my mother, here is my number." She wrote down a number on a napkin and handed it to me. Then she went back to her lunch.

I could see why she wouldn't trust me. My aunt could have sent me. When I came out, Cal was waiting. "Who was that?"

"My aunt is an elder law attorney, and she has a conservatorship over that woman's mother, and she's killing her."

"She blames you?" he asked, looking in at Courtney.

"Maybe. I'm family."

"I could see the anger in her expression."

"I could see it, too. They said they picked up someone who was in a white van."

"There was a video on TV this morning. It was a white Honda Odyssey. Different van."

"So, not the one you got the plate off of?"

"No. I picked a full-sized white van, not a mini-van. Were you worried?"

"No. Not at all," I lied. So the arrest had nothing to do with us. "Maybe whoever they caught really was the person who blew up the shelter."

"We'll never know whether he was innocent now that he's dead," Cal said. "Or whether he even existed—unless there is a funeral."

"They said three people died in the shelter."

"They said nineteen students died at Lancer. Did you see nineteen bodies?"

"I didn't see any dead bodies."

"They claimed that twenty died in Chicago, but Crete said the few names on the police report didn't match any Internet information on students at that school."

"You think those were fake too?"

"If the shootings and dog attacks are staged, what about the explosions at the shelter? The police could have stopped what was happening at the shelter, and they didn't. Then, they catch a guy who commits suicide. Now, which explanation is the simplest? The official one or that the police were supportive of the raid but knew their own actions violated the law. So, they created a non-existent suspect to claim success in their investigation and then pretended to kill him to avoid a trial that would put their misdeeds into the public spotlight. Case closed."

"I see your point."

As Cal drove, Everything sat on my lap, licking me. "Thank you," I said.

"For what?" Cal asked.

"Saving my life."

"What kind of guy would I be if I didn't save my girlfriend from robotic attack dogs?"

"Girlfriend?" *Wow! Does he really think of me that way?* I liked the sound of that, but I wasn't going to let him know. "Aren't you getting ahead of yourself?"

"You're a girl and a friend. Don't you call your friends who are girls, girlfriends?"

"But it's different with boys and girls."

"I suppose."

I guess, he didn't mean it the way it sounded.

The place where he had left the dogs was on the way to Charlie's house. Monarch and Everything seemed to get along well on the way to Charlie's.

I finally got Susie on the phone as we were getting out of the car. I pulled the front seat forward and Monarch dashed out and lay on Charlie's front lawn. I looked around hoping that the neighbors weren't watching.

"Oh my, do I have something to tell you!" Susie said, excitedly.

"I hope it's good."

"We won in court today."

"Yes!" I shouted.

"But there's more," she sounded a bit solemn. "Juliet is trying to get a California judge to grab jurisdiction and overturn the North Carolina order."

"You aren't going to let her, are you?"

"It will be easier to fight her if you are out of California."

"Okay. Should I catch a flight?"

"Is there a chance you could come here under the radar, by car?"

"Yes. Sure."

"Oh, and your principal said to relate to you that you got one hundred percent on the practice exams, which is great, less than a month before the APs."

"Yes, it is." *I should be excited. I want to be back in North Carolina. Why aren't I happier? Something is nagging at me.*

"Cal, Susie and Everett won. I get to go home," I informed him.

"That's great." He didn't sound like he'd miss me. "I'll go with you."

"What?"

"I—I mean, I really like you."

Wow!

"And besides, North Carolina is less dangerous for Monarch."

I had mixed feelings about this. While I didn't want to stop seeing him, I still worried that he might be a stalker or at least obsessive, going thousands of miles out of his way to take me home. *Why had he shown up in Carlsbad and chosen a park close to Juliet's for meeting me?*

At that moment, the front door opened and Jonah ran out, followed by Charlie. I put Everything on the ground and opened my arms, but it was Cal he ran to.

"Jonah, I'm so glad you're safe," Cal said hugging him.

CHAPTER 23

"You came! You came!"

I kind of stood there, feeling like the odd man or rather odd girl out. There was a lot going on here that I didn't understand. Charlie came up to us and quietly said. "We should get inside. GagemEarth and similar stuff."

As we walked in, I pushed past my shock, asking Cal, "You knew each other?"

"Uncle Cal!" Jonah exclaimed.

I reflected on the argument at the church. "Mr. Townscend was—"

"Grampa."

As we entered the house, Cal informed me, "Brian isn't his real father. My brother Preston is."

"You're the son who went to the hospital?"

"That's where I was yesterday. There was another attempt on my dad's life. And thank you for saving his life, twice."

"Well, I'm glad you've got your family back together."

"We're not. Preston is missing. Jonah's mother is missing. About six months ago, Brian swept in and claimed to be Jonah's father. He got Judge Paddock in San Diego to declare him the father and grant him custody without a paternity test or trial."

"That's when the neighbor said this Jonah appeared. He said it was a different Jonah, before."

"We think Brian and Juliet are international child sex traffickers. After they took Jonah, his mother Tammy tried to get help in Washington D.C., and then was picked up and was to be held in indefinite detention, but her detention was discovered.

"Then, San Diego authorities tied to the traffickers illegally dragged her back across state lines to San Diego and held some bogus proceedings against her in San Diego. That's when Dad picked up the place where I'm living in Carlsbad.

"When she got free, Indy reporters escorted her back home, and if they hadn't, she might have been killed. Now, she's in hiding and trying to figure out how to get back her son. If the traffickers get their hands on her before this is resolved, they will probably kill her. We have reason to believe they've already killed a number of people who were assisting her.

"That's awful."

"Jonah was taken from Tammy in the Elizabeth City area and that's where she went back to before she went into hiding. Dad wanted to be there in case she showed up again. Then, Juliet and Brian came to town and you know the rest."

"That's a horrible story. So you saw me at the airport in Atlanta and thought you'd hang out with me until you figured out how to rescue your nephew."

"It wasn't like that. I really did rescue your dog from the trash can. And I meant it when I said I liked you."

"And you lied to me. Or at least, you didn't tell me the truth."

"Jonah, come with me for some hot chocolate," Charlie said, leaving me and Cal to talk.

"If I had told you about Jonah that day on the airplane, you might not have spoken to me further. And worse, you might have alerted Juliet and Brian. If you hadn't later seen what you saw in their house and at that school, you wouldn't have believed me."

"You are probably right. But in other words, all the time you were pretending to be interested in me, you really didn't trust me."

"That's not how it was. I know you're angry with me."

"Of course, she's angry with you. You're still a jerk Callum!" Everything said.

We both turned.

"Becky?" Cal said. "It couldn't be."

"You know each other? First, you know my nephew, and now, you know my dog."

"You didn't even recognize my voice when you pulled me from that trash can. And you didn't even say "goodbye" to me when you left Philadelphia."

"I thought I was going to be back. Come on. It was just supposed to be for minutes."

"You could have taken me with you."

"I genuinely thought I was going to be back in less than an hour. And later, how was I supposed to know you were Rebekka? I'm sorry."

"You two have a lot of catching up to do. And I need to get home. I guess you found the person you were supposed to be with," I said to Everything and walked out the door.

Cal's car was open. I started to pull my stuff out and sat down with my feet outside and my head in my hands.

"Wait," Everything pleaded, as she ran up to the car. "You aren't going to leave me, are you?" She jumped up onto my lap.

"You have Cal. He's the person you were supposed to watch over, right?"

"You're nicer."

"Was he your boyfriend?"

"Yuck. Him?"

"I'm not that bad," Cal said, walking up. "Come on, Sis."

"Sis," I repeated. "She's your sister? Now, I know I'm going crazy. Maybe I imagined the last few days, too." I continued sitting down in the passenger seat trying to get my bearings. *This can't be real. No way is this real,* I told myself.

"You aren't crazy. This is just weird." Cal turned to Everything. "Why didn't you tell me, Becky? We've seen each other a number of times."

"You turned me down. Said you didn't want me."

"What?"

"When Larson offered me to you as a puppy."

Cal looked up and then leaned down to speak with Everything. "I didn't know. I had home-schooling and activities. I thought someone else might be a better owner."

"Owner? So you thought of me as property!"

I sat there in shock listening to a conversation I couldn't believe was happening.

"I'm sorry. It's good to have my little sister back."

"Sister, somebody else. I'm staying with Meadow."

"Rebekka," I said almost trembling at the thought that was starting to pop into my head. "Didn't you say that you were Rebekka centuries ago?"

"Yes."

I passed out.

CHAPTER 24

I had never passed out before, but this was too bizzare. When I woke up, I was lying in a bed. Cal was sitting next to me, and Everything was licking my face. "What happened?"

"I think we hit you with more than you could handle at once."

"So Rebekka is from—"

"The eighteenth century," she finished.

"And so am I," Cal said. It hit me like a shock wave. I hung in there.

"Let me introduce myself by my given name. I'm Callum Jefferson."

"As in Thomas Jefferson?"

"He was my dad's second cousin."

"I see. Next, I'm going to hear that the nation's Founders were from outer space."

"Not as far as I know. My dad was the black sheep of the family. The Jeffersons were very aristocratic and Dad rebelled."

"Mr. Townscend?"

"No. My real dad. His father disowned him. First, my dad settled in Philadelphia. That was where I was born. But, he visited Virginia, where we saw a lot of Tom when Tom was preparing for the Continental Congress and was pushing for independence from England. We returned to Philly with Tom in support of the proceedings. I would listen to Dad and Tom having their discussions. Rebekka sometimes was nearby during the discussions, too. I was really young, and she was only about two years old at the time the Dec was signed."

"I see. Next, I'm going to be believing in Big Foot and the Loch Ness Monster. Go on."

"Well, things went well until I told Uncle Tom off over the slave thing and he threw me out. I guess he didn't have tolerance for kids questioning the hypocrisy of standing up for freedom while owning slaves. Most of our country's Founders owned slaves and didn't see anything wrong with it. So after I shot off my mouth, my father got our family a place in Charlottesville, Virginia so that he could still watch what was happening and try to patch things up with Tom."

"So you were a good guy back when you were really young. TJ did try to get that listed as an atrocity in the *Declaration*. Was that your doing? The *Dec* was before he was involved with Sally Hemings."

"I'd like to think I had an impact. I believed what they were saying about freedom and so slavery didn't make any sense. And despite the section of the *Dec*, which was removed, Tom continued to own slaves. You see when Uncle Tom, as I called him, wrote that 'All men are created equal,' I thought he meant that 'All men are created equal.' It wasn't just Tom who didn't like my attitude. As I mentioned, a number of the other Founders were also slave owners. Because of my mouth, we were close to being run out of Virginia on a rail. We often had to retreat to my dad's other home in Philadelphia, which was close to abolishing slavery at the time."

"Okay. Let's say you were in Charlottesville and Philadelphia back then. How did you get here?'"

"Well, my father was quite an entrepreneur. He had some sound investments and, I hope this doesn't make you think less of me, but like most of the Founders, Dad made a lot of money off the Revolution."

"Money off war? I thought he rebelled against aristocracy."

"He did, but he knew a good investment when he saw one. Most of our country's Founders got rich, too. They didn't just fight for freedom. Most wars throughout history have been fought for economic reasons. Anyway, a number of people came to Father with investment and invention ideas. One was a guy named Jenkens, who claimed to have invented a time machine. He had first gone to Benjamin Franklin before Franklin went to France, and Franklin called him a fraud. Nobody else would touch him after that. So he finally came to my dad, looking for someone brave or stupid enough to try his invention and finance it."

"Definitely stupid enough," Everything interjected.

"It was just supposed to be a trip for under an hour. But he never brought me back."

"Wait," I reacted. "Your dad sent you on an experimental time machine with a near stranger?"

"Jenkens operated the machine. He didn't come with me."

"He let this man use you for a potentially dangerous experiment?"

"He was a believer."

"And a complete idiot. Jenkens got arrested right after he sent you here, and all his equipment was trashed. We thought he'd killed you," Everything said.

"Arrested?"

"He was also part of some scheme to help the British win the war."

"So Jenkens wanted to keep America British?" he asked.

"The way America is going, that might have been a good thing," I remarked.

"Guess Franklin was right," he noted.

"He would have known," I said. "Turns out Franklin may have been a British spy, himself."

"But I lost my brother, and I had to live out my life without the stupid rat. I hope, if you return in your next life, it's as a rat, your true self."

"So you are over two-hundred and fifty years old?" I asked Cal.

"Technically, I'm sixteen."

"How did you wind up with Mr. Townscend, and why do you speak twenty-first century American?"

"I was ten years old when I left the eighteenth century."

"Ten? Your father let you volunteer to travel alone through time at ten years of age?"

"Who do you think Cal learned his stupid from?" Everything interjected.

"He wasn't that stupid. He knew I would check on him one day, and he left a small fortune, now a big fortune, in a special place where he knew I would one day be smart enough to look. Add in inflation, and you know how I bought my car and other things."

"And did you look me up?" Everything glared at her brother or at least, I thought the look in her eyes was a glare. But I suspected that inside she felt hurt.

"I couldn't find any records."

"You said you were ten," I refocused.

"Well, when I appeared out of nowhere, Dad or Anthony Townscend was there. At first, he thought I was some kind of religious figure. But then, I explained things to him and eventually he believed me. I didn't have family, and so he took me in. I didn't fit in at school. My style of speaking was off. There was a lot I didn't know. So he homeschooled me, helping me adjust to the twenty-first century. And here I am."

"Don't schools generally ask for birth certificates?"

"He had had a second son, but the child died of SIDS after getting the hepatitis B vaccine and Dad and my new mother were so distraught that they never checked on the death certificate, and the hospital negligently didn't file it or misfiled it."

"Okay. So, when this really weird dream or whatever it is ends, will you be like a normal guy or will you ride into the clouds on a chariot?"

"I think, I'm here to stay."

Jonah ran into the room, giving Cal a hug. "Cal, when do we see Grandpa?"

"How about if we leave for North Carolina this afternoon?"

"Can we take Monarch?"

"As long as he behaves with Becky, I mean Everything."

Charlie knocked and we invited him in. Derek and Crete, who had arrived, followed him in. Having four guys in the room when I was recovering from a collapse made me feel more than a bit uneasy.

"I've been looking at that dog I got out of the trunk of your car. The technology is extremely advanced," Charlie said.

Derek chimed in. "It's like in Vegas, where Chertoff and Adelman made a fortune off body scanners and metal detectors and other security devices in the aftermath of that shooting. Kids love dogs. So, with the fake dog attacks, they convince people that what they really need is a fake dog. Real dogs are too dangerous. But what they don't know is that the mechanical dogs have secret programming that overrides the owner's commands and they could be used to control the owners if they get out of line."

I looked at Everything. "The live ones are more lovable. The others are just machines."

"They must be planning to make a fortune off these dogs. Three dog attacks in the last two school days?" Derek responded.

"Three?" I asked. "How could any rational person buy that?"

"Fear. Like after nine-eleven. They convince people they are under siege and people will believe anything."

"California, Chicago, and where else?"

"Vermont."

"Blue states where people might require convincing to kill animals," Cal said.

"All big PETIS states. PETIS has spent years telling the world that it's more humane to kill dogs than to keep them alive."

"When you get back from North Carolina, I'll have this all figured out," Charlie told us.

I couldn't bring myself to tell him I probably wouldn't be coming back.

"You can figure it out by yourself?" I asked.

"I have a hacking club. We'll figure it out. And Crete is also a wiz with electronics and computers."

Things were looking up. I was going home. Jonah was reuniting with his real family. There was a growing resistance to the dog insanity and techies would be figuring out how to undo the robotic threat that someone had introduced into the muck. A minor problem, however: I was under the delusion that my boyfriend and my talking dog were around 250 years old. I wasn't sure they even had a name for that form of insanity.

Eleanor had given Charlie her last name and mother's first name. He had learned that Eleanor and her mother had lived in Berkeley before the little girl was taken. Charlie looked up the address for the mother but said it might be out of date. Eight hours out of our way to reunite Eleanor with her mother was nothing. The Mustang was a bit small for the four of us plus Everything and Monarch.

Cal went on Vangurus and found a used Honda Odyssey minivan for thirty-one hundred dollars. There were some minor electrical problems. The rear windows and the lights on some of the dashboard items didn't work. The former owner had replaced the closing mechanism for the side doors and so they at least were functional, a real must. It was a nice shade of dark green and otherwise seemed in good shape.

"It has a good engine and the transmission seems fine," Crete told us after looking it over. "That's what really matters."

Back inside the house, Charlie said he'd take good care of the Mustang until Cal returned. We said "goodbye" to our friends and were about to take off as a Humvee and a Jeep pulled in behind us. Out popped five guys, with muscles bulging from their arms. I prepared for a fight.

CHAPTER 25

Derek came out of the house and gave one of the men a hug.

"This is Lee," Derek introduced us to the guy he had just hugged. "He was in my brother's unit."

"Hi," I said. Cal shook his hand.

Lee pointed to the other men. "These are Jesse, Larry, Kevin and Barry. We were all in Danny's unit. We've contacted other vets, and we are pressing the government with inquiries into Danny's disappearance. We're going to find him."

"That's awesome," I declared.

"We have to go, but let us know if there is anything we can do to help," Cal said.

Crete came out of the house. "Be careful, guys. They just had a dog attack at a high school in New York."

"Another one?" I asked. "In New York?"

"Buffalo. Dogs, nationwide, are now doing copycat attacks."

"Next they'll bring out crazed cats and the bunny rabbits as well," I commented.

"On the Internet, I saw that there had been a dog-attack drill scheduled in Buffalo for today," Derek noted.

"Is there always a drill scheduled for the days of these staged events or false flags?" Cal asked.

"Pretty much," Derek said.

"Derek's right. I've been checking the details of the various attacks on the Net," Crete said. "Be aware, the atmosphere is getting worse and worse all the time and not just in California. I'll never question Derek's theories, again."

"We won't be driving anywhere near New York," Cal responded.

———

With Cal driving, we got up to the Bay area by morning—even with rest breaks. Eleanor had really opened up. She had clearly bonded with Jonah. Everything had slowly won her over, too, and she was realizing that dogs could be nice.

"I once had a dog. My daddy killed it."

"What?"

"He said I was a bad girl because I got dirty playing with the dog. He kicked it in the head. The dog yelped and then just lay there with eyes staring up."

"That's horrible."

"I wanted to bury him. My dad threw him in the trash can. He made me go to my room."

What amazed me was, given how much Eleanor had endured, she was very articulate. She was young, maybe six or seven, but she spoke as if she was double her age or more.

"Well, we like dogs. Maybe your mother will let you have another dog." After I said that, I almost took it back. In San Francisco, how long would the new dog live?

———

Before dawn, we arrived in Berkeley. We drove by People's Park, where students had been shot in the anti-war marches of the sixties.

"This is better," Cal commented. "I don't see any homeless sleeping in the park."

I pointed to a sign, outlawing the homeless from staying in the park after ten at night.

"Does this mean they've housed the population or—" He paused as I pointed to some homeless people sleeping next to a dumpster across the street.

"They just don't want them in the park at night."

"This is not what we fought the Revolution for," he said.

As the sky started to lighten up, we decided to tour the University. It was too early to go knocking on someone's door. The campus police didn't seem to react to our presence. So far, so good. Maybe, the cold and uncaring, but not the crazies, had taken over the Bay Area. We sat down outside Sather Tower. Everything started shivering. I took off a coat I had purchased and wrapped it around her.

"So you got accepted here too?" Cal asked.

"Yes. But I've had my fill of California."

"We've made some good friends."

"True."

"I'd like to go here when I get older," Eleanor said.

"Your mother is here. So, maybe you will. Where is your father?" I asked.

"He's the one who turned me over to those people."

"What? Your father?"

"They made me stay with him. They said I couldn't see my mother, anymore."

I hadn't pressed for her story before. I felt horrible for her. Betrayal from a parent is one of the lowest things that can happen to a child. I thought back to her comment about her dad killing her dog. What kind of court would turn a child over to a guy like that?

"Judges sometimes make wrong decisions," I said.

"My doctor told my mother to take me to the police. I told them what he did. I said I didn't want him to touch me anymore."

"He touched you?"

"It hurt. He made me take off my clothes. I cried. It hurt so much. He hit me to make me stop crying, but I couldn't stop crying."

"That's terrible." I hugged her. "Well, we're going to help make sure that doesn't happen again."

"He took pictures of me without my clothes. He made me do yucky things for the pictures. He put them on his computer. I saw them." The information continued gushing out of her about the touching and the pictures.

"You told this to the police?"

She nodded. "I didn't want to go back to him. He kept hurting me. They said they believed me. Some guy said the judge made him my attorney. I saw my dad give the attorney money and he said I had to go back. He hurt me, too. And they wouldn't let me see my mother anymore."

"Our society has become sick. My first mother passed when Becky was born and my second mother passed away shortly after I was taken in by my second father," Cal recalled. "I always wished I was like the other boys who had mothers."

"I'm sorry," I replied. I turned to Eleanor. "Didn't anyone try to help you?"

"My first-grade teacher had me put into some kind of children's home because my dad made me bleed."

"Bleed?"

She pointed to her lower private area.

"So how did your father get you back?"

"Child Pro, uh pro—"

"Child Protective Services?"

"Yes. They gave me back to him and then again."

"It happened twice?"

"Then my father had to leave the country and I was given to his rel-relatives. They made me do things that I didn't want to do, too."

Cal shook his head.

"How did you wind up with those people you were with when we found you?"

"My dad came back and he took me to them."

"He just gave you to them?" I asked.

"They gave him money. I told him I didn't want to go with them. He didn't look at me. He looked at the money."

"Shit," Cal said. "Sorry. What kind of father sells his child?"

"And CPS played a major part in it," I commented.

"Is he still in California?" I asked.

She shrugged her shoulders. "He kept saying he wanted to take me to Thailand but then he didn't."

"Is he from Thailand?" Cal asked.

"Pak—Paki—"

"Pakistan?" I inquired.

She nodded.

"He's not an American?" Cal surmised.

She shook her head.

"What are you doing here?" Our discussion was interrupted by some students who closed in, sounding angry.

How do they know we don't belong?

"Get that thing out of here," a male student pointed to Monarch.

I slipped Everything from under my coat into my backpack and held it close.

"We're going," Cal said.

We started backing away. "Stop." It was a campus police officer. "I want to see your license for that dog."

"It's in my car," Cal said. "I'll go get it and bring it back."

We moved away from the officer and the students.

"Stop. I'm taking you in." The officer pulled out a Taser and zapped Cal before we could react.

CHAPTER 26

Cal fell to the ground. I rushed towards him with my backpack attached behind me. The barbs had struck and shocked Cal but failed to lodge. As the officer prepared to fire it again in our direction, Monarch jumped and attacked the officer's hand before he could discharge it again. The Taser fell to the ground. The officer pulled out a gun.

The commotion had brought a crowd. I threw myself in front of Monarch. Our dogs were not going to die that day. The officer aimed his gun at my head.

In spite of his Taser injury, Cal jumped up and stood between me and the officer, whose gun was now pointed at Cal. But before the officer could fire, three other students jumped between Cal and the officer. The officer would have had to have fired through the students to get to me, Cal and Monarch.

"They were doing nothing wrong!" a male student shouted.

"We saw it. You attacked unarmed students," another student pointed out. They must have thought we were also students.

"They have a dangerous dog."

More students pushed in between us and the officer. More officers were approaching, as more students joined us. Students were Fastgramming and texting each other and the crowd quickly grew to hundreds with most on our side.

We slipped through the crowd and backed away as the students supporting us argued with the officers and with other students. As we moved in the direction of the performing arts and science buildings towards the east end of the campus, I saw more officers rushing to join the ruckus.

As we continued eastward, away from the Tower, a man in a suit in perhaps his fifties or sixties with grey hair and a beard, came alongside us and whispered, "Come with me. I'll help you." He led us past the law school, into one of the buildings near the upper end of the campus and through the door of an empty lecture hall. "You aren't safe here."

"But this is Berkeley," I said.

"I'm Professor Stone. You need to realize that this isn't the old Berkeley. Gone are the days when this was the campus of freedom and civil rights. The University has been actively reaching out to Wall Street preppies, and the student body is currently mixed."

"A crowd of students rescued us," Cal noted.

"There are even more that are going along with the new agenda. The administrators are using the tuition money for building investments and not on the students. At one time, the students protested when the tuition went up. Now, most go along with it. The Berkeley police have an office on the campus. They have a history of mistreating and roughing up students and have been video-recorded doing just that. There was a time when the student council acted to throw the police off campus."

I remembered seeing a *ScrewTube* video of students roughed up when they protested tuition hikes. I looked at Monarch.

"Hundreds, maybe thousands, of students will stand up for your dogs. Thousands more won't and many will take them off to be killed."

"Dogs are not our enemies. They are our best friends," I declared.

"You are preaching to the choir. Someone is planning to make a lot of money off this crisis."

"That's what Derek said," I recalled. "Someone is making robotic dogs."

"That fits. Did you ever see *I, Robot*?"

It was an older movie, but I had watched it several times. Cal nodded with me. Apparently, he had seen it as well.

"In that movie, the head AI-bot was the bad guy," I remembered.

"In this case, I'm willing to bet there is a more human villain behind what's happening," Professor Stone responded.

"The masses are being lied to and programmed by the media," I said. "They are being encouraged by authorities to slaughter dogs and blow up buildings."

"Mobs are irrational when they are in a pack. Andrew Jackson could not have succeeded with the removals and the Trail of Tears without amassing popular support. Years back, California adopted Proposition 187 which demonized immigrants and made them fear seeing a doctor. The result was an epidemic of tuberculosis."

"Your society has been very active in demonizing immigrants," Cal said. "The government creates refugees with its imperialism and then wonders why the victims need to come here for refuge from what our government is doing."

"And our government responds by treating the victims of our attacks as if they are inhuman," I pointed out.

"This did not turn out to be the country we were anticipating," Cal said.

"And where are you from?"

"I was born in the United States. I meant modern society is not what our forefathers were expecting."

"We all get the blame for where our society is going. Anyone one of us can stand up and make a difference," Professor Stone said.

"And get killed," Cal remarked.

"That's the problem. John and Robert Kennedy stood up. Malcolm X and Martin Luther King stood up. Paul Wellstone stood up. If they knew what was going to happen to them, do you think they still would have stood up?"

"Yes," I said. "That's the kind of people they were. But we don't seem to have many Robert Kennedys or Paul Wellstone's around today."

"There's Dennis Kucinich and Cynthia McKinney," Cal pointed out.

"Who are out of Congress," I replied.

"But they still have popular support," Professor Stone noted. "The Israelis almost killed McKinney over bringing medical aid to children in Gaza, and she was held prisoner for eight days for daring to go back to try to help the children, there. And what did the United States do over the imprisonment by the Israelis of a Congresswoman?"

We shook our heads. We didn't have to answer the professor's question. Our government had done nothing.

"What should we do to protect ourselves, our siblings and our dog?" I asked, pointing to Jonah, Eleanor and Monarch.

"It's odd. You don't look related to each other."

"Adopted."

"I see." I suspected he didn't believe us, but he didn't seem to be wavering in his support for us. "Well, the first thing is for you to get out of here before the campus police search this building." He led us outside to his car, which had a special parking permit. "Let me drive you to your car. You need to keep that dog out of sight."

"We parked on Bancroft," Cal said.

"Hopefully not near the campus police."

"Next to the gymnasium."

Professor Stone pulled out four cards and quickly wrote on the back of each. "If you need to reach me, this is my cell number and email address."

"Thank you," I replied. "It's people like you who keep me believing that America has a future."

"Thank you, sir," Cal said.

Eleanor's mom lived in Berkeley Hills on Buckingham Place. The houses didn't look any better than in the average neighborhood in San Diego County, but, according to Zillow, they were selling for about triple the price of similar-sized homes in San Diego. I used the GPS on Cal's new cell to find the location of the house.

We parked around a corner a few blocks down the street in case of trouble and left the dogs and Jonah in the car as Cal and I escorted Eleanor to the house.

Eleanor was really excited about seeing her mom. It had been years since she had been allowed to see her. Because of the custody order giving Eleanor to her father, Cal had her put on a hooded sweatshirt. We had no way of knowing whether the neighbors were more favorable to the dad or the mother or if they even knew about the case. As we walked, Eleanor kept looking around as if afraid some boogie man would pop up out of nowhere.

A woman answered the door. "May I help you?"

"She's not my mother," Eleanor said.

"Is Shandra Tidwell available?" I inquired.

"Who?" the woman asked and then answered her own question. "Oh, you must mean the prior owner. I was told her visa was not renewed. She is Canadian. So she had to sell the house. Is this her little girl?"

"The father was abusing her, and so we've been asked to bring her back home to her mother," Cal said.

"That's terrible. Well, at least she will get to go home, now."

"Do you have the phone number for Shandra?"

"No. But I can call the real estate agent. She might. Come on in."

We accepted her invitation. She had some lemonade in the refrigerator that she offered us. I thought back to the doctored food at the Pretzel's home. This woman seemed nice. I hoped the lemonade was safe. I sipped it carefully.

The agent did have a phone number for the mother. I called Shandra and told her we had her daughter. "Please get her to the Canadian Consulate in San Francisco. I have a full custody order up here in Canada. The American courts won't enforce it."

"Isn't that a violation of international law?"

"The Americans don't seem to care about international law," she said.

I couldn't argue with that.

"The Canadian Government will get her home to me if you get her to their consulate," she continued.

The house's new owner, Candy Larken, looked up the address for the Canadian Consulate in San Francisco for us.

On the way back to the Odyssey, I spoke to a driver on the near side of the street who was about to take off, possibly to work, in a red Toyota Sienna. He rolled down his window for the conversation. "At this time of the morning, is there a good route for beating traffic to SF?"

"Just take the Bay Bridge and endure it. I do deliveries all day and there are only a few roads into SF."

"You delivering here?" I asked the driver.

"Big one. Good tipper. But you should get out of the street. Not everyone here drives sanely."

The driver opened the passenger door and handed us a paper map. "I don't need it. I'm using my I-phone."

Cal accepted the map and said, "Thanks."

I looked back towards the house and noticed that Candy had followed us out to the street. I waved at her and moved in her direction as she turned and walked back to her house.

I walked back to join Cal and Eleanor at the Sienna and thanked the driver for his help.

"Paying it forward," he responded.

As we walked back to our van, Cal asked, "Does this seem too easy?"

"I guess we're just used to crazy," I said. As we passed Emeryville, Cal got a call from Charlie and put it on speaker. "Stay out of SF."

"What?" Cal asked.

"There is an amber alert out for two teens kidnapping Eleanor."

"Candy must have called the police after we left," I told Cal.

"Do they have our vehicle information?" Cal inquired.

"They think you're in a Sienna."

"Poor guy. He might be late for his next delivery," I lamented.

"Could you look up another Canadian Consulate?" Cal asked.

"There is a small one in Palo Alto but you'd be best going to Los Angeles or Seattle."

Cal turned to me.

"I'd like to get out of this state."

Cal got off Interstate 80 towards SF at Powell and got back on in a northward direction towards Sacramento. "Whether we go to U.S. 101 or along Interstate 80, there will be toll bridges. We need you kids and the dogs to hide when we go past them."

We decided on Highway 101 and stopped along the way at a dog park by the bay. I hoped the dog park would be safe. What greeted us was a panorama of carcasses piled high on almost every square inch of the park. Eleanor looked out the window and started crying.

CHAPTER 27

"Jonah, don't look. Eleanor, keep Monarch down," I said, hoping they wouldn't have to see any more. I turned to Cal. "Let's take a quick look to see if there is any dog that can be saved. Everything, stay here."

As the kids and dogs hid beneath a blanket, Cal and I took a quick walk along the dog park. I carried an extra blanket in case I saw anything alive. The park was its own mini-peninsula sticking out into the bay. The remains were nauseating and I almost threw up. Cal put his arm around me. His touch would have felt good if there wasn't so much carnage around us. So many dogs and dog parts. The violence was unfathomable. There were metal crosses with burned dogs attached to them.

From behind a bush, I heard a whimper. We walked over to it. There was a toy-sized female American Eskimo that looked emaciated and starved. I picked up the little girl and put her under the blanket I was carrying. We started walking back towards the Odyssey.

"Let's get out of here," Cal said.

"We need to find a vet for this dog fast or she won't make it," I told him.

"Well, well, one escaped," a man said as he walked up and saw the blanket twitching. He was about six feet tall, Cal's size, and had on suit pants and a white shirt, covered in blood. If not for the blood, he would have looked like a regular guy walking to work.

"We're taking her back for a ritual," Cal lied.

"Sure you are," the man said, clearly not believing Cal.

Cal stepped forward and the man pulled a knife from behind his back. He lunged towards me and the dog.

Cal tripped him. As the man got up, Cal grabbed and twisted his arm, making the knife fall. Then Cal slugged him hard, hitting his mouth. The man fell down, again. He got up, again, this time with a rock in his hand. He threw it at Cal's head, Cal ducked and then kicked the man down, again.

But the man wasn't finished. He got up, pulled out a bottle opener from his pocket and ran at Cal. Cal stepped to the side and gave the attacker a knockout blow with his fist.

I guess he's not so tough without his knife," Cal remarked, reciting a line I had heard somewhere in a movie.

"Where did you learn to fight like that?"

"My dad got me self-defense lessons."

The kids were visibly upset when we got back to the car. Everything and Monarch were shaking too. I had never seen Everything so unnerved.

"It's alright," I said. "Look who we found." I showed them the dog. Eleanor grabbed her and held her close.

Cal stopped at a nearby Costco to get some supplies and food. I, the kids and our companions tried to stay out of sight in the minivan. The kids, Cal's sister and Monarch stayed low between the seats as Eleanor tried to give the Eskie some water and I, again, placed a blanket over them.

Cal returned with another blanket, a little tub, organic human food, organic dog food, water, a hat for me, a hooded sweatshirt for himself, a raft to put over the seat for hiding the dogs from sight and several large cups of hot water. He inflated and placed the raft over the blankets above the seat tops to allow the kids and dogs to hide. He put the tub in the back and started pouring in the water.

He gave a bag of organic snacks to Jonah and Eleanor. "I know I shouldn't."

"With what he's been eating at the Pretzel's, he could use some treats," I said.

"This is fun," Jonah said. "You're the best, Uncle Cal."

"You got dog food," Everything complained. "If you think, for two minutes, I'm going to eat that—"

"I got you some organic apricots," Cal said.

"Better," Everything responded.

I hoped Jonah was right, that it would be fun as opposed to dangerous. "The organic dog food might be a trap," I warned, looking back at the Costco. "Let's get out of here fast."

We had no problem on the bridge to San Rafael. We cruised through Santa Rosa, only stopping for gas, and then continued up the highway. Cal pulled off into a picnic area next to the highway. We gave the new dog a bath and tried to get it to eat some of the food Cal had picked up. She was very weak but there was hope she would survive. Eleanor and Everything both attended to the Eskie, who had taken their focus off the horror of what was happening in this state. Eleanor sang to her and Everything almost came across as motherly, licking her and cuddling with her.

"Let's call her Sunshine," Eleanor suggested.

"I like that," I replied. "She was a ray of sunshine in a horrid field of darkness." I just hoped the Sunshine wouldn't go out.

According to Crete, it was a pretty drive, taking 101 to Oregon. "Will your dad mind you taking the long way back?" I asked Cal.

"His main concern is that I keep Jonah safe. I called him after we left the Bay area. I was afraid his phone might be tapped after Jonah's disappearance, and so I told him I was delivering a couch and it might take a few days."

"Smart. I wonder if they are monitoring Susie. She got custody of me in North Carolina but, with Jonah missing, they might be ready to pounce when I get there."

"They don't know that you have him, do they?"

"No, but two-faced Candy may connect us with Eleanor."

Along the drive, I did some studying for my APs in the car. Cal had already taken his AP European History exam the prior year and I had already taken the AP World History exam, which he would take this year. So we quizzed each other as we rode along. It turned out that Cal was also fluent in French. He and Everything quizzed me on my French vocabulary. Cal had read Montesquieu's *De l'Espirit de Lois*, which was one of the books I had studied in AP French Literature and we discussed Montesquieu's political philosophy and how his and Locke's philosophy had influenced Thomas Jefferson and other of our nation's founders. Neither Eleanor nor Jonah had difficulty with the concepts of Everything talking or even of her being Cal's sister or of them being around two hundred and fifty years old. They didn't require any adjustment to the idea of conversing with a dog. To Eleanor, it seemed almost natural. There had been a lot of movies about talking dogs. At my age, I had been programmed to think of such things as fantasy. I was having to unlearn the programming I had thought was a grown-up way of thinking.

"You three are smart," Jonah said.

"Almost as smart as you," Cal told him.

Much of rural northern California seemed untouched by the anti-dog violence. We saw people walking dogs. But there was always a look of worry on their faces like they might have to rescue their dogs at any minute.

On the outskirts of Crescent City, we passed a veterinarian's office that was boarded up. Cal stopped at a fast food restaurant across the street. "We need to get this dog to a vet or she may not make it," he whispered to me.

"I know," I murmured, looking at Eleanor, who was softly singing to little Sunshine.

CHAPTER 28

Cal lowered the windows enough for the cool air to get into the car, and we had the kids and dogs stay down while we went inside.

At the food counter, Cal inquired, "What happened to the vet? I see people, here, still have dogs."

"The government came after her and demanded to know who her patients were, and so she closed her office."

"That's terrible," I said.

A woman walked in and ordered some sweet potato fries and a soft drink. "These folks were just asking about you."

"Shop is closed."

"There are still dogs around. They might need treatment," Cal pointed out.

"What's that to you?"

"We care about dogs," I replied.

"So do I. If a dog needs to be treated, I'll help if I can but not as a vet. I'm through with records."

"That means you can't prescribe medicines," Cal said.

"Most things can be treated naturally, anyway, and I'm still licensed."

"If we had a little dog who needed some treatment, could you help?" I asked.

"Maybe."

I looked at Cal. He went to the car and brought back Sunshine. Eleanor followed him in. I gave her a look of concern.

"I want her to make Sunshine better. Please," Eleanor urged.

I could visibly see the expression on the doctor's face melt as she looked at Eleanor and the little dog.

The doctor reached out and checked Sunshine's limbs, eyes and lips. "I'm Liz," she said.

"Pleased to meet you," Cal replied, as I simultaneously said, "Hi."

"I'm Jim, and these are my sisters, Lucy and Carla," he went on.

"Well, little Sunshine seems dehydrated. She needs to be put on an IV."

"Please save her," Eleanor pleaded, almost bursting into tears.

Liz softly put her hand on Eleanor's back. "I'll do my best. I have most of my equipment at home now." The man at the counter handed Liz a bag of food and her drink and we followed her on foot to a nearby house. "Is this your dog?" Liz asked.

"We found her under a bush in a dog park earlier today," I said. "I think she was the only one living."

Liz shook her head. "That's why I closed my practice. I was afraid they would come in there and kill my patients. She's a beautiful dog."

"She really is," I agreed.

"These dog attacks are bullshit," Liz remarked. She looked at Eleanor. "Sorry."

"We think they are planning to make money off robotic dogs," I informed her.

"Stupid. Would you like a robotic wife or sister?"

Cal shook his head.

"Dogs do not attack unless they are provoked and even then, they won't try to kill unless they've been trained to kill. Even the military is having a tough time using them in wars because it's not in the basic nature of dogs to harm humans," she elaborated.

"They have most of America convinced that dogs are dangerous," I told her.

"And they claim another attack happened today at a high school in Massachusetts."

After we went into Liz's home office, she examined our fluffy little companion, put an IV catheter in Sunshine's front right leg and attached it to a line from a bag of fluids. "I think I can help this little girl."

Sunshine started to perk up after being on the IV for a little while.

"Do you want to keep her?"

"If we can't find another owner," I said. I looked at Eleanor. I knew she had taken to the dog and I wasn't going to give Sunshine away if she wanted her.

As if knowing what I was thinking, Eleanor lamented, "I don't know if they will let me keep a dog with me."

"Well, I would love to keep this little girl," Liz said. "I've always had a passion for Eskies. If your little sister wants her back when she's well, I'll honor that."

"Promise you will be good to her," Eleanor said, hugging Liz.

"I promise. And if you give me your address, I'll send you pictures."

"We're traveling, but if you give us your email, Eleanor can contact you when we get settled," I suggested.

Liz handed us her card, crossed off the front, and wrote her cell number and email address on the back. Cal put it in his wallet and pulled out a few hundred dollar bills.

"I'm not going to charge you for treating my new dog," Liz said.

I smiled and gave her a hug, too. "Thank you."

"We need to be on our way," Cal pointed out.

Eleanor gave Sunshine a goodbye hug. She looked back at the little Eskie as we guided Eleanor to and through the door. "I think Liz will be good to her," she said.

"I do, too," I responded.

We made it to Oregon that evening. Cal found a hotel that didn't require credit cards in Gold Beach and we got two rooms. One for the boys and boy dog and one for the girls and girl dog, though it was hard or close to impossible to think of Everything as a dog.

Cal suggested dying the kids' hair. I didn't want to cut Eleanor's long black hair. But she liked the idea of going strawberry blonde. I thought about the damage bleach might do to a little girl's hair. I used a temporary tint to add red highlights to her hair and put it up into a dancer's bun. I went from blonde to black. I was afraid Cal wouldn't like it. When I came out of my bedroom, he said, "Wow. And I didn't think you could get more beautiful."

"I hope you don't think I'm going to keep this color."

"You look sensational both ways."

Jonah, also, used a temporary color to go from blonde to black. It didn't look like enough of a change. Up the coast a little ways in Coos Bay, Cal bought Jonah a wig with early Beatle-styled hair, pretending he was getting it for himself.

Continuing on, we ate lunch in a bayside restaurant in Newport. "I want sleepy toes," Jonah said.

I laughed. "He keeps asking for those."

Cal signaled the waitress. "Could my brother have a plate of sweet potatoes?"

"Sweet potatoes."

"That's what I said," Jonah told me.

"Sorry. I was listening through limited categories."

Jonah looked puzzled. Cal laughed.

We took a couple of to-go orders back to Cal's sister and our other four-legged friend. The kids seemed to be enjoying themselves. Jonah asked if we could stop for a game of miniature golf.

"What do you think?" Cal asked me.

"That's what regular families, who aren't afraid of being imprisoned, do. Why not?"

Jonah and Eleanor won, of course. That's not to say that I didn't play the worst game of my life. Cal accidentally hit the ball in the wrong direction several times. We laughed and had a great time.

Eleanor was very bright for a seven year-old girl. Cal and I quizzed her on math. In addition to regular math, she knew some algebra and geometry.

Everything gave Monarch instructions in dog on how to be more covert. On the road, she struck up a conversation with Eleanor. They talked about dresses and boys and shared their knowledge of the games of their respective time periods.

I called Susie. She asked if I was still in California. "No," I replied. "I want to stay as far away from there as possible."

"I understand Jonah's missing."

"Jonah? That's terrible." You never knew whether anyone was listening. "Do you think he ran away?"

"Juliet and Brian claim he was kidnapped."

"I hope they put out an alert on him. He's too young to be out on his own."

"They did." She paused. "There have been some complications."

"Complications?"

"We got an order in North Carolina, but Juliet got a counter order in California. Brawn said that, since you are from North Carolina and if you are not in California, anymore, California should give full faith and credit to the North Carolina order."

"Should?"

"That's just it. They aren't."

"I see."

"Brawn has filed in the federal court, and there is another hearing, here, in North Carolina, set for May. It would be best if you were here by then."

"I will be."

As we continued up 101, I heard a loud pop and Cal steered the car to the side of the road. "Flat tire."

He asked everyone to stay in the car, but I insisted on getting out to help him. As he pulled off the tire and examined it, a concerned look appeared on his face.

"What?"

"Get back in the car and stay down."

"No."

"Meadow, this looks like a bullet hole."

I looked around. Everyone seemed to be continuing along the highway. I didn't see anyone looking our way. "But the dogs have been down well below the window level and we've got shaded glass."

He showed me the tire. "There's an entrance hole and an exit hole."

"You think we've been spotted?"

"We've got California plates. Maybe someone from Oregon doesn't like Californians. It's possible that the insanity has gotten people shooting at everything in sight."

"But they've confiscated guns, particularly on the West Coast."

"Not for people who don't obey the laws. I would feel much safer with you in the car while I change the tire."

"And I'd feel safer being a lookout while you change it. If I see anything, we rush for cover."

"I'm not going to get you to play it safe, am I?"

"Nope."

He shook his head and quickly changed the tire.

Back along the route, Cal contacted Charlie to see if there were any alerts out on us in Oregon.

Charlie called back and over the speaker, I heard him say, "There is a statewide search in California for the kids. No mention of Oregon."

I noticed that Jonah was looking a little bored.

"I know we're in a hurry, Cal, but maybe we can give them some good memories along the way," I suggested. "We could walk along the ocean or stroll through one of the parks."

"I have an idea," Cal said.

We stopped in Seaside and took the kids to the Promenade, which had a bronze statue of Lewis & Clark and their dog Seaman. Across the dog, someone had painted, the word, "Killer."

Eleanor cringed. Everything was in my backpack and I planned to keep her there. When we got back to the minivan, Monarch was resting below the raft, which was covered by a blanket. We had left the windows slightly open for air while we were gone.

From there, Cal took us to the Carousel Mall. The kids had a good time on the signature ride, and I hoped that this, rather than the nightmare she'd lived through would be what Eleanor would remember of the United States.

Cal found a campground that had a small cabin available for rent. I wondered how a sixteen-year-old was able to get a room.

"Fake ID," Cal said, "but I shouldn't use it more than a couple of times.

"And credit card. You don't have bank accounts under a fake name, do you?"

"With enough cash for a deposit, some places don't care."

The next morning we took off for Washington. Being out of California, I thought we were safe. Then suddenly, the nightmare erupted again.

As night fell and we pulled into Olympia, we passed a park. I saw protesters with anti-dog signs. "Keep Monarch down," I told Jonah.

I called Charlie, who advised me, "It's worse in Seattle. They are having marches, and it's like a scene out of *The Purge*. The slaughtering is worse than in So Cal."

"Why? Seattle is far away from Lancer High."

"Teens are being rallied up in all parts of the fifty states. The ones who won't participate are getting school detention."

"Schools are in on it?" I questioned.

"Gatto says that's where the programming starts."

"Gatto?" Cal asked, listening to the conversation over the speaker.

"John Taylor Gatto. He used to regularly be New York's Teacher of the Year. He quit, saying he couldn't hurt kids anymore. Gatto insisted that schools were intentionally dumbing down kids to create a mindless society that would do as told," Charlie informed him.

"Well, it's looking like he was right about that," I said, recalling the insanity of the last week.

Cal got us a couple of rooms with Wi-Fi at a Motel Seven. We went into the boys' room and watched the news. Cal went out and got three veggie pizzas that the five of us shared, with the lion's portion going to Monarch.

The TV channels showed the marches. Commentators like Raquel Madcow praised the kids who were helping to rid the world of "killer dogs."

"There are up to 4.7 million dog bites per year and many of these result in death."

"You notice she didn't say what percentage of bites resulted in death or how many did not result in death? That's because it's only about .004 percent that result in death."

"In one day," Rachel continued, *"Dogs killed nineteen kids at Lancer High. Those kids would be alive, preparing for finals, enjoying their friends, if our society had rid itself of killer dogs before the incident."* I shut off the TV.

"Did dogs really kill nineteen kids?" Eleanor asked.

"No," I said. "Cal and I were there. The only real casualties were dogs that the officers shot. They slapped fake blood on us to pretend we were injured."

"I don't want them to kill Monarch or Everything."

As she said that, Jonah hugged Everything. "I love you, Everything and Monarch."

"Don't worry. We won't let them." I looked at Cal. "Maybe we should also ask Canada for asylum for us, your sister and Monarch."

"Canada also has some restrictive laws regarding dogs. You have to get permission from the Canadian Kennel Club before you even name a dog there," Cal said. "Charlie got back to me on that yesterday."

I turned back on the TV, hoping the subject had changed. *"In Raleigh, dog owners rallied and sent a message,"* another commentator noted. The TV showed a sign saying, "You'll get our dogs over our dead bodies."

"I'm a liberal and yet for the first time, I'm feeling like I agree more with the people in the South," I said. The others looked at me. "Just because I lived part of my life in North Carolina, doesn't make me a Southerner."

"In my day, the issues were freedom and rights. We had honorable leaders. Now, it seems politicians are nothing but corrupt, greedy liars," Cal said.

"It's no longer about liberal versus conservative. The new division is truth versus suppression and lies," I noted.

"In a couple of years, maybe we can start a 'Truth Party.'"

"That's a party I'd join."

"I'm going to join the Truth Party, too," Jonah said.

"I want to start one in Canada," Eleanor announced. "When I'm old enough to vote. I hope you will come visit me."

"Count on it," Cal assured her.

"That's over ten years away. Don't wait," she urged.

"We won't," I responded, giving her a hug.

I scanned through the channels. As I started to pass Madcow on the TV, her report caught my attention. *"Seven school dog attacks since Friday. One state is taking action to protect its citizens. In Seattle, authorities are going door to door to inspect dogs to see if dogs have been spayed or neutered. Any dogs which have not been spayed or neutered will be euthanized. Additionally, all dangerous dogs, such as shepherds, collies, pit bulls, mastiffs, huskies, chow chows, Chihuahuas, Samoyeds, Eskimos, Spitzes, hounds, poodles, Dobermans, greyhounds, Saint Bernards, and about two dozen other types will be instantly euthanized if found in the SeaTac area."*

From the other channels on the TV, we could see that the marches in Seattle were large and raucous, kind of like the G7 marches, except this time they were not for a peaceful or good cause. The visuals were graphic and shocking and I couldn't believe they were on TV. Lots of people were making a statement by carrying cooked dogs on sticks. One marcher had the head of a dog that looked like a miniature version of Monarch hanging from a chain around his neck. There was even a concession stand with a grill and a sign, reading, "Get your hot dogs cooked here; support PETIS with a donation." I looked at the grill. It wasn't the Oscar Mayer variety of hot dogs they were cooking.

Everything cringed. Jonah and Eleanor started sobbing. As I went from channel to channel, I saw news commentators, who had previously been classified as liberal, praising the teens for their courageous strong stand against dogs.

I kept turning the channel in the hopes of finding something non-violent. Almost every news channel portrayed the violence and was cheering it on. The movie channels seemed to be on vacation and replaced by the continuing propaganda.

"Let's get out of here," I said.

"Don't let them kill Monarch!" Jonah cried. Eleanor was sobbing, too.

"They are not going to kill or maim me, either," Everything said, probably making a reference to not wanting to be spayed.

"I've never had a chance before to ask a dog how they feel about being spayed or neutered," I stated.

"If you wouldn't want it done to you, don't do it to a dog."

"Monarch is pretty big and won't fit in your backpack. Maybe I should get him to the van now."

"If they force open my backpack, they might mistake Everything for one of those 'dangerous' Chihuahuas," I replied. "I think its best if we stay together until we check out."

Cal looked through the curtain. "There is a woman across on the other wing, staring at our room."

"With these kids, the last thing we want is any notoriety," I said.

"We're close to Seattle, but maybe we should turn back and go to a different consulate."

"I think you are right."

Cal ran out to the car and carried in the raft he had purchased at Costco. Deflated, it was more than easy and large enough to wrap around Monarch. Everything was explaining the danger to Monarch in dog language.

"And tell him to be really quiet if someone approaches," I advised.

Cal almost had him wrapped when there was a knock at the door, a loud knock. Monarch looked as if he were about to bark. Everything said something quietly to him in dog talk and he closed his mouth. A key was turning in the lock. Cal looked out. It was the manager.

CHAPTER 29

"What do you want?" Cal asked as he pulled the chain across and leaned against the door to prevent it from opening more than a half inch. The manager would have had to wreck his door to push past Cal.

"We heard you had a dog in there."

Cal, with a gesture, signaled me, Eleanor, Jonah and the dogs to retreat into the bathroom. We piled in and I turned on the shower and then listened at the door.

"My brother is taking a shower. What's going on?"

I was pretty sure they were talking at the door. I couldn't hear the manager's side of the conversation.

"Well, that's ridiculous. There are a lot of crazies out there these days."

The manager was saying something I couldn't decipher.

"No problem. Bye."

Cal came and knocked on the bathroom door. "Someone outside spotted the dogs. The hotel has banned dogs for its own protection during the uprisings. But I convinced him there weren't any."

"Good boy, Monarch, for keeping quiet," I said as we went into the bedroom. Eleanor started crying. I put my arm around her. She sank to the floor and I sank down, too, keeping my arm around her.

Cal looked through the edge of the curtain. "That woman is still outside, staring at our room."

Cal called Charlie and put his phone on speaker. Derek was with Charlie. Charlie brought up a satellite image of the area on feeds that were much more extensive than those on GagemMaps and said he'd call us back.

Cal kept peeking out the window around the edge of the curtain. "There are about five people there now."

"Everything will be easier to hide when we leave. If they rush at us, they might find Monarch in the raft," I noted.

"Well, we're not going out right now. The manager is speaking to them. Maybe, he will be able to convince them," Cal replied.

I pulled out my computer and got on the Internet. Sandy Blackbird had done an exposé of the Lancer attack. She had picked up the mantle of exposés after censorship drove Debbie Lusignan, the Sane Progressive, into Internet seclusion. Sandy showed news footage of me walking away as she pointed out that there was no real evidence of any serious injuries. She asked where the funerals were, the same question we kept asking. Then she spoke about the marketing of the new robotic dogs, designed to create a fortune.

Sandy had a computer expert who had worked on robotics on her Screwtube show who said that there could be a hidden program in the dogs designed to attack the owners if they opposed the government. Her analysis was extremely well researched. I hoped others saw it. As the robotics expert was speaking, Sandy's livestream was cut. Even the first part was suddenly unavailable for replay. No surprise, given the mass censorship that had been going on for some time.

I went to the Walmart News Network. It was the fastest news site on the web, thanks to the end of net neutrality. There was a very fuzzy picture of us and the Sienna minivan with the words, "Kidnappers." The license plate was unreadable.

"It's good Candy is such a lousy photographer," I said. From the news, I learned there was a big childhunt down south for Eleanor.

The former CIA chief who was now the news anchor for the station, reported, *"There is also a search for a little boy Jonah, who is believed to have been kidnapped by a gang of thieves who are believed to be armed and danger-*

ous. Supposedly the kidnappers said they would kill Jonah if they were captured, and so swat teams are saying they will probably have to kill the kidnappers on sight."

"Has anyone ever heard of the *Sixth Amendment* in your century? It was drafted and ratified after I left, but my second dad got me history books to show our government really did the right thing back then."

"The Supreme Court overthrew the *Constitution* on December 12th, 2000, and the pieces that were left have been largely disregarded by our government leaders since. The National Defense Authorization Act provides for indefinite detention of American citizens without any rights. Obama made an executive order providing for the assassination of Americans, all without trial. With the PATRIOT Act, there isn't much left of the *Fourth Amendment*."

"I keep remembering the words Tom wrote into the *Declaration* about overthrowing tyrannical governments."

"Kind of hard to do when they have all the weapons and are trying to take our dogs."

"These rights grabbers have already killed the government that was created. This is not what the Founders envisioned when they fought for a new country."

"Were you there for the *Constitutional* Convention?"

"I was long gone by then. Remember, I left when I was only ten. But I've studied it extensively to see what I missed."

"I was there," Everything said. "But women were treated as second-class citizens. You did notice that your sexist friend wrote, 'All *men*,' not women, 'are created equal' in the Declaration, didn't you?"

"That's not what he meant. He was talking about mankind."

"Even that term is sexist."

The kids were close to hysterical, and the conversation wasn't calming them down. Everything curled up in Jonah's lap. I brushed away Eleanor's tears. I didn't want her to close down again. "How about a game of charades?"

Jonah reluctantly nodded.

"Book titles," Cal suggested. "I'll start." He looked like he was cracking eggs and putting them on a grill while holding his nose.

Jonah guessed, "Green Eggs and Ham."

"Very good. You're a winner," Cal said. He looked out the window. "There are more people out there, now."

I peered out. "More" was an understatement. There were at least thirty people out there. Some had knives. I could see some with wrenches and hammers as if they planned to break down the door.

I called Charlie. "Is there anything on your Net that will show us a way out?"

"I think I have something. I'm using a roundabout route to make a call. When you hear the signal, get out of there."

"What signal?"

"You can't miss it."

Cal wrapped up Monarch in the raft. I put my computer and Everything in my backpack, and we prepared to leave.

I kept listening for another call or for some kind of signal. Nothing. Someone started pounding on our door. "Open up or we're breaking it down."

CHAPTER 30

We didn't have any weapons to fight with, and I wasn't putting our dogs in danger. Cal picked up a chair and moved toward the door as if preparing for someone to break it in.

As if on cue, sirens started blasting through the air, lots of them. The knocking stopped. The crowd may have thought the sirens were for them.

Cal looked out the window. "The crowd is moving towards something past the front of the motel."

We ran to the car and took off as firetrucks and police cars surrounded a building across the street.

"What was that?" I asked Charlie over the phone.

"An internal fire going out of control with radioactive explosives and mustard gas in the building—at least until they discover otherwise."

"I'm glad you're my friend," I said.

"You should head east towards Mount Rainer. There's a desert in the eastern half of Washington. Then, you have Idaho."

"Home of the Aryan Nations. If we aren't with one group of extremists, we're with another," I responded.

"That's just a small group there. Whatever route you take across

Washington, just stay clear of Hanford. You don't want to irradiate those kids. After you get past Idaho, you have the choice of Montana or Wyoming."

"Look up which state has the least number of dog-crazy people."

"That would be Montana. As for Idaho, southern Idaho is potato country with Boise and northern Idaho has Sandpoint, which, as you pointed out, is the Home of the Aryan Nations."

I remembered watching a horrible movie on *Netflix*, called *Betrayed*, a Costa-Gavras film about the Aryan Nations. I hoped Charlie was right about that being only a small part of the population.

"You can also take Interstate 90, but you need to take a roundabout route or you will be going through Tacoma, which I wouldn't recommend. I suggest you go north on 169 and catch 90 further east. There is cover in the trees, too."

I turned to Cal. "How about I get you, Jonah, your sister and Monarch to Idaho and then come back to Seattle with Eleanor?"

"Or I could take Eleanor."

"But you, Jonah and Everything are family. Besides, two girls traveling together would be less suspicious."

"We'll talk when we get to Idaho."

***

We followed Charlie's instructions, and even at night, I found myself in awe at the beauty of our surroundings. I wondered if the crazies would have been out in such strong force during one of Washington's usual rainy days or nights. I guessed we hit Washington on one of its rare dry periods.

I wondered about God. If he really was up there and good, why had this gone so far? I reflected on the children who had been killed in America's imperialistic wars in the Middle East. I thought about all the countries I would be avoiding in my future travels and experiences because of the high levels of radiation from depleted uranium dropped by our government. We had destroyed the people and the land in those countries. Why did anyone living here deserve anything better?

There were lots of trees everywhere, but not walls of trees like in

New York State where drivers often got a claustrophobic feeling. These were beautiful, majestic trees.

As we drove further east, we hit the desert. Through the headlights, I could see that instead of the moist green of Western Washington, the scenery to the east was a dry brown. I wondered if some of what I saw was damage from Hanford, but that was a ways to the south.

"I don't like the idea of you and Eleanor being alone," Cal said, as he pulled into a gas station in Spokane, an oasis in the Washington desert.

"We won't take any chances. Besides, we both have different looks than we did before. If you want, I'll pick up some redneck clothing in Idaho and talk like an uneducated bumpkin to throw people off."

"Is that a dig at people from Idaho?"

"No. I just want to be less identifiable."

As the sun came up, the sky was blue. At Coeur d'Alene, we stopped at a vegetarian restaurant for breakfast and saw a black Mustang with a "For Sale" sign on the side window. According to Cal, it was a model from the nineties. The owner was inside. He was eager to sell it.

"Only has one hundred and ninety-five thousand miles on it and a new engine."

"How much you want for it?"

"Three thousand dollars."

"How about fifteen hundred?" Cal asked. "I can take it off your hands, today. Cash."

"That won't even pay for my new engine."

"Is it a brand new engine?"

"Of course."

Cal looked skeptical. "Okay, you say it's used but in great shape, like new. It's more than two decades old. Two thousand?"

"Two thousand."

Cal went back to the Odyssey and got the cash. I was surprised by how much cash he had, but he had been planning to find a way to protect Jonah since before we met. So I guess it wasn't that surprising.

Cal came back and handed me the keys. "We drove the Odyssey when we escaped Olympia, and it would be best if you drove a different car back into the state."

I guessed he was giving in.

"But I expect you to call me every ten minutes to let me know you are safe." He handed me a new phone. "I picked this burner phone up in Oregon. It has a New York area code. I was concerned that they might start tracking your regular phone. They might get the number from monitoring Susie's phone or one of your friends. According to Charlie, the government has fake cell towers for doing that sort of thing."

I opened my regular phone and pulled the battery. I was glad I hadn't upgraded to a phone with a non-removable battery.

"I've programmed my new burner phone number and the numbers of our San Diego friends into it," he continued. "It also has Canada on its coverage and Shandra's number is in there, but I wouldn't use it to call her until Eleanor is safely at the Consulate. We don't know if they are monitoring her calls."

"Thanks." I gave him a friendly kiss on the cheek.

He smiled. "We have a lot more to discuss when we have some private time."

I nodded. I really liked him, and I got that he really liked me too. Actually, I more than really admired him for his courage and determination to always do the right thing for Jonah and the rest of us in our group. And it didn't hurt that he was really, really good-looking. He was like one of those heroes that you see in the movies but don't believe exists in real life. Yet here he was.

I had gotten quite a bit of sleep in the car on the way to Coeur d'Alene and was eager to get Eleanor to the Canadian Consulate before there were any more complications. So, I said goodbye and gave Jonah a hug. I turned to Everything.

"Please, take me with you," Everything said.

"You are in danger in Washington."

"So are you. I'm small and can hide."

"Please stay here with your brother. If anything happens here, like you said, you are small and can hide. You can tell me the details if something happens and whether I need to rescue someone."

Everything whimpered. Cal took her in his arms. "I'll take care of you, Sis." He put her back into the Odyssey.

Cal escorted me to his new car that I would be driving.

"It's a nice car. Now, you have two Mustangs," I said.

"What am I going to do with two? Maybe I could give one to a friend. I've heard of this great concept called communism, not the totalitarian kind but the sharing kind. Tom would have liked that concept in spite of his aristocratic background."

"And the rest of your family?"

"My grandfather would have thought he was right to disown my dad for raising a radical like me."

I laughed.

He gave me a hug. "Wait a minute, I have something for you."

He went back to his car and got me a pocket knife. "I picked it up at a convenience store by the gas station in Spokane. It seemed a good idea after we almost had to fight killers with chairs and pillows in that last hotel room."

I laughed again. I started to get into the Mustang. He stopped me with one arm. "I'll see you tomorrow *at the latest*, right?"

"Right."

"And call me every ten minutes."

"How about every half hour?"

"Okay. But if I get worried, I may call you more often."

He pulled me into his arms and gave me a hug that lasted for several minutes. "Please come back safely. You are amazing. I meant what I said about really liking you. I would have hung out with you even if Jonah wasn't with your aunt."

"Cal—" I whispered, as he released me.

But the rest of my sentence was silenced as he pulled me back into his arms and his lips met mine and suddenly the world and my ability to think dissolved. I felt like I was going to melt and fly at the same time. I had been kissed before and even passionately but nothing like this. It was as if this kiss was the magic I had always been looking for in a secret search that I had even hidden from myself. Now, I had found everything that mattered and was leaving it all behind in Montana.

As the embrace ended, he softly said, "When you get back, we have a lot of talking to do."

Still in a daze, I answered, "Sure. Yes." I tried to think what I should say next but couldn't. So, I just stared as Cal went back to his car.

Eleanor had been with Jonah by the Odyssey. She hugged Cal and then ran from the Odyssey to the new Mustang.

"Ready?" I asked.

"I just hope I get to see them again."

"You will. We'll arrange it somehow."

The drive back through Idaho was beautiful but lonely. I missed Cal and Jonah. Eleanor was great company, though. She started naming everything she saw along the way, from trees in Idaho and types of cabins and cars to desert plants in Washington State. The more I learned about her, the more I was impressed with how bright she was. I remembered hearing that Indigo children were in the most danger of being trafficked. She and Jonah both seemed way above the curve in intuition and brains.

We started playing the alphabet game. It served a couple of purposes, one of which was to keep me awake.

It wasn't that long of a drive down 90. It was just 312 miles from Coeur d'Alene to Seattle. However, I felt nervous the entire way. There was an Amber Alert out on Eleanor, and in spite of the change in hair, we needed to avoid being stopped and asked for ID. For all I knew, there was an amber alert, also, out on me. So, I made sure to obey all the traffic laws. I didn't tell Cal that I only had a learner's permit. I planned to contact Susie and Everett after I reached Seattle, in case their calls were monitored. Cal had their number, too, and I was sure he'd notify them if we lost contact or if I didn't return by tomorrow afternoon.

I couldn't get my mind off the kiss. I had been so into my studies and dance that I had never had time for a serious relationship. All the prior kisses I had had were kind of yucky, but Cal's was like nothing I had ever contemplated. He was a great kisser.

No. Not great, sensational. I wondered if he had had a lot of practice.

"You, Cal and Jonah will come visit me in British Columbia, won't you?" Eleanor asked.

"Of course. By the way, Eleanor is a great name. My mom's dad was a big fan of Eleanor Roosevelt."

"That's who I was named after. My mom told me she was a great lady."

"She was. She helped Cordell Hull put together the United Nations. And she was a big civil rights leader."

"My mom said she quit some organization because they wouldn't allow Blacks to join."

"The DAR, Daughters of the American Revolution. My dad wanted me to join it, but my mom was against the idea."

"Derek said your parents died."

"A plane crash. My mom was a really good person. But not my dad. He was a terrible person, really mean."

"Mine was too. But my mom was really great like yours."

"We have a lot in common."

"You and your friends saved me. I think they were going to kill me."

"You've saved my life, too. You've given me a sense of purpose. I don't know if I can go back to just hanging out with my friends at school when there is so much in the world to fix."

"Me too. I want to help other kids like me."

"I'm sure you'll have a great future."

We stopped for gas in Tacoma at a cheap gas station. I knew I would miss Eleanor, but I was also envious. She was close to getting to see her mom. I'd never see mine again. I finished pumping fuel and went to get in the car.

Everything was on Eleanor's lap. I got in. "Everything, what are you doing here? They're killing dogs in Washington!"

CHAPTER 31

"I'm your spirit guide, remember."

"No, you're Cal's. On top of that, you're an endangered species in this state. Cal must be going crazy with worry."

"He knows."

"What? You're his sister. He wouldn't put you in danger."

"I told him that, if they got me, I'd take another form."

"Is that true?"

"Who knows? But Cal believed me. He really cares about you."

"And he cares about you. He lost you once. I don't want him to lose you again."

"I'll be okay. I am small. I can go places, and see things that you can't."

"I need to take you back."

"You are almost at the Consulate. It's in Century Square in the Financial District."

"How did you know that?"

"I talked to your other phone before you pulled the battery."

"Oh. Well, I can't risk you."

"You can get Eleanor to safety quickly, and then we can get back to my brother. It won't take much longer than turning around and going back now."

I drove onto a side street, parked and called Cal. "You let her come with me?"

"She passed away two centuries ago. She isn't like us."

"She's a flesh and blood Papillion."

"She talks. Maybe I was naïve and gullible, but she insisted on going and I believed her when she said she'd keep you safe."

"What if something happens to her?"

"The truth of the matter is I told her 'no' and after she presented her arguments, I told her 'no,' again. She went anyway. I didn't know until after she was gone. But I've been thinking about it and I'm kind of glad that you and my sister are looking out for each other."

"Why didn't you say something before?"

"She asked me not to."

"You said, you didn't know she was coming."

"She left me a note."

"She writes?" I looked at Everything.

She put her front paws up in the air.

"I guess she does."

"Any dog who can talk and write two hundred years after her initial lifespan is a lot wiser than we are."

"Either that or we're crazy and delusional. I still don't feel good about this."

"I'm worried, too. But Becky has pointed out to me that I dismissed her concerns during her first lifetime. I want her to know I believe in her, now. You're close to Seattle aren't you?"

"Yes."

"Well then, get that kid into the Consulate, and hightail it back here."

Reluctantly, I said, "Okay."

"You can carry me in your bag. I don't have any metal in me."

"They have x-ray scanners for carry-ins."

"How about under your blouse? The Canadians will use a metal detector for humans. They aren't as paranoid as the Americans."

"You may be small but almost nobody's bust is that big." That part of me was already oversized for my otherwise thin body, and with Everything added, I was certain they'd search me.

"You have me in oversized fatty clothes," Eleanor pointed out. "I can put her at waist level and she will make my fat appearance more convincing. Then you can carry her out in your backpack when you leave."

It seemed plausible. "I guess that could work." I really didn't want to risk bringing Everything, but leaving her in the car also seemed like a bad idea. It was a no-win situation. "This is Seattle."

"The Canadian Consulate is Canada," Everything said.

"But if they throw you out, they'll throw you out into Seattle."

"You are going to have to trust me. I was born around two hundred and fifty years ago. I think I know something about survival."

I finally gave up arguing with my dog, who was really a girl more than sixteen times my age and agreed to go into the Consulate with my fat little girlfriend, who was a Canadian citizen via her mother. With the added weight and new hairstyle, Eleanor looked nothing like the little girl we rescued from the Day Country School.

Walking down the sidewalk, what we weren't expecting were the dogs who were running away from certain executions. Two of them ran towards us half a block from the Consulate. I gathered they had smelled Everything and started barking at Eleanor.

"Hey, are those your dogs?" someone in a police uniform yelled at Eleanor.

"No. We've never seen them before," I said, as Eleanor was formulating her answer.

Suddenly I could hear Everything's dog voice barking from about five feet away behind a planter. The dogs ran over there as did their pursuers, looking for the barking dog. The pursued dogs kept going as the pursuers searched for the invisible barking dog. I started to follow. I couldn't let anything happen to her.

"It's okay," Eleanor called to me.

"I'll join you at the Consulate," I said.

"No, you won't." It was Everything's voice coming from Eleanor's fat tummy. The pursuers didn't notice. They were looking for a dog behind the planter. We continued quickly to the Consulate.

Inside the Consulate, we discovered one of the Chertoff-Adelman human X-ray scanners. "I guess somebody outside the U.S. was gullible enough to buy those scanners," I said to Eleanor. I turned to the security guards. "This is a child. Surely you don't have to irradiate her."

"We could do a pat down," one of the guards said.

"Of a child?"

The men spoke to each other and then the first one replied. "We have a metal detector wand we can use. Do you have anything metal to take off?"

"No. I'm fine," Eleanor said. The wand didn't reveal anything.

"I'll opt for the pat down," I said. "I really don't need the radiation, and I want to have children one day."

They called out a female attendant to pat me down. As we proceeded past security, we were asked, "Do you have an appointment?"

"This is a Canadian child of a Canadian mother who has a full custody order in Canada. We are seeking asylum."

"That will be room nine seventy." We were given directions and guided to the elevator.

Once inside, I had to know. "How did you throw your voice?"

Everything shifted her position inside Eleanor's blouse. "It was one of my abilities, even as a child. There was a ventriloquist who taught me how to do it and then used me in his act."

"Wow! That is very impressive. Is that part of the reason you can talk the way you do?"

"I think talking is part of the nature of my current state of existence. But that could be helping too."

"Next, you'll tell me you can drive a car?"

"I'm from the eighteenth century."

"That hasn't stopped Cal."

"Her name is Everything. I bet she can do everything," Eleanor interjected.

I smiled. "Good. How about minting me a million dollars?"

"You aren't interested in a million dollars," Everything said.

"You're right. But would you do it if I were?"

"Probably not."

———

Upstairs, an intake assistant took the information, offered us each a seat and contacted Mrs. Tidwell. As we sat there, Council General Brandon Leaf came into the room. "Well young lady, my government has been very interested in your case."

"Then, why didn't someone rescue her? She was almost murdered in Carlsbad by a trafficking ring," I said.

"It's a diplomatic issue. The United States is not particularly cooperative with respect to fighting trafficking and honoring treaties. Your President claims to have an official policy of fighting trafficking, but none of his appointees are on board with it." He looked at Eleanor. "I'm sorry that you had to go through all that."

"When can I see my mother?"

He turned back to me. "We understand that California wants her back. It's good you came to Washington State. We will try to get her out of here tonight. But we are working against some very bad people in positions of authority in your country."

"Couldn't you helicopter her out of this building?"

"They might try to flag down the helicopter. We might be better off driving her out in an embassy car. And Eleanor, you can take the dog out from under your clothes now. In Canada, we don't kill dogs."

"How did you—" I started to ask.

"We have been watching you on the cameras since you entered, and either she has a very lively outfit, or the dog has moved under it."

Eleanor stood up, turned around and pulled out Everything.

"She is beautiful," Leaf said.

"I am worried about keeping her safe in Seattle. It's not the safest place for dogs," I pointed out.

"We can give you an escort to your car, but it's best if the dog stays out of sight after you leave the Consulate."

"I'd like to wait until Eleanor is ready to leave."

"Did you park in a lot?"

"Yes."

"Then your car should be okay until then." He turned to Eleanor. "While you are waiting, we have an indoor playground here and lots of food. Would you like a hot fudge sundae?"

"Hot fudge sundae!" Eleanor reacted. "It's my favorite."

"How about you?"

"Do you have anything with almond or coconut ice cream?" I felt like a kid asking for a treat.

"As a matter of fact, we do."

We relaxed in the game room with the indoor playground until nightfall. I pushed Eleanor on the swing and turned the merry-go-round so fast, that she threw back her head and started laughing. I knew they were taking their time to make the journey safe. Mr. Leaf came in. "We have a problem. The U.S. Government has been expecting you to show up at one of our Consulates, and they used facial recognition to spot Eleanor when you entered here today."

"Did they say anything about me?" I asked.

"Are they looking for you too?"

"I hope not. I was going to return home after I got her here."

"Does your guardian know it?"

"Sort of. We were afraid of being tracked, but she knows I'm taking a roundabout route."

"I wouldn't worry about it. They have insisted on getting little Eleanor and expressed an interest in you. But we can take some precautions to protect you, too. At your age, you are a big hero for helping us get back our little Canadian citizen."

"How will you get her out?"

"We could fly her out, but years ago, they forced down the plane of Bolivian President Evo Morales, a world leader, during their search for Edward Snowden. Clearly, they had no qualms about violating international law. I don't think they will go to as much trouble for Eleanor as they did for Snowden. But we're still going to be cautious. We will be trying a two-prong approach. We'll send up a helicopter and a minute later, we'll send out a car."

"Which will Eleanor be in?"

"We're not even telling that to the staff in the Consulate. It will be a last-minute decision. You'll have to trust us. Certain people in the U.S. State Department are working overtime to try to stop the transfer. We've received several threats in the last couple of hours." He turned to Eleanor, who had moved off the merry-go-round and was lying on her tummy and leaning on her elbows while watching us. "Why do they want you so bad, aside from the fact that you are a pretty little girl?"

"I don't know," she said.

"There must be something."

She shook her head.

"She was in a room with men in dark judicial robes. Maybe some of them were real judges who have power and don't want to be identified," I reported.

"Anyone higher?"

"You mean a Senator or Congressman? Would they dare put a little girl in a position to identify one of them?"

"Senator. That's what one guy was called. He made me do stuff that was really yucky."

"I guess they might be afraid she could identify him," I said. "That's why she was to be next when we rescued her."

"Next?"

I shook my head, and I think he picked up on what they had been about to do to her.

"There have been reports that these pedophile rings are tied to the blackmailing of a number of government officials in your country. They get incoming leaders into a compromising situation and, then, they own them. Someone pretty powerful must be afraid of this girl."

From the window, we could see the State Police and National Guard amassing. Someone wanted to make sure Eleanor didn't leave.

———

When it was almost time, Leaf returned to the playroom with another man. "You are about to go back home, Eleanor. First, I want you to meet someone. This is Ambassador David McKnot. He is here to oversee this evening's operation."

"It's my job to make sure my people get you back safely to your mother," David said to Eleanor. "You are a brave little girl, and I'm here to protect you."

Another man came in. "It's time." He turned to me. "I'm the Assistant Counsel General Taylor Brogan."

"Just keep her safe," I said.

"I will."'

"You'll be in the car?" McKnot asked Brogan.

"Yes." He turned to Eleanor. "Come with me."

"So she'll be in the car?" I inquired.

"That won't be decided until the last minute," Leaf said, though that seemed to be the implication.

"It's been a pleasure meeting with you," the Ambassador remarked, shaking my hand. "I have to get to my own car and then back to D.C.," he noted as he left the room.

Leaf stayed with me. Fifteen minutes later, a call came through to the playroom. Leaf answered it, turned to me and said, "The helicopter is in the air. We have diplomatic officials on it and so it would be an international crisis if it were ordered down."

Another call came through. "I see. Thank you." He explained to me. "They've ordered the helicopter down. Our men refused."

A minute later something lit up the sky outside the window. To the next call, Leaf exclaimed, "Oh my God! Did the Americans do that?"

I knew what had happened before he hung up and told me. I prayed that she was in the car.

"The helicopter was hit by a missile." The next call he received was more reassuring. "So the car is out of Seattle?"

The car. She has to be in the car or it would have turned back. Everything curled up in my arms, trying to comfort me. I didn't know if I still believed in God, but I kept praying Eleanor was safe.

A few minutes later, Leaf picked up the phone, again. "No! This can't be happening!"

He made a call, "Ambassador, they blew up the car. I will notify the Prime Minister." He paused. I felt as if my heart had stopped.

CHAPTER 32

"You already called him? And you called the White House? Right, sir. That is best. Are you going to divert to Canada or to Washington to confront the President in person? Yes, sir. A terrible tragedy." I couldn't hear the other end of the conversation, but my end supplied all the answers I wished weren't happening. "Yes sir. Please keep in touch. I understand. Flight might not be safe, even for your trip to Washington at this point. Washington's actions could be classified as an act of war."

Leaf made a call. "The Ambassador has called the White House. He will be meeting up with the Prime Minister and then with the President."

I was too shocked to cry. Leaf came over to me, sat down on the floor where I had sunken and looked into my eyes. "Both the car and the helicopter exploded. We are doing an investigation."

I could barely speak. I couldn't even feel my body. "Eleanor. She's seven," I whispered.

"I know. Someone was willing to risk war with Canada to kill a little girl. I understand how you feel about Eleanor, and in the little time I spent with her, I saw what a beautiful girl you rescued."

An official line. It seemed so inappropriate here. "Some of the men lost were like family to me. I grew up with Taylor. He was my best friend most of my life. This is a loss for all of us." All I could think of was Eleanor. When I looked at Leaf, I noticed there were tears in his eyes as well. He had lost a number of people who had families, loved ones, trusting him to keep the staff safe.

I knew I was being rude, but I just sat, silently, in shock. In the short time I had known her, Eleanor had become like a little sister to me. Everything licked my face, trying to comfort me.

"The press has already been notified. But I need to hold a press conference. I think you should stay here tonight. I'll have one of my assistants show you to a room if you decide to stay."

I nodded. I found myself sobbing. I tried to pull myself together and called Cal to tell him what was going on.

"I heard it on the news. I need to come back to Seattle. I don't like the idea of you and Everything traveling alone."

"You've got to protect Jonah and Monarch. I'm safe in the Consulate for tonight. I can't handle losing anyone else."

A woman came in and identified herself as Jane. "I'm here to show you to your room. I'm very sorry for your loss." Her words sounded like a professional recitation, but her expression and voice showed that she was holding back tears, herself.

I followed her. When I got to my room, I just collapsed on my bed. I lay there sobbing. I had failed. I thought I could keep Eleanor safe. If I hadn't brought her here, she would be alive. It should have been me. It was my decision, my fault.

"I love you," Everything said. She was on my bed snuggling up to me and trying to comfort me. "You saved Eleanor and Jonah from that horrible gang of criminals. You have put Eleanor, Jonah and even me first before your own safety. So, don't be hard on yourself. It will all work out in the end."

"But not for Eleanor."

"I was alive close to two hundred and fifty years ago and right now I'm back. I'm here and happy. Let me rephrase. I'm happy to be with you, not about the situation. There may be evil people hurting kids, here, but there are also forces for good. You are one of the forces for good. You just need to have faith."

"In what?"

"The future. In a way, this life is an illusion. There is more out there than what you see. For tonight, let's pretend that Eleanor made it home."

"But it's a lie."

"What harm will it do to tell yourself that Eleanor somehow made it back to Canada safe and sound? It can't hurt her for you to think of her that way. She wouldn't want you to be so devastated. What would be the first thing Eleanor would do when she got home?"

"She'd hug her mother."

"Picture that. Hang onto that."

I tried to see Eleanor that way, but this dark feeling, the memory of the light in the sky and the phone calls overwhelmed me. Whether Eleanor would want me to feel this way or not, I was devastated by the loss of Eleanor. For the first time, I realized the maturity Everything had about her. It was almost like she was a second mother to me during all these crises. I hugged her tightly.

I thought of the officials on the plane and in the car. Their families had to be in shock as well. I didn't mind losing my dad but my mom. There were people who felt about these officials like I felt about my mom.

There was a TV in the room. I turned it on. It showed a picture of Eleanor as a little girl, chasing a dog and running around. This couldn't be happening. There were pictures of the Canadians who were in the car as well as in the helicopter. One of the officials who was killed was a woman who coached a kids' soccer team in her spare time. Another official, who died, had a newborn baby. Taylor had just gotten married. It didn't specify which transportation Eleanor was in. Leaf appeared on the news and made a statement.

"What has happened today is a great tragedy. We are holding back judgment, but the appearance is that it was Americans who killed Canadian officials and a little girl who had been subjected to child sex trafficking in the United States. Before she left, she informed me that judges and one or more members of the U.S. Senate had been involved in the pedophile ring. This will be investigated, and we will demand that those responsible be brought to justice. The men and women who died today were brave, honest people of the highest integrity. They will be missed and never forgotten."

The news also carried a speech by the Canadian Prime Minister who said he was holding the Government of the United States accountable and demanded it find and arrest the perpetrators to prove this was not an act of war. Strong words against a country that had proved it had no qualms against blowing up weaker nations for money and resources.

My phone rang. It was Cal. "I just wanted to hear your voice," he said. "I think we should create a memorial for Eleanor, something beautiful like she was."

"I like that idea. My uncle was part of that ring. I hope he goes to prison."

"You need to stay safe and we need to make sure he is brought to justice. Derek was afraid to disturb you, but he, Crete and Charlie wanted you to know that they cherished all the time they had with Eleanor and that they care very deeply about you."

"That's sweet. Your sister has been a real comfort. I just hope I can get her out of here without any danger."

"I am still thinking of coming back there for you and my sister."

"No. The Canadians are working on making sure I get out safely."

"We've seen how good their security procedures are."

"Who would have expected our government to go so far as to blow up an Embassy helicopter and car with a bunch of Canadian officials?" I asked. "Leaf thinks Eleanor knew too much. That's why they were going to kill her in Carlsbad and why they—" I couldn't finish.

"I wish I were with you."

"Just keep Jonah and Monarch safe until I get back."

Cal told me he'd call me in the morning.

"Goodnight." I couldn't talk anymore.

I found some candles in a drawer and lit one in memory of Eleanor.

As I was putting it near the window, the phone rang. I guessed Cal couldn't wait until morning.

I didn't recognize the number. Maybe the bad guys had the number of my new cell phone. I reluctantly answered the call but didn't say anything.

"I'm here." Those were the most beautiful words I had ever heard as I recognized Eleanor's voice.

CHAPTER 33

"How? They said you were—How did you survive?"

"I left with David. He had me dressed like a guy. They put these things on me that made me look tall, and we were driven out of town to a private airport. I wasn't supposed to call you, but I couldn't let you think I was dead. Nobody is supposed to know I made it."

"Thank you. Will we talk again?"

"When they let me. This call is against the rules. I love you."

"I love you, too. Until I see you again, stay safe."

"I will. My mom said we may have to hide for a while. Right—" It sounded as if she was speaking to someone at her end. "Mommy said, 'Thank you.' Tell Cal and Jonah I miss them."

"I will."

"Bye." She hung up, but that one call changed my life.

I texted Cal something innocuous, but telling, in case anyone was monitoring the texts. "Miracles happen."

The next morning, I checked my email. To my surprise, there was one from Stan.

"Expect to receive a visitor."

A few minutes later, Leaf knocked on my door. "A man named Gregory is waiting for you in my office. He says you have a mutual friend. I didn't admit you were here. Do you wish to see him?"

"Sure. I guess I'm expecting him."

I went downstairs to Leaf's office. A man in about his forties with grey hair, a beard and mustache, was waiting for me. "I believe Stan has notified you I was coming. I am Professor Greg Holstrom."

"Meadow Clarkson."

Leaf guided us to a private room to chat. I noticed Holstrom carried a cane but was walking just fine.

"If there is any trouble, press that button," Leaf whispered to me, pointing to a button on the desk. I nodded. Both Holstrom and I sat down.

"How did Stan know I was here?"

"He sort of put two and two together."

"Does that mean others know where I am?"

"I think I'm the only one he told, and others in the government seem to think you are hiding out in California."

"I thought I was scanned coming in here?"

"One agency doesn't know what the other is doing most of the time."

"What about Eleanor?"

"That was a different matter. Word is she knew too much. There are some good people in government service and some not-so-good people."

"And which are you?"

"Semi-retired. They say you can never fully retire. So I have to go back from time to time for special assignments. I was just finishing something up when Stan called."

"And before you were semi-retired, were you good or bad?"

"A mix, but I try to be on the good side as much as possible so I can sleep at night."

"Do you sleep?"

"Not as well as I'd like. Stan asked me to do some checking into Daniel MountClaire."

I leaned forward in my chair. "Do you know where he is?"

"Not where, but I saw something that has me concerned. I was looking into the electronic file on him and, as I was looking at it, it disappeared. So I went to check the hard copy. It was missing and there was another person's file with that number."

"What does that mean?"

"It might be a bad filing system. The NSA collects information on virtually all Americans."

"You're NSA?"

He nodded. "We're not all bad. Edward Snowden is my hero. But if anyone official asks me, he's a traitor."

"You don't think it's just a filing error, do you?"

"Have you heard of the NDAA?"

I knew what that meant. "How do we find someone who is in indefinite detention?"

"That's the problem. There are a lot of places they could hide people who have disappeared. I seriously doubt he's in Washington State. North Carolina, Virginia or Texas are the most likely. Though Colorado, Wyoming, Wisconsin and Georgia are possibilities."

"That's a lot of territory. You say people? How many has this happened to?"

"You will sleep better not knowing."

"A lot more than the American people know about?"

He gave a quick nod. "I'm going to continue to look and ask some of my trusted contacts to look. If he's alive, maybe we can turn up something."

"If he's alive?"

"You've heard of the executive order Obama gave back in 2011."

"Has that been used?"

"What do you think?"

"Eleanor?"

"That wasn't officially sanctioned. Some of the not-so-good people working for the government have gotten too used to the killing. Loss of human life, even a child's life, doesn't affect them anymore."

"Does that happen a lot?"

"I don't know the percentage. But the desensitization and programming are very pervasive. What do you think is happening to the morality of those kids playing video games with those drones that blow up schools in the Middle East? Rumor has it that it was a drone flown by a teenage recruit that blew up the helicopter, last night."

"I see."

"Be careful. You could be treading in dangerous waters."

"Are Brian and Juliet tied to the government?"

"They're not on the official list. They definitely have connections. Their little trafficking operation is on the 'Do Not Touch' list, meaning the government doesn't want to get involved or to stop it."

"Any thought about what they planned for me?"

"Let's just say that it's good that you got away from them. You should go out of your way to stay out of their reach in the future."

I nodded.

"I have to get back to work before I'm missed."

"Did they see you enter?"

He leaned over onto his cane. "I don't have a beard in real life, either."

"They saw through our disguises."

"I am pretty good with make-up."

"A regular Ethan Hunt."

"Not quite, but there are people who shouldn't know I'm looking into this."

<hr>

Derek's line was probably being monitored. My location may already have been given away. Leaf handed me a phone he said couldn't be tracked and I used it to call Derek's cell.

"I'm already in Washington," he said.

"Really?"

"I looked up my brother's next-door neighbor in the White Pages and the guy claimed Daniel had never lived there. That was a big mistake. I've visited Danny at his apartment."

"What about your school?"

"I generally do my homework by uploading it. The most important lectures are recorded. Crete is keeping track of my classwork until I get back."

"Guess you, me and Cal are on distance learning for the time being."

"It's the way of the future."

Derek was staying at the Crown Plaza in downtown Seattle for the time being. I arranged to meet him at the second-floor lounge a couple of hours later. Leaf said he had had my car checked out for tampering and it was untouched.

After I had breakfast, Sandy Johns, a secretary, entered the building and agreed to let me borrow her clothes. I did my hair like hers and put on a hat. Leaf found a pair of non-prescription glasses that appeared to match hers.

Soon, I was off with Everything and my backpack in a laptop case, similar to Sandy's but with air holes for breathing, and was on my way to the Crown Plaza, which was less than a mile away. I took a detour through Ross Dress for Less and TJ Maxx in an effort to confuse anyone who was trying to follow me. Derek was ordering breakfast on the second floor when I arrived and gave me a pass key to his room and the elevator. The room was on the twentieth floor and had a nice view. I was only there a couple of minutes when he joined me with breakfast.

As Everything and I ate the breakfast fruit he had picked up for us, Derek and I discussed our plan to find out what had happened to his brother. When Derek had visited his brother's condominium building, the manager had given him the run-around.

So, I was to go in alone, pretending to be looking for a place to rent. Derek had a fake beard in case he was spotted and I picked up a business suit at TJ Maxx that made me look much more sophisticated. I also picked up additional underwear and cleaned it in the hotel laundromat.

As we got back to my Mustang, Leaf was there, trying to look casual to outsiders. "I had one of our men double-check your car. We don't want any more losses."

"Thank you." I had to trust someone.

———

"Do you have something with a good view on the second floor?" I asked the apartment complex manager.

"Not currently, but in about a month." He showed me to Daniel's apartment. It was a beautiful place overlooking Puget Sound. "This one is being rented by a lady from Australia, who has been here for a couple of years, but she is planning to move away next month if you can wait that long," he said approaching the door.

"That coincides with when I'll be moving, here, from Oregon. How long has she been living here?"

"For a couple of years."

The manager knocked and then opened the door with his key. "You startled me," a woman said.

"Excuse us, Gretchen. Andrea here is considering renting the place when you go back to Australia."

The apartment was clearly decorated for a woman from Down Under. There were Australian calendars on the wall and fashion magazines on the tables with knitted pink tablecloths.

"I haven't had a bathroom break since before breakfast. Would you mind if I visit your bathroom?" I asked.

The manager and woman looked at each other. "Of course," Gretchen said.

I went into the bathroom. I suspected, they hadn't expected a potential renter to do more than a cursory glance in the bathroom. On the sink were hand lotions. In the shower were shampoos and cream rinses. Toothbrushes were in a holder attached to the wall. I opened the mirrored cabinet. There were bottles of medicine with the name "Gretchen Carlson" on them.

Okay. They were prepared for an inspection. I opened the cabinet under the counter. There were cleaning solutions. In the drawer were hairbrushes and combs. I lifted the tray. Nothing.

I had to look where they would expect. I went to the toilet and opened the tank. Inside was a watch, hanging from the chain. I freed and examined the watch. It contained the inscription, "D.M. from L.J. with love."

CHAPTER 34

I slipped it into my pocket. Then I closed the tank, flushed the toilet and turned on the water to clean my hands in case they were listening.

"Have there been any problems in the time you've lived here? "I asked Gretchen upon returning to her and the manager. "Loud neighbors?"

"If one of our tenants is loud, we get rid of them pretty fast," the manager said.

"I've been here for six months, and it's been really quiet," Gretchen said.

"You mean in the last six months that you've been here," the manager corrected.

"Yes. I didn't mean I had only been here six months." She had apparently deviated from the script.

"Well, this place looks really good. I will give you a call when I make my final decision," I told the manager.

"If you are concerned about quiet, this building has thick glass and you can't hear any of the exterior noises. The entrances are key-locked, and you need to have a key to enter or else know someone here to let you in."

"That's actually just what I'm looking for. Thank you so much for your time."

I went out to my car. Derek was away, but Everything was inside. "Derek is taking pictures," Everything said.

"Oh. Probably a good idea."

When he returned, I showed him the watch.

"That's my brother's. His former girlfriend Louise gave it to him."

"It also seemed the tenant was confused as to whether she had been here for six months or two years."

"He must have suspected someone was after him before he went to school that day and left the clue in case something happened to him. He said on the phone he thought they were after his gun. Then, later, he must have had his phone ready to text me in case they grabbed him."

"If not for the call and text, would you have been worried?"

"Not right away. Let's get out of here and go by Daniel's work."

"You said he was a professor at U of W?"

"Yes. But I've been getting the run-around there too."

As we drove away, I asked, "Did you ever see *Capricorn One*?"

"No."

"There was this scene where Elliott Gould's character Robert Caulfield went to his friend Elliott's apartment and some woman was there, claiming it was hers and that his friend hadn't lived there. Then, Caulfield went back to his car and it went out of control or maybe in control of someone else and it drove into a body of water."

"Good thing the Consulate guy checked out your car."

"Yeah."

Students milled around the university, but the staff wasn't there, and there were no classes until Monday, two days later. When Daniel asked about his brother, he got a couple of strange looks, but otherwise, his brother was unknown. That seemed odd for a professor who had been teaching there for years, up until three weeks ago.

Derek got a second room at the Crown Plaza, telling them his mother had shown up.

"Do I look like your mother?"

"You could stay in my room, but Cal would be high-tailing it from Idaho, and beating on the door if he got wind of it."

I laughed. "He likes me, but—"

"I've seen the way he talks about you and the way he looks at you."

I called Cal and told him I was staying until Monday.

"I don't like it."

"Have some fun with Jonah. Go out on the lake."

"I'll be worried about you and my sister."

"We're staying high up in a five-star hotel with security entrances. And there is Wi-Fi."

I turned on the TV. The deaths of the Canadians had replaced the dog attacks as the number one news item. The reporters spoke as if the Venezuelan government had planted bombs in an attempt to turn the Canadian and U.S. Governments against each other. Of course, they didn't present any specifics or evidence to back up that allegation. At the break, there were ads for Arrowcorp's safe and loving robotic canine companions.

"Who is this Arrowcorp that is profiting off the school attacks?" Derek asked.

"Profiting?" I inquired.

"Exactly. This is all part of the military-industrial complex. And people are buying up their robotic dogs before they are even on the market."

"That's a disaster waiting to happen."

"Charlie put up the footage Cal got of Doug being told not to say he wasn't there."

"And?"

"They keep pulling it down. Charlie continues to respond by putting it back up, but it's down almost as fast as he gets it up. Also, he's been uploading the footage of the woman whose German shepherd was killed."

"Do you think people will start coming around?"

"There is a growing dog rights group in California that is working to defeat the hysteria."

"Let's hope they can make a difference. Washington State is over the top."

"So are Michigan and New York. It's the influence of PETIS. They are lying about a dog overpopulation."

"They've been doing that for years," I noted. "I read in Nathan Winograd's book, *No Kill Nation,* this started with HSUS. Before it was founded, dogs would wander from door to door and people would put out bowls of food. HSUS started locking them up and then claimed there were too many dogs for their limited space facilities. Next, came the executions."

"Nice. Really nice. If a dog doesn't have an owner, instead of simply giving it food, they call killing the dog humane."

"Our whole society has gotten crueler. My mom used to tell me about how nice people were when she was younger."

"I heard that from my parents too. Back when they were younger, divorces were considered failures and looked down on. Now, look at the divorce rates. How can anyone trust a person who betrays the person they promised to love forever?"

"And that's more than fifty percent of our society," I pointed out.

"Most of the Millennials have chosen not to marry. Our generation might be able to bring back families and do away with the hate if it ignores the MSM."

"When I see teens killing dogs, I wonder."

"It's the programming in the schools and the media. They try to create a mob mentality and commercialism. It's all part of the NWO."

"I know. I got hit with that in school, too."

From there we went to visit Professor Phillips, a friend of Daniel's who taught sociology at the U of W. As it was the weekend, we thought it would be best to visit him at home. He hadn't gotten back to Derek or answered his phone calls and Derek was worried.

The house was a nice one-story with a garden in the front yard, but it looked as if it hadn't been kept up recently. We knocked at the door and rang the bell. We noticed a female neighbor watching us from across the street. After receiving no answer, we walked over to the woman who was watching us. "I was looking for Professor Phillips," Derek said.

"And you are who?"

"He taught at the University with my brother and he asked me to look him up when I got into town."

"Oh," the woman said. "Well, I'm sorry."

"Sorry?"

"Would you like to come in?"

We went into her house. A man in his fifties, with dark hair and glasses, stood up from his chair.

"This is my husband, Chuck. I'm Lia. Chuck saw the whole thing."

"What thing?" I asked.

Lia turned to her husband. "They're here to see Keith Phillips."

"Keith passed away close to two weeks ago," Chuck said. "Were you friends of his?"

CHAPTER 35

"He was a friend of my brother's," Derek said. "They taught at the university together."

"This is terrible," I responded. "What happened?"

"He was hit by a car, a hit and run." Lia informed us.

"Hit and run?"

"Someone in a black SUV hit him and took off."

"An accident?"

"It didn't look like one," Chuck said.

We waited for more information.

Chuck continued. "It was almost as if the guy was aiming for him. The driver actually crossed onto the left side of the street, hit the professor and then took off."

"A man?"

"I couldn't tell. The windows were too dark, blacked out. The police never caught him."

"Did you get the license plate?"

"It didn't have one as far as I could tell, but it was moving so fast, I couldn't have gotten a number if there had been one."

"Professor Phillips was a good man," Derek said. "My brother disappeared, and he was checking on what happened to him."

"Do you think there is a connection?" Lia asked.

"This whole situation is strange. I wouldn't be surprised," Derek responded.

"I remember Keith mentioned something about a missing professor," Chuck said.

"That was my brother."

"He said that he thought he had uncovered something very sinister in connection with the disappearance of that professor. That was minutes before the accident."

"I had a missed call from him about two weeks ago. He didn't leave a message," Derek related.

"About when he died," Lia said.

"He was a good neighbor," Chuck added. "If you find out what happened to him, let us know. We had a memorial for Keith. His sister Fran came in from out of town."

"It was a beautiful service. The whole neighborhood and a lot of college students and professors came," Lia recalled.

"Do you think he might have told any of them what he learned? Maybe his sister?"

"Fran said she hadn't spoken to him in some time," Lia replied.

"Maybe someone at the university," Chuck noted. "Keith also spoke of wanting to contact the press. He said what he had learned could be dangerous. Next thing we knew, he was dead."

As we left, Derek and I spoke about the Professor. "He must have started checking things out right away," Derek surmised.

"And found something."

"You might want to take a backseat, Meadow. I don't want to have your demise on my conscience."

"I'm already a wanted woman, remember?"

"Black SUV with darkened windows. That sounds like the government. Crete used to think my ideas were just—"

"Conspiracy theories."

"Right. But after seeing the dogs, he said he was starting to turn into a conspiracy theorist, himself."

"Conspiracy is actually in all the penal codes, including the USC. In other words, the government is the biggest conspiracy theorist of all."

Saturday night, we went to see Daniel's old girlfriend, Louise.

"Daniel? I haven't seen him in more than a year. Didn't he go back to California?"

I sat down on the couch while Derek paced around the living room. I figured he was looking for clues.

"Louise, he brought you with him when he visited us at Christmas."

"No. I've been with Jim for the last year." I noticed there was tension in her voice. "I've got something burning on the stove. It's been nice hashing over old times."

She opened the door for us to leave. Instead of leaving, I remained seated on her couch, and Derek went through the kitchen door, just inside the entrance to her place.

"There's nothing on the stove," I heard Derek say.

"I meant I have to put something on the stove," she said, her voice wavering.

"She's lying and she's scared," Everything whispered to me through the opening in my backpack that I was now holding in my lap. "Her voice is shaking and her pitch doesn't sound natural."

"Someone has gone to a lot of trouble to erase Daniel's life here," I whispered back.

I excused myself and walked outside to look around. Louise had a nice two-story townhouse, set among pine trees, on Lake Washington. I wondered how someone who claimed to be a cocktail waitress could afford a place like that. It occurred to me that Jim, whoever he was, might be footing the bills.

It was getting dark. Washington was the most beautiful state I had visited. The trees, mountains and lakes reminded me a bit of home. North Carolina had those, but the state also had the grueling humidity that made it less fun to be outdoors. As I looked at the lake, I heard a sound beside me. As I turned, I felt something hard smack my head and the lights went out.

CHAPTER 36

I think I only lost consciousness for a second, but I was in a daze, in pain on the ground, and my eyes couldn't focus on anything.

My first thought was that my backpack had fallen away. Was Everything okay? Had she fallen into the lake? My vision was blurry. It looked like my backpack was off to the side, open but it was hard to be certain what I was seeing. *Where is Everything?*

I was pulled up. Someone, with a strong build, put me over his back. A voice drifted across my woozy state. "You know what curiosity did to the cat." I could feel a beard against my back as he turned his head. I was shoved into the back seat of a car.

The person shoving me suddenly fell, then got up and started to turn. Through my blurred vision, I could see a branch slugging the man across his face. He fell again. The branch came back down with a loud crackling sound a couple more times. He didn't move anymore. He was shoved into the front seat of the car.

The aching in my head increased at the sound of the front car door slamming shut. I was having trouble keeping my eyes open and focusing on anything.

I was lifted up and was on someone else's back but my vision was too fuzzy to make out who it was.

"We need to get out of here." It was Derek's voice.

"Everything."

"She got me."

"My backpack."

"We'll get you another one. Your valuables are in the hotel room, right?"

"Yeah."

He walked, carrying me for quite a ways, as I repeatedly slipped in and out of consciousness. We had parked a quarter mile from Louise's house, but it hadn't seemed that far of a walk when we arrived.

In the car, I had trouble staying awake. At times, when I became lucid, Everything was licking my face. "Don't tell Cal," I got out. "I'll tell him when I see him."

"Did you say something, Meadow?" Derek asked.

"Don't tell Cal." I drifted out again.

Next thing I knew, a doctor was examining me. "She has a concussion," he said. "But her EEG and CT scan look normal. I don't think there's any internal swelling, but we will have to keep her alert for the next twenty hours."

The doctor gave me some kind of injection. I didn't know what it was. I was starting to come out of the daze.

"They are going to keep you here overnight," Derek informed me when we were alone in my hospital room.

"I can't be in the hospital. I don't want Juliet to find me."

"Don't worry. Crete called with his sister's medical insurance information. You are technically Jemma."

"They almost killed Cal's dad under the nurse's noses at the hospital in Elizabeth City."

"I'm not leaving until you are leaving. I got special permission to stay. I'm supposed to keep you awake."

"Everything?"

He went to the chair and pulled up the hood on a sweatshirt he was carrying. She was there. "We are going to have to discuss this very interesting dog."

"Oh?"

"When she got me, I distinctly heard the words, 'Meadow's being taken! Help her!' coming from this dog."

"I guess you and she have some kind of mental connection."

"I don't think so, but I won't push you until you are better."

"Do you have any idea who the guy was?"

"His name is Jim Fischer. I lifted his wallet."

"Jim. The guy she was talking about was named Jim."

"He has a card indicating he is working at the university."

"So he may have been watching your brother."

"Very likely. Behind another of his cards is a government ID: Department of Homeland Security."

"Well, we've got dog killers, child sex traffickers and DHS after us. Next, the government will be drone-bombing us."

"Do you want to call your friend in the CIA?"

"For all I know, they're in on it. When it's safe, I'll send Stan an email."

Derek brushed some hair out of my face. "For someone with a concussion, you don't look bad."

"Thanks. You should do cheer-up in the hospital gunshot wing."

He smiled. "Seriously. There is a little bruising on your forehead near the hairline, but it could be worse. The doctor says the concussion is mild. You staying here is a precaution."

"Thank you for hanging out with me."

"Safety in numbers."

"I wonder if there is a way I could do my schoolwork as long as I have to stay awake."

"What's the subject?"

"AP French literature is my toughest subject."

"I pulled your cell from your pocket and texted Cal that you were catching up on some rest. He texted back to call him in the morning."

"Thank you."

"He's not going to be happy with me when he finds out what happened."

"It's for a good cause. It won't do him any good to worry and he might even do something crazy like come back to Washington with Monarch."

"Slippery slope. Not good for relationships."

"We don't have a relationship. Not yet, anyway."

"Denial."

Derek pulled out his phone and tapped a few buttons. "It's a new smartphone that I am going to start using. Here." It started playing a UCSD video on French literature. When one video finished, it played another one.

The next morning, Crete called. Derek put his cell on speaker so I could also hear.

"I have a profile on Fischer. He has ties to an organization called Safe Accountant Professionals. It's contracted with DHS, hence the ID card," Crete informed us.

"That was my dad's company. But Stan said that my dad had ties to the CIA, not DHS."

"Your dad died in a plane crash, right?" Crete asked.

"You don't think it was an accident?"

Derek looked at me. "You haven't questioned it yet?"

"You think there's any chance Fischer might have killed my parents?" I asked Crete.

"I can't say. It's a connection worth looking into. Get this, one of the subsidiaries is Arrowcorp."

"The company that sold the robotic dogs to Brian."

Shortly, after our conversation with Crete ended, my cell rang.

"Hey, Cal," I said.

"You okay? You sound weird."

"Just resting. I lost a lot of sleep over that situation with Eleanor."

"Understandable."

"I'm going to take it easy today. We're going to go by the university on Monday, and then I'll rejoin you."

"I don't like you being there."

"It'll be alright. I'm planning to stay out of trouble. You having fun with Jonah and Monarch?"

"We've been out on the lake and we'll be going back out on it, again, today. Jonah's a good swimmer. We all miss you. I've rented a cabin there. I'll text you the address."

"I miss you, too. Give my love to Jonah."

"I will. Is Derek behaving himself with my beautiful girlfriend?"

"Girlfriend as in a friend who just happens to be a girl?" I asked, remembering his earlier comments.

"No, girlfriend as in the girl I'm crazy about."

Twenty-four hours after the attack, I was allowed to leave. Back at the hotel, I tried to get some rest. But it wasn't restful rest. I kept turning over and waking with thoughts of the events of the last couple of weeks. I still missed my mom. The more recent events had been a bit of a distraction, but they hadn't taken away the loss and the pain.

I got on my computer and tried working more on my studying. Something was nagging at me. My dad was somehow tied to a very bad DHS operation, and the CIA was asking for his documents. The agencies reportedly didn't collaborate that much. My dad had turned me over to Juliet and Brian, two child traffickers. I thought about how abusive my dad was towards my mom. Juliet and he were cast from the same mold.

Derek used another burner phone to try to contact more of his brother's neighbors via information from the White Pages. None of them seemed to recall Daniel at all. "Must have been before I moved in," was a common mantra.

Monday at the university, Everything was in my new backpack and I was wearing a hooded college sweatshirt. While Derek went by Daniel's former office, I went to speak with the head of Daniel's Department.

"I'm looking for Professor MountClaire," I told the department head, Dean Marvin White. I noticed he was working with a student in his office.

He excused the student, whom he referred to as Jackson. "You must have the wrong Department. We haven't had any professors by that name in the Political Science Department since I've been here."

"But he was my inspiration for coming here. He was here last month, and we spoke about my educational plan."

A harshness formed in White's voice. "You must be mistaken. Maybe you spoke to Professor McCarrin."

"No. Daniel MountClaire."

"You are mistaken. There is no such person here."

"Sorry for bothering you," I said.

I walked out of the office as Dean White closed the door a bit harshly.

I hadn't gone more than two feet when the student who had been in the office grabbed my arm. "Daniel was my professor. One day he was here, and the next day he was gone, and they told us he had never been here. A couple of students got angry and demanded the truth. They were put on suspension for creating chaos. When they returned, they clammed up, but I could tell Jason wasn't happy."

"Jason?"

"Jason Moore."

"I see. I'd like you to speak to a friend of mine."

"Sure."

White opened his door. "Jackson, come back in here. We aren't done with your session."

The student moved his eyes from side to side as if he was shaking his head without doing so.

As he went inside, I went to the room Derek had said was Daniel's former office. Derek was having an argument with a woman who claimed it had been her office for the last three years.

"You are lying!"

"Get out, or I'll call security!"

I pulled Derek away. As we moved down the corridor, I said, "I found someone who remembered him."

As we walked back toward the Dean's office, I saw Jackson leaving. "This is the friend I wanted you to speak with."

"Hi," Jackson said.

"Would you tell him what you told me?"

"I said that I had no recollection of that guy you mentioned."

CHAPTER 37

I stood there, not knowing what to say next.

"Perhaps if we go elsewhere to talk."

"No. I don't know your friend, and I don't want you to bother me, again." He walked away.

"The Dean got to him," I told Derek. "The Dean has to be in on it."

We went to the student union. I asked a couple of students if they knew Jason Moore. The first two didn't know him.

The third pointed to a student. "Martin is his best friend."

Martin looked like a younger version of Michael Jordon. As we approached him, his expression changed from jovial to almost hostile as if we didn't belong. Maybe he knew all the students who hung out here and realized we were out of place. "You want something?"

"I'd like to speak with Jason Moore. I understand he knew my brother," Derek said.

"Who's your brother?"

"I'm Derek MountClaire."

Martin swept his hand over the top of his hair. "You need to get out of here."

"What?"

"Just go."

"Why?"

"If you don't want to get hurt, go."

"You threatening me?" Derek asked.

"Not me," Martin whispered. "Go."

He turned his head towards the door.

We started to move. A couple of men came in and looked at us. We took a different exit.

"Whoever is behind this doesn't want anyone asking any questions," I said.

"We need to find this Jason Moore."

"If he hasn't been silenced, too."

As we walked, we saw the two men we had seen earlier coming closer to us. We kept moving. As we passed a tree, the voice of someone we couldn't see said. "Go to the gymnasium. You're being followed. We'll handle it."

We looked at a college map and started on a roundabout route towards the gymnasium. I looked back. The two men were surrounded by several tall muscular guys in basketball uniforms. They had formed a circle around the men and weren't letting them through. We continued moving, going through an entrance to another building, out another door and then hurried on to the gymnasium.

A guy sitting on the bleachers called to us as we entered. "It's about time someone came asking questions." I gathered this was Jason. Even sitting, I could tell he was tall. He resembled a younger version of Chris Rock

"What's with the secrecy?" Derek asked.

"I saw him taken away by two men with bulges, gun bulges, in their coats. My guess: it was the Feds. I followed them in my car and they drove to SeaTac, to the private plane section."

"I was told, by a Fed that it was unlikely he was still in Washington State," I said.

I followed Jason's gaze to the door.

"Why is everyone so afraid?" I inquired.

"Staying in college until graduation matters. Have you checked out the economy lately?"

"And you?" Derek queried.

"I'm the star basketball player and the star football player. The coach threatened to go to the press if I wasn't reinstated."

"Reinstated?" I questioned.

"I was taken off the team by someone higher up after I tried to report what I saw. As part of my reinstatement. I was supposed to keep quiet, but I'm not good at following orders."

"Will the coach talk to us?" Derek asked.

"No. He just cares about the team. He doesn't care about Professor MountClaire."

"Do you have any idea why he was taken?" Derek inquired.

"I'm not sure, but in one lecture, the prof asked us what we would do if we uncovered evidence of a scheme to create a series of false flags to take away our freedoms."

"Like the attack at Lancer High?" Derek asked.

"Yeah. That was nasty."

"It was also fake. I was there," I said, joining back into the conversation.

"Hmm. That was after he was taken. Maybe the prof was onto something."

Martin opened the door and nodded.

"You should go before someone notices us talking. They don't like questions," Jason warned us.

"Who?" I pondered.

"Somebody. I don't know. But they have the ear of the Dean of Students and the department heads. A couple of students who weren't players never returned after they asked questions."

"Did their parents inquire?" Derek asked.

"Not as far as I know. Maybe they just quit school."

Jason pointed his finger towards the far door. "Go now. If you find any proof of what happened to him, my email address is topofthefield@washington.edu."

"Thanks," I said. "Good luck with your games."

"I don't need luck. I'm good."

We went back to my car and got in. Everything started squirming in my backpack, but she didn't let out a noise. I unzipped it and she stayed inside.

I put the bag between the front bucket seats at the back side of the shift knob and drove off. I should have paid attention to her squirms. Out, from under a blanket in the back of the car, popped a man with a gun.

CHAPTER 38

"Keep driving."

"I am."

"Take 520 towards Bellevue."

As I got partway across the bridge, he said, "Now turn the car into Lake Washington."

"I forgot my swimsuit."

"I remembered mine." With the hand that was not holding the gun, he held up a face mask attached to a tube. Presumably, the other end was attached to an oxygen tank.

Derek turned and started to reach back.

"Which of you wants to die first? It really doesn't matter to me whether I shoot you or whether you go into the lake."

"Well if you say so," I said turning the car towards the right lane, cutting off another vehicle and almost getting hit.

As I did so, Everything jumped up out of the backpack and bit the wrist of our carjacker's gun arm. She drew blood, apparently knowing exactly where to bite. He yelled in pain.

As Derek grabbed the gun out of the man's weakened hand, the gun went off and a shot went through the windshield.

In the gun-wrestling struggle, the firearm fell to the front floor at my feet.

Derek jumped in back and started pummeling the man, who was barely fazed and fought back. Somehow, they both wound up over the top of the front passenger seat as I tried to maintain control of the car and steer towards the left or number one lane of our side of the bridge.

I saw the passenger side door swing open. The man was trying to push Derek out, but Derek leveraged himself inside the vehicle with his right leg wedged against the windshield, the other leg going through the opening in the bucket seats and his left ankle tucked behind my seat. His attacker used his strength to try to force Derek out as Derek managed to clasp onto his assailant and pull the man over him into and out the open doorway. The assailant tried to grab onto the door but failed and flew onto the highway.

Derek pulled himself back in and closed the door as I pulled to the left. I heard a screech and looked in the mirror as the front driver's-side wheel of a car ran over the assailant. As that car braked, it was hit by another car from behind and spun to the left, getting hit by a third car in the left lane.

More and more cars piled up. From the mirror, it appeared that several vehicles were likely totaled but the passenger compartments looked okay as far as I could tell. Maybe that was just hopeful thinking.

"Let's get out of here, fast," Derek encouraged.

As I got to the other end of the bridge, I could see responders coming in the other direction towards the scene. I could hear sirens way back behind, as well.

"If you can pull in somewhere, I'll put on the correct license plate," Derek said.

"You switched them?"

"My brother disappeared. I didn't want us to meet the same fate."

We pulled off onto a side road by a housing tract, between a couple of cars. Derek went to the back and pretended to be working on the trunk as he discretely switched the plates.

"What about the front?"

"There isn't one right now. I can put it back on later. I didn't want the owner of the other black Mustang to get too suspicious if he looked at the front of his car."

"Hope he has an alibi."

"He probably does."

"Back to Seattle?"

"My brother isn't there. Let's go to North Carolina and see if we can drill your friend in the CIA."

"Sure. Would you mind driving? I'm sort of shaking."

"Concussion. Near-death experiences. No wonder. Of course, I'll drive."

I called Cal to let him know we were on our way, but he wasn't answering. It would be about a five-to-six-hour drive back to Coeur d'Alene at a reasonable speed. I hoped there was no trouble on his end.

"Glad you have a real license. I only have a permit."

Derek looked a little surprised. "If you can drive without a license, I can make it to Coeur d'Alene in less than four hours." He called Charlie, putting his phone on speaker. "We're taking 90 East at top speed. Can you use the Net to check for cops?"

"Easy."

"Make that three hours," he told me, increasing his speed.

We followed Crete's directions to the cabin Cal had previously texted us about. It was at the end of a dirt road, backed up against the lake. We parked as close as we could get. Other vehicles were parked between us and the cabin, which I figured must have cost Derek quite a bit to rent. I kept forgetting that Cal must have a decent monetary supply. We opened the car doors. Everything started sniffing and shook her head. Monarch ran up. He quietly barked at Everything as we got out and started towards the cabin.

"Wait," Everything said.

Derek turned. "Your dog does talk."

"What's happening?" I asked her.

"Trouble. In the cabin."

Cal hadn't been answering. Had something happened to him? Was Jonah safe?

"Is Cal alright?"

"I don't know," Everything whispered to me. "He sent Monarch out to wait for us. But Monarch heard men and loud noises."

There were a number of bushes and trees between us and the cabin. We stayed low in the brush. The cabin was sticking out a little into the lake on its own tiny peninsula. Trees were close to the visible sides of the land jetting into the lake.

"There's a door on the other side, next to the water," Everything informed us.

"Wait here," I told Everything.

I slipped quietly into the lake and swam, partially underwater in the freezing cold, only made tolerable by the warm day. As I pulled my head up, I saw the main cabin door open and Brian's head poke out. He wasn't looking toward the lake. He started to turn his head in my direction, but then pulled his head back in and closed the door.

Toward the end of the small peninsula, there was a private pier with a small boat tied to it. A boardwalk connected it to the front side of the cabin and appeared to continue around to the other side.

I dove back underwater, swimming toward the boat and grabbed onto a post under the pier before resurfacing and looking in the direction of the cabin.

I heard movement in the water. I started to turn as the blade of a knife was pressed against the front of my throat.

CHAPTER 39

The knife was attached to the hand of someone in the water behind my back.

"You aren't so tough without a dog to protect you." It had to be my watcher from California.

'You've recovered well from Brian's attack dog." I was still holding onto the post, wondering if he would next try to dunk me in the water or slash my throat.

"The injuries were superficial. I'm a trained Night Stalker."

"I'm sure you are. A Night Stalker who stalks by day."

"I could take you up to the cabin with your boyfriend. Your aunt sold you to a Senator in Washington for a nice price."

"How much am I worth?"

"Over a million. Only a fraction of what the boy is worth."

"Over a million. I'm honored."

"But I consider this a business loss." In other words, he planned to kill me.

I tried to move, but the knife pressed deeper into my throat.

Suddenly, it loosened as my attacker yelled, "No!"

I turned. It was Monarch chomping into his neck. The watcher tried to use the knife on the dog but, in the stalker's weakness, I grabbed the knife and twisted his arm. Monarch seemed to have him under control, and I swam to the boardwalk on the other side of the cabin and pulled myself up. Keeping below window level, I went to the door. It was unlocked. I slowly and carefully turned the knob, opening it just a crack but not enough to see inside. I heard the front door, again. I opened the one near me enough to see. Brian was on his way out the other side.

Cal was lying unconscious on the floor near a couch. His hands were tied, and his shirt was bloody. Jonah was roped to a chair.

I moved inside towards Cal. Brian started to come back in the main door, and I hid behind the couch. I peeked around the one side.

Brian was heading to the couch with a gun, looking at the trail of water drops I had left between the door and the couch on my way in. "I know you're there." He started to point the gun at the couch. Then he moved over to Cal and pointed the gun at his head. "Or you could stand up, and I won't finish what I started with your boyfriend."

I rose and moved away from Cal, hoping Brian would point the gun at me instead.

"No!" Jonah yelled, causing Brian to turn his head. It was enough of a distraction that I ran at Brian before he was able to fire. He knocked me back and pointed the gun at me.

But he never had a chance to fire it as a shot came from the door. A familiar-looking man who was built like the Terminator walked in, followed by Leaf, some other men and Derek.

I rushed over to Cal. His heart was beating. I didn't know how badly he was injured.

"They showed up just a minute ago," Derek said, moving to Jonah and starting to untie him.

Brian moved a little on the floor but still looked unconscious. The familiar-looking muscular man, whom I was pretty sure I had seen at the Consulate, came over to Cal.

One of the other men spoke on a radio. "Get emergency personnel up here. We have some injuries."

One man turned Brian over, and another entered the cabin and pulled some bandaging out of a bag he was carrying, and gave a package to the man attending to Brian, who quickly started wrapping

Brian. The guy with the bag knelt down next to the muscular man and they took off Cal's shirt and used it to blot his chest. It appeared the blood had been flowing from the side of his upper torso. Cal was starting to come to and then passed out, again.

Once Jonah was freed, he and Derek rushed over to Cal. "Please, please," Jonah seemed to be praying.

"He'll be alright," the built man said as he poured some iodine on the wound and then spread some silver nitrate on Cal's side. The other man placed bandaging over the wound and started applying extra bandaging around Cal's torso. "The bullet just grazed his side. He may need some blood," the first guy added. The two men taped down Cal's bandages.

Brian, who was now conscious, said, "I'm suing your government."

"It would be tempting to just leave you. The paramedics always take so long in these backwoods. But we'll do you a favor and take you to a hospital we trust. You'll get a chance to see first-hand how good our medical treatment in Canada is before you see how humane our prisons are."

The men moved Brian out the door.

"You can't do this!"

"We're helping you. Thank us for saving your life," Leaf said as two of his men handcuffed and took Brian away.

"You shot me!" I heard Brian yell. He was well enough to yell.

Someone hauled in the watcher's lifeless body. "We'll take him with us too. There's enough paranoia in your country about dogs. Your shepherd deserves a Medal of Valor," Leaf said.

Monarch came in and barked, followed by Everything.

"The shepherd saved my life," I told Leaf. "That man would have killed us both."

Leaf leaned down and petted Everything. "I used to have a cute little dog like you."

Everything gave a happy bark.

Then, Leaf gave Monarch a brief hug. "Good work, pal."

I turned to Leaf. "How did you find us?"

"Several of our diplomatic corps are dead, and a Canadian child was kidnapped and killed." He winked at me. "We've been trying to keep a watch on you in case you could lead us to the people who did all that damage. We lost you over the weekend. Found you on I-90. Not many cars hit over two hundred kilometers per hour on a major highway. I'm surprised the Washington State Police weren't watching the same satellite feed." He looked at Jonah. "Is this child Canadian, too?" Leaf asked.

"No. He's Cal's nephew. Brian, the guy you just took out, kidnapped him," I replied.

"I understand someone broke protocol and made a phone call. We'll make sure that person stays safe."

"Thank you—for everything. Oh, I have a question. I heard Juliet talking about selling a mini-Dachshund and an Afghan. But I never saw any."

"Trafficking terms. The little boy was likely the mini-dachshund."

"She said he was a little over half a year old."

"Dog years. Is he four?"

"And fifteen would be two and one-seventh? The guy your friends dragged out of the lake said that I sold for over a million."

"Not nearly what you are worth. Be careful."

A couple of men carried Cal into the middle seat of the Odyssey as no paramedics had arrived yet. Derek moved the Mustang out of sight and then drove the Odyssey while I kept an eye on Cal. Everything sat right next to her brother. The kids and Monarch were in the third row. I pulled a blanket out of the back, in case we had to cover Monarch.

"Good boy, Monarch," I said giving him a hug. "You saved my life."

On the way to the hospital, Cal drifted into consciousness and said, "God, I'm so sorry. I almost got you killed."

"Thank God you're alive and awake. I was so worried about you."

"We were getting off the boat and Brian and that guy came out of the water. We ran into the cabin and I pushed Monarch out the other side. Jonah kept refusing to leave. I tried to get him out. Then, Brian pulled out a gun on me before Jonah would leave. I told Jonah to run, but he still refused to leave me." He turned his head as if trying to spot his nephew. "Don't disobey me again, Jonah."

"I didn't want you hurt, Uncle Cal," Jonah said.

"We're mostly safe now. We need to make sure you're alright and you might need a transfusion," I told Cal.

"You can have my blood," Jonah said.

"That's really great of you. But I don't think I'll need blood. It looks worse than it is."

At the hospital, the doctor said there was blood loss but it was not critical. He expressed confidence that, with antibiotics and rest, Cal would recover without a transfusion.

"I'm not sure it's safe to stay here," I told Cal after the doctor left.

"I agree. Let's see if we can make it to Helena tonight," Cal encouraged. "You up to driving?"

"You do know she doesn't have a license, don't you?" Derek ratted me out.

Cal looked a little miffed. "If I had known."

"I made it back here okay with your sister and a friend."

"I'm not sure you should drive without a license."

"I drove three hundred and fifteen miles to Seattle without a license. I did fine, and I only killed one person."

Cal laughed, apparently thinking I was joking. Derek and I looked at each other. Derek seemed to silently agree with me that now was not the time to tell him about the stowaway.

My phone rang. It was Leaf. "I thought you should know that Brian got away from us and tried to kill one of my men."

"That means he'll come after us, next."

"No. He didn't get completely away. We had to take him down to prevent him from killing my assistants."

"He's dead?"

"Unfortunately. We were hoping he could help us round up the child trafficking ring. Now, that's a dead end."

"There is the daycare school in Carlsbad where we found Eleanor. I bet you could get one of the people associated with that place to talk."

"If your government wanted to stop the ring, they would have already. We don't have jurisdiction in Carlsbad."

The doctor came back into the room. "The police would like to speak with you about your gunshot wound. An officer will be here in twenty minutes. There have been several problems downtown at a dog show. Some crazies showed up and started shooting the dogs. The perpetrators also shot two of the breeders, and they are being ambulanced here. Otherwise, there would have been an officer here already."

"The breeders. Do you think they'll make it?"

"From what I understand, the injuries are serious but not life-threatening."

"We'll help out by giving up the bed and dropping by the station on our way out of town," Cal lied.

We took both vehicles. Derek drove Jonah and Monarch in the Mustang and I drove Cal and Everything in the Odyssey. Cal wasn't happy I was driving, but he was in no shape to do so himself.

We had camping equipment in the car, but it was too cold to camp at Glacier National Park. We found a Motel Seven along I-90 at Missoula, Montana. I was surprised. There were actually people walking dogs there.

Cal decided it was best not to use his fake ID, again, in case Brian had notified others in the trafficking ring about it when he tracked down Cal and Jonah. Derek was the only one of us over eighteen, and so it was decided that he would do the registration for the two rooms, explaining to the manager that the rest of us were his younger siblings.

The manager liked my "brother's" black Mustang. He wasn't nearly as impressed with my other "brother's" Odyssey. Cal asked about the gunshot in the Mustang's windshield. He guessed that had happened during the shootout at the cabin. Neither Derek nor I said otherwise.

I suggested that Jonah stay in my room so he could have his own bed.

"Can Monarch sleep with me?" he asked.

"I don't see why not?" I told him.

"Do I get to pick the TV shows?"

"Of course," I said. "Let's hang out with the guys for now, though."

"Alright."

I put the battery into my regular phone and called Susie.

"How you doing, honey?"

"Fine. You should probably know that Brian was taken into custody and was killed trying to escape. That may be confidential, so don't mention it to anyone besides Everett."

"That will help. But there's been another complication. Mars, the attorney handling the case for us, had a serious accident earlier today."

"What?"

"His car went off a cliff. He's in critical condition."

CHAPTER 40

"These people are dangerous. I don't want you to put yourselves in any peril," I told Susie.

"We're taking precautions."

"I was told that Juliet had sold me for over a million dollars."

"Sold?"

"The guy Brian had watching me said that. He's no longer a threat, but I don't know if they have anyone else chasing us."

"Maybe he was making it up?"

"He said it when he had a knife at my throat."

"Oh, honey. We need to get the police and Feds involved."

"The man is dead. So, he won't do that, again. Juliet has other friends, but I don't know how far they would go. I've had some official help, but I shouldn't talk about it."

"I thought they were after your parents' money."

"Money?"

"Your parents amassed a lot of money. It's yours when you turn eighteen. Your guardian is supposed to supervise it until then."

"I'm sure that 'steal' it is a better term for what Juliet has in mind. You need to be careful. If she thinks you will come between her and money, she might go after you. Courtney is convinced Juliet's killing her mother for her money."

"Since you are fifteen and should be able to decide for yourself, I don't understand why there is a question about your guardianship. Also, when you turn sixteen, as a high school graduate, you can seek emancipation. I think your graduation will weigh heavily in the judge's mind. That would allow you to take charge of your own inheritance."

"I'd rather have my mom back than all the money in the universe."

"I know, honey. I miss her too and I know she loved you very much. I've heard from the school. The work you've sent in is top quality. Principal Carmen said she expects you to do well on your exams. Also, I think they will cut you some slack with the missing time, given your circumstances."

As I was hanging up, Derek got a call from Charlie that he put on speaker. "I and a couple of my friends have been looking in some satellite feeds where we officially haven't been looking. Using some other programs that we don't officially have access to, we got a facial recognition on the man who took Daniel away."

"Yes?"

"It was Fischer and someone whose face wasn't clear. But the other guy appeared to be the one flying the airplane."

"Where?" Derek asked.

"It looks like it went to North Carolina, Elizabeth City."

"Why would they fly Daniel to Elizabeth City? There is nothing there. Just a big old Coast Guard base that has some seaplanes," Cal commented.

"Coast Guard, as in taking people to Guantanamo?" Derek asked.

"It's not just a Coast Guard base," I said.

"She's right," Charlie continued. "It's the largest Coast Guard base on the East Coast. It's an aviation logistics center and an aviation training center. It houses a National Strike Force Coordination Center and provides support to the other bases on the East Coast. It's also got Administration facilities. Nobody can get on or off the base without an ID. One review says the people running it are very unfriendly."

"Where was your dad flying out of the day of the accident?" Cal asked.

"It wasn't the Coast Guard base. He took off from a runway for private planes at the regular airport."

"We need to get to North Carolina fast," Derek said.

"You can fly," Cal told him. "But Meadow might be on a list, and we can't trust the airports with Everything and Monarch."

"I suggest you guys stay together. If Daniel's alright, he'll probably still be when you get to him. There is safety in numbers," Charlie chimed in on the other end. "It's already been several weeks."

"Agreed," Derek responded.

"My dad should be out of the hospital in the next few days. That will be about when we get there."

I realized it was best to put my concerns about Juliet and the court case on hold. Maybe things would be resolved in the couple of days that it would take to drive there.

"I don't have a good feeling about going to North Carolina," Everything said. "That's where this all started."

"Cal, Brian had multiple passports for Jonah under various names, and the ones I looked at listed Juliet as his mother, also under different last names."

"Jonah's real mother is Tammy Riel."

"Jonah Riefenstahl was on one of the passports. It had Brian and Juliet Riefenstahl listed as his parents."

"According to witnesses in the courtroom, after Judge Paddock granted Brian and Juliet custody without a trial or paternity test, Paddock also told them to get Jonah out of the country fast and authorized them to have passports made under new names."

"That should be illegal. Why was he still with them?"

"Maybe they were waiting for someone to meet their price."

"Where did they come up with the name Riefenstahl?"

"Riel was shorted from Riefenstahl."

"Is Tammy related to Leni Riefenstahl?

"A distant relative. Tammy's also part of the Habsburg and Rothschild lines."

"Bloodline trafficking. I've heard that term, but don't know what it means. The file at Juliet's said 'bloodline-high profile.' Is that what this was?"

"There are rich pedophiles who want bloodline children. It makes them feel more powerful. When the kids get older, they try to groom them to be elites in the trafficking industry as opposed to killing them for their adrenochrome."

"Adrenochrome?"

"The people running the most elite of these trafficking rings believe that drinking the blood of a terrified child will help them live longer or maybe forever."

"That is so sick. At the school, they were trying to get the kids to drink what looked like blood. They had killed a girl and were about to kill Eleanor when Derek rescued her."

"That's a common practice with those megalomaniacs."

"How awful. It's a world that's hard to believe exists. If I hadn't seen what I saw, I wouldn't have."

"And that's why most of America closes their eyes and pretends that Pizzagate was just about some pizza parlor—as opposed to something much more embedded and sinister. People sleep easier not knowing."

"Eleanor said that her family had ties to royalty too. Why did they try to kill her?"

"Maybe she refused to cooperate and they wanted to scare her and then later, they were willing to sacrifice her to protect the operation."

"They scared me. Juliet will probably make another grab for Jonah, just like she is trying to do for me."

Cal thought about it. "When we get to Elizabeth City, maybe we should put you and Jonah up at a hotel just outside of town while Derek and I check out the situation there."

I turned on the TV and flipped through the stations. The news was still covering the tensions between the U.S. and Canada. The anti-dog frenzy was continuing to take a backseat to the flare-up. I hoped this new focus continued.

Derek turned off the TV and called Charlie, again. "We need to know which states to avoid. Which ones are anti-dog?"

"Be very, very careful in Wisconsin, Minnesota, Indiana, Iowa,

Ohio, Missouri, Kansas, Michigan, Kentucky and Arkansas." I recognized Crete's voice over the speakerphone. Apparently, he was with Charlie.

"There's no way to avoid all those."

"Wisconsin, Michigan, Illinois and Minnesota are the worst of those in your path. Definitely avoid those states," Charlie noted.

"Will do," Derek said.

"Let's go out for a walk," Cal suggested. I nodded.

The air was a little chilly, and Cal put his arm around me. I wasn't used to having a guy's arm embracing me, but it felt nice. I suspected his injured side probably still hurt, but I didn't want to remind him.

"Do you miss the eighteenth century?"

"I was only ten when I left, but I still have some really good memories. I've acclimated to the twenty-first Century. So, I probably wouldn't fit in there, anymore."

"How about your dad and your friends?"

"I have some good memories of my birth father, but I'm much closer to my current dad. Father was always busy, chatting about the future of America or checking out new inventions. I hung around with him, but I never got that I was a priority. My dad, here, is very devoted to me and Preston. He's more of a family man."

"But this century is a lot different than that one, right?"

"There are good people and bad people in both. The way women are treated is different, here. Not as respectful."

"But we have more rights. More choices. More opportunities."

"It's an illusion. Women had rights before. It just wasn't so official. There were evil men then, but most men honored their wives and daughters. Despite the laws, women had more rights than they do now."

"You didn't have women in government or leadership roles."

"Maybe not officially. Have you noticed that most of the women in leadership roles now try to be the best men possible? That doesn't advance the rest of the womankind."

"You have a point. And women once had the right to raise their own children. Now the courts are taking them away and giving them to the men."

"Married men used to show more respect for their wives. Now, there has been a dramatic increase in domestic violence, infidelity and incest with children."

"According to my history books, it was going on before."

"But it was frowned upon. Now it's accepted."

"I see pluses and minuses, but you are right about one thing. My mom was afraid of my dad. He had all the power in their relationship and beat her up a lot, but there was no safe way for her to get away. I used to hold that against her, but now I realize she did the best she could."

"Society is colder, less caring, now."

"That I believe. My dad, Juliet, and most people turn a blind eye to the rights of women and children. I agree that women who aren't in danger often don't care about the ones who are. Judges side with abusers. What kind of cold and inhuman judge would take Eleanor and Jonah away from their mothers? I guess you are right, but I say that with some reservations."

"There are some advantages to your time. For instance, bathrooms and fast cars. And there are good people. My adoptive parents. My second mom passed away shortly after they adopted me, but she was wonderful and a lot like my real mother. They both died too soon. My twenty-first century dad already loves you. You saved his life twice. He is a great guy. I got very lucky."

I smiled. "And there are our friends and my next-door neighbors, who are all going out of their way to help me. And it sounds like your brother Preston was pretty fab."

"I thought Preston was a good person. But he put his college ahead of Tammy and Jonah, and then he disappeared. The right thing would have been for him to immediately accept responsibility and take care of his family."

"He probably wanted to make sure he could provide for them."

"That's no excuse. He brought a child into the world, and he needed to man up. I want you to know, I would never do as he did."

"Hopefully, you won't be in that situation."

Cal leaned in and I was sure he was going to kiss me.

"Cal!" It was Jonah's voice sounding almost shrill, close to crying. "My picture was on TV."

Derek came up behind him. "Sorry, man. He got away from me."

"What is he talking about?"

"TV," Jonah said.

"There's an APB, but it's an older picture."

"You shouldn't be out here," Cal told Jonah. We walked back inside.

Even knowing which states were the worst, we couldn't be certain that the frenzy hadn't affected the other states. Cal insisted that I be a passenger since I lacked a license. He took over the driving of the Odyssey and Derek drove the black Mustang. As for us non-driving human passengers and dogs, we switched off between cars, making sure that each vehicle had two humans and one dog. While I liked being with Cal, I also wanted Jonah to get more time with his uncle. Everything insisted on staying with me at all times. Knowing that we could be monitored by satellite, we chose to travel at a more or less legal speed—most of the time.

We took a route that led through Saint Louis, Missouri. We couldn't avoid Missouri while missing other worse states. It was a beautiful day. We went into a restaurant with a sign saying, "All the Organic Soup and Salad you can eat for lunch." Everything was in my bag. Monarch was in the Odyssey out of sight. As we came out with leftovers for Monarch, we saw that the Odyssey's front passenger window was destroyed and Monarch was missing.

CHAPTER 41

Derek analyzed the direction of the break. It was broken from the inside outward. "Monarch wanted to get out."

Where did he go? It could have been in any direction.

Everything was frantic, as well. "I can drive east and you can drive west," Derek suggested.

A girl about my age came over to us in the parking lot, crying. "They took my dog."

"What?"

"My dog. She was a Samoyed, Sadie. PETIS came and took my dog away in a van," she sobbed.

"Did you see what direction they went in?" I asked.

She pointed to the east. "That dog of yours followed the van. I don't think they saw your dog or they would have taken him too."

"Let's go get our dogs!" Derek reacted and invited the girl into his car. I heard her say her name, Charla, as he helped her into the car. Derek jumped into the lead as we followed.

Derek called on his phone. "Charla's cell says that there is a PETIS shelter on Clark Avenue. We're going to try to catch up with the van before it gets there."

Cal stepped on the gas to catch up while a speeding Derek, drove even faster, ignoring red lights, and swerving around oncoming cars. Up ahead, I saw the Mustang shoot around a van and turn to block it.

The male driver of the van, who had managed to stop without hitting the Mustang, stepped out. Monarch jumped off the PETIS van's back bumper. A large woman exited the passenger side as we pulled up behind it.

"What do you think you are doing?" the PETIS driver demanded as Cal exited our vehicle towards the van driver.

"Stopping a murder," Cal said, throwing a punch and knocking the guy to the ground, unconscious.

The woman came around the back as Monarch ran up towards her. She pulled out a Taser, preparing to tase Monarch.

From her other side, Everything jumped on her and I launched a kick to her face, knocking her down. Monarch grabbed the Taser out of the woman's hand and seemingly accidentally fired it at her as she got up, causing her to fall back to the ground screaming and wriggling.

"Imagine what that would have done to a dog who weighed less than you," I reproached her.

Derek and Charla went to the back of the van and opened it up. A dozen dogs jumped out. A couple of dogs were in cages and we let them out. Everything was barking something at them. The Samoyed rushed over to the girl and jumped into her arms excitedly, almost knocking her down, as the other dogs ran off.

Charla kneeled on the ground and hugged her Sammy. "I love you, Sadie. I'm never letting anyone take you away, again."

"We should all get out of here," Derek said, as we lifted the unconscious driver into the back of the van. "Nice knockout punch. He'll have a headache when he wakes up."

I escorted the dazed woman into the back of the van while Monarch, holding the Taser in his mouth, continued to point it at her. Cal had her go into one of the cages and then attached a lock Derek found in the van to it.

As we got back to our vehicles, Derek asked, "Did you notice how many people didn't stop?"

"Maybe they were afraid their own dogs would be confiscated," I replied. "Or it's that 'somebody else's business' attitude."

We returned to the restaurant. "How can I thank you?" Charla asked.

"Keep your dog out of sight until the insanity is over," Cal said.

"I will. They'll be looking for you."

"Don't worry," Derek said as Cal started changing the license plates. "Those weren't our real license plates, and we've collected a lot more."

"The window," I pointed out.

"Across the state line, we'll get it repaired." Cal rolled down the Odyssey's front passenger window. "Temporarily fixed."

We had a group hug that Everything joined in on.

The plan was to drop me and Jonah off in Camden, and then for the boys to circle back to Elizabeth City and check out the scene. As Derek went to check us into the hotel, I said, "I want to go home. Jonah and I could probably sneak into Susie's place. She has a basement."

"That's the first place they'll look," Cal said.

"I'd really like to go home."

"I don't think that's a good idea," Everything said.

"I agree with my sister."

"I want to help you two figure out what happened to Daniel. I might be able to stay with Tara."

"Tara?"

"She's on my dance team."

"If you must go to Elizabeth City, let's check you into a hotel. That way you won't have to trust anyone."

"How about the housing near Elizabeth State University?" Everything asked.

"Haven't you had enough of student marches over the last couple of weeks?" Cal inquired of her.

"I've seen dogs outside in North Carolina. Maybe it's—"

"Just waiting for another false flag, Sis."

"The one in Carlsbad wasn't real. You were there, remember?" I responded.

"Well, there are the old warehouses," Everything noted.

"Yes. In the district where you dropped into my life. How did you do that?"

"I had been following you for a while. I was near the airport and I saw you run away, crying. There was something different about you. You were sweet and sad. I decided you were the person I wanted to be with." She glared at Cal.

"More than your brother?" Cal asked.

"You turned me down. I tried to hang around you, but I got taken to Elizabeth City and I ran away. I didn't even see you in Elizabeth City before I left."

Derek came out to the car. "Hate to do this to you, man," Cal told him. "But the team has decided to stay together. We're going to go to Elizabeth City, and I'll get you the money to rent a loft."

"Me?"

"I don't want them to suspect my nephew or Meadow are in town. They might check out any place I rent."

"I guess I'll have to try to check out of this hotel and get my money back," Derek said.

In Elizabeth City, Derek found a real estate office with a number of listings, including one for a townhouse that he liked. The rest of us were hanging out in a park just outside of town when he came back for us and held up the keys.

The townhouse was actually a really nice place with a view of Chesapeake Bay.

"Are you going to tell Susie you are in town?" Derek asked as we looked around.

"Not until she says it's safe. How can you afford this?" I asked Cal.

"I think I mentioned that money was passed down to me. My

father left valuables in a location where he knew I'd find them," Cal said.

My apparent boyfriend had picked up most or all of the cost on this trip. I felt kind of guilty about that but planned to pay him back when I could.

"These days, the government confiscates valuables when someone finds them."

"My second father also has a lot of money and clout, just not enough to save Jonah from the trafficking ring."

"I see."

"No really. His dad, my adopted grandfather had huge tobacco farms and made a lot of money that he invested. Dad sold off the farms after his father died from smoking. Dad had learned his lesson watching his dad die. I know. It's confusing. Two dads and four sets of grandparents."

"There is a lot of that in our society and usually not because of time travel."

"I'm going over to the hospital to see how my dad is doing."

"Give him my best."

"I will. Like I said before, he likes you. You saved his life twice."

"I didn't do anything anyone else wouldn't have done."

"That's not true. There are a lot of cold people in this society and a lot of 'I don't want to get involved.' And then there are some warm ones, and I've got the warmest here." He started to lean towards me.

"Uncle Cal, can I take Monarch out for a walk? There's a girl with a white dog, big like Monarch, next door."

"How old is this girl?"

"Five."

"You have to watch out for those older women," I joked.

"I'd rather you stayed inside for now," Cal told him.

"How about if we play a game of charades?" I thought back to Olympia. "Or maybe another game. How about hide and seek?"

"Okay. But you better hide well because I'm an expert at this game."

"I'll be back soon," Cal said.

"I'm going over towards the base to take a look and then I'm going to head over to the college. I thought I'd see if one of the ROTC students at ECSU could get me onto the base." Derek informed us.

"Good thinking," I complimented him.

I had fun looking around and somehow avoiding finding Jonah for five minutes. Of course, he found me right way. "Guess I'm not as good at hiding as you are," I told him after the third time that happened.

Hoping it was safe if I was fast enough, I called Susie. "Any changes?"

"Yes. Courtney Cohen is here. She wants to collaborate on your case and hers. She is terrified her mother is going to die if something doesn't happen in the next few days."

"We're afraid they are monitoring your home."

"She doesn't want to come here," I heard her say to someone. Into the phone, she said, "She has a friend in town she is staying with. You can meet at his place."

Susie gave me the address. I went to check on Jonah. He was napping.

I turned to my companion. "Everything, you stay here."

"Not a chance."

I tried to call Cal, but his line was busy. So I left him a note. "Look if Cal comes back, I'm counting on you to tell him where I went."

"Growl," Everything said in a human way.

"Can you watch Jonah or should I take him to Cal at the hospital? You aren't just a dog, and I know you can keep him safe."

"I'm a babysitter now? I'll make certain Jonah is safe."

Even with Everything watching Jonah, I planned to be back soon. I put a scarf over my head and walked to the address Susie had given me.

I had missed Elizabeth City. After so much riding in the car, I enjoyed walking. It was a sunny, clear day and the area was beautiful. Sure, there were some not-so-great areas, but overall, it was one of the most beautiful cities I had ever lived in. Maybe instead of going out of state, I'd go to ECSU, also known as Elizabeth City State University.

"Hi, Courtney," I said when she opened the door. "I'm glad we're going to be collaborating together. I felt so bad about what Juliet did to your mother."

"Did you know that a lot of elderly women in Juliet's care die? They die and she collects the money."

"That's awful. I plan to do anything I can to help."

"That's good. Because I've found a way to save my mother."

"Good. What is it?"

I heard the sound of an inner door opening behind me. As I started to turn in that direction, a bag went over my head.

CHAPTER 42

I yelled for help and tried to pull it off, but someone strong gripped my hands and cable-tied my wrists together. I felt pretty helpless and even stupider. I tried to feel for my phone in my pocket. If I could reach it, I could press resend and contact Cal. It wasn't there. I must have left it back at the townhouse. I was lifted up, carried down a staircase and placed in what felt like the hatch or trunk of some kind of vehicle. I gathered a door was open for a while as I heard Courtney say, "I did my part. Now, Juliet better do hers."

"Your part? I wouldn't mention it to anyone or you're an accessory to kidnapping and trafficking." I had heard that voice before but where?

"My mother."

"Juliet thanks you for your services."

"My mother."

"Juliet's got a restraining order against you."

"No. That wasn't the deal."

"Doesn't matter. She died yesterday."

"No!" Courtney screamed.

I kept hearing her scream and wail, but the sound was cut off as I heard a door close and the car start to drive off.

I didn't know how far it drove, but suddenly, there was an impact, a hard one. The car stopped.

"What the—" It was the man who had spoken to Courtney. Even in the back, I could hear the man's voice. "You can't do that!" the voice shouted.

I heard a shot and then the back opened and I was lifted out. As the bag was pulled off of my head, I saw Cal sitting on Juliet's partner, Jed. A gun was on the ground near them. Derek cut the bands from around my wrists.

The Odyssey was in need of some serious body work on the passenger side. The black Mustang was parked behind the SUV I had been in.

My cell phone fell off the back bumper of the SUV as Everything jumped off.

"It seems someone doesn't just talk but can make phone calls. She guided us to the car," Derek said.

I picked up Everything and hugged her. "You were supposed to be watching Jonah," I whispered.

"Aren't you glad I came after you? Besides, he's sleeping and I locked his door from the inside so nobody could get in and I left Monarch to watch him," she whispered back.

"Monarch's a dog," I said, having mixed feelings as if it were a bigoted comment.

Derek escorted me to the Mustang as a police officer arrived on the scene.

"This man put a bag over my head and was kidnapping me." I pointed at Jed.

"She's lying. I was driving her back to her guardian when these two hoodlums—"

"We've got cell footage on it and he also tried to shoot my friend," Derek said. He pulled out his cell phone and showed the sequence of the aftermath of the accident: Jed starting to get out of his SUV with the gun as Cal slammed the door against Jed's arm with a kick to it as the gun misfired. Cal grabbed the gun and tossed it in the street and then dragged Jed out of the car and kicked him to the ground. The video then showed the opening of the SUV tailgate with me inside with the bag over my head.

The officer collected the bag and picked up the remnants of the cable ties that had fallen to the ground. Cal got off Jed. The officer handcuffed Jed and read him his rights. Then, he shoved Jed into the police car and had Derek forward him the video.

The officer gave me his card. "My name is John Thompson. I have a sister about your age. I'll see that he doesn't bother you again."

Derek gave the officer his name and driver's license, and Cal gave him the made-up names of Aaron and Lisa Jackson for ourselves. As the officer started to ask for Cal's license, I pretended to almost faint. Cal caught me.

"I can see that you are shaken up. You better get her home or to a doctor. I'd like to get a statement from you in the next day."

I nodded as Derek said, "You will."

Officer Thompson got in the car and drove off.

"I don't know if the police are in on the trafficking. The courts will probably turn Jed loose with honors, but at least Thompson seemed an honest cop," I noted.

"He's young. Wait until he's been on the force longer," Cal responded. "You wouldn't believe how many judges and police officers assisted Brian with stealing Jonah. We better get back to him."

"I shouldn't have left him alone."

"You weren't the one who left him alone, but I'm glad she followed you."

Cal's car was drivable, but there was some serious damage on the front passenger side. He dropped the Odyssey by a body shop, and we went back to the townhouse in the Mustang.

"Well did you find out anything?" I asked Derek when we got back to the townhouse.

"There is a dance for the officers on the base Tuesday night. They are letting girls from the U.S.O. in, specially for the event."

"I'm a girl," I said as Cal shook his head, trying to discourage me from volunteering.

"I'll call Charlie. Maybe he can tap into the USO's list and get you on it."

"I don't want Meadow's name on any lists associated with this situation. She's already almost been killed at least three times."

"Five, if you count Seattle," Everything said.

"Rat," was my reaction to her comment.

"You take too many chances," Everything continued.

"What happened in Seattle?" Cal asked.

"Um, I got hit over the head and had a concussion."

"From a guy who tried to kidnap her," Everything threw in.

"Did you have it checked out?"

"I spent the night in the hospital."

Cal shook his head. "And the fifth?"

"When we left the University of Washington, there was a guy in our car with a gun. Everything bit him and Derek knocked him out the door of the car. I'm pretty sure he's not going to be coming after us, again."

"No more chances. Let's find another way to get onto the base. And Derek, why didn't you tell me?"

"I asked him not to."

"Sorry, Bro. Should have told you. I thought it was Meadow's place to say something," Derek said. "Tuesday night is a dance—not a war. Charlie can send me the template for a fake school ID that she can use to get in under a fake name."

"She is not a detective."

"My brother introduced me to a lot of servicemen. Most are pretty loose-lipped around American girls when they try to impress them."

"How would we know they aren't just making things up to look impressive?" I asked.

"You don't, but if there is any truth in any of what they say, we might find out something important."

"What if they go too far in their interest in girls?" This seemed to be Cal's main concern.

"There will be officers around to keep them in line, keep up appearances for the USO."

"Do you really believe that?" Cal asked.

"He's right. They will want to keep up appearances for the USO," I threw in.

"If they try anything, they could get detention or court-marshalled," Derek told him.

"Not if the officers are in on it." Cal shook his head. "I don't like it."

"I'll keep an eye on her," Everything said.

"Now, you take too many chances," I responded to Everything.

"And can I count on either of you to tell me if Meadow is in any real danger?"

"If anything happens, Derek and Everything have my permission to let you in on it, right away."

"And Sis, you won't wait days to tell me either, right?"

Everything glared at me. "I will make sure you know if Meadow is in danger."

"I haven't asked. How is your dad?" I felt guilty for not inquiring before.

"He's doing great. They want to keep him for a few more days, though, so they can do some extra tests." Cal turned to Derek. "I'd like to talk privately to Meadow."

I nodded.

We walked out along the bay. "Look, I am not good with girls. I was ten when I came here, and I spent most of my years here trying to fit into the twenty-first century and get through my education."

"You've done great at that. I didn't know you were from the eighteenth century until you told me. You certainly don't seem like someone who is shy around girls."

His voice waivered as if nervous. "Then why haven't I found a way to tell you—" He paused. I had never seen him nervous like that before. Then, as if afraid of my reaction, he quickly said, "I've-I've fallen completely in love with you. I want to spend the rest of my life with you, going to whatever college you go to, maybe getting married one day and I hope I'm not pushing you away."

For a second, I couldn't breathe. "Wait," I said halting him before he went further.

He looked down as if embarrassed. I didn't know what to say. I felt very light-headed as if I could almost pass out. *What is wrong with me?*

"I-wow. Nobody's ever said anything like that to me before." I tried to think, but my thoughts were too jumbled. My fears for him from the last week flashed before me. "When you didn't answer the phone in Carlsbad and later when you were on the floor of the cabin, I thought I was going to die if you weren't okay. I—it's not just your sister who is everything. You—"

He pulled me to him and kissed me before I had a chance to say more. I found myself melting as if the universe had exploded around me. My knees started to give out, and Cal held me up as our lips parted and asked, Are you okay?"

I nodded, unable to speak. As our lips met, again, it felt as if we had dissolved into each other. Never had I felt like this before, and I never wanted this kiss to end.

When he finally pulled away, still holding me up, I was in a cloudy daze. "I love you, too," I managed to whisper. "Even when I thought you were a dog thief, I think I was falling in love with you."

"Does that mean I should buy you a ring?"

"Whoa. I'm fifteen. I really want to do graduation and college before I get married."

"How about I get you a promise ring that you'll wear until you're ready for a real engagement ring?"

"I accept."

He picked me up, whirled me around, and kissed me even more passionately than before. As he released me, I tried to figure out how I'd pull myself away from him long enough to go to a dance without him. This was totally unfair timing.

He put his arm around me and we walked back to the townhouse. I was still wobbly.

As we stepped in the door, Everything looked back and forth

between Cal and me. "It's about time you got together. I was about to lock you two in a closet."

"Been there. Done that," I said. I picked her up. "You little matchmaker."

"How else was I going to watch over both of you at the same time?"

I noticed that I had a call from Susie. I called her back. "Honey, Courtney called. She told me what she did. I told her never to go near you, again. I am so sorry I trusted her."

"It's alright. I trusted her, too. Jed is in the hands of the police unless he's already made bail."

"Everett checked. He's still being held, but they probably won't be able to hold him past tomorrow. Everett has requested an emergency restraining order on your behalf against both Jed and Juliet. Courtney provided him with an affidavit. But she could get down on her hands and knees and I'd never trust her, again."

"She was worried about her mother's life. When someone is protecting a loved one, sometimes they do things they wouldn't otherwise do. And poor Courtney. Jed said her mother was dead."

"You're pretty understanding, and very mature for your age."

"My mother took beatings for me. I will be living with that guilt for a long time."

"She wouldn't want you to feel guilty."

"You and Everett have been such good friends. Thank you."

"Your mother was my best friend. You're family."

As I hung up, Derek said, "You know in the movies, it's usually the person you trust the most who is the bad guy."

"Susie is prepared to help me get emancipated and be on my own. She didn't have to suggest that. She was my friend long before all this stuff started happening. Her daughter was my best friend. And she and my mother are very much alike—except that Susie had a good husband."

I pulled the battery from the phone again.

"If my girl is going to a dance, she's going to have the nicest outfit in town."

"I actually have some clothes at Susie's, but you're right. I should stay away from there in case someone is watching."

***

The next afternoon, Cal took me by the Southgate Mall in Elizabeth City. It had changed over the years but still had some of the best clothing stores in the city. We went into Fashionlove, where Cal found me a silver and green dress that brought out my eyes and showed off my dance legs. It wasn't a formal dance, and so a short skirt seemed like the best way to go. Besides, Everything loved it, and I had learned to respect her opinion.

As I was coming out of the dressing room, I heard my name.

"Meadow, is that you? What did you do to your hair?" I turned. It was Tara.

"Hi. How is everyone doing on the dance team?"

"Really missing you. Jenna tried to take over, and we kicked her off; told her to get her own dance team."

"Poor Jenna."

"Don't be so kind. You should have heard the horrible way she used to talk about you, always putting you down."

"Well, it helped to have you always building me up. At least, I had one friend."

"Everyone on the team loves you. We have been lighting candles in the hopes you will be back."

"That's sweet."

Cal came up to us. "Cal, this is my friend Tara."

"And you are Meadow's—"

"Boyfriend, if she'll have me." He put his arm around me. I felt myself blushing.

Tara let out a broad smile and gave him a light punch on his free arm. "You better treat her well."

"Tara is my spiritual support person on my dance team. She's also a great dancer."

"I'm okay. Nothing like Meadow. Maybe we can do some practicing now that you're back."

"That would be fun, but my being back is supposed to be a secret. There is a custody dispute between my mom's best friend and my evil aunt."

"I know how those go. Usually evil wins."

"Not this time. I'll whisk Meadow away if Juliet wins in court," Cal said.

"He's a romantic and cute too. But one wrong move with my friend, and I'll get the dance team after you," she teased him.

"I'll watch myself. Can't have those dancers coming after me."

"I'm free this evening. I wouldn't want to mess up your plans with Mr. Romantic, though."

"How about you come over this afternoon and stay for dinner," I suggested. "Then, we can go over any new steps I've missed while I've been gone."

"I'd love that."

Cal gave her the address. "Park down the street and be discreet coming over, though. We don't know if Meadow's friends are being watched."

"Will do. And I won't tell my mom which friend I'm seeing."

Tara showed up later that afternoon. We practiced some of our dance routines in the upstairs den. As we finished the second one, I noticed Cal was quietly watching. Seeing me seeing him, he applauded. "You two are really good."

"Thank you. But we weren't expecting an audience," I replied.

"Consider me a fan. Those were some great flips you did, Meadow. I've seen people, who have been doing tumbling for years, who aren't that fast or poised."

"That's why she's the star of the team. That and the fact that she's really nice," Tara said.

"Tara is super nice, and she does great flips too," I said.

Tara rolled her eyes. "Thanks."

As we walked downstairs, Derek came in the front door, "Wow. Who is this?" he asked, looking at Tara.

"This is Tara, the nicest girl in the school," I said.

Tara waved my comment off. "No. That honor belongs to Meadow."

"I can see that you two are the presidents of each other's fan club," Derek commented. "I picked up some Chinese at an organic restaurant downtown. You cool with that, Tara?"

"Sure," she said.

During dinner, I noticed Tara and Derek staring at each other. Afterward, Cal and I opted to do the dishes.

"I think there is a budding romance out there," Cal said.

"They'd make such a cool couple. Tara's also a senior but she's already eighteen."

"Derek's also eighteen. Maybe it will work out."

As we got back into the dining room, Derek announced, "I would like to take Tara to a movie, if the two of you don't mind."

"I was kind of hoping for some alone time with Meadow, myself," Cal said. He turned to me, "If that's okay with you."

"It's fine," I replied, excited about how well Tara and Derek had hit it off.

After they left, we settled back on the living room couch.

"I don't really want you to go to that dance tomorrow night. Maybe, Derek and I could pretend to be officers."

"Risky."

"Besides, I don't want my girl in the arms of some other guy."

"Possessive."

He laughed.

"It's just a dance and I promise to be um—" I paused. "I promise not to do anything you wouldn't do, um, besides dance with some guys."

CHAPTER 43

"You are not coming." I was having an argument with Everything. Cal, Derek and I were standing by the living room couch on which Everything was sitting.

"Come on, big brother. You need me to protect your girlfriend."

"I also want to protect my baby sister."

"You are only sixteen. I lived longer than sixteen years last time around. So technically, you're my little brother."

"The military really might just shoot a dog," Cal said.

"I'm no ordinary dog. I talk. I write. I make phone calls. For all you know, I may have other abilities."

"It's dangerous," I insisted.

"I'll be an extra set of eyes and ears, and my ears are bigger than yours. Nobody will worry about what they say in front of a dog."

"They might have metal detectors and X-ray machines for any possessions. Derek, you used to visit your brother on his base, didn't you?" I interjected.

"Don't get me involved in a family argument. Cal, is she really your sister?"

"Long story," Cal responded.

"As impossible as this is, after seeing her speak, I'll believe just about anything," Derek said. "Did you used to be a dog, too?"

Both Everything and Cal answered, "No."

"How do we know she's not some kind of government spy pretending to be your talking dog sister?"

Cal and I looked at him.

"Okay. Okay. She's your sister."

"Let me finish my question," I said. "You used to go to base events, didn't you? Did you ever get scanned?"

"No, but the number of base shootings has increased. So they may have changed procedures."

"Okay, you can put me down outside and I'll sneak in. Nobody saw me sneak into Courtney's."

"There were only two people."

"I'll throw my voice like in Seattle. I can get them to look the other way."

"What?" Cal asked.

"She has ventriloquist abilities."

"If you ever decide to go public, do you know how much money you could make doing TV shows?" Derek asked.

"And she could get dissected that way, too," I pointed out.

"I promise, I'll be careful at the base. Besides, you know how hard it is to tell me 'no,'" Everything insisted.

"Even as a child, she never listened to me," Cal agreed.

"Alright, but if they start shooting, I plan to throw myself on you and take the bullet. Do you want that on your conscience?" I hoped trying to guilt her would get her to back down.

"You won't have to. Look, if you lock me up, I'll find a way out. Wouldn't it be better if we worked together?"

"I don't like the idea of either of you going," Cal said.

"And I can call the boys if something happens."

He put a new smartphone in a small soft silk purse that had a flexible band to attach it to my wrist. "Our numbers are programmed into it. They'll probably confiscate your phone if you get caught. So don't get caught."

"Which is why you need to remain careful," I told Everything.

Cal pulled out another new phone, put it on voice activation and placed it on the couch near Everything. "For the unlocking mechanism, say something."

"Cal loves Meadow."

I wrinkled my nose.

"Good password," Cal said.

Before I left for the base with the fake ID Derek, with Charlie's help, had created for me, Tara arrived at our townhouse. "Um Tara, I'm busy tonight. Maybe we could get together, tomorrow."

"I'm coming with you."

"What?"

Derek came out of the living room into the entry. "Tara, you're right on time. Beautiful dress to go with a beautiful girl."

"What's going on?" I asked.

"I told Tara about my brother and she wants to help. So Charlie got both of you on the guest list."

I turned to Cal. "Did you know about this?"

"Derek mentioned it."

"Tara, this could be dangerous. And Derek, how could you put her in such danger?"

"She insisted and threatened to sneak onto the base if I didn't include her. She and Cal's sister have a lot in common."

"Tara," I started to scold her.

"We're a team."

"A dance team."

"And there is safety in numbers. If you disappear, Tara will call," Derek pointed out.

"Cal's got a sister?"

"Long story," I said.

At the base, Tara's name and my fake one were definitely on the list, thanks to whatever hacking Charlie had done. I hoped nobody connected with Juliet was there.

I went inside the event room as a DJ was playing retro music. As Coldplay's "Viva la Vida" started up, a Seabee with a stripe and a star on his sleeve clasped my hand and kissed it. "May I have this dance?"

"Sure." I looked around. Next to a planter, having successfully snuck in, was Everything, shaking her head. The Seabee kept staring at my face. It made me feel a little uneasy.

Socializing was part of the plan. So, I nodded, hoping he wasn't recognizing me from somewhere. "Dance. A good idea."

He put his right hand on the side of my waist and took my right hand in his left as I put my left hand on his shoulder.

He seemed gentlemanly enough and I hoped he was one. "So you're an officer?"

"Ensign."

"How do you like it here?" I asked.

"I just got back."

"Really? Building a base in our next war zone."

"No, actually, in America. You wouldn't believe where they have us building."

"Where?"

"It's not for public knowledge."

"Hey, they trusted me enough to put me on the list here. I'm good at keeping secrets."

He looked thoughtful.

I continued, "You seem like someone who works hard and is moving up. I bet they have you working on some pretty important stuff."

"Really important. Almost right away, they put me working on improvements to an underground facility in Denver. Huge. Luxurious high-rises inside."

"Really. But that's no secret. Lots of people are talking about Denver's underground city for the elite."

"That's nothing compared to my last assignment. They pulled me away to work on a state-of-the-art facility in Georgia. It's also an underground facility."

"Georgia?"

"They wanted it near the sea."

"Luxury places for Congressmen in case of an asteroid disaster?"

"No, this one has lots of cells. High-tech cells, like a prison."

"Prison. For federal prisoners?"

"Not regular prisoners. It's designed to house dangerous people that nobody is supposed to know are being detained. NDAA and so forth."

"Are there a lot of those underground prisons?"

"Some. But this one is built to hold a lot, I mean, a lot of prisoners."

"I suppose it's probably just in case they have to make mass arrests if there's an insurrection."

"No. They already have lots of people in the cells. They weren't even waiting for us to finish it before they started bringing in the prisoners. There was this woman, about your size. When I saw you, I almost mistook you for her."

"Me?"

"I guess I'm just feeling guilty. She was really sweet. I shouldn't be talking about this. You said you could be trusted. Please, don't mention it to anyone."

I removed my hand from his shoulder and made a zipping motion across my mouth. I didn't know if he was trying to impress me or if he was just bursting with guilt and had to speak with someone who wouldn't get him court-martialed for speaking out. I thought back to how Chelsea Manning must have felt. This was probably a much safer way to ease a conscience than uploading information to *Wikileaks*.

"You know you are a very impressive officer. And I can tell you care about people. So there were just women there?"

He hesitated for a few seconds and then continued. "No. There were a lot of people, both men and women."

About where in Georgia is it?"

"That's what's so funny. You remember hearing that the underground city in Denver extends under the Denver airport?"

"Yes. Jesse Ventura did a video."

"He is right on the mark about a lot of things. You know he was a Navy Seal, don't you?"

"He talks about that."

"The one in Georgia is partially under the Savannah International Airport."

"That's not far from the water."

"I know."

"So what if there's a tidal wave?"

"They have it sealed up from the sea. But we built a seawall that opens onto the Savannah River to let in the water and drown the prisoners if they need to disappear and another seawall and underground channel that opens to the Atlantic for submarines and flushing out the debris. I'm sure they wouldn't actually lower the wall and then wash prisoners out to sea—except for real enemies of the country. We're the good guys."

I shuttered. It was as if he didn't understand how wrong that was or what our government was capable of. I wondered why he was telling me as much as he had, and then it occurred to me that he might have thought a girl would give him validation, make what he did okay and not something to be ashamed of. If I talked, nobody would believe me, and if I provided details, he could say I must have had a different source.

"You mentioned people. Is that where they put soldiers who desert?"

"Maybe. I know there were some former servicemen down there. I talked to one."

"Why was he there?"

"Someone said that he was mouthing off about some theory that turned out to be right on point."

"What? They wanted to silence him?"

"Just temporarily, I think. So as to not get people riled up."

"But why would anyone listen? There are a lot of crazies around with wild theories. Isn't it best to ignore them and act like they are too stupid to listen to?"

"He was a professor."

"How many prisoners are there?"

"Only about six dozen when I left, but there were cells for perhaps a hundred thousand."

"It's a good thing they have someone like you working on that project. Another serviceman might have told the wrong person."

"I'm pretty careful who I talk to."

"I'm sure you are. You seem like a really smart guy. Wait, you aren't just saying this to impress me, are you? I mean this project sounds a little too fantastic to be real."

"No. I'm serious. Look if you'll come with me, I'll show you something."

I looked for Tara. She was dancing with an officer and the two seemed to be engaged in an interesting conversation. Everything was watching the people enter on the other side of the room, theoretically listening with her big ears. She continued to look the other way as we started to leave through a patio door. I hoped to delay to grab her attention.

I turned back to see Fischer entering. I recognized him from the picture on the driver's license Derek had stolen. Everything was focused on him. He looked around as I turned my head away and put it on my new friend's shoulder, making an effort to seem like a giddy groupie type without any real agenda.

Outside, I said. "I don't even know your name."

"Chris. Chris Bernard."

"I'm Connie Jensen."

"Pleased to meet you. You're much prettier than the girls who normally attend these events."

"Thank you. That's very sweet of you to say."

"And you seem really nice. I wouldn't tell just any girl about this stuff."

"I'm sure you wouldn't." Though I suspected that any normal girl would do to alleviate his conscience via confession.

We walked out past the patio and then strolled between several sets of buildings, stopping by one. "Wait here while I get something from my barracks."

I looked around. I didn't see Everything anywhere. I hoped she was okay. I pulled out my phone and set it to record. Then I slipped it back into my purse.

Chris came back with a set of drawings. "I hand-copied the plans. I know, it's not standard procedure, and I could get in trouble, but it was such an impressive operation. Maybe one day, when it's declassified, I can write about it. You promise you won't tell?"

"Who would I tell? I'd get in as much trouble as you. You said it was under the Savannah Airport."

"Only partially. Remember, I said it went all the way to the ocean."

"So one way in is also through the ocean."

"That way requires a submarine or underwater gear and it's sealed anyway. The best way in is through an almost abandoned building about a mile away from the airport. The building is next to a bar that is still in operation, so it doesn't look suspicious when people go over there. It looks like they're just going to the location for a drink. The facility is accessible by an entrance through a basement."

I wished Everything were here to hear this, but I could relate the information to the others, later. I, myself, felt guilty about using this guy, but all is fair under the NDAA. Maybe I could check it out later, without revealing my source. *Where is Everything,* I wondered. I hoped she hadn't been caught.

Chris put his arm around me as we walked back towards the dance. I knew I'd have to watch out for Fischer as we entered. I didn't have any romantic feelings for Chris, but I wanted to play along. I know it was a jerk thing to do.

"You are so amazing. I hope we get to see each other after tonight," I said in a gushy way to keep up my pretense.

"Of course. Maybe we can go out tomorrow night."

"I'd like that. Then, we can have some fun without all this supervision."

"Supervision is the name of this place. It's as if it is harboring the nuclear arsenal."

"Wouldn't it be funny if it were?"

We both laughed.

"Well, well, well, you certainly do get from coast to coast."

Chris turned as I tried to look for a way to run from the voice I recognized but it was too late.

"Is your friend with the branch around here, anywhere?"

"You must have mistaken me for someone else."

"I don't think so, Ms. Clarkson."

Chris laughed. "You are mistaken, sir. This is—"

"Meadow Clarkson."

"What a ridiculous name," I said.

Fischer grabbed my arm.

Chris shoved him back. "You are not an officer. Contractors don't have the right to—"

"Beat it kid, or you'll wind up in that place you've built."

"I plan to report this to my superior officer. Now let go of Connie."

Fischer laughed as he continued to hold my arm with one hand and pulled out a gun with the other. "Loose ends. Loose ends."

Pointing the gun at Chris and dragging me by the arm, Fischer moved us in a different direction that led onto an airfield. As we passed the last building, I tried to pull free, kicking. I barely got out of his grasp when he grabbed me again. I let my bag slip from my wrist down my right side next to a bush near the airfield as I slugged at him, first with my left fist and then my right arm which was now empty.

He laughed. "You should give up on fighting. You're not good at it."

"You won't get away with this," I said, hoping he hadn't noticed my purse. He grabbed me again and continued on.

He marched us out onto a runway right up to a plane.

A man stepped out of the plane onto the steps: a man with a face that made me do a double take. How was he alive? "Dad, I'm so glad you survived," I said flatly, wishing he hadn't.

CHAPTER 44

"Of course you are. And I'm happy to see you again, too," he said in a happy, pleasant tone and with a friendly smile. "Unfortunately, now you will have to disappear."

Chris and I were ushered onto the plane. I knew my dad. He was the most evil man I had ever met. A man who regularly beat a woman he had promised to love and cherish until death do them part was not a nice guy. He would have beaten me, too, but my mom kept jumping between us. "How did you survive?"

"Parachute."

"You went up there with mom and set up the plane to crash, but parachuted out so you would survive?"

"You were supposed to be on the plane, too."

"And you would have killed me, as well." He looked away and then back as if his regret was only momentary. "Why?"

"Certain people felt I needed to disappear."

I knew I had to be careful. I wanted to kill him. He had killed my mother, and he would have killed me. Now he was either going to kill me or was taking me to some kind of prison, maybe Chris's prison that could be used as a death chamber.

"Does Juliet know?"

"Not yet. I figure I can show up sometime and demand my money back. She won't want to go to prison over her little operation."

I thought about Everything back at the dance. I wondered if she would look for me. I hoped she waited to look until my dad's plane was gone though. I didn't want her hurt. My dad had never liked dogs. I may have lost my freedom, but I wanted Everything, Becky, to live a long life.

Inside, Fischer held us at gunpoint, as my dad went into the cockpit to prepare the plane for the flight, until Dad came back to where we were. There was no running from this plane. I thought about the purse. I had dropped it by a bush next to one of the buildings overlooking the airfield. It wouldn't have done me much good to bring it as I knew it would certainly be confiscated at some point.

If I was going to a prison, they'd likely force me to change into prison garbs, anyway. I figured that probably security would pick it up during their late-night rounds. If they listened to the recording, Chris would be in trouble—even if my dad let him go, but none of the Seabees would likely act against anything they thought was official.

If only Everything had heard what was going on. She was probably at the dance collecting information and listening to conversations. I wondered if she had gotten worried about me, yet.

"You could at least let Chris go. He's military. He's not going to talk."

"Like Chelsea Manning didn't talk? Wasn't he talking to you a minute ago?" Interesting that Dad would bring that up. Had he been watching us?

"Not about anything important." I hoped he hadn't heard the conversation. "Besides, I'm sure he has a top-secret security clearance, and you don't get those for being snitches."

Chris just kind of sat there frozen as my dad went back into the cockpit. He probably realized by now that I had lied, and he undoubtedly hated me for getting him into this. I felt horrible about what I had done to him.

I had no doubt that my father, who had killed my mother, wouldn't hesitate to kill someone he considered a loose end or to lock them up for life. I wondered if Chris had a family like Daniel. Did he have a brother who would come looking for him? I had to convince my dad that Chris hadn't revealed anything. I hoped he had disposed of his drawing, just as I had disposed of my purse.

As I sat there, I wondered about why my dad had needed to play dead. Had he killed the wrong person or persons? He was clearly capable of killing. Did he have information that whoever he was working for wanted secret and did he think the best way to protect himself was to pretend he was dead?

After we were in the air, my dad came out of the cockpit, again, probably having placed the plane on autopilot. "Dad, couldn't we work out a deal? I'm your daughter. Maybe we could forget all this, and you could go back to being dead, and Chris would know that his life and career depend on his keeping his mouth shut. I'm taking my AP exams in less than two weeks, and then I'm off to college. I don't have time to worry about who's alive and who's not. Military matters don't interest me."

"Ah, but I know you, Meadow. You've always been too independent. That's why you ran away that day. I wish I could trust you, but I don't."

I looked at Chris. He remained silent. *What is he thinking?*

I remembered a Stevie Wonder song from my youth. My dad used to sing it to me. It was a side of him that masked who he really was. *"You are the Sunshine of my life,"* I sang. *"That's why I'll always stay around you.* Come on Dad, sing it, like you used to."

"You are the sunshine of my life. Forever, you'll stay in my heart." He stopped. "It's true. You are sunshine. I will never forget you, Meadow." Not the fatherly response I was expecting.

The plane landed. Some men in bulletproof vests with towels covering big somethings entered the plane. One of the towels slipped and to no surprise, there was a gun underneath.

They roughly grabbed me and Chris and escorted us to a jeep. They drove into a parking garage. The door closed behind them. One got out and inserted a card into a reader. He got back into the jeep and the garage floor started moving, downward. It went lower and lower. They drove it forward as a hidden door in the wall opened and the car rolled forward onto the floor on the other side. That floor descended as well.

This wasn't the airport entrance and had to be part of the abandoned building. It would be easy to move lots of equipment in and out through this garage entrance. The jeep continued through a paved tunnel until the underground road ended at the loading dock on the side of some massive underground concrete structure. We were escorted on foot through a door and down a maze of hallways.

We were turned over to two other men. They appeared to be military, armed, of course. One of the new captors held me at gunpoint and sat me and Chris down on a bench in a room as he waited for instructions on what to do with us. With us under control, the other one left the room.

A door to a corridor was open. From my seat, I looked out to see if my father was coming. I didn't see my dad, but someone was marched by the door. I had never seen him in person, but I recognized Daniel from Derek's pictures of him. "Daniel!" I called out. He turned.

"You know him?" Chris asked.

"Not personally. I've seen his picture."

"You do know we're never getting out of here alive," Chris said.

"I'd like to be optimistic even as the waves crash in." I tried to smile, but I knew he was right.

"They have nastier things they can do to us."

"At least, you are talking."

"I was an idiot. Screwed up."

"I'm sorry. I am responsible."

"No. I knew what they were doing was wrong. I tried to tell myself that there was something good, heroic even, behind it. But this is wrong, and I am getting what I deserve." A conscience. I had been right about his reason for talking.

"Hey, guilt is usually my thing. My dad killed my mother. If I hadn't run that day, maybe I could have saved her."

"Your dad doesn't seem like the kind who is easy to stop. You'd probably both be dead if you had tried."

"When I lost her, I thought about all the things I never got to say to her. She was always there for me. She always loved me, and in the end, I repaid her by running off."

"If that's what your mother was like, I'm sure she saw you running off as the best thing that could have happened. Mothers have a way of loving their kids and wanting the best for them—even if they can't be part of their children's joy."

"Was your mother like that?"

"And then some. That's why I joined the military. My dad was violent and I wanted to get out of there. After I got in, I started sending checks to my mother so she could get out and take care of herself."

"Did she?"

"She got out, but she sent back all my checks."

"My mother would have done the same thing." I smiled at the memory of my mom as tears formed in my eyes.

I looked at Chris. I found myself wishing that I had gotten someone else, someone evil, in trouble and not someone who cared about his mother and opposed what was going on.

The next person I saw gave me some hope. It was Justin. The officer who was watching us went out and closed the door.

"Justin, you don't know how glad I am to see you."

"I'm sorry you wound up here," he said matter-of-factly.

"Can you get us out?"

"I'm sorry. You weren't supposed to learn about this place." *What was he saying?* Had he infiltrated the operation or was he part of it?

"Is Stan here?"

"This is a need-to-know facility."

"Weren't you working under Stan?"

"Technically. But—"

"You aren't part of this, are you?"

"Sometimes we need to make decisions, often unpleasant ones, to help our country."

"That day when you came to my home; were you part of it then?"

"Not at that point. But I did some checking and was offered an opportunity to better serve my country. You see, I'm a patriot, and we need to have facilities like this for those who may be dissenters."

"You have three hundred and forty million holding cells?"

He laughed. "Most people won't care. In every rebellion, there are those who would become leaders. Without them, any rebellion would fail. This is a place for those leader types. There are vets who refused to give up their guns and who taught classes criticizing our government. They belong here, too."

"What about me? I'm just fifteen. I could change a lot, maybe see things your way."

"You weren't going to give up on looking for Daniel, a nobody to you, until you found him. Fischer tried to stop you. Another of our men was killed trying to discourage you."

"He was a professor at U of Washington," I said, trying to come up with a cover story.

Justin looked dubious and I didn't know what Stan had said to him about Daniel and Derek.

So I changed the subject. "And when did you decide to take me?"

"I didn't. Your dad did when you showed up at the base. It was clear you were motivated to continue looking until you found this. And now you are here."

"So you aren't going to help me?"

"That would be counterproductive."

"How did you know I was looking for Daniel?"

"We got a call from Charlotte Emerson."

I looked puzzled.

"Known to you as Gretchen Carlson. Somehow, you followed the path to MountClaire's former residence and job. How did you find out about him?"

His question told me one thing. Stan hadn't told Justin about our communications regarding Daniel and he hadn't told him about Derek.

"I was studying for AP exams, and I heard Daniel had the inside track on the AP American Government exam. I didn't realize it would come to this. I'm not planning to talk about this center or cause trouble. I just wanted to ask Daniel some questions so I could ace my exam."

"I might be able to arrange that. I can't tell you how long you'll have to talk. That isn't part of my pay grade. I don't believe you will be taking that exam, though. Them's the breaks."

"Meaning."

"This facility is supposed to be secret. We can't leave loose ends around."

"I see. You know, Chris is recruitable. He is very loyal. I couldn't get any information out of him, no matter how hard I tried."

Chris sat there and looked at me, not saying a word.

"I don't know Chris, but as an officer, he knows there will be collateral damage and that collateral damage could be him. It's a chance recruits take when they sign up. We wouldn't want him to develop a conscience over your demise."

Great. The "demise" word. "In other words, you are planning to kill me."

"I'm sorry. You really are a sweet girl. Pretty too. And that was a sweet dog you had. If your friends don't want her, I could use a pet."

If he killed me, Everything might well get him or help somebody else get him. The thought gave me some satisfaction but also some worry about Everything's safety.

"So, are they offering you something the government, alone, can't supply?"

"Oh yes. Independent contractors have a lot of privileges and much, much better pay."

"Well, do I get to speak to Daniel? If he's the reason I'm going to die, it might be good to find out if he's worth it."

"You'll be able to see him from your cell. Maybe we can arrange a visit with him and perhaps someone else. The cells are monitored for sound and watched twenty-four/seven. There is no escape."

Escape. This reminded me of a movie by that name starring Stallone and Schwarzenegger. Stallone kept being placed in prisons where escape was supposed to be impossible. In the end, he got away with Schwarzenegger's help. No Stallones or Schwarzeneggers were here to get me out.

I was separated from Chris and put into a room with an X-ray scanner. "I'd rather have a pat-down."

The guard looked up at what I suspected was a camera and a voice came over a loudspeaker that I recognized as my dad's. "Go ahead."

I was a little surprised that my dad was okay with some yucky guy putting his hands all over me, but the guard appeared to be more interested in searching for whatever than in me.

I was forced to put on an orange jumpsuit. It had snaps around the bottom of the torso, like a child's onesie. *Wonderful.* I was glad I didn't bring my phone, but it was probably just sitting where I dropped it or in some lost and found locker at the base.

I was escorted down to the cell block. It was at a much lower level than the intake office, probably something to do with the planned flooding of the prison area. The cells had walls that appeared to be made of glass, possibly bullet-proof. There were no cots inside, but each one had what looked like a porta-potty, stuck to the transparent floor.

There were elevator shafts that appeared to go down a long distance. If the seawall were opened, the prisoners on the bottom level would be the first prisoners to drown, but I wouldn't be too far behind. I felt guilty about that thought. They had just as much right to live as I did. Ahead and to the sides, the rows of cells seemed to go on for miles, as far as I could see. Maybe it really could hold three hundred and forty million Americans. The main walkways were suspended out from the cells with narrower planks or walkways leading to the individual cells. There was some kind of metal frame that held the transparent walls in place and suspended the upper cells above the ones below. I noticed metallic pipes running from underneath the toilets to just below the walkways that ran between the rows of cells. Looking down below, I could see many cells were filled, at least the ones I was able to look into.

As my escort walked me down a path toward my cell, I saw a man pounding on the glass. He appeared to be yelling, but I couldn't hear the sound of his pounding or his voice. The cells were seemingly soundproof. But were they waterproof? The pounding man looked familiar, but I couldn't place him.

"Who is that man?" I asked. My escort did not answer me. I tried to move towards the man's cell. My escort held my arm firm. I wondered if I could pull off a backflip and kick my escort off the walkway. But then, I would be a killer, just like my father. I realized that my escort was just doing his job.

At the next cell, he ushered me onto the entrance ramp. "How long has that man been here?" I asked, still looking at the cell we had just passed. Again, my prison guard ignored my question.

The cell opened. Either it was in response to our walking on the ramp or we were being watched and it was being remotely opened. Maybe there was some kind of robotic programming like the self-driving cars contained, that operated the prison. I didn't know.

The floor was not soft and there were no beds. I gathered I was expected to sleep on the glass floor. I wondered if I could pull the toilet free to smash the walls. However, when I tried, it wouldn't budge. There was a hand sanitizer dispenser attached to the side. I wondered if it was toxic enough that prisoners could commit suicide by imbibing all the contents.

The glass was thick, undoubtedly bullet-proof, definitely sound-proof. But if it were bulletproof, wouldn't it also be waterproof, unless it was designed to open just enough to let the water in when the seawall was lowered or lifted? I looked more closely at it and thought of the transparent aluminum from the original *Star Trek IV* movie. It wouldn't surprise me if someone had already invented that stuff.

I sat down and felt like crying. My mother had been murdered by my father, who turned out to be even more evil than I had believed. I never should have left her with him. I wondered how many others he had killed.

I hoped Everything had made it safely back to Cal. Cal would be worried about me. Maybe someday I'd come back as a dog. Cal hadn't recognized his own sister. Would he recognize me?

Chris was in a glass cell across from mine. He sat down, looking sad. I wondered if he would ever forgive me for getting him into this. Heck, I didn't deserve forgiveness for that. They were planning to kill him because they thought I got him to talk. I thought about the plans he showed me. If they had found them when he changed, they probably would have already killed him. He must have found a way to dispose of them before entering the plane.

Across the path and just past Chris's cell was Daniel's cell. He had never met me. I couldn't be sure he had heard me call his name. I wondered if we were in the political prisoner section. From the ramp, it had appeared that the layers of cells went down a quarter of a mile or more and we were on the highest level, though lower than the office section we had been marched from. If the water did come in, Dad would be safely above in the office area as the prisoners drowned. On my level, we would watch those in the cells below us drown first and then drown, ourselves.

In a cell behind mine across another drop and attached to a path on its other side was a woman, young, maybe in her twenties, nice look-ing. Had she gone looking for a friend and wound up here?

The cell just past mine was empty. I wondered if they were executing people and then reusing the cells. I remembered one time discussing the death penalty with my dad. I was opposed. He said, "People have to die sometimes. Does it matter when?" I thought that was cold then. But I figured he was just talking theoretically as he was just an accountant.

I thought about the escape that Stallone and Schwarzenegger pulled off in the movie. Was there even a lunchroom here where we could meet other prisoners? In the movie, they were on a ship. We were near the ocean. I couldn't get out of my mind Chris telling me that they could wash us out to sea. They could claim we had died on a joyboat ride. Maybe, once the prison was filled, they would simply wipe everyone out so that all the cells would be fresh and ready for the next round of prisoners.

I waved at the girl in the cell behind mine. She waved back. I had taken a course in sign language, but it wouldn't help unless the person I was signing to also knew it. But there were gestures I could make that could convey some messages to non-signers. I looked up. They were undoubtedly watching everything we did. They had said the cells were monitored.

My AP exams were coming up in less than two weeks. I thought about how I was going to fall behind here. I had planned to re-review all the material before the exam. I didn't even have my books. I started to cry. With all that was going on, how could I cry at the thought of my exams? Was I so selfish that I could hold it in for so much tragedy and then cry at the thought of blowing my AP exams?

I fell asleep and dreamed. I pictured Cal, leaning down and kissing me. "I told you not to go to the dance," he was saying.

"You were right. I was stupid."

The picture changed to Everything. "I need to get you out of there," she whispered.

"No. You could get caught. I want you to be okay. Just tell Cal I love him."

The picture shifted to my dance team. We had performed for the student body before the Christmas break. The students gave us a standing ovation. One of the schools that had accepted me was Juilliard. I was debating between a life of dance and something more meaningful, like ending poverty and saving animals. I was a little too squeamish to become a veterinarian. Maybe I could become a dog trainer.

I dreamed of my dad's words to me the day he flew off with my mom. I pictured what should have happened. I should have been on that plane those weeks ago and ripped the parachute off him, given it to my mother and saved her.

"Mommy, I need you. I'm so sorry," I screamed in my dream. "Mommy, mommy."

"It's alright," her voice said. "You saved me." I opened my eyes. Was I still dreaming? It was her. My mother. In my cell, next to me.

CHAPTER 45

She was thinner. She looked tired. Tears were visible in her eyes, tears she appeared to be trying to hold back. At that moment, she was the most beautiful sight I had ever seen. Was I delusional? Her touch was real. She was real.

"How?"

"You ran off. As he was finishing preparing to take off, I managed to jump out after you as the door was closing."

"You weren't on the plane?"

"I would have been if you hadn't run off. You saved my life."

"But why did you let me think you were dead?"

"You're a faster runner than I am. I was hoping to pick you up on the drive home, but I didn't see you along the main road."

"I went through the warehouse district. It was faster walking that way. But you should have arrived home before me."

"I came home and was about to go inside when that man Fischer grabbed me and hauled me away in a car. I didn't realize until later that I was supposed to be dead, that we all were. It's a good thing I wasn't with you."

I hugged her. "I love you. I didn't mind him dying. He was so evil." I practically shouted this, knowing my dad's people were listening and hoping he was too. "You were the one person who was always there for me."

"And you were the one person who was always there for me."

"They plan to kill us. Us prisoners, I mean."

"I don't believe we've survived this long, just to die at the hands of a gang of murderers."

"At least we're together."

"I wish we weren't. I was hoping you were safe."

"Safe? They turned me over to Juliet."

"Juliet! I'm so sorry. Did she hurt you?"

"She kept me prisoner and Brian got some stupid robotic dogs to keep me from escaping. But I did. And there's someone." I stopped. I didn't want my dad to hear about Cal.

She looked around as if she understood. "I've kind of lost track of days. But I don't think it's been long enough for you to have had your APs."

"I was just thinking about that. I don't know how I'll study for them in here."

"How about you review by telling me what you remember of your subjects."

"Okay. I'll start with European history." I proceeded to summarize the significant points I had learned from ancient times to the present.

As I finished my summary, a voice came out of the glass ceiling. "Mrs. Clarkson, it's time for you to go to your cell."

"No!" I cried. "You took her from me once. You'll have to kill me to take her away again."

"Meadow!" my mother cautioned. She turned her attention to the ceiling. "You've stripped us and searched us and you know we have no way to escape. Let us stay together. What harm can it do?"

"Mrs. Clarkson."

"Is my husband that much of a monster that he would separate us again after we've just found each other?"

"He was kind enough to let you speak to each other."

"That isn't kindness. It's a form of torture to pull us apart. If he has any humanity left in him, let us be together."

It sounded as if the first voice was talking to someone while partially covering the microphone. "We will let you stay with her for now. But there is no guarantee as to how long we will let you stay."

"Thank you," my mother said.

"Pigs," I uttered quietly.

"Let's not talk about them. They hear everything we say. So, what was it like in California?"

"They are killing dogs on the West Coast. I think it's all so they can sell those robotic things."

"That's terrible."

"And Juliet kidnapped a little boy and got control over an old woman and killed her, I think."

I knew I probably sounded conspiratorial and as if I was exaggerating. "I am not making it up." I had to cover for Jonah and so I added, "And who knows if the kid will get away to safety."

"You never make anything up. If you say it, it's true. Juliet contributed to my mother's death."

"What?"

"Juliet helped your dad get his hands on my mom and she died. It was long ago."

"I'm sorry. From what little I remember of Grandma, you two were really close."

"Juliet belongs in jail for elder abuse, and from what you have said, she belongs there for kidnapping, too."

"She sold me."

"What?"

"That's what some guy said. I got away, but he said she sold me for over a million dollars."

"I knew I couldn't stand her. And her husband is a piece of work."

"I heard someone say he died."

"Couldn't happen to a more deserving guy. How's the dance team?"

"We're supposed to dance at the graduation."

"That's wonderful."

"And Principal Carmen wants me to speak there. I'm the youngest graduate and with the highest AP passage rate so far. I'm not the Valedictorian, but I get to do a speech."

"I have always been proud of you. You've been amazing ever since the day you were born."

"You always say that."

"How are Susie and Everett?"

"They were fighting Juliet for custody. I don't think Juliet'll have a chance now that her partner tried to kidnap me and got arrested."

"Was that that Jed guy?"

I nodded.

"That's awful. From what I could gather from her calls to your dad, he's a terrible person."

"He's a snake."

"I'd have to agree."

"If they represent what elder attorneys are like, they should rename that area of law, 'elder abuse.'"

She looked around.

"The lights, are they always on?" I asked.

"Yes. You should get some rest."

"I don't want to miss any part of being with you," I told her.

"You'll enjoy it more if you are rested. I'll be right here beside you."

We both lay down. I don't know if she slept, but I dozed in and out of consciousness in her arms.

———

At some point, food was put under the door.

"Is it safe to eat?" I asked. "Juliet was drugging my food when I was staying with her."

"We can only hope. I think they have a different plan for killing us. I've been eating the food and haven't found any problems—except that it's not particularly good."

It looked like some kind of fruit. "Hopefully it's not genetically modified."

"It's better than what I'd been given to eat before you arrived. Your dad knows you're a vegan. So maybe he ordered it special."

"That doesn't make up for what he's done."

I tasted it. The taste wasn't bad and so I decided to eat it slowly. I was still awake and alive at the end of breakfast.

"Mom, why did you put up with him for all those years?"

"I was afraid of losing you. He used to threaten to have me committed and obtain full custody of you. He was so driven, I knew he'd pull every dirty trick, not because he loved you but because he wanted to punish me by taking you. I couldn't let him do to you what he did to me."

"But you could have left and saved yourself."

"You were the most important part of my life. What life would I have had if I had left?"

"But all those beatings."

"I didn't like the beatings, but I'd go through them a million times and over to keep you safe. I wish you weren't here."

"It's not so bad as long as I'm with you." I meant it, too.

"They have me and they know you wouldn't do anything to hurt me. We might be able to convince them to let you go. With me here, they can trust that you wouldn't talk," she said, looking upward.

"I won't leave you."

"It might be the only chance you have."

"When I walk out of here, it will be with you."

"Meadow."

"Last night or, at least, I think it was night, you said you didn't survive this long, just to die at the hands of a gang of murderers. I've been thinking about it overnight and you're right. Something, somehow is going to save us and we are going to walk from this place together. Well, we might run."

She smiled. "Now you sound like yourself, spirited and determined. Who is the guy across from us? He's been looking our way a lot."

"His name is Chris. It's my fault he's here. I was looking for a professor named Daniel, and they thought Chris was a liability because he talked to me." I raised my voice, "About other stuff."

"Do you like him?"

"I barely know him. But I have a boyfriend back home. He's probably wondering where I am." I figured saying that much wouldn't hurt.

"A boyfriend. My little girl is growing up."

"And I have a dog. A really cute, little dog."

"That's wonderful."

My mom had always been sweet and positive, probably to make up for my dad's personality. I had sometimes resented her sugary attitude, but now, I was so glad for everything about her.

"So what's your little dog's name?"

"It was Rebekka. But I call her Everything."

"That's a great name for a dog."

"I know."

"I bet she misses you."

"I'm sure she is unhappy that I didn't come home, last night."

I looked at the man pounding on the cell next to mine. "Do you know who he is?"

"I think someone said his name was Presley or something like that."

Presley. The name sounded familiar. I had heard a similar sounding name somewhere before.

It was a man's voice saying it. Brian's. When? Where? I tried to remember, but my thoughts were jumbled.

"Ms. Clarkson." The voice from the ceiling came. "You are about to have another visitor. It would be easier on you all if your mother left."

"You can hear everything we say. I have no secrets from my mother, and apparently, I have no secrets from you, either."

"It seems you are very popular," my mom said.

A few minutes later, a guy who looked a little like an older version of Derek arrived at my cell. "Daniel, hi," I said.

CHAPTER 46

"Do I know you?"

I looked up at the ceiling. "It's Meadow. Someone in the family suggested I contact you regarding my AP homework," I said, emphasizing *"the family."* He looked confused. Then nodded, understanding.

"Well obviously, someone in the family has gotten you into a lot of trouble."

"Family is good at that. But where would we be if our family weren't out there alive and well."

"Alive and well and free is the key."

"Absolutely."

My mom looked confused.

"Mom this is Daniel MountClaire. Danny, this is my mother, Theresa Clarkson."

"Pleased to meet you. Sorry you are here," he greeted my mom.

"Pleased to meet you, too. Sorry, you are also here."

"As long as you are the reason I'm here, I'm curious how you got here," I said.

"Well remember when they were confiscating guns from anyone with PTSD, which included most veterans."

"I remember hearing about that."

"Well, I refused to give up my gun. And then I started looking at information about the roundups. I'm not the only vet here. There are a lot of us."

"So they are worried about vets and guns."

"It's not just that. A lot of veterans served their country, only to come back and find out that we were routinely lied to, just as we were about the false flags that led up to the gun confiscations and the scanners in all the buildings. Remember Standing Rock and how Wesley Clark, Tulsi Gabbard and other veterans went there to protect the water protectors? Well, a lot of us have been questioning the underhanded actions of our government."

"I remember."

"There were Oathkeepers, a group the government wanted to get rid of. You know why?"

"Go on."

"Because they knew that we veterans had taken an oath to defend and protect the *Constitution of the United States*. The Oathkeepers were demanding we keep that promise. So the government went after the guns and the Oathkeepers, themselves, and then started making veterans disappear."

"But a lot of veterans are still out there."

"For now. I was teaching about what the government was up to, and they didn't like it. Others are standing up and then disappearing."

"I've heard that a lot of profs get fired for telling the truth."

"I expected to be fired, not confiscated, myself. My only disappointment is that my unit didn't come looking for me."

"They probably don't know where to look," I said.

"If you are here, you must be a fighter, too."

"In my own way. I'm fifteen. As far as I can tell my dad runs this operation. He is not a nice person."

"Bad choice in sperm donors," he said. He looked at my mom. "Sorry."

"You're right," she replied.

"If he's the guy in charge I've met, he's not military. He doesn't even have proper military protocol down."

"No. He's a contractor," I informed Daniel. "He's never served in the military to my knowledge. But I didn't know he was working with the CIA or that he was a contractor for stuff like this."

Daniel looked out. "I recognize that guy. He was one of those working on the facility—even after I was incarcerated."

"Chris. They mistakenly think he talked to me and so he's what they call, 'collateral damage.'"

"Shame. He was nice."

"He is. What about that guy over there?" I asked, pointing to Presley.

"He keeps ranting about a son."

"Son?"

"Go home or you'll meet the same fate as Tammy or Preston." Brian's threat to Townscend. Not Presley, Preston, Mr. Townscend's older son. Cal's brother.

I stood up. My dad knew about Juliet's operation. He had expected her to help him, and he was helping her by keeping Jonah's real father prisoner.

"How long has he been here?"

"Longer than me. He never gives up. He must really want to get to that son of his."

I didn't want to let on to the voice in the ceiling that I had put things together. "So, I understand we're pretty much trapped here for life."

"Or until they drown us."

"I guess we can't swim out of these cells. Are they watertight?"

"You're a smart girl. What do you think?"

"I think I want a new dad." I turned to Mom. "Is it too late for you to remarry?"

She smiled. "Mr. MontClaire, my daughter is supposed to take her AP exams next month. Is there any chance you could help her with her studying?"

"Mom," I chided.

"It beats sitting in a cell staring at six glass panels," he said. "What subjects are you taking?"

I went over my coursework with him and told him about the exams I had already completed.

"You must be going for a record."

"She's already an AP Scholar with Distinction and a National AP Scholar."

"If you do well this year, you'll probably be number one in your state. You'll have your pick of colleges. May I suggest the University of Washington?"

"Your Department Dean pretended not to know you, and he threatened a kid who remembered you."

"Mr. White. He's a bit of a coward. Puts the school first and avoids getting involved in anything controversial."

"But pretending you were never there?"

"He can come across as more than a bit of a jerk."

"That's an understatement."

"You'll find that a lot of people just go along and don't want to get involved as long as it's other people whose lives are at stake. That's how the Nazis got away with killing so many Jews, Arabs, Russians, Blacks, Gypsies, professors, journalists, the mentally disabled and others."

"And we were told it could never happen here. Look where we are." I pointed to the surroundings.

The cell door lifted a little and three lunches were pushed into the cell.

It wasn't the food that caught my attention. It was Dave, Susie's son, the Marine who had pushed the lunches in. "You're working here with Dad? "

"I've been assigned to assist him." I felt a sense of relief. *Dave wouldn't kill me, would he?*

"But you were at the funeral."

"I was on leave."

"You let me think my parents were dead."

"I didn't know your dead parents were alive, back then. I was assigned here later."

"I understand they are planning to kill us."

"You? Your dad wouldn't."

"Does Susie know you are here?"

"This is a top-secret facility. She understands I can't talk about my duties."

"I guess we'll never go out on that date. I thought you meant what you said to me at the funeral."

"I did. If your dad thought he could trust you, I bet he'd let you go."

"You think so?" I asked flatly.

"He's a great guy. He's been mentoring me."

"In holding Americans prisoners without due process?"

"We're at war."

"With who?"

"We have enemies all around the world."

"With good reason," I remarked.

"I was in the service," Daniel said to Dave. "Did you ever see the look on the face of a child when a soldier shoots his mother or just before the soldier shoots the kid? That's what war is all about."

"We don't kill children, except when we have to."

"And you don't think my dad intends to kill me."

"No. He would only kill if our government's security is at stake. I have to go. I'm sorry about your lunch."

I looked at the lunch. It was a mixture of beef and vegetables. At least I could eat part of it. My mother offered me her vegetables. "Then what will you eat? I know you don't eat beef."

Dan solved it by offering to give his vegetables to me and Mom while we gave him our meat. Later that afternoon, another serviceman I didn't recognize came to the cell. "That's enough time together." He removed Daniel.

My mother and I stood as he left and then sat back down on the floor. "Daniel seems like a nice man," she said.

"He does," I noted. "Have they had you in solitary this whole time?"

"Pretty much."

"It would be nice if we had access to reading material."

"This is a form of torture. I don't think they want to make it easier on any of us."

A while later the guard came back. I hoped it wasn't to take away my mom. I was prepared to fight to stay with her. "Mr. Sims wants to see you?" He was addressing me.

"Tell Justin Sims I do not wish to see him."

"It's not optional."

I looked at my mother. Would this be the last time I would see her?

"No. You have held me, my mother and the professor prisoner and we haven't done anything wrong. Even that poor guy," I pointed across to Chris, "who was so loyal to your cause, he refused to tell me anything. You've locked him up and he was on your side."

"You have to come or—"

"What are you going to do? Shoot me? How is that any different from what you've been planning to do?"

He went over to my mother and grabbed her. "I guess I'll just take her away, right now."

"Leave her alone! I'll go, as long as my mother will be here when I return."

"As far as I know."

"No. I want a promise."

"I promise that I won't remove her." *In other words, someone else might.*

CHAPTER 47

"I'll go. But just to see what they want. However, if my mom is not here when I return, that's the end of my cooperation."

The guard moved me onto the path between the cells, and the door automatically closed with my mom on the inside.

"How many military personnel do you have working here?" I asked.

"That's no concern to you."

"Let's see. You have one or more soldiers watching the video feed and listening to everything we say. There's you. You searched me and escorted me to my cell last night while another guard escorted Chris. You're the one who later brought Daniel into my cell. There's Dave. You probably have at least 8-hour shifts. So if there are three sets of you, there are at least twelve. With my dad, Justin, Fischer, the two guys on the plane, and the two who escorted me from them to where I met Justin, that's nineteen, including my dad. Do you have a skeleton crew or are there a lot more of you in hiding somewhere than meets the eye?" It did occur to me that there could be guards for every section of the prison, but maybe he would counter my guess with the real number.

"You need to stop talking."

"Seriously. Is this place mostly automated and understaffed? After all, you are afraid of someone being here who will leak out the location and information."

"Quiet." We continued to walk. I got that he didn't know what to make of me. My father ran the facility. Yet, I was my father's prisoner.

We walked up the stairs, through a door into a corridor. Suddenly, the lights went out. I started to scramble back in the direction we had come from to get to my mother. A hand grabbed me and pulled me forward into, I believed, a corridor. Then we turned and climbed up some more stairs.

The person with me had a flashlight that he was pointing at the floor. He spoke. "When you get out of here, you won't tell anyone about this place, right? You wouldn't want anything to happen to your dad."

I answered Dave's question. "My mother is in here."

"I don't know if I'll be able to get her out, but I'll keep her safe."

"I'll have to come back for her."

"That could endanger the whole operation."

"What? Endanger this concentration camp where people might wind up dying."

"Look, I'm taking a risk to help you."

"Risk? I just talked about virtually nothing to Chris, and they locked him up for just talking to me. You'll be lucky if they don't wind up putting you in a cell right in front of the seawall."

"I'm helping you. But this operation is important to national security."

"This operation is evil and so are the people running it. It needs to be closed down."

"Okay." He flashed the light at a closed wall. "This entrance is likely blocked by the power failure. We'll have to go the other way. I've always loved you. I never told you, but I want you to know that, to remember that."

"You are very sweet, Dave. I hope I see you on the upside after I leave."

He guided me back down a staircase, then through a different corridor and continued through a door. I wondered where the other exit was.

The lights went on. We were in a room. A door opened.

"Nice of you to bring me my daughter," my dad said entering.

"You were right, sir. She planned to talk."

"So, this was all a hoax," I said.

"A test," Dave responded. "I so wanted you to pass it."

He turned to my father. "Should I take her back to her cell?"

My father handed him a gun. "No. Shoot her."

CHAPTER 48

"Sir?"

"I said 'shoot her.'"

"I can't do that."

"You are disobeying a direct order?"

"The Geneva Conventions."

"You've already broken those."

"I'm sorry, sir."

The iciness I had seen before in Dad's eyes returned as he pulled out a gun from behind his back. I found myself silently saying prayers that my mom, Cal and Everything would be alright.

"Please, sir. Give her another chance."

"I'm not going to shoot my daughter."

"Good," Dave said. My father turned the gun at Dave as I saw the realization hit Dave's face. My dad didn't hesitate. He fired instantly into Dave's forehead, dropping him to the floor like a rock.

I went over to my dad, ignoring the gun, and slapped him.

"That's your last one, dear. The next time, I won't give you another chance."

"You killed him, our neighbor. You watched him grow up, and you killed him."

"We only moved there five years ago. Before that, I didn't know him."

"Please, release my mother. As long as you have me, she won't say anything."

"I can't do that. People might suspect I survived the plane crash."

"You did. You can say she didn't make the flight."

"And they'd wonder why she didn't go home."

"You could come up with something. You're creative."

I looked down at Dave. The tears I didn't want to shed in front of my father came pouring out. "He was my friend. You killed my friend."

"You'll get over it. It gets easier with time."

"Really and how many people have you killed that you've gotten over? This is why you had to disappear, wasn't it? Someone you couldn't kill was onto you."

"That's none of your business."

"I guess they picked the right guy to run a death chamber."

"Meadow, you need to fix that attitude. I would like to save you."

"If you are going to kill the rest of the people here, I want to join them."

"You are going to stubborn yourself to death."

"I take after my father. I'm supposed to be stubborn." I thought that might have an impact on him.

I looked at Dave and as hard as I tried not to cry, the tears continued to flow.

I kneeled down. "What will I tell Susie?"

"She'll be sent a message that he died a hero in Somalia."

"Like the lie, they told about football player Pat Tilman, who turned out to have been killed by friendly fire in Iraq?"

"Dave was a coward."

"No. He wasn't willing to kill me."

"It was a test. Just as we were testing you."

I dropped down to the floor, almost blinded by the tears that wouldn't stop pouring from my eyes, and picked up Dave's gun where he had dropped it as he fell.

I pointed it at my father. "I want my mom out of here."

"That's not loaded. I wouldn't have my own daughter killed."

"Then, what do you want with me? You threatened to kill me and Mom so many times."

"But I haven't yet, have I?" He paused as if waiting for an answer. "You've always wanted a dog, right?"

"What?"

"I got you one."

My mind went to Everything. *Had he gotten his hands on Everything?*

"Come with me."

He took me to a room the size of a large warehouse. There must have been hundreds of dogs, robotic dogs, inside.

"Pick one you like."

"They aren't real. They're robots."

"Daughter, these dogs are going to make us richer than you would believe. I've got a military contract for thousands of them. I've already sold hundreds of them to people who could afford them. You can go to the college of your choice, and live the kind of life you want. Isn't that better than dying in this prison?"

"Are the others going to die?"

"Every now and then, we need to clear the cells. Until we have a full military unit here, we can only have so many prisoners. Most of the system is controlled by computer but the military wants guarantees on an operation like this."

"How many prisoners do you have here?"

"About two-fifty. Too much work for the staff I have if there are ever any computer glitches. But full backup is coming, very soon. Especially now that the prison is completed. Soon, I plan to do a demonstration of how easy it is to rid the world of terrorists without a trace."

"My mom is not a terrorist. Neither are Dan nor Chris. Chris is one of you. He refused to tell me anything." I kept hoping they hadn't retrieved the plans Chris showed me.

"They aren't like us."

"I don't want to survive if my mom dies."

"You got that attitude from your mom. She always cared more about you than her own husband."

"She cared about her husband's daughter. That's what wives are supposed to do."

He looked as if he took that in a little. "She was oppositional, questioning me, standing up to me."

"Well, maybe she didn't know the real you," I said, softening my tone. "You are nothing like the accountant we thought you were. If she saw the real you, she might think differently." I wanted him to think she'd like the real him, not hate him, even more.

"I don't know."

I was trying to talk my way out of a corner and felt like I was too deficient in persuasion skills to talk my way out of a paper sack. I could only hope that something I said would have an impact on him. I didn't want my mom, Daniel, Preston, or Chris to die. A picture of the girl I didn't know but had waved to flashed into my mind. I didn't want her or anyone else to die either.

"Mom and I could assist you with the dogs. That's a lot of work to do on your own."

"Mr. Fischer is assisting me with that."

"But certainly he has other duties."

<hr>

Back in my cell, my mom was missing. Where was she? Had something happened to her?

CHAPTER 49

I screamed at the ceiling. "Liar. When I left the cell, I was told she would be here when I got back. You are a liar." That wasn't exactly what was promised but it was a reasonable interpretation of what was promised.

"Lying to me is dishonorable. I want my mother back," I continued.

There was no response from the ceiling. I started thinking back to my AP subjects. I had gotten a five on chemistry. I was close to getting a five on physics. Could I rig up something that would destroy the locks on the cells or blow the electrical system? I was taking AP computer science, but there was no way I had the knowledge Charlie or Crete had. I missed my team of friends. Would I ever see any of them again?

Had I gotten through to my dad? I had seen him wavering at the idea of killing me. Still, he had ordered Dave to kill me and killed him because he had failed. I didn't know for a fact that Dave's gun wasn't loaded. I didn't try to fire it. I knew when I had it in my hand that, as much as I hated my dad, I couldn't kill even him.

Back at home, Dad was a typical abuser. He would escalate to the point where my mom was afraid for her life. I was afraid, too, but I had always known my mom would save me and, if necessary, give her life to do so. There was a pattern, though. There were times when Dad was more tranquil. I had read that that part of the cycle was called the honeymoon phase. Then it would escalate to a peak. It was a circle.

I had read Lundy Bancroft's book, *Why Does He Do That?* It described various types of abusers. My dad fit into three of the worst kinds, one of which was classified by Bancroft as "The Terrorist." He also fit into what Bancroft called, "The Demand Man" and the "Drill Sergeant." I guess it showed consistency to his true self that he was ordering Marines around, killing people and running a prison.

I thought about Lancer High. My dad was planning to make a lot of money off the robotic dogs. Was he involved in the fake attack? Did he know I was there that day?

I regretted all the times I had held my mom's not leaving against her. No wonder my mother stayed with him. He was such a control freak that he would have killed us both if she had left him.

After watching him kill Dave so easily, I knew he would have had no qualms about killing either me or Mom if we had gone against him. He was still contemplating killing both of us.

The room was relatively soundproof so I didn't realize my mother was being brought back until I looked up and saw the door opening.

She came in and hugged me. "I was worried about you," she said. "When the lights went out, I hoped that somehow someone had helped you escape."

"It was all a set-up, a test for me and for Dave."

"A test?"

"Dave is gone. Daddy told him to shoot me and he refused. So Daddy shot him."

"He killed little Davey?"

"Well, he's not so little anymore. But yes."

My mother sank down. "He was such a sweet child. He always looked at you like he was totally smitten. I often wondered if the two of you would wind up together."

"He died because he refused to kill me. It's my fault."

"No, dear. You aren't responsible for what your dad does. Dave did the honorable thing. Susie will be devastated."

"I know. She was so proud of him. And Trish. I don't know how I'm going to tell her."

I started tearing up again.

"At least, he died saving you. That means something."

"It doesn't make him any more alive," I sobbed.

I looked across. Someone was coming for Chris. The guard, who had escorted me a little while earlier, entered his cell and spoke to him for a minute. Chris nodded. Then the two of them left together. Would Chris be asked to shoot me or die? After I got him into this place, I couldn't blame him if he did wind up shooting me.

"You've been through a lot. Why don't you rest?"

"One of my best friends is dead. I don't know if I can sleep."

My mom encouraged me to put my head on her lap. Then she sang me to sleep. My mom had never been much of a singer, but right now, hers was the most soothing voice in the world to me. I didn't want to lose her again.

It wasn't a restful sleep. I kept dreaming about Dave being shot and trying to change the outcome. I didn't know how long I slept. "How long do you think it's been since I was first brought here?" I asked when I woke up.

"I don't know. There aren't any clocks. I don't even know how long I have been here."

"When I came here, it was a little over three weeks since you didn't die."

"It seemed like months until you arrived."

"Time passes quickly when you are having fun."

My mom smiled.

"This is the place where the lights don't go out. You know, the Ministry of Love."

"And my husband is Big Brother."

"I wonder if I inherited any of his traits."

"No. You take more after me."

"Well, that's a good thing. Has he killed anyone besides Dave since you've been here?"

"I don't know. These walls are pretty soundproof."

I nodded. "So, are they glass or transparent aluminum?"

She smiled. "Apparently, your father was running a tech team of profiteers all the time we thought he was doing numbers and figures back at his boring accounting office."

"Never marry an accountant."

"I've certainly learned my lesson. So tell me about Daniel. He's a professor somewhere?"

"University of Washington."

"Good university."

"What does he teach?"

"Some kind of social justice classes in the political science department. His students really like him."

"He seems very nice."

I looked at her with an expression that caught her attention.

"Darling, he's too young for me, if that's what you're thinking."

"I don't know how old he is. But I understand he has tenure and has been teaching for quite some time. I also know that his former girl-friend covered up his disappearance for the people who took him."

"Terrible."

"I'll say. That's where I met Daddy's friend Fischer. He gave me a concussion."

"What?"

"He hit me over the head. I was in the hospital overnight."

"The Fischer who is working with your father? Big beefy guy, red hair?"

"That's him."

"He's the one who picked me up at the house. I heard him say his name when he made a phone call before he brought me to your dad."

"They're apparently partners. I guess likes attract."

"I was too busy playing mom to realize what was going on. I was such an idiot."

"No, you weren't. I didn't pick up on it either."

"You were a kid."

"Mom, I've grown up."

"You certainly have."

"In 2011, Obama gave an executive order allowing for the assassi-nation of American citizens without trial. At least, Daddy is holding most of these people, instead of killing them. Maybe he is only partially evil."

"You said he shot Dave."

"Yes. I guess he really doesn't have any saving grace. Also, one of Daddy's men tried to kill me. He was hiding in my car and told me to drive into Lake Washington at gunpoint. He had equipment for his own survival but not for mine."

"Oh angel, what you must have gone through." She looked confused. "You have a car?"

"Well, it was a borrowed car. It's a long story. Juliet was trafficking children, like the little boy I told you about, and her law practice involved stealing money from elderly women under her care, like that woman I told you about who died."

"I am so sorry I married into that family. I keep thinking again and again if I would change things if I could go back, would I marry someone else or not get married? But in the end, I'd do it all over again if it was the only way to have you. Then after you were born, I'd do things a lot differently."

"A guy like Dad would have killed us both years ago if you had tried to leave him. As much as I try to mitigate what he's done, he's a monster with no redeeming qualities. Otherwise, he wouldn't have imprisoned his wife and daughter."

The door opened. It was Chris with food.

"He released you?"

"He was short a man and realized that I hadn't revealed any information to you." His eyes went up to the ceiling. I certainly wasn't going to tell them differently. But from the serious look on his face, I gathered his divergence from orders was over and done with. His life depended on that. I could see where Chris would be an asset to my dad. He and some of the other Seabees built this place and he probably knew every square inch of it.

I looked at the plate. More meat. No vegetables. My dad was trying to change my eating habits. "Tell him, I'll starve before I eat an animal."

"That's not wise. Your dad doesn't like insubordination. You'd best do as told."

"Like you?"

"Like me," he said firmly. I guess he really had learned his lesson.

I looked at the food he had placed on the floor and decided it could sit there for the next year if necessary. My mother also didn't eat hers.

We just relaxed for a while and then Chris's former cell opened up and someone I recognized was escorted in. I sat there in shock. "How did Tara get here?" I murmured.

CHAPTER 50

Before I knew It, I was pounding on my transparent wall. "Tara, Tara," I called. She seemed to be looking at me, but it didn't appear as if she could hear me.

I didn't stop screaming. "Tara." After a while, I settled down.

Tara was staring at me. I knew it wasn't by accident that she was here. She must have come looking for me and gotten caught.

My escort came back to my cell and took me to what I surmised was my dad's office.

"There are too many strays here. We may have to execute some more," my dad was saying to Fischer as I walked in.

"My understanding is you plan to kill us all," I interjected.

My dad turned to me as if shocked that I would dare to intervene in his conversation. I could see anger in his eyes. Then, the anger simmered a little. "In due time, unless there's a raid."

"You called me to your office for some reason."

"We talked about you liking dogs. I thought you might help with testing them out."

"Testing them out?"

"Yes. See if they follow basic commands."

"And if I do."

"It will buy some extra time for your mother and that girl we just brought in."

"Why did you bring that girl in?"

"That girl." He laughed. "That girl, Tara Martin, went to the base and demanded to know where you had been taken. She stated she was going to start a Federal investigation. We really had no choice but to help her disappear."

"She has family."

"It seems that someone went into her home, packed her things and left a note that she had taken off with you to California. Her parents should be packing for the West Coast by now to find their daughter. They won't think to look on the base."

"In a little over a week, we take our APs. I don't think they'll buy that one."

"They won't be able to prove otherwise. She'll just be one of those missing girls."

Cal and Derek might have known where Tara went, but if she told Derek, he would have probably tried to stop her and have gone himself. So they were probably still clueless.

"Alright, show me the dogs."

CHAPTER 51

Chris came in and escorted me to the warehouse. We started pulling dogs out of boxes. "Your dad said there is a button at the right side of their necks below the jaw. You press it in to test them on learned commands."

"Do they understand English?"

"They've been programmed to understand eighty thousand words in English. Your dad has foreign models as well."

"If they are going to work for the military, 'sit,' 'stay,' and 'roll over' will be kind of lightweight."

"We're also supposed to test them on the military-grade commands. They have state-of-the-art programming and should pass all the tests."

"Is there a passcode?"

"Now, they are in training mode. After the testing phase, we will be turning off the open command programming so that only those with passcodes can tell them what to do."

"These dogs are pretty strong, aren't they?"

"They can chew a man to shreds in seconds."

I thought about Brian's stalker friend. He had been chewed but survived and then some.

"They may not be as capable as my father thinks," I said.

"He would know what they can do. If previous ones had deficiencies, he would have taken care of that by now." He stopped and glared at me. "You aren't trying to mess me up again, are you? Because if you do, my loyalty is to my commander. In this circumstance, that's your father." Wonderful. I guess he didn't want to go back into detention with his execution pending. Still, I was glad not to have his death on my conscience.

I tested several of the dogs on sit, stay and fetch. Chris pulled out some dummies and tested the dogs on disarm, though he only used water pistols. He followed up by having them attack and kill. The dummies were torn to shreds.

I thought about how Brian's assistant must have been lucky that he remembered the passcode and that the dogs got distracted by me. Maybe there was there a flaw in the early programming that allowed him to survive that long or maybe those particular dogs were programmed to attack but not kill. I was hoping to find a flaw I could use against these, but I didn't see one.

Chris also tested them on disarming fake bombs. They had skills that most humans lacked and their paws doubled as actual hands. I didn't want one of these dogs anywhere around Everything or Monarch. I, myself, was now getting an education on dismantling bombs.

A couple of times, Justin came in to check on us. He seemed to be satisfied by what he saw as he left.

"I'm really sorry I got you into trouble," I told Chris.

"I don't want to talk about it," Chris replied. "I've learned my lesson. Never trust a pretty girl."

"I understand. Well, now you are back to working long eight-hour shifts."

"Twelve."

With the first several dogs, we set up a demonstration for my dad. He was impressed. "Chris, these dogs are supposed to be able to swim. You'll be taking them out into the ocean and testing their water skills."

"We will?" I asked, hoping for an escape path.

"Chris will."

"Dad, Tara is a bit of an airhead. If you tell her you'll keep me alive and well if she stays quiet, she won't tell anyone about this place. She is good with secrets."

"Isn't she on your dance team?"

"I didn't think you ever paid attention to my dance team. We're supposed to dance at graduation. But first, we need to take our AP exams."

"I wish I could help with that. But I can't take any chances."

"Dad, do you really think I'd turn you in?"

"That's what you told Dave."

"I was angry and was letting Dave know I was angry. Since I've been working with you, I've seen the importance of what you are doing."

My escort brought a prisoner I didn't recognize into the prison warehouse. The person's hands were bound behind his back. He stood there at attention, like a soldier. The escort left and returned with another prisoner. His hands were also bound. He took a similar stance.

"Who are they?"

"Soldiers who were caught contacting the news media. The government considers them a liability and doesn't want the negative publicity they got from Chelsea Manning's court-martial."

"I see. So are most of the persons in here military or former military?"

"Quite a few. We also have a number of professors and journalists."

"I see."

"So, even as prisoners, these former servicemen act like good soldiers," I remarked, noticing the two men still standing at attention.

"Our government does a good job of programming them in the boot camps. They drill the brains out of the recruits, particularly out of the Marines. It doesn't work with all. Some continue to think for themselves. That's where the problem is. The lesson here is that thinking leads to trouble."

"So, when they leave here, they'll follow orders better."

"They won't disobey any orders after they leave here." He smirked. "Number 102 and 103, attack the subjects." The men flinched a little but continued standing at attention. Before I had time to react, two dogs ran at the men, opened their mouths and aimed their teeth at the throats of the subjects. I couldn't let this continue, even if it meant my life.

"Salmonella, stop the attack!" I yelled. The dogs paused and pulled back.

"Override. Kill," my dad shouted. The dogs jumped back in, tearing at the throats of their subjects. Seconds later, it was clear the men were dead, but the dogs continued until my dad told them to return to their spot and freeze.

CHAPTER 52

He turned to me, disappointment showing in his eyes. "Where did you learn Salmonella?"

"Brian bought two of your dogs."

"Well, Salmonella is a weak command that can be overridden. I've already programmed them with a superseding code word and to recognize my voice. Unless they hear the higher code word, my voice commands will supersede any other commands."

"Oh. Well, it was a good test," I said, trying to keep from falling apart and from appearing as unraveled as I felt.

"You countermanded me."

"I don't like the idea of people dying."

"You're weak. That's always been your problem."

"Doesn't killing ever bother you?"

"You get used to it. In this world, killing has become a necessity. When it's time to drone bomb a school or a hospital, loyal servicemen never show any weakness, and neither do our Presidents."

"Since they think you're dead, you'll never be President."

"No. I'll be the man behind the President once I prove what I can do."

"And behind teens thinking they are playing video games as they operate the drones?" I had heard about the teens but didn't know if it was true.

"They think it's a game and they love hitting those targets. After we test them out and offer to recruit them, we inform them they could be arrested for their gaming abilities unless they accept our offer to continue. If they hesitate, we've got this and other facilities. This is how you weed out the rogue elements of society."

I was sure I was one of those rogue elements.

In spite of the horrors of what he was doing, he was outwardly keeping his cool much better than at home. He was probably feeling proud of himself for pushing past me to kill those men, showing me he was in charge. I still had to be cautious. One minute at home, he was normal. The next, he was a raving lunatic and I often didn't know what made the difference.

I tried changing the subject. "May I speak with Tara? I haven't had a chance to speak with her since she arrived."

"You just finished going against my instructions to the dogs."

"Yes, but you won. I lost. I learned."

He looked thoughtful and then I believed I detected a faint smile.

My escort took me toward my cell. I kept wondering how many people were working at the prison.

Chris said they were on twelve-hour shifts. I had only seen two escorts in addition to Chris and my late neighbor. They undoubtedly each had a relief. Was that just for my section or were there two to three guards for each section? And were they all loyal? Then, there was my dad, Justin, Fischer and the four guys who had escorted me after my arrival. The viewing staff and kitchen staff could have been wholly or partially AI. I could be up against a significantly large crew or a relatively small crew, but I suspected it was small as they needed a quick replacement for Dave and that's what saved Chris—though I didn't trust they wouldn't execute him later as an example, anyway.

Instead of escorting me to my cell, I was escorted to Tara's. As soon as the escort left, I asked her, "How do you like the glass walls with someone watching and listening to every word we say?" That was to ward off her saying anything about Cal, Derek and Everything.

"It's an interesting place. I was wondering if we could do a dance for the servicemen who work here. Sort of like a USO show. You can do those new dance moves that everyone loves." She was undoubtedly using a roundabout way to talk about the flips.

"I've been wanting to practice those steps too."

Did she honestly think we could flip our way out of here?

I wasn't sure if she had seen my dad, but she might be safer if she didn't know he was here. "They've given me some assignments. I don't know if they trust me enough to let me live, but I'm hoping. Maybe they could do likewise for you," I said, lifting my eyes up to the ceiling. She lifted hers up, too, and then seemed to nod her eyes as if she knew I was also talking to the audience.

"I'd love to help. I saw your dad earlier."

That answered that question.

"I thought he was dead," she said.

"So, did I. Isn't it lucky he survived the crash?"

I moved my eyes from side to side as if shaking my head but really just my eyes.

"Yeah, real lucky. Maybe he'll let us out and we can show him our dance routine."

"I was talking about our dance routine earlier."

"I guess we think alike."

"So, when you left was Everything or I mean was all well?"

"Oh, yes. Everything was just fine."

I breathed a sigh of relief. "I kind of miss California. I suppose it's doing okay." Of course, I was talking about Cal.

"Well, California is still out there, but I'm sure California misses you, too."

"You know it was crazy to go and demand to know where I was. I wish you weren't here."

"But I really wanted to see you. That's why I did it." She seemed almost cheerful. She was a better actress than I had realized.

"Everyone here is slated to die," I whispered.

"Now?"

"No. Later. I don't know when."

"As long as I still have some time."

"You aren't worried about being here?"

"This is a very interesting place. I could use some relaxation time. Too much research, studying and searching for answers."

I wondered how much Derek had told her. If she had known how dangerous these people were, would she have gone back to the base? She was so nonchalant about it all.

I gave her a hug. "I wish you weren't here, but I'm so glad to see you."

"Same here. Is that your mother in your cell?" She pointed right at my mom who was watching us.

"Turns out, she survived, too."

"See sometimes you just need to have faith. Just when things look dark, everything turns light."

"Here the lights don't go out."

"Like in the Ministry of Love."

"That's right. My mom and I were talking about that. I guess you read that book for school, too."

"Just so long as they don't bring out the rats."

"Maybe some large dog-sized ones."

"Oh."

Chris came to Tara's cell and the door lifted. "Your dad wants to see you."

"Can I see my mother before I leave the area?"

He looked up.

"Five minutes," came my dad's voice. I was sure he had been listening to everything we had said. I hoped that we were not obvious in any of our communication.

Chris escorted me across to my mother.

"I always liked Tara," Mom said.

"She is really nice."

"I remember when she came here from Chicago. She seemed so shy, and then you put her on the dance team and she started to glow."

"And she turned out to be my best friend on the dance team. I'm going to see if Daddy will let us do a performance and if he'll let you be there."

"Don't count on it. He hasn't had much to do with me since I've been here."

"Maybe I can fix that."

"Meadow, kids can't fix their parents' problems. It's unfair of any parent to make a kid even try."

I heard my dad clear his throat over the speaker.

I hugged my mom. "Dad only gave me five minutes. I'll be back."

"I love you."

"I love you, too."

Chris escorted me back to my father.

As we walked into the warehouse, I was met by my dad, who was standing with two men and a woman I had only seen on TV. I quickly recognized Secretary of State Max Pompous and DHS Secretary, Christy Nelson. Also present was journalist Mark Bluepill. I remembered him once being a hero and later spouting the Administration's propaganda as if he had taken a bribe or something. The fact that he was here as a free person and not as a prisoner meant he was a government insider, not an independent journalist.

"My daughter has been helping to test our new dogs," my dad seemed to be bragging.

"This is a very interesting operation," Mark said. "I'd like to see what these dogs can do." Obviously, it didn't bother him that my dad had faked his own death or had a squadron of killer dogs.

"105, come forward."

One of the dogs trotted forward. It looked like a golden lab. Mark went up to it.

"We can put these dogs in homes to help with disabled vets as their service dogs," my dad continued. "105, do a demonstration for Mark, who is standing right by you. Mark, you can name the dog."

"How about Oro?"

"105, you will respond to the name Oro."

"Oro, roll over," Mark said. The dog rolled over. "Oro, jump." As if having power boosters, the dog jumped up twenty feet and then landed back on the floor. "Very impressive."

My dad pulled a device out of a cabinet that looked like a nuclear bomb. "Tell him to deactivate the bomb."

"Oro, deactivate the bomb," Mark instructed. Nails came out of Oro's paws and using his paws like hands, he opened a panel with wires underneath in the bomb or rather fake bomb. He looked at the wires he had exposed, sniffed and pulled one.

"He has special hearing and can actually hear and smell the current flowing through the live wire. Additionally, he has been programmed to sniff for bombs and listening devices. So if someone plants a bug in your residence, he'll find it."

"He's very impressive. And if an intruder comes to harm you?"

"Oro, demonstrate. Oro, Mark is a dangerous intruder. Demonstrate how you would deal with him." Mark gave out a laugh as if he were waiting for a punchline.

The dog approached Mark. "I suppose he stops the intruder and holds him for the police."

In a flash, the dog pounced on Mark and severed Mark's throat. I tried not to respond, but I felt like I was going to either throw up or faint. I had to keep standing.

"Now that's impressive," Max said, seemingly unmoved by the loss of life.

"And with such speed and determination," Christy added. "So, it will even attack owners or those who have given it commands when a higher authority demands it?"

"That's the most important feature."

"No more revolutions," Max remarked, giving a one-clap applause.

"Not here, anyway."

"I think we'll order seven hundred and fifty thousand to start," Christy said. "I'm told you have a marketing firm that can sell and distribute millions to the American public; keep them in line."

Dad chuckled. "These dogs can do more than that. They can record and transmit private conversations. But the cost would be prohibitive for most people."

"The government will subsidize the sales. I will get an authorization for special funding. There is a slush fund that has been accumulated for projects of this nature. That way, we don't have to go before Congress with the request," Max assured my dad.

"I suggest we adjourn to the dining room. I've had lunch prepared and we have planned entertainment." My dad touched the wall as we exited the warehouse and the door slid closed behind us.

"Entertainment?" Max asked.

"My daughter and one of the top members of her dance team will be performing." I looked at my prison oranges. They were loose but I could perform in them. I didn't know if I was up to it, though, given that it was all I could do to stop shaking.

We entered a dining room and my dad's guests sat down at a table. Tara came in escorted by Chris.

"Could my mother be here?" I asked. "I really would like her to see this number."

The others looked at my father. At first, he seemed perplexed, trying to come up with a response. Then a look of resolve hit his face.

"I don't see why not." On the screen was a picture of one of the seawalls. "During lunch, I've got another demonstration planned."

"The flooding of the prison?" Max asked as if he were asking about apple pie. "You said there would be no traces of the prisoners after they were washed out to sea."

"Well, eventually their bodies might be found by fishermen, but they would probably be sufficiently decomposed by that time and we can handle the DNA processing to make sure they are not identified."

"You do think of everything," Christy marveled.

"May I have the dance shoes I came in with?"

"You brought dance shoes?" Tara asked.

"Yes. Not my regular jazz shoes but shoes I can dance in. I am sure you want a top-quality performance, Daddy."

"In that case, may I have my shoes as well?"

"Chris, could you go get the clothes that were removed when they were brought here?"

Chris left again.

A few minutes later, my escort returned with my mother. She was seated in a chair at the table.

"This is your wife?" Max asked.

"Yes."

"She is lovely." No mention of the fact that she was wearing prison orange, like me, and was clearly an inmate.

Chris returned with Tara's dance shoes and also the shoes I had worn the night I was captured. It seemed odd that she had on dance shoes when she went back to the base.

"Tara's shoes are good, but on second thought," I said. "Mine aren't up to the task. I'll be doing it barefooted."

"What music will you two be performing to?" my dad asked.

"We have a dance routine to an old song, Tears for Fear: 'Everybody Wants to Rule the World,'" Tara said.

My father pressed some buttons on the wall and the viewing screen showing the sea wall reappeared. "I think that the fall of the seawall will go well with the dance music."

"Won't this area be flooded too?" I asked. "I mean we're higher, but not that high." Normally, my dad would have objected to my questioning him but not when he was trying to impress people.

"That's the beauty. When the water reaches the inner wall of the prison, it will trigger a barrier that will protect us here."

"So, we're going to dance while the prisoners drown?" I asked, doing my best not to sound bothered. Preston's image, banging on the walls of his cell, flashed in my mind.

"Something like that. Of course, when the dance ends, your group will be going back down to join them for the finale." Max and Christy looked almost surprised but recomposed themselves immediately.

We didn't actually have a dance number to any of the Tears for Fears songs, but I knew the number we used for the Christmas show would fit the music. I got the impression that Tara was making a statement of some kind with her song selection.

I was really doubtful about our getting out of this alive. I was kind of glad that the dogs were locked out in the warehouse. I didn't really want them ripping us apart as the encore to our dance.

My father opened a panel and pressed a button. I could see water starting to come in from under the very slowly rising wall. Preston and Daniel were among the other approximately two hundred and forty-eight prisoners still incarcerated below. Hopefully, they were still located on the top layer. I knew it was selfish to think that, given all the others below, but I wanted them to have as much time as possible.

The music started. We began with turns, cartwheels, jazz squares and some fast partner dancing. As the words, "Everybody wants to rule the world" repeatedly played, I thought about how my father wanted to be the man behind the President, the one pulling the strings. I reasoned that his two guests were also Deep State, part of the Establishment gang running the show while the President was merely a figurehead. Those watching us were or planned to be the rulers of the world. One of the real-world rulers who was missing was the head of the Council on Foreign Relations. He may have been too busy orchestrating another war to show up.

We were back to doing fast turns, which we did around the table. Next, we did leaps to the walls of the room. We danced around the sides of the room positioning ourselves at opposite corners of the room from which we were to do a series of handsprings and flips into the center of the room. The table was blocking us from the center and I guessed what adjustment Tara had in mind.

Suddenly, I heard explosions. That grabbed my dad's attention. Were those something he had been planning?

I proceeded with the apparent plan, doing a line of handsprings and flips and hoping I didn't break any parts of my body. My final one landed on my dad's head, knocking him to the floor unconscious. I wasn't certain I hadn't broken one of my feet. To my not-surprise, Tara landed her final one on Max. Christy appeared to be freaked. My dad was unconscious and Max lay on the floor, not moving as well.

"You! This is insurrection!" Christy yelled at us.

Chris pressed some buttons to stop the opening of the seawall and to close it. The next thing I knew, Cal, Derek, Charlie, Crete, along with Jason from the U of W, Jesse, Larry, Kevin, Lee and Barry of Daniel's squad, and a number of other beefy-looking guys ran into the room.

"The rest of Daniel's unit?" I asked.

Jesse nodded.

"Hi, Jason. Found your proof. And now we need to free Daniel and the other prisoners."

"If we cut the power to the prison, all the cell doors will automatically open at once," Chris said.

"And the seawall?"

"It will automatically close and stay closed, absent the use of an emergency lever."

"You sure?" Tara asked Chris.

"I helped build this place."

Everything stepped forward from behind the other newcomers and jumped into my arms.

"Boy, have I missed you. Excuse me, girl, have I missed you." I turned to Tara. "Please get my mom and Everything out of here."

"I'm not leaving without you," my mom said.

"Neither am I," Tara insisted.

"Oh, no," Chris said. "I forgot about the dogs."

"The dogs?"

"When the power goes down, the warehouse door will automatically open. We won't be in danger unless your dad gives commands. We've got to help the prisoners out. The oxygen will last until we're out of here, but the ventilation will go out with the power."

"What about lights?"

"There's automatic emergency lighting that goes on when the power is cut."

"So as long as my father remains unconscious, we're fine."

"There are Seabees, Marines and other servicemen down there taking orders from your dad. They might be trouble."

"Why are you helping us after what happened the last time?"

"Geneva Conventions. I am not a murderer."

Chris and Crete went to the power room. The rest of us started towards the prison. Cal put his arm around my waist. I took my mom's hand and said, "Mom, I'd like to introduce you to my boyfriend, Cal."

"Pleased to meet you," my mom said.

"How did you find us, Cal?"

"Everything heard your conversation with Chris and got the map of the inside of the prison and your cell phone, but we didn't know how to find the exact location. So Tara insisted on getting them to bring her here with GPS devices in the soles of her shoes."

"You planned to get caught?" I asked Tara.

She smiled. "That's what friends are for?"

"That's way more than what friends are for." I hugged her. "Thank you," I whispered. "You are amazing."

"She certainly is," Derek proclaimed from behind her. I released her and he put his arm around her.

"Derek, how could you let her do it?"

"She's just as stubborn as you are."

"I'm not going to let some guy tell me what to do or what not to do," she said.

"You guys are all great."

As we arrived at the upper floor of the prison, I noticed that the cells hadn't opened. We turned back to see if Chris needed help. We ran past the dining room as my father appeared at the door with a gun. A second later, Chris came in followed by Fisher at gunpoint and Crete came in followed by Justin, who was holding him at gunpoint.

"Into the warehouse," my father said, pointing the gun in that direction and then back at us. We were being given a choice of being shot or having our throats ripped out by the dogs. There were three of them and a lot more of us. Correction. Behind us, about a dozen servicemen appeared, all with guns.

"Well, well, it looks like you've got these terrorist kids under control," Christy said, coming to stand by my dad.

I looked at the friends and veterans who had come to rescue me. None of them had guns. The government had been very effective at confiscating guns from everyone in the public, including veterans.

We moved towards the warehouse, with Crete and Charlie taking the lead. "They have thousands of those robotic dogs in there," I informed them.

CHAPTER 53

My mom looked terrified as Dad opened the warehouse door. I put my arm around her and she did likewise. "This is my fault," she sadly told me.

"No," I replied.

"Don't worry, Mrs. Clarkson. Your daughter is stronger than she looks," Cal said.

"I personally prefer the living version," Crete remarked, looking at the dogs. "They are better lickers."

"I've watched these robotic dogs rip out the throats of three guys in no time flat," I informed him.

Charlie clasped his throat. "Those dogs should learn some manners."

Charlie and Crete certainly had courage. I was terrified, but they seemed to be taking everything with more courage than I had in me.

As we entered the warehouse, my father gave the order. "You two talkers. Go stand in the middle of the room." He pointed to Charlie and Crete. "You, Chris, join them. Your betrayal will be short-lived."

Chris joined my friends in the center, looking as if he was resolved to seeing his own end.

"Numbers 107, 108 and 109—"

"Chris, we're the superstars," Charlie said, over-speaking my dad. "See, everyone is watching,"

Charlie was meeting his fate with more relaxation than I had seen him exhibit in all the brief time I had known him.

Crete looked at Derek, who looked at Cal. Something was going on.

"Derek, I told you this wasn't going to work," Cal said.

"This is your fault," Derek replied. As attention turned to the argument between Cal and Derek, Jason, Jesse, Larry, Kevin, Barry, Lee and their co-rescuers turned and yanked the guns out of the hands of our primary assailants and then knocked them, including my father, to the floor. The remaining guards pointed their guns at our team. Behind them, through the warehouse door, came Stan and Professor Holstrom.

"I guess this is the end of your CIA career, Justin," Stan said, pointing his gun at Justin.

"Command: 107, 108 and 109, attack the targets," my father said as Justin helped him up off the floor.

The dogs were all charging. Crete and Charlie whipped what looked like small flashlights out of their pockets and each pushed a button. One second the dogs were charging at them. The next, they stopped and dropped lifeless to the floor. My dad called out more dogs and Chris and Charlie kept repeating this action as the dogs charged at them.

My dad called out. "All, Command, attack," and an army of dogs started to come forward.

"Salmonella," I yelled. "Stop." They stopped cold.

"Override," my dad yelled. "Kill all of them." The dogs were now running at all of us.

"How do we override his 'override?'" I muttered, visualizing the end.

"Wedding cake!" my mom yelled. "Stop. Down. Deactivate."

The dogs dropped and seemed to go lifeless.

"Wedding cake?" I asked.

"It was a guess. Your dad claimed our wedding cake gave him salmonella poisoning. It was a running joke during his nicer days."

My dad pulled another gun out of his waistband and pointed it at my mother. Everything jumped up and bit his hand causing him to drop the gun. He picked Everything up and reached for her throat. She was a tiny Papillion and didn't have a chance.

I don't know how I wound up with it but suddenly the gun was in my hand firing. My dad dropped her as he fell to the floor.

Everything looked unconscious. "You have to be alright," I cried. I ran to her and dropped to the floor. She started moving, and next I knew, she was in my arms.

Cal was at my side. "It's okay."

"You didn't kill him," Chris said. "That's an entry wound in the back of his head and the exit wound is in the front."

"I don't understand. I fired the gun."

"Lower down and to the side. You got his hip," Cal said. "You must have been aiming to avoid hitting Everything." He could have been right. I had been on automatic and didn't really recall my aim, just that I fired.

"I don't remember firing twice."

"I shot him in the line of duty," Stan said.

"I fired. I'm capable of killing," I lamented, questioning my morality as I shakily stood up.

"Meadow, he was prepared to kill all of us. He was a monster," my mom said, putting her arms around me.

Derek leaned down and felt my dad's neck. "This time he's not coming back."

Cal wrapped his arms around me and gave me a passionate kiss, right in front of my mother. I thought about being embarrassed, but he was so hot.

Tara and Derek joined in with their own embrace.

As much as I loved being kissed by Cal, I had to be upfront with him. So, I pushed him back. "I've got a surprise for you, a really big surprise."

While Stan and a team of CIA agents who had come with him zip-tied the new prisoners' wrists, Chris and Crete cut the main power and got the cell doors open as the rest of us assisted the prisoners out. We sent most of the rescue team to empty the bottom floors first.

"How fast can you run?" I asked Cal. I was moving towards the cell next to mine. Everything was in my arms. I didn't want her trampled by any prisoners leaving their cells.

Preston was already standing outside his cell looking around when we arrived. When he saw Cal, his stunned glance turned soft. He took a breath and smiled.

Cal gave him a big hug. "Don't ever disappear on me like that again, Bro."

"Where's Jonah?"

"At home, playing with Dad and our new dog."

"And Tammy?"

"Missing. Is she here?"

"I don't think so," he said.

A minute later, my mom and Derek came running by us to Daniel's cell just down the row. We followed and watched as Derek gave his brother a hug. Hugs were in vogue today. "What took you so long, little brother? I've been waiting here for weeks."

"I told you to leave a forwarding address when you moved. I went to your place, but no forwarding address."

Jason, who had followed us to the cell block, gave Daniel a fist bump.

Those of us who could, assisted prisoners who were in bad shape. The prisoners on the bottom level had to stand on their toes to avoid drowning.

Crete restored the power as Charlie and Chris worked the controls to evacuate the water. Christy, Max and my dad's staff were locked up in cells in the prison they had worked to create.

———

As my mom, Cal, Everything, Tara, my new friends and I were walking out of the complex into the open sky, Daniel spoke to my mom. "I understand they've refilled my position at U of W. So, I have some free time on my hands. I, well, I was wondering if you'd like to go out on a date now that we're out on parole."

My mom looked at me, seemingly hesitating to say anything.

I was bolder. "She'd love to. I guess you'll be staying with Cal and Derek in Elizabeth City for a while?"

"Sounds good to me. So how about it, Theresa?"

"It would be nice," my mom finally said.

I turned to Stan. "So, were you part of this team?"

"Me? No. Your dad had a contract to supply robotic dogs to the CIA for use overseas. Justin was supposed to be my junior partner, but it became clear he was hiding stuff. So, I started monitoring his activities. I wasn't expecting this."

"But my dad was doing this for the government, wasn't he?"

"There will be an inquiry as to which sub-agency was contracting for this—" He paused. "Concentration camp. There is no way these inmates could be classified as enemy combatants."

I might have been naïve, but I hoped that once the American public learned of the prison, someone would be held to answer for it.

———

We made a web video of the prison and of statements from those released prisoners who were willing to talk.

After we got home, Susie knocked and said, "It was crazy. Despite Courtney's testimony, the judge gave jurisdiction to California and custody of you to Juliet."

"You want to bet," my mom said, stepping out of the den.

"Theresa!" Susie exclaimed. "Thank God." She pulled my mom into a hug. "How did you, I mean, why didn't you let us know?"

"You can thank my dad for that," I said.

"Is he alive?"

"Not anymore," I told her.

My mom turned to me. "Would you like to vacation at Tara's house until the end of the school year?"

"Juliet knows where my school is, I think." I looked at my mom and Susie. "Alright, I'll pack."

"And I'll keep watch to make sure your sister-in-law doesn't get anywhere near her," Cal assured my mom.

A knock came at the door. "This is law enforcement. Open up."

I went upstairs and my mom went back into the den, as Susie opened the door. I positioned myself where I would have a view while remaining out of sight from downstairs.

"Yes?"

"I have come for Meadow," I heard Juliet say.

"She isn't here. I've been looking for her," Susie replied.

"I guess we'll have to search the house. She was seen entering it."

"I don't think you are taking her anywhere," my mom said, re-entering the living room.

"Ma'am, this woman has custody," the deputy sheriff, who had accompanied Juliet, announced.

"I'm the mother."

"Well, you no longer have rights. I have orders to see that the girl is placed on a plane to California."

"Over my dead body."

Juliet smiled. "That can be arranged."

The deputy shook his head at Juliet and then looked at my mom. "Ma'am, if you interfere, I'll have to arrest you."

"Mom, I'll handle it," I assured her coming down the stairs. "You try to take me, and I'll have the Feds prosecute you and this deputy for kidnapping."

"I don't see any Feds lining up to help you, Miss," the deputy said.

"My husband is an attorney," Susie told him. "And this woman has a history of creating bogus orders. My husband will have to review whatever order you have. I'll call his office." Susie went to the phone.

"What you are doing is a crime," my mom lectured Juliet. "You held my daughter prisoner and you don't get to do it again."

"You don't know much about family court, do you?" Juliet snidely remarked to my mom.

"It's the money, Mom. She wants Dad's money."

"I see," my mom responded.

"Of course, I'm after the money," It was Juliet's voice, but her lips weren't moving.

The officer looked at her and said. "Quiet."

Juliet shook her head as if she was in disbelief she had said that.

"That's why I bribed this officer and the judge." Her lips still weren't moving, but her voice came out loud and clear.

The officer turned around. "Stop joking. Someone might take you seriously."

Stan, who had accompanied us home came out of the kitchen. "I heard that. Now, if the two of you don't get out of here, I'm taking you both in on a federal warrant. I will deal with that judge later."

He showed the officer his card. "Her partner just confessed. How many years in prison do you think you could get for assisting her?"

Stan escorted the two of them out of the house.

"That's not going to hold, you realize," Cal warned us as Stan returned.

I looked at Everything and picked her up and got a face full of licks. "I think I should get emancipated before they figure out how talented somebody's sister is."

Stan shook his head, seemingly not understanding. Cal smiled.

My mom and Susie looked a little confused. Trisha came running through the front door and gave me a hug.

I knew I had to break the news to Susie and Trisha, but I didn't know how. "There's something I need to tell you about Dave."

Susie looked sad. "I know. We got a call from his commanding officer." Her eyes began to tear.

Trisha's eyes were red and she also looked as if she had been crying.

Susie continued, "He said that Dave rescued a family from a building that was under siege and took several bullets saving them. I'm proud of him for being a hero, but I'd rather have him back alive." She let out a sob.

I didn't have the heart to tell her the truth. "He was a hero," I said.

Dave had saved my life, and that's why he had died. Susie would probably never forgive me when she found out I was the reason. And it would break her heart to know that Dave was involved in my Dad's operation. Maybe the only thing that was important was that she knew he was a hero.

EPILOGUE

Those of us who had been held prisoners and our rescue team were subpoenaed to testify before Congress, but not before Cal, Tara and I took our AP exams.

"How did you feel about yours?" I asked Tara on the way out of the school.

"All fives, I hope."

"Me too."

"Cal, how did you do?" I asked. He gave me a sad face and then broke out into a smile.

We went to my home for a celebration. There was a knock at the door. *Not again*, I thought. Cal went over and answered the door. Jonah ran in and gave me a hug as Preston gave Cal a hug. Then Jonah joined Preston and Cal in a group hug.

"Good to see you again, Pres," Cal said, smiling.

"Jonah and I didn't come alone."

Jonah ran back to the door and escorted a woman, whom I suspected was his real mother, inside. Tammy was beautiful. She looked a lot like Liz Montgomery had in the reruns of the *Bewitched* TV series.

"And Tammy. It's great to see you," Cal said. He reached out to hug her, but she walked past the guys towards me. "Are you Meadow?"

"In person."

"Thank you. You saved my son and you saved Preston."

"Um, I think Cal deserves equal credit for saving Preston and Jonah. In fact, my mom and a bunch of other people might not have survived but for Cal, my friend Tara and my dog."

At the mention of my dog, Tammy looked perplexed. She gave me another hug. "I was in hiding, working with some of the Feds while other Feds were involved in doing the trafficking and trying to stop the truth from coming out. I didn't know whom to trust."

"I'm just glad that you are all safe and together. You are together, right?"

"Yes. When Preston disappeared, I thought he'd run off. I was forced to fight Brian and Juliet on my own and the judges were bribed. The judge, in my state, turned jurisdiction over to California and the court there gave custody to the traffickers without a paternity trial and authorized fake passports for Jonah."

"I know how that is. I'm about to get emancipated to make sure Juliet will stay out of my life."

"I wish someone could stop the corruption within the family court system."

"I'll say. Are you going to stay around?"

"Preston, I and Jonah are in protective custody until we testify about the trafficking operation and are safe. But we convinced them to bring us here, today, to thank you in person."

I looked past her and saw a couple of black SUVs with darkened glass.

My mom and Daniel really seemed to have hit it off. He was kind, even-tempered and considerate, qualities my dad had lacked. In fact, they were spending a lot of time with each other. I was glad for that, especially since outside of preparing for graduation, I was spending a lot of my time hanging out with Cal. The more I got to know him, the more I loved everything about him

The Indymedia had picked up the story of the secret prison and had been broadcasting about it for a couple of days. The broadcast news mentioned it and then went back to pro-war propaganda. The robotic dogs had been exposed and people were starting to realize that real dogs were safer. California and Washington were still a problem, but California had been anti-dog for decades.

At graduation, I was number two in my class. Principal Carmen announced that I was a National AP Scholar and the top AP scholar in the state. I hoped she was right about the latter as this year's results weren't even out yet. Cal's educational units were transferred to Elizabeth City High School. So, he was able to graduate with my class.

Our dance team performed to an old Queen song, "We Are the Champions." Everything joined the team as its newest and most impressive member. It turned out that Rebekka had loved dancing and that hadn't changed since she became Everything. She was better at aerials than I was. I wasn't sure that the law of gravity applied to her. It was no wonder she wound up in my arms that day in early April.

We got a standing ovation. A talent scout offered me a contract to come to Hollywood to be in a movie.

"California?"

"Yes."

I looked at Everything. "There is a lot I like about California. But I'm going to hang out elsewhere until the state becomes more dog-friendly."

After the graduation, I got the best present of all. Everett handed me the official order emancipating me. Juliet was out of my life.

I still hadn't decided where to go to college. I liked being near my mom. Daniel had been offered a teaching contract at Columbia and had asked Mom to marry him.

"Hmm. Guess you do get your redo after all," I told my mom.

"I told him I want to take my time deciding. I've learned how things can seem very right and then go very bad."

"Dan's nothing like Dad. You love him, right?"

My mom didn't answer, but the smile on her face told me her answer.

"Do you miss graduating in your century?" I asked Cal as we walked with Everything and Monarch through Charles Creek Park, near the Elizabeth City waterfront.

"I miss the idealism of my century, but I wouldn't go back. I plan to recreate that idealism here. What do you think about our picking Georgetown, so we can keep an eye on our government?"

"Well, if you're going to Georgetown, I may have to decline their invitation. After all, I don't want you to get tired of me."

"Does the word, 'never' mean anything to you?"

I laughed. "Sure. Georgetown. It doesn't really matter where I go, as long as I'm surrounded by people I care about. And if Mom is hanging out near New York, she and I will only be a train ride apart."

Cal took me in his arms and kissed me and it was as magical as the first time.

"Georgetown, I can handle that," Everything proclaimed.

"I wonder what trouble we can get into," Monarch mused.

We all stared.

"You can talk too?"

ACKNOWLEDGMENTS

First I want to acknowledge the millions of protective parents who are fighting to protect their children from what has become known as "Court-Sponsored Child Trafficking." So many moms I have met have heart-breaking stories and are praying for the safe return of their trafficked children. San Diego County is considered to be a major trafficking hub within the United States for American children who are removed from the country into the horrors of international slavery. Among those assisting protective mothers is Malinda Sherwyn, who has been tirelessly fighting to restore parental rights to good, loving parents seeking to locate and regain custody of their children.

It is important also to acknowledge the work of Janet Phalen, a great reporter, who has educated the public about the Public Guardian system and senior trafficking, wherein court-appointed guardians steal the money of seniors and force them into low-cost, sub-standard nursing homes where the seniors too often die, sometimes of starvation. Another supporter of the rights of the elderly is current Orange County, California, District Attorney Todd Spitzer, who exposed the Public Guardian scandal in Orange County in 2010 and saved the lives of a great many seniors in his county.

The late Teddi Alves also deserves credit for her work over many years to protect the health and welfare of dogs and the rights of the owners who love them. She was a great and very wise lady and a wonderful inspiration. She and Debbie Lusignan will both be missed.

I would like to thank Rosie de Guzman for her work in editing this book and for arranging some wonderful write-ins.

This book was drafted in 2018 during the April Camp Nano Event in less than twenty days, but it took until 2024 to decide to have it published.

Last, but not least, the character of Everything was based on a five-pound Papillion named Ever Everything.

Note regarding Canada: There was a time when Americans went to Canada for freedom and when Canada put human rights and lives above narratives. It is hoped that, in the future, Canada will return to those policies of the past.

ALSO BY NATALIE TRIUMPHS

Want more Everything? Coming Soon: Everything II: Rebekka's Story

Everything II. Follow the continuing adventures of Meadow, her talking Papillion Everything, Cal and their friends as they work to save the lives of dogs and other animals in a world that will forever be changed by judicial corruption, defense industry corruption, murders, dognappings, and trans-species experimentation.

Also coming: *Everything III*, the final book in the series, where once again Meadow, Everything, Cal and their friends fight to expose government corruption so extreme that it threatens the future of humanity.

Now Available: Amazon Best Seller Kakistocracy of the Technocrats

#1 in Young Adult Politics & Government and #1 in Young Adult Fiction Alternative History

As White House researcher for a non-existent department that oversees a demented robotic President, Karissa James finds herself in the middle of a string of murders, fires, earthquakes, embassy bombings, assassination attempts, bribes, wars and an Administration that can best be described as a Kakistocracy.

ABOUT THE AUTHOR

Amazon Best Selling Author Natalie Triumphs is an attorney, private investigator, journalist and educator with a background in criminal defense and in assisting victims of domestic violence and child trafficking. Natalie is a dog-lover who has fought to protect the rights of dogs and the people who love them.

9 798988 768142